Love Songs for the Shy and Cynical

Robert Shearman

Praise for *Tiny Deaths*

Times Literary Supplement:

Space age Beckett... Robert Shearman is probably best known for having reintroduced the Daleks into the new television series of *Doctor Who*. In *Tiny Deaths*, he shows the same perverse ingenuity that gave us killer robots crying out for love. Blackly humorous and absurd, his stories examine death from a variety of off-kilter perspectives, upending cliché, jumbling together good and evil, encouraging us to side with the villain and the underdog. Shearman shows up reality as a slippery business, liable to come unstuck through the unstitching of our most hackneyed rigmaroles and rituals.

The Guardian:

Disturbing and caustic, the stories in this entertaining first collection robustly tackle their unusual subject matter – from the authorities who decide that mere knowledge of mortality is insufficient and therefore notify each citizen of the exact cause and time of their demise, to the child victim of a hit-and-run accident who is reincarnated as her parents' ashtray.

The Metro:

Far from morbid, each bizarrely comic tale has a peculiar interior logic and, although the humour is invariably gothic, it's also clever and oddly passionate... Wistful, dream-like... strangly beautiful... Shearman applies an oddball comic whimsy that doesn't deny the darkness of his stories, but transmutes into something that, through its oddity, becomes comprehensible.

The Independent:

This is an excellent and highly imaginative first collection of stories by a writer who is not afraid to approach the big subject, mortality, but who does so from interestingly oblique angles and with a light, kittenish gait. Rather profound, ingeniously plotted.

Australian Specfic In Focus:

Robert Shearman is a gentle writer. That is to say, his style is quite tender, and his touch on the page is light. So light, actually, that it takes you a while to realise that what he's writing about is actually a bit scary and possibly downright awful. By then it's too late – you're hooked and you just can't stop. These stories display their brilliance in ways both sly and shy, as if lifting their skirts to show off their knickers and then acting as though nothing happened.

About the Author

Robert Shearman has worked as writer for television, radio and the stage. He was appointed resident dramatist at the Northcott Theatre in Exeter and has received several international awards for his theatrical work, including the Sunday Times Playwriting Award, the World Drama Trust Award and the Guinness Award for Ingenuity in association with the Royal National Theatre. His plays have been regularly produced by Alan Ayckbourn, and on BBC Radio by Martin Jarvis. However, he is probably best known as a writer for *Doctor Who*, reintroducing the Daleks for its BAFTA winning first series, in an episode nominated for a Hugo Award; he has also written many popular audio dramas for the series produced by Big Finish.

His first collection of short stories, *Tiny Deaths*, was published by Comma Press in 2007. It won the World Fantasy Award for best collection, was shortlisted for the Edge Hill Short Story Prize and nominated for the Frank O'Connor International Short Story Prize. One of the stories from it was selected by the National Library Board of Singapore as part of the annual Read! Singapore campaign. In 2008 his short story project for BBC7, *The Chain Gang*, won him a Sony Award, and he provided a second series for them in 2009.

He is now at work on a third collection of short stories, and – his wife will be pleased to hear – his first novel. (His wife prefers novels.)

First published in November 2009
by Big Finish Productions Ltd, PO Box 1127, Maidenhead, SL6 3LW
www.bigfinish.com
Project Editor: Xanna Eve Chown
Managing Editor: Jason Haigh-Ellery

'Be of Good Cheer' appeared in Midnight Echo issue 1, 'Pang' in The Lifted Brow issue 5, 'Luxembourg' in Andromeda Spaceways Inflight Magazine issue 39, 'Love Among the Lobelias' in Andromeda Spaceways Inflight Magazine issue 42, 'One Last Love Song' in Hope issue 1 and 'George Clooney's Moustache' in The British Fantasy Society Yearbook 2009. 'Roadkill' was released as a novella by Twelfth Planet Press. 'Love Among the Lobelias' and 'At the Crease' were both broadcast on BBC Radio 4 in Jarvis and Ayres productions; 'Sharp' on BBC Radio 3 in 'The Verb'.
'The Hidden Story' hasn't appeared anywhere before, nowhere, not at all. But it is in this book. Somewhere. You'll just have to look.

ISBN 13: 978-1-84435-436-8 (hardback edition)
978-1-84435-460-3 (paperback edition)
978-1-84435-461-0 (leatherbound edition)

A CIP catalogue record for this book is available from the British Library.

Cover art 'Private Members Only' by Rachel Goodyear, 2005. With thanks to Paulette Terry Brien.
Cover design by Alex Mallinson.

Typeset in Baskerville
Printed in Great Britain by the MPG Books Group, Bodmin and King's Lynn

She'd always imagined he'd be crushed to death by all those books of his. He had hundreds of them – no, thousands, probably; he kept them all in his library, and it really was *his* library, she had no reason to go in there. She wasn't sure where he got the books from, but if he even so much as went for a walk he'd come home with bags of the things – and then he'd put them on his shelves, proudly stacking them two or three books deep, she felt he enjoyed that stacking just as much as he enjoyed reading them. She'd tell him that sooner or later the shelves would give way, they'd collapse and he'd be crushed to death by them all. And he'd just smile politely, and he'd say he couldn't imagine a nicer way to go! There weren't many laughs in the house, but plenty of polite smiles, they could certainly stretch to that. He'd say that she really ought to give some of his books a try, there were lots of good ones he could recommend her, but she always said no. And after dinner she'd go and watch television in the sitting room, and he'd go upstairs one flight further and read in his library. She'd hear the creak as he sat down in his favourite armchair, and she'd know he'd be settled for hours. And then, when she'd watched enough TV, she'd go and knock on his door, and he'd get up from his chair, put his book back on the shelf, and dutifully follow her to bed. "Good night," he'd say, and "Good night," she'd say, and they'd kiss, and then go to sleep. Sometimes she'd dream he was crushed by his books. It'd be a nightmare sometimes, and sometimes it'd be really rather reassuring.

So when he died quite peacefully in his sleep, and she woke one morning to find him next to her stiff as a board, the scream she gave was not so much that she was cuddling a corpse but that he'd died in completely the wrong way. There wasn't even a book in sight.

The children both came to the funeral, and that was nice of them, she knew they had busy lives of their own. Afterwards they offered to help her sort through all the husband's things, but she told them there was no need, she was quite capable, thank you. First she took down all his old clothes to the charity shop. Then she took down all his *new* clothes too, might as well, she couldn't see what use she'd have for them now. The man in the charity shop got quite used to her. "Hello again!" he'd always say. She asked him whether the shop wanted any books. "Oh yes," said the man, "we're always looking for books." "I'll be back soon," she promised.

She soon realised that books were very heavy things; she could carry no more than a dozen at a time, jammed inside old carrier bags. This was going to take forever, she thought, as she waddled her way down the street to Oxfam, it really was thousands, not hundreds but *thousands*. And she also thought how lucky she was that he hadn't been crushed by the books after all, they were so heavy it would have made an awful mess. When she lugged into the shop the sixth bag of books, the man was waiting for her. He looked serious. "Can I have a private word?" he asked. He led her to the back, and through a door marked 'Staff Only'. She felt a flutter of fear – was there something illegal about her husband's books? Were they pornographic? Really, what did she know about what he'd ever got up to in that library? The man closed the door behind them, and told her that they'd found envelopes tucked inside the books. Sealed, addressed to her. "Which books?" she asked, a little uselessly, since she didn't know the books, why did it matter which books, but it felt the right thing to say, it felt she was taking an interest. "Well," he said, and gave a slightly embarrassed laugh, "well… all of them."

She fetched the stepladder from the understairs cupboard, so that she could reach the highest shelves. Then she worked her way through every single book, left to right, A to Z. Sometimes the envelopes were easy to find, right at the front. Others took a little effort, and she had to take the book down and give it a proper search, he'd have wedged it tight against the spine so that it wouldn't simply come out with a shake, it might be pressed flat between pages three hundred and two and three hundred and three. Each envelope contained a letter. A lot of the letters said the exact same thing: "I love you," in big letters, nothing else, as bold and simple as you'd like. Others made attempts at little poems, or whole sprawling paragraphs in which he'd try to explain what he meant by this love. "You're always there for me, I know," read one. "I know it isn't a passionate love, this love of ours – but you're always there for me, and I'm always there for you." One envelope contained an essay so long that it took her a whole twenty minutes to read, before she tossed it on to the pile with all the others. "I love you," she read, "I love you, I love you," so often, so many times, until the very word *love* began to look odd and misspelled through repetition. "I do hope you'll read my books some day, just so you realise the way I feel!" joked one letter. In another, "I love you so much. And I'm so sorry that I need you to read it rather than hear it. I'm so sorry I'm too shy ever to say it out loud."

She began on the Monday afternoon. By the weekend she had finished. The last letter wasn't anything special, stuck inside a 'Thérèse Raquin' by Emile Zola. "I love you," it said. Yes, I know, she thought.

She walked her way through the love letters that now covered the entire floor, a sea of white broken up by occasional bits of black and blue scribbling. She stepped on them, kicked them aside. She wouldn't read them again, she didn't need them any more. And when she reached the shelves, she took down the first book that came to hand. She sat in her husband's favourite armchair, it creaked under her weight. And she turned to chapter one, and she began to read.

Contents

Introduction

Steven Hall

This introduction shouldn't be here. I mean, it is here, obviously. It's here because quite a few people wanted it here – the brilliant Rob Shearman wanted it here, as did his publishers, and I wanted to do my bit to help promote this very fine book, and so here I am doing just that. But now... I'm worried that having this here is like sticking a button badge on an emperor butterfly.

Because here's the thing – *Love Songs for the Shy and Cynical* is such a very delicate, beautifully understated and fantastically well-balanced book. Rob Shearman's prose is so deceptively simple, and his emotional touch is so very gentle, that sometimes it seems that too much ink on a full stop here, or an over-indented paragraph there, would be all it'd take to overbalance this fragile creature you're reading and send it tumbling out of the sky. And yet here I am, hanging an introduction around its neck like some big, cheap gold chain from Argos. I'm sorry, I promise I'm trying to be quick.

Over the following pages, you'll meet ghostly cats, winged rabbits and see Luxembourg disappear, amongst many, many other strange, wonderful and absurd things. Ultimately though, this is a book about people: ordinary, stupid, love-struck, empty, happy, broken, cheating, devoted, laughing, crying, confused people. People trying to deal with themselves, with the people around them, and with a world that's blatantly more insane and unfathomable than any disappearing European country could possibly be.

Within the covers, you'll find heartbreaking humanity nestling quietly in every page. I almost wrote 'shining from every page' but that's not true – like everything else, it's delicate, it's subtle, it's the kind of thing that might sneak under your radar for a little while (in fact, I think Mr Shearman may have constructed this book so that it does exactly that) but the effects are cumulative and *Love Songs* will find a way to get you eventually, I'm sure of it.

I'm also sure you'll laugh a lot – this is a very funny book – you might also be a little bit scared, and if you're anything like me, you'll cry at the end and feel a little melancholy and odd when you finally put the book down. It's a great testament to Mr Shearman's skill as a storyteller that when this happens to you, you won't quite be able to put your finger on why.

So many people seem to believe that 'heavy' is what's important in stories – weighty, depressing writing about weighty, depressing issues. Yawn. Please understand that when I say this book is light, I don't mean it's thin or throwaway or ephemeral by any means, I mean it's light in the way that a hummingbird is light, in the way that a Zen koan or Chinese calligraphy is light, in the way that Muhammad Ali was light as he danced around that ring.

Light is good. Light is beautiful.

Now forget all about this introduction, or even better, neatly remove this page with a Stanley knife, so this book can find its proper balance, flutter its wings and really get some air.

Steven Hall, 2009

Love Among the Lobelias

'You might want to sit down for this. Because I've got great news! I hope you think it's great news, we're all very excited here. Are you sitting down?'

'Yes,' he said, though he wasn't. He didn't like sitting down, and tried to do so as little as possible. Sitting down, he felt, undermined his authority, and authority was all he was about. Besides, it wasn't comfortable, the tail got in the way.

'We read your manuscript,' the voice on the phone went on. 'And we love it! And we're going to publish it, what is it, *Love Among the Lobelias*, that's the one. There you are! Was I right to say you'd be excited? Was I right to tell you to sit down?'

He found he *was* excited, and he hadn't been for so, so long. 'Thank you,' he said, and meant it, and that felt good, because he hadn't meant that for so, so long either.

'No problem!' said the voice. 'Thank *you*, for writing such a great novel! Hey,' he said, and a note of alarm crept through the cheer, 'is everything okay, is that screaming I hear?'

'Just the TV set,' and he kicked the door to his office shut with a hoof. 'I'm going to be a real-life author?' he went on. 'With my name on the cover and everything? You've no idea how long I've been trying, the rejection letters I've had...' And he decided to shut up, in case he ruined everything.

'Real-life author, that's it,' chuckled the voice. 'Now, let's not kid ourselves, okay? This isn't going to be a bestseller. Let's say that from the outset. So there won't be much money. And the romance genre, it's not the sort of thing critics like. So there'll be precious little respect either. But your name on the cover, definitely, Nick, definitely, that, alone, I can guarantee. You don't mind that I call you Nick?'

'Sure, go ahead,' said the author, who wasn't called Nick, who wasn't called anything remotely like Nick. He'd been hiding behind pseudonyms for so long, he only now realised it wouldn't be his name on the cover after all. But that was okay, it was a name he'd picked for himself, that was the main thing. Not like some of the others, people could be so *cruel* – especially when they were scared.

The rest of the conversation passed in a whirl. And once it was over, his head full of barely understood chat about cover illustrations and royalty payments and foreign rights, Nick found he couldn't stop smiling for a good half hour. He hadn't smiled for a long time, and at first he found the expression somewhat disconcerting, but it grew on him. He opened the doors, gazed out on the whole yawning inferno that was his home, and pointed at the first creature he could find. 'You,' he called. 'You'll do. Come into my office a minute.'

'I'm going to be published! I'm going to have a novel out,' and then he added, because it made it seem all so much grander, 'in the *shops*.'

The demon stood before him, expressionless and dumb, dropping ash and clinker on to the carpet.

'Good, isn't it?' prompted Nick.

'It,' rumbled the demon, in a voice scraped from the underside of Hell's bowels, 'is good.'

'Do you want to hear what it's about?'

The demon tilted his head to one side, weighing the options. 'Yes,' was the answer he plumped for.

'There's this boy called Tom,' said Nick, 'and there's this girl called Susan. And they're just right for each other, you know, just a perfect match. But at the beginning, you see, they don't realise that! And before they can get together, there are a few obstacles in the way!' The demon said nothing, just licked his lips with a tongue too large for his mouth. The plot seemed remarkably flimsy now Nick had to say it out loud, and seeing the nonplussed reaction from his horned colleague, he remembered why he'd kept the book a secret in the first place. 'I don't know, it's sweet,' he concluded, and the demon nodded.

Post for Hell was delivered to a PO Box in Croydon; a goblin collected it on Thursdays. When his author's copies arrived, Nick ripped open the cardboard box, held the books up for inspection. The covers were nice and shiny, and, making sure the door was closed, he couldn't help but stroke his cheeks with them. When his cheeks had been given as much stroking as they could take, he at last put all five copies on to the shelf. Nick didn't own many books – his job didn't allow much time for reading – but he had a Bible, it was good to see what the opposition were up to. Besides this massive tome his paperback volumes looked dwarfed and pathetic. But then he remembered that the Bible was a whole compendium of books, really; he opened it up, measured all the fifty chapters of Genesis between thumb and forefinger, and with satisfaction noted that of the two debut novels, his beat God's on word count hands down. And that made him feel much better.

Inspecting the new crop of dead souls for punishment had always been a fairly tedious part of the job – all that pleading, all those tears – but he fairly whistled with good humour as he did the rounds nowadays; he only had to think of those books in his office, and the way those fresh pages smelt so *good*, and he was happy. 'Hello, hello!' he called up to Mr Jones cheerily, 'what are we in for, then?' and looked at his chart. Then, 'Good God,' he swore, 'get him down from there.' And Mr Jones was unwinched from the chains suspending him over a cauldron of oil.

'It says here,' said Nick, trying to sound as nonchalant as possible, 'that you've been reading *Love Among the Lobelias*. Tell me, just curious. What did you make of it?'

Fifteen minutes before, Mr Jones had been speeding down a motorway with his ear being licked by a girl who bore not even a passing similarity to Mrs Jones. Even had he been alive, his mind was not in the best frame for a literary discussion. But Nick waited patiently as the corpse got his thoughts in order. 'It was all right,' Jones said, at last.

'Oh, good,' said Nick. 'That's good. So you liked it? That's good. You know,' he added shyly, 'I wrote that.'

'Did you?'

'Yes. What did you think of the characters? Did you find them engaging, warm, likeable? Who was your favourite?'

'I don't know. Erm. What was the bloke's name?'

'Tom?'

'Yeah, Tom. He's my favourite.'

'Not Susan? You didn't like Susan?'

'Susan was good too,' said Mr Jones.

'Okay,' said Nick. 'Okay. Any other favourite bits?'

'Not really.'

'Okay. But you really liked it? That's great. It's so nice to meet a fan.' And Nick gave him a smile, and had him strung up for disembowelling.

The demons soon realised that their boss liked to have his readers pointed out to him. 'It's selling better than I'd hoped!' he said, one particularly gratifying day, when there were no fewer than four of them rotating on a wheel of spikes. And it wasn't until the seventeen members of the Women's Reading Group in Margate pitched up in his domain that he realised what was wrong.

The receptionist asked him whether he had an appointment, but then she looked up and saw the unbearable reality of him, and that where he had trod was still smouldering from the heat. 'I think he'll see me,' said Nick.

'I wish I'd known who the author was,' said the publisher, 'I'd have rethought our marketing strategy altogether.' Nick was offered some bottled water; he refused. 'I can't see what you're so bothered about. So anyone who reads your book is going to Hell. Isn't that sort of thing right up your street?'

'But it wasn't meant to be like that,' said Nick, and he hated how whiny his voice sounded. 'It was something for *me.* At work all I get is destroy this, destroy that, and I just wanted to *create*, to carve out a little piece of something nice. Tom and Susan, they're ever so nice, aren't they, and, okay, they've got their obstacles, but even the obstacles are fairly nice. We've got to get all the copies back,' he said decisively, 'and pulp them.'

'Hmm,' said the publisher. 'Or, tell you what. We could put a warning sticker on the cover.'

'DO NOT READ,' the sticker read, in bold, and, underneath: 'These are the words of the Devil. Read and you'll BURN in Hell!!!' And they'd added three exclamation marks to Hell, and put a little fiery effect on BURN. And Nick saw the sticker, and saw that it was good. 'If that doesn't stop them, nothing will.' And yet very soon Hell got busier, Nick had to lay on extra staff. 'We need to make the sticker more lurid!' Nick told the publisher. 'You're the boss,' the publisher said, and soon there was nothing but stickers to see, the lobelias were all buried beneath them. And the damned turned up in droves. The novel was read by professors and lorry drivers, those who worked at the stock exchange and at the counters in Burger King. 'What did you think of the *story*?' Nick would ask them all, but they never had much to say about that. 'For God's sake,' said Nick, 'what the *hell* is wrong with you people?'

And the saddest thing was that he couldn't look at his novel in the same way. Tom and Susan, everything they said was a lie, their first meeting on the bridge, that misunderstanding about the will, just lies. And he knew that all stories were lies, but deep down, weren't the best of them true as well? He was the Prince of Lies, after all, and those evenings bashing out chapters on his old typewriter, fortified by nothing more than black coffee and the joy of creation, they were the biggest lies of all. He took his author's copies from the shelf, threw them into the back of a cupboard, and determined to forget about writing altogether.

One day the phone rang. 'Are you sitting down for this? You've got an Oscar nomination!'

'They made a movie of my book?'

'Check your contract,' said the publisher. 'I got you a producer credit.'

Nick rented a tuxedo, and flew to Los Angeles. The screenwriter looked about twelve years old, big and hairy and enthusiastic. 'I'm such a fan,' he told Nick. 'I've tried to be as faithful as possible, only changed things here and there for dramatic effect. I must have read the book a dozen times, forwards and backwards, every which way.'

'You are in *such* trouble,' Nick told him.

And when they won there was such a round of applause, and the kid and the devil got up in front of the podium to collect their golden statuette. And Nick wanted to tell them that this whole thing had been *wrong*; that it should be about the art, not the artist. That if he hadn't been a celebrity, no-one would have touched his book, and maybe that would have been for the best, then Tom and Susan and all those lobelias could have spoken for themselves. But he knew the audience wouldn't understand – the clips they'd played had renamed them Brad and Jennifer anyway, there weren't any lobelias but bloody tulips, and there was a spotlight in his face, and millions watching at home on TV, and was that Jack Nicholson in the front row? It was, it was Jack! And Nick heard himself thank the Academy, thank his agent, and thank the parents he couldn't remember and wasn't sure he'd ever had.

Nick liked Hollywood. It felt so familiar to him. The heat, the bare flesh, the fact so many of its residents had already sold their souls to him. He stayed on to produce the next two instalments in the *Love Among Tulips* franchise, and then helped to create a whole slew of summer blockbusters. He wasn't a writer – he soon realised writing wasn't his forte – but he was an Ideas Man, his skill was giving his ideas to other writers to make sense of. And he knew that anyone who saw his movies was damned for all eternity, but then, he supposed, they were probably all damned anyway.

And once in a while he'd pop back to Hell. It seemed to be managing fine without him, although it had all got so busy now it lacked the personal touch he'd liked.

'Thank you,' said a voice by his side. And he was surprised to see a little old lady, wholly unafraid, smiling up at him.

'Hello, sweetheart,' he said, in that drawl he'd picked up in spite of his best endeavours.

'When I was very ill,' she said, 'my husband read your book to me in bed. A chapter a night. It was so romantic.'

'Where's your husband, sweetheart?'

'Over there, in the pit of fire.' Nick waved at the man, and he thought he might have waved back, but he wasn't sure. 'One chapter a night, and then we'd make love. Nothing much, but just like in your book. Gentle, and very, very sweet.'

'Thank you,' said Nick. 'That makes it all worthwhile.' And he felt that it really did.

He went back into his office, opened the cupboard, took down his novel. The cover was still shiny, the pages still smelt fresh. And, although he didn't like sitting, as he began to read he sank into an armchair, and lost himself in a world that was innocent and naïve and romantic.

Roadkill

i

He'd said he liked companionable silence, that it was a sign of friendship. But when it came down to it, what they had was just silence, really, wasn't it? As they sped down the motorway in the dark, no sound except the low roar of the engine and the occasional grunt of the windscreen wiper, she felt drowsy, she thought at least that she might get some sleep. But she didn't dare – it'd seem rude – they *weren't* companions, not really, in spite of what they'd done – and he kept on stealing little looks at her, throwing her awkward little smiles, and saying, 'Sorry I'm being so quiet, sorry.' If he wanted the companionable silence then why did he keep popping up with such stuff as, 'Oh, look, only twenty-two more miles to the nearest service station,' or 'Oh, look, cows'? Always with that apologetic grin she'd found rather endearing only a day before.

'Do you want some music?' he said at last, 'would some music be nice?' He fished around for a wad of CDs with his spare hand. 'I think some music would be nice,' he said, 'I'll see if I can find Elton John.' And then she didn't so much hear it as *feel* it, there was a thud, and a quick streak of something very solid against the windscreen. 'Jesus,' he said. He didn't drop the CDs, she noted, he put them back safely into the glove compartment. 'Jesus, what was that?'

'Pull over,' she said. And he looked at her with bewilderment. 'Pull over,' she said again, and he did so. The car stopped on the hard shoulder.

'Jesus,' he said again. 'We hit something.'

You hit something, she thought. 'Are you all right?' she asked.

'I think so,' he said, 'yeah. Yeah, I'm fine. Are you all right? What do you think it was? I mean, it just came out of nowhere. You saw that, didn't you? There was nothing I could have done. Jesus,' he looked up at the windscreen, 'I hope it hasn't damaged anything.'

'You should check,' she said, and he just gave her that bewildered expression again, so she sighed, undid the seat belt and opened the door. She wondered whether he might be in shock, but she'd seen him look bewildered a fair amount that weekend, and it couldn't *always* have been shock. She wondered whether she might be in shock too. 'Fuck,' she said, as she stepped out into the dark and the rain, 'fuck fuck,' but actually she felt good, some fresh air at last, and something was happening, there'd be no need for a companionable silence now, she didn't feel like saying 'fuck' at all. She gave the windscreen a cursory inspection, and from inside the car he gave her a hopeful thumbs up. She gave him a thumbs up back, but she hadn't looked, not really, there could be shards of glass all round for all she cared. And then she turned and walked back down the hard shoulder to look for a body.

It wasn't rain, not really, just a bit of wetness in the air, and it was refreshing. She liked it out here in the black, on her own, and she wondered how long she could get away with it, with not returning to the car, returning to him – pretending instead to look for whatever it is they might have hit, she'd never find it now. And then she saw it, maybe about two hundred yards behind the car, a little mound that had been knocked into the middle lane. She stood parallel to it, but couldn't make out what it was. She thought it might be moving. She waved back, indicating he should reverse the car. For a moment nothing happened and she thought she'd have to walk all the way back and tell him what to do. 'Fuck,' she said, but then, slowly, surely, the car began to back down the hard shoulder towards her, he'd got the message.

'It's just there,' she told him, as he wound down the window. 'Try to angle the car a bit, so we can see what it is in the headlamps.'

'What is it?' he asked her.

'I don't know,' she said. 'Try to angle the car. You know. So we can see what it is in the lamps.'

He did his best. She still couldn't identify it, it was sprawled in such an odd position, she couldn't even see if it had a head. But there had to be a head, because it was definitely alive, whatever it was it was twitching, you couldn't twitch without a head, could you? 'Probably a bird,' he said, and she jumped, she hadn't heard him get out of the car, 'you saw the way it flew at me, probably a bird.' And he sniffed. But it looked a bit large for a bird, and besides, surely that was fur? 'We should go and get it,' she suggested, and he looked horrified. 'It's in the motorway,' he said, 'we can't walk out into the motorway.' But there were no cars coming, no headlights in the distance, and the creature twitched again, for God's sake it was *twitching*. 'It's not as if we'll be able to help,' he said, and she gave him a look, said a 'Sod it' under her breath, and then ran out into the road.

Up she scooped it into her arms, and she made to dash back, but as she did so she felt that the creature had been stuck down on to the tarmac, she fancied there was resistance as she pulled it up, and she was suddenly terrified that she'd left bits of the body behind, that she'd make it back to the safety of the hard shoulder with only half an animal and the rest of it trailing after her. 'Are you all right?' he asked, and his arms were out wide, and for a moment she thought absurdly that he wanted to *hug* her, after all that had happened, and she thought, no, he wants to take the animal from me, he wants to *share* this – but not even that, now his arms had dropped uselessly to his sides, he was doing nothing to help, nothing. And as she reached him she had a sick urge to drop the creature to the ground, but what would be the point of that, why bother rescuing it in the first place? And though she suddenly felt such revulsion to it, she kept it in her arms those few seconds longer, she knelt down and laid it out gently on the hard shoulder. And she realised at last that it *was* fur, matted fur, and she wondered whether it was matted with blood or with rainfall. 'There,' she said, as she pulled away from it at last, 'there you go,' and, stupidly, 'you'll be all right now.' And it did have a head she saw, thank God, and it turned that head and fixed her with its eyes.

'It's a rabbit,' she said.

'Yes,' he said. 'Or a hare. I always get the two muddled up. Aren't hares supposed to have longer ears? Or is that the other way round?' He thought for a bit. 'Do you think those are long ears?'

'I don't know.'

'Nor me. If we had another rabbit here, you know, side by side. You know, we could compare.'

They stood there for a good half minute, just looking down at it. And it lay there, for the same length of time, just looking back. 'It's not moving much,' he said.

'No.'

'Do you think it's dying, or what? There isn't much blood. I mean, unless there was in the road. Was there a lot in the road?' She didn't answer. 'What do we do now?'

'I think,' she said heavily, 'we have to put it out of its misery.'

'Right,' he said, 'right. And are you sure,' he went on, licking his lips, 'that it's actually *in* misery? I mean, it's not making much noise. It's not squealing or anything. Surely if there were misery, there'd be squealing and stuff.'

'Help me find a rock,' she said. And they both went up to the embankment, scrabbled around in the grass. It didn't have to be a rock, anything sharp or heavy would have done, but it was rocks that they found. Hers was better than his. When he saw that, he dropped his to the ground.

'How are you going to do this?' he asked her.

'I'm not going to do it,' she said, and she'd never been more sure of anything. 'You're going to do it.' And she gave him the rock.

'You could have just left it in the road,' he said. 'Why didn't you just leave it in the road? Some car would have come eventually, squashed it, there'd be no need for rocks and shit.' And she felt such a flare of anger at that, but she didn't raise her voice, 'Go on,' she said. Go on, finish it. Finish what you've started.

So he stood there, all five foot six of him, weighing the rock in his hands, aiming downwards. 'You're going to have to get closer than that,' she said. 'Jesus,' he said. 'What, right down in the, you want me on my, right, Jesus.' And he got down on his knees. 'I hope you're happy,' he said. 'I hope this is what you want. Jesus.'

'You're going to have to hit it pretty hard,' she told him. And she almost laughed at the look he threw her then, and it wasn't funny, not really, she really *mustn't* laugh. But he'd tried so hard all weekend to accommodate her, to keep smiling no matter what, and here on his face at last was something like fury. 'Go on,' she said. And he muttered something, and lined up the rock with the rabbit's skull, as if he were taking a snooker stroke, for God's sake, as if he were swinging a golf club. 'You might want to hold its head,' she added.

'I'm not *touching* it,' he said. 'I'll kill it, but I won't touch it. Oh. Oh. Wait. Look.'

And she'd had enough suddenly. 'I'll do it,' she said, 'if you can't.' I just want to get home, she thought.

'No,' he said. 'What's this?'

She stooped beside him.

The rabbit had a wing. It was thick and black and leathery. And *wide*, it lay stretched out to the left, a wider span than the body from which it had unfurled. The rabbit blinked at them, as if it was as surprised as they were.

'It can't be real,' he said. 'It must be stuck on.' And he hadn't wanted to touch the creature before, but now his fingers were all over it, feeling the wing, prodding at where it met the fur. 'I can't see any join,' he said. 'I thought it must have been stitched on or something, but it just comes out of the skin.' The rabbit gave a little cough, almost politely – and from out of its right side a second wing unfolded. It spread even wider, and it fluttered a little under the drizzle.

The rabbit shuddered and gave a single grunt. It was only for a beat, it was very quiet, but they both heard it. 'I don't see what difference it makes,' she said.

'Maybe there's some sort of scientific base nearby,' he was saying. 'You know, where they put ears on mice and things.' He was on his feet now, looking about, as if expecting to see a laboratory on the horizon. 'Do you think that could be it? I mean, maybe it escaped. Maybe they want it back.'

'Give me the rock,' she said.

'What are you talking about?' And for a moment he genuinely didn't know. Then he grinned at her, talked very slowly, very patiently. 'But, no. But we can't kill it now. That would be terrible. I mean, look at it,' although he was doing nothing of the sort himself, he was beaming with a big smile now and his eyes were bright. 'I mean, what if this is even *better* than an experiment from a lab? I mean, this could be a new *species.* Can you just think of that?'

'No,' she said.

'Look,' he said. 'Look.' And then he was silent for a moment, as if trying to work out what she should be looking at. 'Okay, look. We came out here for something magical. Didn't we? I mean, that was the whole point. And maybe this is it. This is something magical.'

'It's in pain,' she said.

'We'll get it a towel,' he said. 'There's one on the back seat, I think. Yeah, we'll make it nice and comfortable. Go on,' he said. 'Go and get the towel. Go on then,' and there was just a touch of impatience in his voice now, and as she looked at him his eyes were gleaming in the rain, it was raining for real now and it made his face look shiny and alive.

And she fetched the towel, and he wrapped up the rabbit in it as gently as he could. Lovingly, she thought, almost lovingly. She tried to help, but he waved her away. He stroked the wings and he stroked the fur, and told the creature it was going to be okay. The creature looked at him a little doubtfully, but at least it didn't make that grunt of pain again, that was something. And they carried it to the boot, they shut it in, and then they drove away.

ii

And on the way up all they'd done was talk. After a few hours, halfway up the M5, he'd admitted to her he'd been a bit nervous, what if they hadn't found things to chat about? And she'd laughed, and said fat chance! The words had just spilled out of both of them, sometimes there were about three different conversations going on at once – she thought it was rather exhilarating and laughed every time she lost her train of thought only to find another altogether. First off, of course, they'd talked about work – he'd only been at the office for a few weeks, whereas she'd been there for *years*, she could tell him all the gossip – and he said he was relieved, that the people he thought he was beginning to like were the ones it was safe to like, and those he hadn't taken to were precisely the ones to steer clear of. It was good to get such inside information! And they'd discussed their families, why it was he didn't get on with his mum, why she didn't get on with her dad. 'It's the same sort of thing,' he told her sympathetically, 'but in reverse. Jesus, what's wrong with our parents anyway?' They'd even touched on politics, and although she rather suspected the views he held were just watered down versions of her own, at least they weren't going to argue, at least they were in the same general ballpark. He'd picked her up from the top of her road first thing that morning; as it turned out, he could have done so from the house, she'd sorted everything out, but he said it might be safer his way. 'Is that all your luggage?' he'd said, and she'd smiled, and said she didn't think she'd need much. And she'd sat in the passenger seat beside him, and there wasn't any crap lying on the floor, and there was a smell of lemon. She thought he must have cleaned the car especially – and then thought, why not just ask him? So did. And he blushed and said he had, actually, was that really pathetic? 'No, no,' she said, 'it's nice, it's nice.' And meant it.

She navigated. He told her he didn't have a satnav. 'Well, I do,' he said, 'but I don't like it, I think the voice is a bit creepy.' And she'd laughed, and agreed, those voices *were* a bit creepy, weren't they? Although she didn't find her satnav creepy in the slightest. And he'd said that maybe they only hired actors to record those satnav things if they had creepy voices, and he'd tried to picture the auditions involved, even acting it out, turning down Mel Gibson, Jack Nicholson, because they didn't sound enough like axe murderers, and the joke must have run on for over half an hour, and somehow never quite stopped being funny. She was pleased to see he didn't mind when she gave the wrong directions, when they came off the motorway at the wrong junction. 'It's a holiday!' he said, 'it's not as if we're in any hurry!' They pulled into a service station, and he bought them both a coffee. He noted how she insisted it come with soya milk, he told her with mock grimness that was important knowledge he would store away for future reference, and then grinned.

'Look,' he said. 'Silly to ask. But just so I'm sure. What we're doing is what I think we're doing, isn't it?' And he played with his plastic stirrer. 'You know. We are shagging, aren't we?'

'Yes,' she said.

'Oh, good,' he said. 'Oh, that's what I thought. But it'd have been embarrassing if... I mean, I only got us the one room. Good.'

She leaned forward across the coffee and the soya milk. And the detritus of how many other travellers, maybe they were all going down the M5 for a spot of shagging, why not. He looked surprised, and it took him a few moments to realise he should lean in too. And she kissed him on the lips. He responded very well, actually. There was a bit of movement on his part, a sort of nibbling, but not too much, he didn't get carried away. And although the tongue did make an appearance, it didn't hog the party the way it sometimes could, it was just a push against her teeth, a quick hello and goodbye, a quick see you later maybe.

'You've done this before,' she said.

'What, kiss?' he said, and was puzzled. Then he realised she was teasing, and said, 'Oh yes, kissing, I've kissed a few times, yeah.'

'Good to know,' she said.

'But never,' he added, as they got up and put on their coats, 'someone who tasted of soya. That was a new one on me.'

'It's a lovely part of the country,' he told her as they drove on. 'I grew up there as a kid. And I hope you like the hotel. It had a nice website. It's a family hotel, you know, nothing posh, but I don't like those posh hotels much, do you? They're not very personal. I like personal, personal's nice. This one looks nice, the pictures are nice, it has off-street parking.'

'So long as it has a bed,' she said, 'we'll be fine.'

The landlady was waving at them from the front window. 'This must be it,' he said, and they pulled up in the driveway. 'Hello, hello!' said the landlady, opening the door to them. 'And welcome!

We spoke on the phone, yes? I'm Marcia. I hope you'll be very happy here.' Marcia was fifty-ish and grey-haired, with arms thick enough to churn butter.

They introduced themselves. 'Married?' asked Marcia.

'Yes,' she said.

'No,' he said.

'Only the one of us,' she said. Marcia laughed. 'Say no more!' He looked embarrassed, but she didn't mind – she'd rather he'd been mistaken for her husband than her son. Marcia led them through to the back of the house. 'And here's your little part of our home,' she said. 'Here's the key, and there's a separate door through the garden, you see, if you want to come in late at night. Just so you won't worry about disturbing me or my husband.' She watched them take in the room, the wardrobe, the TV mounted in the corner, the bathroom door, for some reason a painting of a goose. And the double bed, big, bold, bloody unignorable, right there in the centre. 'Have fun!' she said, and left them.

'I like her,' he said, 'she seems nice.' She put down her bag on the bed, kissed him from behind on his neck. 'Oh!' he said. 'What are you doing? We haven't even unpacked yet.'

'I'm sorry,' she said.

'No,' he said, 'I'm sorry. Sorry.' He opened his arms, and she thought, a hug, he wants a *hug*. She stepped into the embrace anyway, and he held on to her gingerly as if she were cut crystal, and he rubbed his cheek against hers, and gave her a peck. Then he thought about it for a moment, grinned, what the hell, and kissed her full on the lips. It was for longer this time, and the tongue gave more than its cameo performance. 'Okay?' he asked.

'Oh yes,' she said. 'It's very nice here.'

'It is, isn't it? I love hotels!' He released her, went to open drawers, cupboards. 'There's a kettle here! And an ironing board. And look!' He'd found a little folder, right by the Gideon Bible. 'They do room service. Just like a proper hotel. Shall we order something?' She assured him she was fine. 'Oh, it'll be fun. We can have breakfast in bed! I think we should! Hang on,' he said, winked at her, and lifted the receiver. Dialled a number. Waited. 'It's ringing,' he told her. And then, 'Hello! Yes, we thought we'd order breakfast in bed for tomorrow! We thought, why not, it's a holiday, if you can't do it on a holiday... No, we're staying in your house. Yes. In the guest room. Yes. Yes, at the back.' She lay down on the bed and waited for him to stop talking. 'Yes, then would be fine. Looking forward to it. Thank you.' He hung up, smiled at her. 'Breakfast in bed, what a treat!' And she smiled back. 'Come here,' she said to him.

He lay on the bed next to her. 'Okay if I take this side?'

'You're fine.'

'It's quite soft, isn't it?'

She made to shrug, but she was supported by one of her shoulders, so it came out as a twitch. They snogged for a while. 'You're really special,' he told her at one point. 'Whatever happens this weekend, I want you to know, it's just great to have such a good friend at the office.' They snogged a bit longer. 'I should unpack,' he said. 'Do you want to unpack?'

'We're only here the one night,' she told him.

'I know,' he said. He got up, unzipped his suitcase. Took out three, maybe four, shirts, and a spare pair of trousers. He opened the wardrobe. 'Okay if I take this side?'

Marcia recommended them a restaurant in town. They wouldn't need the car, it was only ten minutes' walk, and besides, the weather was lovely. 'Neil swears by the crab,' she told them, 'you must try the crab!' They found the place easily enough, it wasn't too busy, they got a table for two, and a waiter lit a candle for them. 'I don't like crab,' he confided to her, and she agreed, she couldn't abide shellfish, so they giggled, ordered a steak and a lasagne, and joked that they'd *tell* Marcia they'd had crab when they saw her. The house red had no label, but was rather good, and they got through two bottles of it. 'Coffee?' asked the waiter. 'I won't, but my girlfriend here will, but the milk has to be soya.' Girlfriend, she thought with surprise, it almost sobered her up. 'I'm not sure we have soya milk, sir, I'll check.' 'It has to be soya, that's what she drinks.' 'Listen,' she said to him, and touched his hand gently, 'I can have other milks, it's just soya for preference.' But no, no, he was adamant, it'd be soya or nothing, only the best for her, for his girlfriend – if there was no soya milk to be had he'd bloody well go out and get some, leave the restaurant, find some supermarket, and bring back his own. And fortunately the waiter returned and said there *was* soya milk, so no-one had to find out whether he'd back down or not. Mind you, she thought as she sipped at the coffee, it didn't taste like soya. By the time he'd paid – his treat, he insisted – it had begun to rain. Just a drizzle, really, they were both so hot after the wine it was welcome.

And he told her he'd protect her, and did his best to hold his hand flat over her head as they walked back to the hotel. It did nothing to keep her dry, of course, but it made them both laugh.

When they got back they snogged again for a little while. As soon as she'd stepped into the room he whirled her around, and caught her mouth with his. It was quite nice, but as she stood there straining her face up to meet his, she couldn't help feel there were more comfortable ways to do this. 'I'm going to get ready for bed,' she said gently, and indicated the bathroom, 'all right?' Of course, he said, did she want him to come with her...? No, no, she assured him, she just wanted to clean herself up a bit, nothing sexy or complicated like that. He said okay, and she thought he looked a little relieved. 'I'll only be a minute,' she said, kissed him again, stepped into the bathroom, and closed the door behind her. As she washed her face she noticed that he'd carefully laid out all his toiletries side by side at the top of the sink, toothbrush, toothpaste, shampoo, a pair of tweezers.

She opened the door, and nearly laughed. He was standing there naked. Arms to one side, as if presenting. It wasn't that there was anything funny about his body, not in the slightest, it all seemed to be present and in roughly the correct dimensions. It was just the surprise at the whole reality of it. He looked down, smiled a little awkwardly. 'Sorry about him, he's got a bit excited.'

'So I can see,' she said. 'No, it's very flattering.'

'Thanks.'

'Do you want me to strip off, or...?'

'Oh, absolutely. Yes.'

'Okay,' she said, and did so.

'Wow,' he said. 'You're really beautiful.'

'Thanks.'

'No, really,' he said, with utter sincerity, his face was frowning with so much sincerity. 'Really beautiful.'

'Well,' she said. 'That makes two of us.'

He smiled at that. 'Look,' he said. 'This is the sort of last chance to turn back, isn't it? I just want you to know that's an option. We don't have to do this if you're not ready...'

'Oh, shut up,' she said, kindly. 'We might as well, I'm here now.'

'I think I'll just use the bathroom myself,' he said. He wasn't in there for long, she heard a couple of bursts of deodorant, and he was out again. 'Right,' he said, with an entirely new confidence. There was a ribbed condom slightly weighing down his penis. 'You lie on the bed. I'm going to make love to you as you've never been made love to before.'

'Okay,' she said.

He knelt at the foot of the bed, looked at her feet, narrowed his eyes, *inspected* them. And then, with a suddenness that was probably meant to look very dramatic, but came across as just a bit too deliberate, he darted his head forward. And began to suck at her toes.

'What are you doing?' she asked.

'I'm going to lick you all over,' he told her, very earnestly. 'Every single inch of you, you're going to be kissed on every inch. From head to foot.' He corrected himself. 'Foot to head, I'm working upwards.'

It was quite a pleasant sensation, she found. And, thank God, mostly dry. He only dabbed at her with the tongue, and then any little spittle he left was hoovered up by his lips. That was fine, actually, she wasn't quite sure how well she'd have suffered lying there glistening and soggy. As he poked his tongue between her toes, she actually allowed herself to be aroused. 'You've done this before,' she teased him.

He stopped, looked shocked, serious. 'No,' he said. 'No, really. All of this... this is inspired by you. This is what you bring out in me.'

'Okay,' she said, and closed her eyes. She lay back and blissed out as she felt his tongue climb ever higher up her body. 'It's okay,' she breathed at last, 'that's lovely. You can enter me now.'

'But I've only reached the knees.'

'It doesn't matter, I'm ready.' And she pulled him up closer, and looked him full in the face, and it wasn't a bad face, she thought, a little bewildered but it was trying hard. And she fed him inside of her.

'Jesus,' he said. 'Oh, Jesus.' 'Yes, I'm Jesus, baby, I'm Jesus,' she said to him, 'now keep going. Go on... Oh.'

'Oh,' he said. And then, 'wow.' And then, 'I'm sorry, I got a bit overexcited.'

'That's okay,' she said. 'I was excited too.'

'Did you come?' And however politely he asked, the question sounded so blunt that she wasn't quite prepared for it. She had to hesitate before saying yes. 'You didn't, did you? I'm sorry.'

'I'm pretty sure I did,' she said.

'I'll stay inside. He's been hard all day, I know he'll wake up again.'

'If you like,' she said, and they both lay there, not saying anything for a while. He smiled down at her. She smiled back. It was all very friendly, really. And then he began to start thrusting again. 'Look,' she said gently, 'if you're not ready...'

'No, something's happening down there,' he assured her. And then began to grunt along with each thrust. Come on, he seemed to be saying with those grunts. Wake up. Wake up. And she thought she should do her best to help, she began grunting too, just to chivvy him on. The grunting got louder and louder, it was like some caveman metronome, his light boyish voice given up as he growled ever lower in pitch. Her own grunts sounded embarrassingly tinny beside his, she thought, and she tried to deepen her voice too. And then, 'Can you hear that?' he panted.

'Don't stop,' she said.

'Next door,' he said, 'listen!' And he was right, through the thin walls she could hear their hosts having sex too, Marcia and Whatsisname. Neil. 'Don't stop,' she said, 'use them. Use them to help you keep time.' And on they grunted, all four of them, until at last with a sigh of relief and an exhausted gasp of 'Jesus' it was all over and he was able to roll off her.

'Well done,' she said, sincerely.

'Thank you.' He looked very pleased with himself.

Next door the grunting went on. Her lover smiled indulgently. 'Listen to that,' he said. 'We probably inspired them. Do you think?'

'Maybe,' she said.

'Old married couple like that. We probably reminded them what it was all about.'

'Yeah,' she said, 'look, I'm quite tired now, do you think we could get some sleep?'

'Sure,' he said, and he seemed so serenely smug, she could probably have requested anything, he'd have said yes. 'I'll just pop to the bathroom, be with you in a tick.' She was asleep before he came back.

A few hours later – the neon alarm said it was gone two – she stirred. For a moment she forgot where she was. Then she saw the picture of the goose, and she saw him too, sitting on a chair in the corner, right beneath the TV set. She saw the red glow of a cigarette. She didn't even know he smoked.

'What's wrong?' she said.

'I'm surprised you can sleep,' he said softly. 'They're still at it. It's been going on for *hours.*' And she hadn't noticed it, it'd been so regular that she'd screened it out somehow, but now she could hear it. The same grunts from next door. Keeping rhythm, keeping time.

'Jesus,' he added, and sucked on his cigarette.

'I don't think you're supposed to do that in here,' she told him.

'Sorry,' he whispered, and stubbed it out.

iii

They didn't talk about the grunts. She might even have thought he couldn't hear them over the burble of his own chatter, but she watched his face, when there was a grunt she could see him *flinch*, he could hear them all right. They were very erratic. At one point there wasn't a grunt for a good three or four miles, and she thought, it's dead, it must be dead now, and *thank God* – but then it came again, just as clear as before. It's still hanging on, she thought. What's it hanging on *for*?

He'd given up any pretence at companionable silence. He was lively, told jokes even. She didn't have to pretend to respond, he kept talking anyway, she could have been in the boot as well for what difference it made. 'We ought to think of a name for it,' he said suddenly. 'Scientific discovery like this, it'll have to have a *name*. Won't it?' He paused her for a moment. 'They don't name animals after the people who discover them, do they?'

'I think that's inventions.'

'Yeah,' he said, and was disappointed for a while. But he quickly perked up. 'Half bat, half rabbit. What about "babbit"?' They drove in silence for a few seconds, then he laughed. 'Even better! "Rabbat". I like that, what do you think?'

'You said it could be a hare.'

'Oh yes.' He thought about this, weighed up the permutations of syllables, found them wanting. 'I hope it's not half hare,' he said. 'Let's keep our fingers crossed.'

He'd already rhapsodised about the legacy of their achievement, the great worth of what they'd found. Not that he meant financial worth, he quickly assured her, although actually, why not, why shouldn't there be a bit of money in it? The two of them would be famous. They'd be on the news, and in programmes for the Discovery Channel. That had made him pause for thought. That could be a bit complicated, he'd realised. You know, considering what they'd been up to.

'Oh,' she'd said. 'I suppose.'

Maybe, he'd gone on, only one of them should step forward. One of them should get the attention, the media coverage, whatever. And the other one, of course, wouldn't be left out. The other one would be fine. Any money that came his way, he'd split it with her fifty-fifty.

'I wouldn't worry about it,' she'd said.

No, no, straight down the middle. He wouldn't cheat her. They were friends, weren't they? Good friends. Look, it was up to her. I mean, *she* could be the one. If she really wanted to be. She could be the one to step into the limelight...

'No,' she'd said. 'I think this is your discovery. You're the one who ran it over.'

He'd laughed at that and said, yes, he had, hadn't he? He'd been the one. He'd do all right by her, though, she'd see. He'd take care of her. And he'd reached for her with his spare hand, tried to give her a friendly squeeze. And she hadn't been sure what part of her body he'd been aiming for, but what he'd found was her knee, he was at it for what seemed like ages, squeezing away down there like there was no tomorrow. She'd felt her flesh crawl.

'Oh, look,' he said eventually. 'Eighteen miles to the next service station.' About six miles from it he said, 'What do we reckon? We could stop for a coffee. Stretch our legs.'

'I'm fine,' she said.

'Okay,' he said.

Three miles from the service station he said, 'I might get myself a coffee, though. Stretch my legs.'

They pulled into the car park. It was mostly empty, just a few overnight lorries over in the corner. 'Last chance,' he said. 'Can I get you anything?'

'I'll just stay here,' she said.

'I won't be long.'

'Okay.'

He disappeared into the darkness. She sighed with relief. And for a couple of minutes she just sat there and enjoyed it all. The peace of the car. The rain against the windscreen. The grunting from the boot. Then she opened the glove compartment, rummaged inside. Travel sweets, a few CD cases, they weren't much use. She picked up instead the book from which she'd been navigating, a hardback road atlas of Great Britain. Not perfect, but the best there was. She reached under the steering wheel, felt the boot release. She hesitated, then got out of the car.

She swung open the boot. 'I'm sorry,' she said, she was apologising already and she hadn't even seen it yet, she couldn't have told you what she was sorry for, for what she was about to do or that it had taken her this long to do it. For a moment she thought it wasn't even there – the towel was empty, it had been scuffed aside. And then she saw it, hiding in the corner. It shuffled forwards, to the light, to the rain, and to her. 'Hello,' she said, and felt a bit stupid.

It gave another grunt – quieter this time, as if it knew it no longer had to make itself heard through layers of aluminium and plastic. It blinked, and fluttered its wings uselessly. She looked for a wound. The stomach was all but bare, the rabbit had nibbled away at its fur, and the skin beneath looked thin like cellophane. Something moved beneath it, bulged.

'Oh God,' she said. Warily she put her fingers to the belly. And then she was ashamed of herself somehow, that she was being so squeamish, this poor animal wouldn't even be in a Welcome Break car park if it wasn't for her, she put her fingers to the belly and *pressed*. And the belly pressed back against her, a kick, just a little kick.

The rabbit grunted again. And then it just lay back, its distended stomach waving up at the woman brandishing the atlas. It almost made her laugh. Go on, the rabbit seemed to be saying, displaying itself. I'm ready, love, take me. She got a sudden insane urge to lick the rabbit's toes, I'm going to lick you all over. And then she really did laugh, out loud and barking, and the rabbit tutted impatiently.

The skin was so thin, it just needed the littlest help to break. She wasn't one to grow long fingernails, they were a bugger to type with at work, but they were sharp enough anyway. Just one little slit, and that was it, there was something a little wet running over her fingers which she supposed might have been blood but felt different somehow – and the skin pulled back of its own accord from the puncture, opening out into two flaps. And poking free, a little nose, no, several noses behind it, all trying to jump the queue. They were all pushing through the open door at the same time, if they were only that little more patient there'd have been plenty of room, but the babies were blind and stupid. So she put down the atlas, and with both hands held open the flaps a bit wider. And flop – out came the first. And then there was more space, out came all the others, mewing and cooing as they hit the bottom of the car boot with a bump.

Five came out altogether. She waited for a sixth, wondered if she should pick up the rabbit, try to squeeze one out. But at last the mother relaxed, it was all over. Her head lolled back against her own fur pluckings and a couple of empty crisp packets. Her babies kept bouncing around, into each other, into her, chattering away for all they were worth, but she didn't seem to mind. The eyes stared upwards, fixed upon her human midwife. One of the children took a jump right over her head, but she didn't break focus, it didn't distract the severity of that look. Well, lady, the eyes said, what now?

The first baby out, clearly the most entrepreneurial of the bunch, took the leap to jump back over its mother. It jumped higher this time, and as the woman watched, she could see a tentative flap of something small and leathery. A tiny wing slid out from the baby rabbit's side, then back in again, as if it didn't know whether it belonged on a rabbit or not.

And as the rabbit mother stared at her, so she stared at the babies, all of them starting to stretch their wings, to realise they had wings in the first place. And they, of course, didn't stare at anything, their eyes still sealed tight, crying out not in distress but obvious bewilderment.

The expression on their faces reminded her that her lover would be back soon.

'Come on!' she urged them, out loud. 'Come on, quickly!' And she flapped her arms by her sides. They couldn't see her, of course, and even if they could have done, and had had even a *glimmering* of what she was trying to encourage them to do, they'd have found the demonstration somewhat impractical. The mother rabbit grunted at her, and even seemed to roll her eyes.

She picked up one of the babies, the one that appeared to be the genius of the litter. It was soft and wet and seemed composed of nothing but clay skin and those ridiculous tiny wings, she felt its little heart beat as it sat confused in the very palm of her hand. 'Come on,' she said to it again, 'please,' and it bounced around as if summoning up the nerve for a test flight. And then it *did* it, it did, it actually flew, it made the jump out of her hand – and she thought it would simply drop to the ground, and it did drop, that's true – but before it hit the surface it rallied, steadied itself, gained height again. She watched it fly, it was flying, not in a straight line, there was no confidence to it, it was like a drunkard tripping his way home, but flying all the same.

And she turned back to the boot, and saw its siblings, all of them too, jumping about, taking experimental little hops into the air. 'Please,' she said again, as if that would do any good – and then, one by one, each of them rose up out of the car, and took to the night sky. They *soared*. Only a minute old, two minutes, out in the wet, and the cold, and with no mother to suckle them: what chance could they have? And for God's sake, they were blind, they were flying *blind* at a motorway. Their eyes were still glued tight, she ought to get them back, she could catch them and stick them back in the boot, anything would be better, surely? But they were gone. She looked up at the lamp-post, there were creatures buzzing around the light – but they'd never have made it that high, they must be gnats.

She looked back to the mother. She couldn't see the wings, they must have slipped back inside the body, it didn't look special any more. She knew it was silly, but she couldn't help it, she studied that rabbit face for something – gratitude? blame? But there wasn't anything to be seen, it was just a rabbit, that's all. She supposed she should finish what she'd started. She ought to bludgeon it with the hard spine edge of the *A to Z Great Britain Road Atlas (2002 edition)*. But as she picked up the book the rabbit closed its eyes, gave one shuddering breath, and was still.

She got back into the car.

She really thought she'd like to cry now. She really thought that would be nice. She gave it a good go, too; she scrunched up her eyes, tried hard to force something out. The effort made her head smart. It was no good. She clearly wasn't the crying type.

There was a knock at the glass, and she started. He was there, grinning, motioning for her to wind down the window. She did.

'Sorry I've been so long,' he babbled, 'I made a couple of phone calls, they were very excited. Don't think they minded I woke them up.' He passed her a plastic cup, she accepted it dumbly. 'And I got you some coffee anyway. And yes,' he laughed, 'I know, I know, it's soya milk, don't you worry, I got you the soya, don't you worry about that.'

And she told him she didn't want any fucking coffee, if she'd wanted any coffee she'd have fucking got some for herself, what did he think she was, an idiot? What did he think she was? Because he didn't *know* her, he didn't have a clue, he didn't have the faintest fucking idea. And how *dare* he talk to her about soya milk, as if it were some private fucking joke between the two of them, he hadn't earned the right for that, he hadn't earned the right for anything – some joke about soya milk they could be nostalgic about one day, do you remember the time we first met and you'd only drink soya milk, blah blah, that was the same weekend he'd run over the rabbit, how hilarious, she *liked* soya milk, that was all, okay, and it hadn't got the slightest fucking thing to do with him.

And they drove off. If he noticed that the grunting had stopped he didn't say anything, but then he'd hardly bothered to react when there *had* been grunting, so there was no surprise there. In fact, he didn't say much at all, and if it wasn't companionable silence, it was at least silence, so thank God for small fucking mercies.

iv

He'd clearly gone to bed eventually, because when she was woken up at half past eight by a knock at the door he was fast asleep next to her. He wasn't exactly at the far end of the bed, he could have moved further away from her had he really put some effort in, but there was still an appreciable gap between her naked body and his. In sleep his face was utterly without expression, turned towards her. He was cuddling a pillow tightly.

'Just a second,' she called out, and got out of bed. She looked for her nightie, then remembered she hadn't actually packed one. She thought to get a towel from the bathroom instead.

He stirred. 'What is it?' There was another knock at the door. 'Oh!' he said, and his eyes were open, he was wide awake, and he bounded to his feet. 'You go back to bed,' he told her, 'my treat, this is my treat... Just a second!' he called out, and hurried over to the wardrobe. He took out an ironed pair of pyjama trousers, struggled into them.

'Good morning,' he said, as he opened the door. 'Is it breakfast?'

'Breakfast ready,' said a man.

'Do you want me to take it from you, or do you...?'

The man came in, pushing a little trolley in front of him. On it were a couple of plates of steaming food, she thought she could smell bacon, and a mound of toast. 'I'll leave it here,' said the man. He was short and ugly and had a sort of beard, although she couldn't be sure whether that was intentional or simply because he hadn't bothered to shave for a few days. He looked across at her, now safely back under the duvet, nodded. 'Morning,' he said.

'This looks nice,' said the vision in pyjama trousers, flapping after him. 'Lovely. Are you Neil?'

'Yes.'

'You're married to Marcia?'

'Yes,' said Neil.

'Your bedroom is just through there,' and he pointed at the wall. It wasn't really a question, and Neil could have ignored it, but he confirmed that this was the case. 'And you were there last night.' Neil didn't reply. 'Nice.'

'Enjoy your breakfasts,' said Neil. Formal to the end, no hint of a smile, he gave another nod at them both, first to him, then to her. Then left.

'So,' he said. 'That was Neil.'

'Yes,' she said.

He looked over the trolley. 'Quite a feast here,' he said. 'Sausages, baked beans, mushrooms, egg, fried tomato. Are you hungry?'

'I don't really do breakfasts,' she said.

'No,' he said, 'nor me. But breakfast in bed. How could we not?' He brought her over a plate. 'There you go,' he said. She held it in both hands, it was uncomfortably warm. 'Oh,' he said, 'and you'll be needing...' and went to fetch her a knife and fork. 'There you go,' he said. He went to get his own plate, got into bed beside her.

It was hard to eat without a surface to lean on. She'd have rested the plate on the duvet, but she'd have worried the tomato sauce from the beans would have washed over the side. She speared anything that was small, she made short work of the mushrooms. 'Do you want my sausage?' he asked her, and she said no, she hadn't even started thinking about the mechanics of eating the one she already had. 'Fair enough,' he said.

They ate there in silence for a while. She wished she could turn the television on, just for a bit of company.

'What do you want to do today?' he asked her. 'We're on holiday, it's up to you. There are some quite nice things around here. I was looking at some of the leaflets last night. There are some underground caves, not a million miles away. There's a gorge. Do you like gorges?'

'I don't know. What's it like? You grew up here, didn't you?'

'I've never been. You know what it's like. You don't do gorges on your own doorstep. Thank you for last night,' he said, suddenly and seriously. Oh God, she thought. 'I couldn't sleep, you know what it's like. I just sat there and felt, well. So lonely, actually.' Oh *God.* 'But you were so lovely. I came to bed, and you opened your arms, and I thought, she wants to hug me, she wants a hug. She wants to look after me. And you held me. It was really nice.'

'That's okay,' she said, and remembered nothing.

'No, it really meant a lot. And I felt so at *peace.* Peace I haven't felt for... well, quite a while. You know what I've been through recently, well, you can guess, you know what it's like. I could have slept like a baby. I didn't actually, ha! I was enjoying it too much, your arms around me, I just kept myself awake. Ha! And you smelled so nice. Quite tired now, actually.'

'Well,' she said.

'And I thought, she's one in a million, she's really special. A great friend, whatever else happens. Thank you,' and he leaned across to kiss her. She wasn't sure if it was meant for the lips or not, she wasn't sure even what she *wanted* this kiss to be, and she was pretty sure he didn't know either, his mouth hovered in front of her face for a bit. Then it made a decision, fell upon the forehead, and she blinked under the earnest pressure of it, and thought, well, that's it then, that's the choice he's made. And she felt oddly relieved and oddly saddened, and she splashed some tomato sauce on the duvet anyway.

'Come on!' he said, and laughed. 'We've a whole day ahead of us. It's a holiday!'

They never saw Neil again; they found Marcia in the kitchen, and paid her. 'My treat,' he said, although she tried to pay half, 'no, my treat, you get next time.' 'You two have a lovely holiday,' said Marcia, 'nice couple like yourselves.' They asked her about the gorge, and she said, yes, it was very beautiful, well worth a visit – no, she hadn't been herself, but the leaflets made it look very nice indeed. But they didn't visit the gorge – next time, he said, if we come back – it was a longer drive than he'd thought, and there was a long drive back ahead of him, he didn't want to spend all his holiday driving. 'There's a twelfth century church,' he said, 'we could pop inside for a bit.' So that's what they did, and wandered around for a good twenty minutes – a woman asked if they wanted a guided tour, and they really didn't, but it felt rude to say no. So she bought them a tour for a fiver, he tried to pay, and she said, no, her treat this time, her treat. As they stood there, listening to a treatise on medieval pulpit-making, he tried to hold her hand, and for a while she even let him do so. 'That was very nice,' he said, when they came out, 'I liked that,' and he went on to say that religion wasn't really his thing, how anybody could believe in religion in this day and age was beyond him. He walked on, just solving the mysteries of life and death so glibly, and she felt the urge to say she was a devout Christian, to take offence, but she couldn't quite be bothered, and besides, she didn't believe in God. She never had before, and she certainly wouldn't now, she had no reason to believe in God; she had a few Christian friends and after all that had happened she was *deluged* with sympathy cards and maudlin emails and best wishes on the answering machine, for Christ's sake, and all of them assuring her that the pain would pass, the pain *would* pass if only she could give up her troubles to God, she had to put her strength in God. And her husband had said, well, maybe that isn't such a bad idea, and she'd been utterly floored by that, he'd never believed in *anything*, he'd been the one who insisted they get married in a registry office, he'd been the one who'd upset her parents because he said he couldn't go through the whole hypocrisy of pretending to believe when he just, frankly, couldn't. It really pissed her off, this sudden turnabout on his part, the way a tragedy could turn him into someone so patient and caring and sanctimonious; he said they had to find faith in something, otherwise how could they go on, how could they go on?

They walked one end of the town to the other. A stretch of road had been pedestrianised, and now had cobblestones everywhere. 'Very olde world,' he said, and he pronounced the 'e' on the end of 'olde', and she supposed that was correct, but it still made him sound a bit of a tit. It began to drizzle, and they took shelter in a

WHSmith's. It was a very nice WHSmith's, he said. She bought herself a copy of the *Radio Times*.

'Do you fancy some lunch?' he said to her at last.

'I've only just had breakfast,' she said.

'I know.' But it was still raining, so they went into a café anyway. They ordered toasted sandwiches.

'You can talk about your husband if you want.'

She thanked him politely, and asked him exactly why she would want to do that.

'I don't mind,' he said kindly. 'I'll tell you about my girlfriend. If you'd like me to.' He breathed in, smiled bravely. 'Okay, I'm ready,' he said. 'Now, this is a bit complicated.' And he told her just about the least complicated thing she'd ever heard.

'It's not fair,' he said eventually. 'She seems so sure. How can she be so sure? Love, it's a complicated thing, isn't it? How do I know that what she feels is the same thing I feel?'

'Quite,' she said.

'I mean,' he went on, 'I'd have thought you could only love one person. Or what's it all about? What can it mean otherwise? But now, I can't be so sure. She'd like us to get married. She'd like us to have kids. Can you see me as a father?' He laughed. 'I mean, can you?'

She couldn't see why not, lots of people were having kids, there were kids running about all over the place. They had to come from somewhere. 'I suppose not,' she said.

He smiled at her. Tilted his head. 'Why is that, do you think?'

'What?'

'I mean, you know me. What is it about me, what makes you think I couldn't be a father?' He sat a bit closer to her. 'Please tell me. I'd really appreciate your insight.'

'I don't know,' she said. 'Maybe you'd make a great father. I bet you would.' His face fell a bit. 'Yeah,' she went on, 'I can see you doing it all, the school run, changing nappies, everything. Yeah.' By now he looked thoroughly wretched. 'I bet you're very fertile, why not?' He perked up at this, supposed yes, he might be.

'But what sort of role model would I be?' he asked her seriously. 'I mean, I don't think I'm a bad man. I wouldn't, you know, hurt anyone. But what sort of man would betray... I mean, here we are. And what we've done is bad, isn't it? All that stuff in bed. I mean, it was very nice, but really, come on, let's be honest, it's filthy. It's a filthy thing to do. Isn't it?'

'Yes,' she said.

He let her pay for the sandwiches, they went out on to the cobbles again. The rain had stopped. They did a bit of window shopping.

'Look,' he said. 'I'm sorry. This was supposed to be a magical weekend for you. I wanted this to be really magic. And it hasn't been.'

She assured him it'd been fine. It certainly beat being at home on a Sunday afternoon.

'And last night should have been magical too. I think... I just wanted it too much. It felt like all or nothing. Which is silly, because we're friends, aren't we, you're not going anywhere.' He took her hand. 'We shouldn't be here, looking in Marks & Spencer. We won't get much chance to do it, we should be shagging, we should be shagging each other's brains out. That would be good.'

'Oh, I don't know,' she said.

'Please,' he said. 'Please. Let me try again. Let me finish what I started.'

She checked her watch. It was only quarter past three.

They drove back to the hotel. Marcia was surprised to see them, wasn't nearly as welcoming. 'Did you leave something behind?' He asked her if they could have their room again. Not for a whole night, just for a few hours. She looked unhappy about this. 'I haven't made up the bed yet,' she said. He told her that was no problem. She said okay, but she'd need to be paid a full night. He said fine. And she'd need to be paid *now*, if they were just going to take off when they felt like it. Fine, he said, and gave her the money right there and then.

The room was just as they'd left it. The stains of red she'd made on the duvet looked rather lurid. He'd brought his suitcase in from the car, she couldn't see why, and he started to unpack. 'For God's sake,' she said, and he explained it was just for the toiletries, he had to be clean, she'd want him clean, wouldn't she? And he went to line them all up in the bathroom.

'Let's make magic,' he said. He asked if he could undress her, and she said she couldn't really see the point, there was no magic in getting undressed. But he pleaded, he promised it would be fun, so she let him, and it wasn't. 'You're beautiful,' he said, at last, looking at her naked body. She told him she already knew. 'You don't want me to undress you, do you?' she asked, rather sternly, and he said that on balance that wouldn't be necessary.

'Lie on the bed,' he told her, and she did. 'I'm going to lick you on every inch of your body. I'm going to do it properly this time. You'll see.'

'No,' she told him. 'Enough of that. If you want to fuck me, you fuck me. All right?' He looked as if she'd broken his favourite toy.

'Listen,' she went on. 'You want this. Do you hear me? You're the one who wants this. I don't want this. I don't need this. It's you who wants a fuck. In which case, for God's sake, for God's *sake*, just get on and do it.'

'You don't want this?' he asked.

'No,' she said. '*You* want it. I want to make that very clear.' She looked at his penis, and it didn't even have the decency to wilt a little.

'Okay,' he said softly. And struggled with a condom wrapper.

'You're not listening,' she said. 'No fucking condoms. No nothing. Fuck me now, fuck me right this *second*. Or fuck off. Don't you see?' He stared at her. 'I don't care. I just don't *care*.'

So he fucked her. It was tight, and it hurt, but at least it *felt* like something. And he began to grunt, and she joined in too, one grunt from him, one from her – utterly out of time now, but it was honest, the grunts just came out the way they wanted to.

And from next door, too, the grunts began in earnest.

'I don't believe it,' he said, and froze.

But there they were. Louder than theirs. Bolder. And much much happier.

He pulled away – she tried to hold him back, keep him inside, but he had rolled off her now, his face a picture of fury, his penis already dropping and giving up the ghost. 'Shut up!' he cried, and banged on the wall.

'Come back to bed,' she said.

But he was having none of it. His fists pounded against the homely wallpaper. The goose picture jumped at the impact each time, as if in surprise. 'What are you doing?' he screamed. 'What's in it for you? Have you even *looked* at each other? She's a tub of lard, he's... he's a fucking *dwarf*...! Why are you doing this to us?'

'It's funny,' she told him. 'Can't you see it's funny?'

And he began to howl a little, as he kept those fists banging uselessly against the wall. Because they didn't care next door, they must have heard him, of *course* they had, but the grunting didn't even pause a beat, on and on it drove, and he was crying now, actually crying, angry tears, streaming every which way. She watched with utter fascination as he at last lost the energy to rail any more, and sat down on the edge of the bed, sobbing and bawling like a baby.

What it must be like to cry like that, she wondered coolly. She hadn't cried for such a long time. She hadn't even tried for a while. She should some time, she decided then and there, she'd give it a bash, see if anything came out.

'She doesn't deserve this,' he was saying, 'I mean, yeah, she pisses me off, she's such a *child*, I'm so sick of being the adult all the time...' And this was so funny, she had to laugh out loud.

He stared at her, surprised, his face wet and red. 'Don't you feel any guilt at all?'

'No,' she said.

'Jesus,' he said. 'What's the matter with you?'

'I'm dead inside,' she told him. She said it very simply, but the words still sounded gloriously melodramatic, she just had to say it again. 'I'm dead inside, that's how they put it,' she said. She laughed at that, and his face was such a picture of horror and confusion that she laughed at that too.

They didn't speak for a while. He sobbed a little more, then was still. The grunting next door just went on.

'I'm very tired,' he said at last. 'I didn't sleep much last night.'

'You should get some rest,' she said.

He nodded, lay out on the bed. She got up. 'Just shut my eyes for a while,' he said. 'Might as well, the room's paid for.' He cuddled up to a pillow. She drew the curtains. 'Thank you,' he said.

She got dressed. It was still light enough that she could read the *Radio Times*. She sat on the chair under the TV, read the listings, found out what programmes she'd been missing. There was an old film she quite liked playing on BBC2; she switched on the set, but turned the sound off, followed the last half hour on subtitles.

And a little while after that she climbed into bed next to him. He didn't wake, but moved to her anyway; she opened her arms, and in he came, and she held him. And she even gave him a kiss – just the once, mind, and gently, and on the forehead. And at some point the grunting must have stopped – she didn't notice it any more, anyway.

v

He said he'd drop her off at the top of the road. It'd be safer that way, and the rain had stopped, she wouldn't get wet walking home. She said she didn't care. Then he thought, and said, no, he'd drop her outside the house. Why not, he wasn't ashamed. And it was so late at night, surely that'd be okay, unless – and he laughed – her husband was given to staring out of the window at four-thirty in the morning. If he was, he'd be very odd! If he was odd like that, no wonder she was having an affair! And she said she'd meant it the first time, drop her where he liked, she really didn't care.

He parked the car, looked at her. 'Well,' he said. And smiled.

'Well,' she said.

'I know that wasn't quite the weekend we'd been looking forward to. But I want you to know, most sincerely, I had a really good time.'

She nodded. Fumbled for the door handle.

'We're okay, aren't we?' he said. 'We're still friends. We're still going to have those gossips by the third-floor lift at lunchtime?'

'Why not?' she said. 'I'll see you tomorrow.'

'I love you,' he said.

And there was nothing to say to that. He broke into a shy grin.

'Well, it's out there now,' he said. 'That's put my foot in it!'

She pulled at the door handle. And forgot she was still wearing her seat belt. She sighed.

'I didn't know you could love two people at once,' he said. 'It's a funny thing, this love thing. And I do still love Alice,' and it took her a moment to puzzle out who Alice was, 'but, you know, if I have to choose between the two of you, I'll go with you. I will. It'll break Alice's heart,' and she now just pictured poor Alice, lying on a bed somewhere, glistening with his spit as he licked every inch of her body, wet and sticky and bored out of her tiny fucking mind, 'but if that's the way it has to be, then... You don't have to leave your husband,' he added helpfully. 'You know. I'm not asking for any sacrifice on your part.'

'Thanks.'

'I'll just fit right in.'

'I get it. Thanks.'

'You want to go, don't you? Sorry.' And he undid her seat belt for her. She pulled it away gratefully. 'I just think. What you said. You're a very unhappy person, I think. And that just breaks my heart. Because I know I can make you happy. I can *fill* you with happiness, if you just let me.' He opened his arms out for a hug.

She looked at him. She supposed a hug wasn't worth much, not after what she'd given him already. But she was damned if she was going to feel his body around hers again.

He frowned, waiting. 'I'll take care of you,' he said.

And then, from the boot, she heard a grunt. She checked his face. No doubt about it, he'd heard it too.

It broke the moment. He lowered his arms. They both looked behind them, even though obviously there'd be nothing to see.

'No,' she breathed.

His silly boyish face broke into a beaming smile. 'He's all right!' he said. 'What a relief! Isn't that a relief?'

'Yes,' she said, softly.

'Do you know, I thought he'd died on me. I thought he was back there, you know, already rotting away. I thought I was going to have to slap him straight in the freezer!'

And all she could think of were the babies. The mother hadn't finished giving birth to her babies – there'd been others inside her broken body, needing to be rescued.

'I've changed my mind,' she said. 'I'd like to look after it.'

'What,' he said, 'the rabbat?'

She had failed them. She should have picked up the mother, she should have checked. She should have picked her up, put her fingers between those flaps of skin, her whole hand if need be. She should have rummaged around, found whatever else was incubating inside, should have pulled them free.

'You said I could,' she said. 'You said it could be *my* discovery. And I want it to be. I've got the perfect room to keep it in. It's like a little nursery, it'd be lovely. It'd be happy with me. She'll be happy.'

'Yes,' he said doubtfully. 'I'm sure. But I've got a nice room too. I'm sure we've both got nice rooms.'

'You love me,' she said. 'Give me the rabbit.'

There was another grunt.

He licked his lips. She didn't take her eyes off him.

'It is ours,' he agreed. 'I said it was ours. We've so much to share. But I'm going to be the one who cares for it.'

And she could have insisted, maybe. She could have fought him, she could even have offered to hug him, to accept his love, to go on as many weekend shag sessions as he liked. But it was half four in the morning, and she was tired, and the seat belt was off now, wasn't it, and the door was open too – and she got out of the car.

'Don't worry,' he said. 'I'll take care of everything.'

And as she walked up the road, she thought she could hear the grunting from the boot – louder, more desperate. It was calling for her, she knew that, the grunts were for *her*, where are you *going*, and she kept walking, and she didn't look back.

There was a note from her husband waiting for her on the kitchen table. It told her that he loved her and that he hoped she'd had a good weekend and hadn't worked too hard at the conference, and that he'd had to go to bed, he couldn't wait up any longer. It wasn't that long a note, but her husband had appalling handwriting, and she was only halfway through deciphering it when he quietly entered the kitchen.

'Hey,' he said softly.

'Hey,' she said. 'Why aren't you in bed?'

'I was,' he said. 'But I don't know. I suppose I was waiting for you to get in.' He gave her a kiss on the cheek. 'How was it?'

'Oh, you know,' she said. 'I'll tell you tomorrow.'

He nodded.

'Go on,' she said, 'you go back to bed.' Please. 'I'll be up in a minute, I'll just have a cup of tea, then I'll join you.'

'I'll make you some tea, I don't mind.'

'It's okay,' she told him, firmly but gently, the way she'd been advised, the way they'd both been advised, 'I can make tea.' And he smiled, and agreed, and they both knew he'd been told not to fuss her, they mustn't fuss each other, and then one day everything would be magically back to normal.

The kettle took a while to boil. She walked into the sitting room, turned the lights on, just looked at it pointlessly. Then she turned the lights off, and closed the door behind her. Then she went into the dining room – well, they called it a dining room, they ate in the kitchen mostly – and she turned the lights on there, she looked at that too. Then she turned the lights off, and closed the door behind her. The kettle still hadn't boiled, so she went upstairs, very quietly. And she opened the door to the nursery. Their useless little nursery.

They'd even stripped the wallpaper, just to put up something more colourful and childlike. She turned the lights on, looked at this room as well. They should turn it into a spare bedroom, she thought, be useful for when guests stayed over. Assuming guests would want to stay over any more. And maybe that boy had been right, maybe loving two people at once would have been a bit complicated, maybe it was for the best. And she pulled at a hanging flap of wallpaper, and turned off the lights.

She went downstairs, and drank a cup of tea.

Then she went up the stairs to bed. Her husband was already asleep, just this mound in the darkness. She quickly got undressed – she was getting used to that, she thought, and then it was gone, that really was the last attention she paid that weekend, it was now behind her. She slipped in beside him. He grunted a little, nuzzled against her. And then didn't make another noise, all they had was this companionable silence. She felt warm and safe and utterly unreal.

'Listen,' she said, softly. 'I don't love you any more.'

He didn't reply. But his breathing became less regular.

'Listen,' she said again. 'I did love you. Oh, God, I loved you so much. And I wish I loved you now. But I don't. I want to end this, whatever it is we've got. Listen. I want to put it out of its misery.'

She wished she could cry. That would be so great, right now. Make the whole thing so much more momentous. But no, dead inside was all she felt.

She had an idea. She turned on the bedside lamp. She wanted to see the expression on her husband's face. And, more importantly, if it made any difference. She studied it carefully for a good few seconds. 'That's what I thought,' she said at last, then rolled over, and turned out the light.

Sweet Nothings

He was in love. He knew it was love, too, it wasn't just lust, it wasn't like all the other animals, going at it hammer and tongs all through the night. It was true that he liked to look at her when she bathed naked at the pool, and that he did it hidden, behind the trees where she couldn't see – it was spying on her, yes, but it wasn't spying *furtively*, that wasn't it at all, he just didn't want her to feel she had to make polite conversation with him as she performed her ablutions. It was considerate of him, that was all. And as he watched her cup the water in her hands, and tip it over her head, so that it flowed down her long black hair, off her perfect nose, down her perfect chin, on to her perfect breasts – it was true, he supposed, yes, he felt the little pink sausage between his legs stiffen. Indeed, whenever he thought of her, and that was quite a lot, the sausage would balloon every which way, it made it a little hard to walk straight. But it wasn't lust, or not merely lust at any rate, it was love, he knew it was *love* as well, whatever else might be going on downstairs in the sweaty areas love was definitely a major part of it.

He knew it was love, because of the love songs. They gave poetry to his passions, they dignified the sausage. He'd watch as she rubbed herself dry with leaves – if she dried herself at all! sometimes she just walked from the pool glistening in the smooth heat! – he wouldn't dare blink, not wanting to miss a single second. And his every nerve was thrilling with desire. But he wouldn't masturbate, no, not any more. He'd return home, and there he'd stamp down with his trotters, he'd thwack his haunches against the trees – and out of that he'd find a syncopation, and out of that a basic melody. And he'd sing. He'd let his feelings out. The first songs had been descriptions of her body, all those fleshy parts he himself didn't possess but which looked so *ripe*; but soon the lyrics became more sophisticated, they told of her innocence, of her spirit, of what she symbolised to him every day dripping wet, the most perfect of creatures in the most perfect garden. Sometimes he'd sing of himself too, of the preposterousness of his love, of the impossibility he could ever do or say or give anything that could make her happy. And these songs were the most beautiful of all. As he sung them he'd be taken out of himself quite, be so lost in the rightness of the music that he forgot how bruised his poor heart felt, enjoy the song for its own sake and be happy.

His wasn't the first music in the garden. Not whilst the birds hungered for worms, or the lions purred in their sleep, or the monkeys rutted all day long screaming in frenzy. But his were the first love songs. The first songs in all the world that weren't simply cries of impulse, that appreciated something other than the singer's own wants and needs. The strange sound made a lot of the animals wary. Most of them gave it a wide berth. But some, in spite of themselves, couldn't resist the call of it, something which could be so mournful and yet still so celebratory – and they'd spy on the singer secretly, hiding behind trees to hear his music, just as he hid from the naked woman who inspired it.

One day the man came to see him. He didn't much like the man, and he was pretty sure the man didn't much like him either. It wasn't that they were enemies, nothing like that; they'd politely nod a greeting at each other if they crossed paths on their way to church. But the man was a shallow creature, he hadn't a poet's soul. Rumour said he'd already shagged his way through half of the animal kingdom, anything vertebrate that caught his fancy, he'd love it and leave it. His longest relationship had been with a penguin, and they'd just broken up rather messily; the man hadn't been after anything committed, but the penguin had felt used, penguins mated for life. 'Hello, pig,' said the man.

'Hello,' said the pig. 'How are you?'

'Yeah, I'm doing good, yeah, yeah, I'm fine. Actually,' said the man, and he hunkered down in the straw next to the pig, although the pig hadn't invited him to sit, 'actually, that's what I came to see you about. I need a bit of advice.'

'Oh?'

'God's having one of his strops. Told me it was high time I stopped fucking around – his words – and settle down with a mate. For life! And you won't believe who he's picked.'

The pig felt his heart go cold.

'"Can't I pick another one?" I said. But he did insist. We look about the same, it's going to be like doing it with your own *reflection*. Well, apart from the udders. Where's the fun in that? And he said that if I refused, he'd expel me from paradise.'

The pig licked his lips nervously. 'Maybe it'll blow over.' God was always threatening expulsion from paradise for something or other.

Smoking, swearing, dropping litter, eating fruit. It was usually best not to take him too seriously.

'I think he really means it this time,' said the man. 'He had his frowny face. And he says that if I do it, he'll raise me high above the other beasts and give me dominion over you all.'

'That's nice,' said the pig.

'I didn't say there weren't perks. But, shit, though, yeah?'

The pig agreed politely that it was shit. But he didn't see what any of this had to do with him.

'Oh come on,' said the man slyly, and gave a grin that showed all his teeth. 'Everyone knows how you feel about that woman. It's obsessive, that's what it is. What's she going to see in you? You're a fat pig.'

It could have been put more tactfully, but the pig knew it was true. So he sighed and nodded and did his very best not to look put out.

'All I want from you,' the man went on, 'are a few tips. Just tell me what's so great about her. All furless and tailless like that, walking about on hind legs, I don't get it at all. Help me out, and I'll tell you what. I shan't be angry with you. I shan't be angry that you've been ogling my fiancée. Yeah? All right? Is it a deal?'

So the next morning the pig and the man hid together behind the tree, the one that commanded the best view of both pool and breasts. The pig had promised that this was the time of day when the woman was at her most compelling, her most hypnotic, her most magical – and the way that the nipples stood up in the cold water was just great. They watched for a while as she washed. 'Yeah, I don't get it, piggy,' said the man at last. 'Tell me what I'm supposed to be enjoying here. All I see is some broad getting wet.'

And the pig wanted to explain it wasn't to do with the wetness per se, it was the little details surrounding it. The way that as the woman cupped the water she deliberately let it run through her fingers wastefully, clearly enjoying the sensation as it trickled back into the pool. That at first she'd flick the water over her shoulders drop by drop, as if teasing herself, as if pretending she wasn't going to let them get soaked, not really – only to drench them moments later as she all but flung entire waves behind her. That, as she did all these things, she smiled – but it was a strange smile, a slightly sad smile, as if there was something else she wanted from these visits to the pool but didn't yet know what. The pig didn't know either, of course. But that was the beauty of her – all the other animals were out there eating and shitting and sleeping and fucking, that was how they filled these perfect days – and here there was this one creature, this one solitary creature, alone in all the world, that was *enigmatic*. But the pig couldn't find the words. He didn't know the words. So he stamped his trotters, he thwacked his haunches. And he sang instead.

The man listened to the song. He said nothing. Then he shrugged his shoulders, and stepped out of hiding.

The pig watched the man wade into the pool. The movement of his legs produced ripples which flowed out and expanded and hit the woman's own. The woman watched too as the man came nearer. She looked at him blankly, without curiosity. The pig had seen many creatures try to seduce the woman, but all had been rebuffed: the rhinoceros that tried to tempt her with a bit of rough, the serpent with his honeyed words. The pig wanted her to reject the man too. The man came to a halt beside her. She didn't move. Nor did the man. The water came up past his thighs, just grazed his testicles. The ripples dispersed, and the water around them was clear and unbroken.

Then the man began to sing. And the pig was astounded, at first he thought the man had been inspired to create a love song of his own, but no, hang on, this was *his* love song, wasn't it, this was his. He hadn't recognised it immediately because the man had no trotters to stamp, instead he was kicking at the water – and this was better, somehow, the drum beat was subtler that way – and rather than thwack his haunches he was using his hands to clap, and the claps were brisk and crystal clear. But it was the pig's tune, and the pig's words, even if the words came out in a rich baritone far more suited to the expression of love than the pig's reedy squeal. The song was over. The offer of love had been made. The woman just stood there and stared, her mouth hanging open a little. And then she stepped forward – yes, she moved towards *him* – and she kissed the man on the mouth. He kissed her back, and they swayed together in the embrace of it, her breasts now squashed flat against his chest, his testicles bobbing about on the water like dinghies in high seas – and it didn't stop, they made love right there in the pool, rutting away like the monkeys would. It was exciting stuff, the pig had to admit, and he couldn't help but watch the performance from behind the tree. But it made him feel awkward too, and very sad, and there was a new sick taste in his mouth as he saw the man enter the woman and heard her give a cry of pain and delight, and then he felt his swollen sausage dwindle to a chipolata and knew it was time to go home.

For a few days the pig continued to compose his music. But it wasn't very good; there comes a point when songs about heartbreak, no matter how earnest, are no longer artistic but merely petulant. And besides, the gravel he needed to put into his voice to convey how miserable he felt made his throat sore. So he gave up, he went back to doing what pigs were supposed to do, eat filth and shit filth and get fatter. He no longer had the urge to see the woman bathe. He knew logically that she was no more lost to him now than she had been before, but it seemed different, it seemed wrong. But he did see her, again, one last time.

God pronounced himself well pleased with his favourite son, elected himself best man, and promised that the night before the wedding he'd throw the most pissed-up stag do in the whole of Creation. He pronounced too that the bride and groom would be at home to receive congratulations and presents from all the beasts of the garden. The pig watched as the giraffes and the cows and the mosquitoes traipsed their way to the man's lair, all clutching collections of berries and shiny pebbles and interestingly shaped pine cones, all with smiling platitudes on their lips – or, at least, those that had lips to smile. The pig could not be such a hypocrite, and stayed at home. But the more he skulked and sulked the worse he felt; at last he could resist it no longer; one morning he went to the pool. This time he didn't hide behind the tree, but stood out from it, boldly. The woman was washing her hair and humming to herself softly. The pig cleared his throat. She didn't notice. He cleared it again, louder, and hated the way it sounded, so shrill.

'Oh,' she said, turning around, seeing him there on the bank. 'Hello!' And then she smiled.

'Hello,' said the pig.

There was silence for a little while, and still she stood there, smiling at him, and the pig basked in the warmth of it. At last it wobbled, she frowned a little. 'I'm sorry,' she said. 'Do I know you?'

'No,' said the pig. 'No. Sorry. We've never been... I've never quite... I'm the pig.'

'Hello, pig!' said the woman, brightly.

'Hello,' said the pig again.

'Did you want to give me a wedding present?' asked the woman.

'No,' said the pig, honestly.

'Oh.'

The pig nodded sadly at that. And she nodded, not so sadly, not to worry, said that nod, I don't need any more berries anyway! And he nodded again, with a rueful smile, I can quite see that you don't! And they stood like that for a little while, both smiling somewhat awkwardly, and the pig broke first, he felt very self-conscious and blushed rasher red. 'Bye, then,' said the pig, and turned to leave.

'Bye, pig,' said the woman. She started humming again. And now the pig was close enough to recognise the tune. And he knew then, if he had ever doubted it, that the love song was the reason she had accepted the man, it was his song, all the song's fault. So this is how it would be, the human race founded upon a lie, the words of a pig taken by a thief.

'Yes,' said the pig. 'Yes.' The woman turned back, puzzled. 'Yes, I have a present for you.' And he sang to her. He sang his favourite song, so familiar to him that some nights he was sure he dreamed it – but it was different this time, it was to *her*, he didn't like his voice but it was richer and stronger for her presence, it sounded good to him at last, and when he stamped his trotters he did it with such conviction that it hurt, it *hurt*. And the words were of the glory of love, how it gave him a reason to live, but also its cruelty, what was the point in it being so very hopeless? And the whole truth of it stung him, as his voice soared to the upper register, to notes he'd never dared reach before, he felt tears spring to his eyes. And then – and then. And then she smiled, and then she sang too, she sang along with him. Her soprano took the melody and he deferred to her in descant, and for the first time he felt connected to something, for the first time he had a place in this brave new world, and the tears rolled down and burned on a face now glowing with pride.

And then the song ended.

'Thank you,' she said. 'Thank you.' She walked out of the pool towards him, and the pig shivered with her closeness, but he didn't back away, he bravely stood his ground. And she kissed him, just once, very softly, on his snout.

'It's my husband's song,' she said. And for just a moment he still thought she might have understood, and then, 'He taught it to you, didn't he?' And he couldn't say anything, he wanted to say something, but no, here she was, still speaking, and with such innocent enthusiasm, 'Could you sing it at our wedding?' And she seemed so happy, that warm smile, and he was nodding, he was nodding at her like an idiot, 'I'll ask my husband right now, you can sing it to us all,' and he tried to say it, no, don't tell him, no, he'll know why I sang to you, *he'll know what I was trying to do...* But he nodded, he nodded all the same. 'That's settled then,' she said cheerfully. 'I'll see you at the wedding.' And she turned right round, and she walked away.

She did see the pig at the wedding, but he wasn't part of the choir the woman had asked for. The man had taught the song instead to a gaggle of geese, and a few squirrels, a dog, a llama or two. But he wasn't a patient teacher, and the animals weren't good students, and though no-one could fault the gusto of the performance, the love song didn't impress the way it might have done. Still, everyone clapped politely all the same, and said how wonderful, what a lovely song, how very *nice* it was, you must be very proud, Mrs Man, to have such a poet for a spouse. And the man stood up and grinned with all his teeth, as he was wont to do, and let the wedding feast begin. And there were goblets of wine pressed from God's own private vineyard, and bowls brimming over with once forbidden fruit, and platter upon platter of delicious roasted pork.

Pang

When he came home from work he found her sitting at the kitchen table. Smiling sadly, she tapped the chair next to her and indicated he should sit down. So he did.

'We need to talk,' she said, and, of course, he knew straight away something was wrong. They didn't ever need to talk, they never *needed* to talk. If one of them ever wanted to say something, it was easy, they'd just come out and say it, it didn't need to be prefaced by anything, it didn't need an *announcement.* One talking, one listening, that was the way it worked, and then back into that affable silence they both enjoyed.

'It's my heart,' she said. 'It's been giving me, I don't know. Pangs.'

'Pangs?'

'Pangs, yes. I think that's the best way to describe it.'

He didn't know what to say. He knew something was probably expected of him, but God only knew what. One of her hands, the one that wasn't gripping a mug of cold and forgotten coffee, lay on the table. She didn't seem to be inviting him to touch it or hold it or do anything in particular to it, but he could reach it without it looking contrived, so he did so. He gave it a sympathetic squeeze. It was cool with sweat.

'There,' he said. And 'There,' he said again. And then, in a voice he hoped sounded helpful, 'Well, it's something we'll sort out. Isn't it? We'll just have to jolly well sort it out. Take care of you. You're not going anywhere!'

'Darling...'

'You'll have to take it easy. We'll go on a holiday, somewhere restful, wherever you like. I've got holiday due, I expect, in August, can you hold on till then? And I can do more work round the house, get you off your feet a bit...'

'Darling, I've been to the doctor's.'

'And that's a start too. Yes, good.'

'They've done lots of tests. And I'm fine. Really, fine. There's nothing physically wrong with me whatsoever.'

'But that's. Well. That's great. Well!' And he gave the hand another squeeze.

And that sad smile she'd been wearing throughout the whole

wretched conversation got a little sadder. 'But I've still got the pangs,' she said. 'It can only mean one thing, I think. I think I don't love you any more.'

Absurdly he didn't know what to do with her hand any longer. It seemed ridiculous he was still holding it. He shouldn't be, surely, not like this, not now? He didn't want to let go, though, just like that, it might make her think he was being angry, or cruel, or wanting an argument. But he knew he couldn't cling on to the hand indefinitely, she'd be the one to take it away if he left it too long, and he didn't want that extra rejection. He came to a decision. He gave it another squeeze, as friendly as anything, and then swung his own hand upwards, very deliberately, to scratch his nose.

And there was silence. Just that sad smile from her, and the nose scratching from him, working at an itch that hadn't even been there in the first place.

'Is it something I've...?' And she was shaking her head. 'Or something I've not...?' And still the head shook. 'Well, what?'

'I don't know,' she said. 'Maybe love, it just stops sometimes. Do you think? It just stops.'

'Maybe it hasn't really stopped,' he said. 'I mean, if it were just a pang, a pang doesn't sound so bad.'

She frowned, gave it a little thought. 'No, I'm pretty sure it's stopped.'

'But you can't, one day, after fifteen years...'

'Seventeen years.'

'Seventeen. Good God, is it really?'

'Oh yes.'

'Seventeen. God. Well. Even more reason.'

'You must feel the same way,' she said. 'Just a little. Don't tell me I'm the only one.'

And he wanted to help her. He'd always tried to agree with her, to like the same films she'd liked, to enjoy the same food. He'd always thought if it mattered so much to her that he shared her opinion, he'd do his level best to accommodate. But he couldn't now. Not this time. And he wished he hadn't let go of her hand so easily, because it began to dawn on him that he might never get the chance to hold it again.

'I've got something for you,' she said. 'I want you to take this back.' For a moment he thought she meant the wedding ring, and said so, and she told him no, it was a *beautiful* ring, they'd chosen it together, and it symbolised seventeen years, seventeen wonderful years, she'd always treasure it. He felt a little better for that. And then she plonked a Tupperware box down on the table.

He peeled off the plastic lid.

'Do you recognise it?' she said gently. And no, he didn't, of course he didn't, he'd given it to her all those years ago.

He wasn't sure if he was meant to inspect it, but she gave him a nod of encouragement, and so he prodded it gingerly with his finger.

'Seems in pretty good nick,' he said.

'Oh yes,' she said. 'I've taken good care of it. Do you know, I've not so much as looked at another man all the time we've been together. No, that's in good working order, that's as new.'

'Well done,' he said gruffly.

'Thank you.'

'I don't want it back. You can keep it.'

'Oh, darling, you say that now. But you might need it again.' She looked a bit embarrassed, then said, 'And there's no rush, but at some point I'm really going to need mine...'

'Oh yes.'

'In your own time. There's no rush.'

There wasn't much to say after all that. They waited out the time it took her taxi to arrive with conversation as polite as it was artificial; he wished they could simply have retreated into those happy silences they were used to, but now even that seemed too intimate. And then the doorbell rang, she let him carry her luggage out to the car – she'd hidden it, already sorted and packed, in the spare room, so that he wouldn't see the evidence of her leaving him before she'd had a chance to explain, and later that night as he lay in a bed which seemed much too big and much too still, he wondered whether that had been a kindly or a cruel thing for her to have done. And then, promising she'd be in touch, and exhorting him to take care of himself, she got up on her tiptoes to peck him on the forehead, as if all this time he'd been not so much a husband as an infant, got into the cab, gave him a wave, and was driven away.

He didn't expect to sleep that night. He surprised himself and drifted off fairly easily, and, yes, he had nightmares, but they were only the nightmares he *usually* had, ones about ageing and unpopularity and ugliness and spiders and his mother and pressures of work, nothing at all about being abandoned by his wife. When the next morning he lay in bed on his own he felt so perfectly normal that he even thought maybe everything was all right, that he didn't *care*. And then it occurred to him that this was his first day waking up into a world in which no-one loved him, and he felt something very like a pang himself.

He got up, shaved, washed, dressed, went downstairs to pour himself a bowl of cereal. He'd forgotten about the Tupperware box sitting on the kitchen table, and seeing it there, lid off, its grisly contents exposed, made him lose his appetite. He didn't want to look at it, he'd put it in a drawer somewhere, eat his cornflakes and have done with it. But something about that little pang he'd felt made him think he should give it a closer look, and reluctantly he poked at it with his finger once more.

And to be fair, it wasn't *especially* grisly. He just wasn't comfortable having body organs lying around the breakfast things, he was squeamish like that. His heart lay, fat and gleaming, in a pool of thinly pinking water. He put his nose to it, gave it a cautious sniff: he didn't quite know why, because he had no idea what hearts ought to smell like, and all he could detect was something slightly stale and coppery. He felt a thrill of alarm, but when he raised his head and sniffed again, he realised that it was even stronger away from the heart – the kitchen always smelt a bit funny, there was something wrong with the fridge. No, as far as he could see, his heart was fine. He probably should have kept the lid on overnight, though, as a couple of moths were floating inside the tub, drowned in the bloodied water. He fished them out, wondered why they'd been attracted to the heart in the first place, did hearts glow in the dark? He decided that, in his lunch hour, he'd pop over to the library and find a book about biology and see.

His wife had always been a woman of firm resolve. Once she'd made a judgment – whether it be on shellfish, that B&B in Wolverhampton, or the decline of the Conservative Party – it was not to be altered. So he certainly didn't expect that she'd have changed her mind, that when he came back from work that evening she'd be cooking dinner in the kitchen, all forgiven, all forgotten, with his heart safely stowed somewhere away from his view. But as the day wore on, he began to allow himself a little hope, that her natural stubbornness would weigh against throwing over so many years of marriage, and by the time he put the key in the front door he had almost believed that all would be well. But it wasn't. And the heart was still, unarguably, implacably, *there*, the only living thing in the house waiting for him to come home. He peered at it, and it beat a little harder at his presence, like a dog wagging its tail at the arrival of its master. Three more moths were floating at its side; he fished them out, binned them, and went upstairs to get changed.

That was the Tuesday. She didn't come home on the Wednesday either, nor on the Thursday. By the Friday he'd stopped expecting anything at all, but there it was, a little flash on the telephone, he'd no reason to believe it was her, but it was – one click, and there was her voice, playing on the answering machine. His heart gave a little flip of excitement. (He heard it splash back down in its plastic box.) He called the number she'd left him straight away.

'Where are you?' he asked.

'Oh, don't ask, darling,' she said, 'I'd rather not tell you. I need a little space to sort out how I feel.'

He realised that all hope was not lost, then. She might still come back to him. 'So, all's not lost. You might still come back to me...'

'No, darling,' she said firmly, 'no.' And he thought, she's just saying that, she can't know. But this time he kept it to himself. 'How are you, darling?' she asked. 'I've been worried about you.'

'Oh,' he said. 'Thank you. But I'm fine.'

'Are you sure?'

'Yes,' he said. 'Really.'

'It's okay,' she said, after a pause, 'not to be fine, you know. It really is. You've always been so big and strong for me, you've been wonderful like that. You don't have to be strong any more. Have you cried yet? You can cry if you want.'

'No,' he said, irritated. 'Why, have you cried?'

'Oh yes,' she said. 'Buckets.' He felt ridiculous, as if this were some sort of contest. 'But then, I've been crying for *ages*, darling.'

'Right,' he said. 'So. Anyway.'

'Anyway. I wanted to ask if it would be all right if I called around tomorrow.'

'Of course. You don't have to ask. I mean, this is your house.'

'No, I *do* have to ask. I really do. I just want to pick up a few odds and ends, you know. Can you have my heart ready?'

He'd decided he had to be the one who hung up first, but somehow she still got her goodbye in ahead of his. He stood by the phone for a while, then realised he hadn't yet taken off his coat, hadn't closed the front door even. 'Right,' he said, as he did so, 'right,' he said, as he changed out of his work clothes into something slightly more casual, 'right, best get to it, then. Best jolly well get to it.' And he began to look for his wife's heart.

Realistically, there were only a few places it could be: the cupboards in the spare bedroom, the hatch under the stairs, a small chest of drawers in the room he'd privately felt it rather pretentious they called the study. His wife was not so sentimental that all the keepsakes and knick-knacks she kept cluttered up the house – some married couples, of course, kept their hearts on the mantelpiece beside the wedding photos, but she'd found such public displays of affection in rather poor taste. 'What is it they're trying to prove?' she'd ask her husband after a dinner with friends, 'if you truly love someone you don't need to put it on *display*,' and when they were safely at home away from prying eyes she'd lean forward and give him a little kiss on the lips. He worked methodically through all the likely cubby holes, but no heart was to be found. It had to be *somewhere*; he wouldn't have thrown it out, surely; it couldn't have been given to Oxfam, what would they want it for? And instead, pouring from these hidden pockets around the house, all the little remnants of their marriage. The valentine cards he had given her. Long-expired passports they had acquired for a single holiday in Tenerife they hadn't enjoyed and never repeated. Their wedding certificate. And before he knew it he was crying, at last he was crying, but it wasn't what you're thinking, really it wasn't – these were tears of *frustration*, of course they were, where was this bloody heart, why the bloody hell wasn't the bloody thing where it was supposed to be? Emptying out old shoeboxes, spilling junk to the floor, but nothing beating, nothing alive. And as he sobbed he allowed himself to resent his wife, just a little bit – sod her, *sod* her, why was she disrupting his life like this, why was he looking for something she'd so freely given him only to demand it back again, you can't *do* that with presents, it wasn't *right*. He hadn't asked for her bloody heart in the first place; she'd been the one who'd pursued him, she'd done all the pursuing, she'd chased him and hunted him down and told herself that he was to be hers, and she always got what she wanted.

A sudden pain in his chest. It only lasted a couple of seconds, maybe not even that. But it took him a full minute to get his breath back, to rise to his feet, step over the debris of the past, and make his way down to the kitchen.

He looked at his heart. It was still beating, of course – if anything, it seemed to be beating rather faster, which was reassuring perhaps. He idly picked out the fresh moths it had acquired, and thought to go. But as he looked more carefully he made out little pinpricks of white, spotted all over. Had they been there before? He couldn't be certain. He remembered his heart being a perfect sea of rich pink, but he had to admit that when he'd looked at it, his mind had always been on other things. Maybe it had always been a bit... well... *speckled.* He fetched the book he'd borrowed from the library, wondered again why diagrams on the page never look remotely like the real thing when it's sitting in a Tupperware box. Yes, see, the line of spots started at the tricuspid valve, then spread up to the... right atrium. He flicked through the book but could find no mention of white spots at all; he supposed he could have looked the white spots up in the index, if only he could have guessed what on earth to call them. So he looked up both 'Tricuspid Valve' and 'Atrium (Right)' in the index instead, but had no joy there either. He put the book away. Rather nervously, fearing another spasm, he pressed down on a cluster of spots gently – then harder, then harder still. Nothing.

He could take it to a doctor, he supposed. Sit in a waiting room for a couple of hours, only to find out that the white spots were perfectly normal. And, by doing so, show the whole world that his wife didn't feel it was a heart worth keeping any more. Most likely the pain was because he hadn't stopped to eat before he'd gone hunting through the cupboards upstairs; now that he was in the kitchen he realised he was ragingly hungry. He rinsed his bloodied hands under the tap, opened a tin of baked beans, and tried to work out what he should do next. And as he filled his stomach, and began to feel so much better, the answer became clear.

The next morning he got up early, and was standing outside the butcher's when the shop opened. 'I want a heart,' he told the girl behind the counter, 'as close to a human's as you've got, a thirty-nine year old woman having pangs.' When he reached home, and opened it up on the kitchen table, he wondered whether the girl might have looked a little harder. He compared it to his own, side by side, and even allowing for the growing proliferation of white specks across its surface, his was clearly in better nick. For a start, this pig heart was unashamedly *blue.* It had its pink bits, to be sure, but only as little islands in these vast oceans of discolouration. It was the wrong size as well, just a little too small, and had bits sticking out of its side which he was quite sure shouldn't be there in the first place; after he'd trimmed off some of the weirder looking crags, the heart looked even more pathetic. He considered nipping back to the butcher's, getting a second heart – maybe he could bolt it on to the side, somehow, give the whole thing a bit more body – but even in his rising panic he realised that wouldn't fool anybody. The greatest problem, though, was the heart's texture. His own, beating away softly in the tub, fairly gleamed; this pig heart looked as dry as death. He rooted through the cupboards, trying to find something he could glaze it with to give it some extra sheen; with great care he painted the pig heart with vinegar using the back of a soup spoon. Most of the vinegar ran off the sides, but enough of it got between the cracks that after a little while the whole thing sparkled. Of course, it now stank. He tried to mask that by spraying it with old perfume he found on his wife's dressing table, and that was so strong he was forced to paint the whole organ with a new coat of vinegar to try to take the edge off.

The doorbell rang.

'Hello, how are you?' she said, and there was a smile of practised cheer as if they'd just been introduced at a party. He asked her if she'd like a coffee. 'No, no, I won't stay, I'll just pick up the... is this it?... thanks.' And she dropped the bagged heart into her handbag, without bothering to look at it or sniff at it. He was relieved, of course, but also a little hurt.

'We need to talk,' he said, and hated the very words.

'I know. I know. We do need to talk. And I'd hoped we'd talk today, but something popped up, I have to go and... But soon. I'll call you. Well. Thanks for this,' she said, tapping the handbag, 'thanks for looking after it,' and she blushed, realising what she'd said.

'Are you giving it to someone else? Is there someone else?'

'No. God. No. It's not been a week...'

'I'm seeing someone else,' he said.

'You are?'

'Yes.'

'It's not been a week.'

'You don't mind, surely?'

'No. No, I don't mind. God. Well, good for you. Well. What's her name?'

'Sharon,' he said, without hesitation. He was pleased by that, because he'd no idea he had a single word left in his head before it popped out of his mouth like that. It could just as easily have been anything, it could have been 'Pipe cleaner', or, or 'Sandpit'.

'Well,' she said, and smiled again, but it was a different smile this time. 'As I say, thanks. As I say, I'll call soon.' She left her keys on the table, and the spare keys, and the back-up set. She wasn't coming back.

He closed the door behind her as gently as possible – it somehow seemed all the crueller that way. And he heard a clatter in the kitchen, and, hurrying back, saw that his heart was on the floor, writhing about in some distress. At least this time there'd been no pain, and he supposed that was an improvement; it had clearly spasmed so hard that it had flipped out of the Tupperware box altogether. Having spent hours hacking away and polishing the pig's heart he no longer felt quite so squeamish handling his own. He picked it up, blew the dirt off, turned it over, and promptly dropped it on the floor again in surprise.

The underside of the heart wasn't so much covered with spots as welts. Studded into the pink tissue, a couple were the size of ten pence coins. They looked like bones growing there – could they have even been bones? he didn't know – he ran his finger along the surface of one of these white blobs, pushed hard, and he thought that maybe it yielded a little under the pressure. He set the heart back in the box, looked at it thoughtfully. Then he decided to turn it back over, because it looked slightly healthier that way up. And then he decided to put the lid back on, put a blanket over it, and shut it away in the cupboard where they kept the best china, because it looked a *lot* healthier that way.

His first weekend as a single man was pleasant. He watched television programmes he'd never have watched with his wife, and realised that although they were no better than the ones they'd watched together, they were now, at least, *his*. There was an unmistakeable thrill to be in charge of the remote control, and when he tired of what he was watching, he'd flip through all the channels as fast as he could – by Sunday night he'd got pretty speedy. He ordered in fast food on the

Saturday, and enjoyed it so much he ordered the same thing for the Sunday. 'Yes, it's me again,' he told the delivery man as he handed him his pizza, but he couldn't be sure whether it was the same chap or not inside his motorcycle helmet. And he tried not to think of his heart. And he tried to think instead of Sharon.

Sharon worked in the Human Resources department, which meant that her entire job was a mystery to him. He didn't know why his brain had come up with her name, but he supposed it might just know something he didn't. Back at work on Monday, he looked at all the women in his open plan office. They were a pretty unprepossessing bunch, but at least Sharon wasn't married, and was probably a bit younger than most. In her early thirties, he guessed, maybe even in her twenties – it's so hard to tell girls' ages when they get that overweight. When she went outside for a cigarette break he followed her.

'Hello,' he said. 'I thought I'd like to get to know you better.'

She blew smoke out of the side of her mouth, said nothing.

'I mean,' he soldiered on gamely, 'only if you'd like that too. I wondered if you'd like a drink some time. If you'd like that too.'

'You mean on a date?'

'Oh,' he said, as if surprised by the very concept, 'I meant a drink. But, yes, it could be a date, yes.'

She looked him up and down. He felt irritated. He knew he was past his best, but at least he'd had a best, he didn't look like a beached whale in a skirt. 'Aren't you married?' she asked.

'Yes. No. Well, sort of. A bit.'

She shrugged to shut him up. 'I don't really care either way.' So why did you ask, then? 'You like Italian?' Yes, he liked Italian. So she gave him the name of a restaurant in town. 'See you there at eight-thirty.' She took a final puff on her cigarette, crushed it under her heel, and waddled back to work.

After he'd scrubbed and brushed and deodorised, and tried to recall other preliminaries he should perform before a date, he opened up the cupboard, took out the tub, fished out the moths that had impossibly got inside, and gave his heart an examination. At first he assumed that he was looking at the underside, it was so covered with those bony welts, but then he realised that all the little spots had clustered and hardened all over it. He weighed it in his hands, and guessed it must be a good three, maybe four pounds more since he'd last held it. He put it down, thinking hard. He checked his watch. There was plenty of time – he'd got dressed and ready to leave a good two hours early, as usual. Then he came to a decision, and went to fetch the knife.

He worked on the bigger of the blotches first. He considered that so much damage had been done there already, he could hardly make it much worse. He hoped the nodule wasn't too deep, but as he inserted the blade into the gap between pink and white and pushed carefully at an angle, it met resistance. He pushed deeper still, and just as he thought he didn't dare push any further, that sticking knives into his heart may not after all be the wisest course of action, he felt the bony substance at last giving. He prised it out with a slight sucking sound; at first he was a bit too timid about yanking the thing out once he'd got a purchase, and it sank back into the tissue with a plop, but he'd now seen what needed to be done and that all it took was a bit of gusto. He freed the pebble, put it into a saucer; where it had been cutting into the heart most deeply there was a bit of gristle attached, a bit of blood, but all in all it was a remarkably clean excision for a beginner. Mind you, there was now a hole in his heart, but it wasn't a *hole*, not really, it was just a little pock mark.

By the time he was attacking the seventh lump he was almost enjoying himself – he got a little careless and knifed through some living tissue, and that gave him a shock of discomfort. He staunched the bleeding as best he could, then put an elastoplast over the cut. He held the heart up to the light, appraised it dispassionately. Not too bad at all. Of course, there were lots of bone bits left, like rivets, but they seemed too small to worry about for now. He felt around the rim of one of the holes he'd created, and it had been so numb during the surgery itself he was surprised to feel that it itched to his touch. A furious itch, and he couldn't help himself, he had to scratch away at the crater, scratch deep and for all he was worth, and the more he scratched, the greater the itch, it felt so *good* and yet it was *burning*, he wasn't scratching now he was tearing, and he literally had to pull his hand away from it with the other to stop. Under his fingernails now were fine shreds of pink, he'd got spots of blood on his cuff. He checked his watch again. There was still time to change his shirt – thank goodness for that!

* * *

She was waiting for him. Black nail varnish, a nicely patterned top, her skirt a little shorter. 'Hi,' she said, and let him kiss her cheek. There was a bottle of white wine in front of her, and she'd already drunk about half of it.

'Sorry I'm late,' he said, although he wasn't late or sorry.

They talked as they waited for their food to arrive. They didn't watch the same TV shows. He hadn't even heard of her music. She seized upon the garlic bread when it arrived. 'I love garlic bread!' she positively enthused, 'do you love garlic bread?' He said he did, and she smiled; it was the first thing they'd found in common. She pushed an entire piece into her mouth, and it barely touched the sides. 'It's very wide, my mouth,' she told him, and grinned. He wondered what her heart was like. Wide and plump and rubbery, like a trampoline.

And as they ate it turned out they had still more things they could agree on. The people she hated at work were, by and large, the same people he suspected hated him. He'd never liked Denise from Marketing. 'No, she's a bitch,' Sharon agreed, devouring a tiramisu and draining the second bottle of house white.

'Things have gone rather well,' he said. 'Do you think? I mean, this could happen again.'

'Sure,' she agreed. 'Why not?'

'I mean, we could be friends. *Really* friends.'

'Sure,' she said, and shrugged.

'I have something for you,' he said. He reached into his bag, and offered her his heart.

'Oh,' she said. 'Now look. This is just a date. Isn't it? I mean.'

'You don't have to take it now,' he said. 'I was just saying. You know, if in the future, you *wanted* my heart. For any reason.'

'Sure,' she said. 'Wow.' She tried to pour herself another wine, realised the bottle was empty, and accepted his glass when he pushed it towards her.

'I'll get the bill,' he said. 'This is on me.'

Outside it was starting to rain. 'Better get a taxi,' said Sharon. 'Too pissed to drive.'

'I'll get you one,' he said. 'You stay here, in the dry. I'll get one.' He stood on the pavement for a full three minutes waving his arms like a windmill. And he thought, this is nice, I'm being protective of her, she'll think this is nice.

He held the door open for her, as she told the driver where she lived. 'Thanks,' he said. 'This has been nice.'

She looked at him in surprise. 'Aren't you coming with me?'

'Sure,' he heard himself say.

Inside she lit a cigarette. The driver told her there was no smoking in the cab. 'It's all right,' she said. 'I'll open a window.' He told her there was no smoking at all. 'If you don't like it, then chuck me out.' The driver said nothing, and drove on. 'Don't give him a tip,' she said loudly, and blew smoke in the direction of the window when she remembered to do so. 'Can I see that heart again?' she then asked unexpectedly.

He gave it to her. She peered at it curiously, holding it close to her face, ash dropping on to it. 'Looks like a Swiss cheese,' she said. 'And what are all these knobbly bits?'

'It's not much of a heart,' he admitted. 'I just need someone to take care of it. It needs taking care of, you see.'

'I've never been given a heart before,' she said. 'Not by anyone.' She kissed him in the ear. He wondered whether she'd been aiming for somewhere better and had missed, but now she was there she coated the inside of it with her tongue. 'Did you like that?' she asked him. He told her it was very nice.

In spite of what Sharon had told him, he gave a generous tip. The taxi driver glared at him and drove off. Sharon staggered into her house. 'Denise!' she called. 'Denise!'

'Who's Denise?'

'My flatmate. You know Denise. From Marketing. Good, she's in bed. I told her to make herself scarce. Come on. Do you want a drink?'

He told her he didn't need another. She fetched a bottle anyway. She sat him down on the sofa, then stuck her tongue once more in his ear. He tried to tilt his head so that she could work her way to his mouth, pretty soon she got the general idea. And before long they were all tongues and teeth – well, to be fair, most of the teeth were hers, and he thought at least two of the tongues – and he was trying to remember how you breathed during kisses like this, it was through the nose, that was it, and she didn't taste like his wife whatsoever.

'Come on,' she said, and all but pulled him to his feet.

On top of her duvet were half a dozen stuffed toys. He felt a twinge of affection for Sharon; here she was, all hard-drinking and hard-smoking, but deep down she was still just a little girl who slept with teddy bears. He felt he'd caught the real person unawares, seen beneath the brassy exterior something small and sweet she liked to keep hidden. Then he remembered that she'd obviously planned on bringing him back here, so always knew he'd see her toys, and didn't know what to think any longer. 'Listen,' she said, as she swept a Snoopy in World War I flying goggles on to the floor, 'I should say. I'm not going to give you *my* heart.'

'Of course not,' he said. 'That's okay.'

'I mean, I *can't.* You see? When I was fourteen I sent it to Robbie Williams. I was a really big fan of his.'

'He must get a lot of hearts.'

'Yeah. I had such a crush. Thing is, I'd really like it back now. I've written to him lots of times, put in stamped addressed envelopes, he wouldn't have to pay the postage. But nothing.'

'He must get a lot of post.'

'Sometimes I think,' she said, and she *was* thinking, she was tilting her head to one side as if to egg her brain on, and it looked odd to see her think whilst quite so drunk, 'I think that we give away our hearts too easily. You know? We're all in such a hurry to get out there and fall in love as soon as we possibly can. And maybe we're missing out, that maybe our hearts would feel so much better if we just kept them inside our chests. I mean, what does Robbie Williams want with my heart anyway?'

'He must,' he said again, 'get a lot of hearts.'

'It's the reason I smoke,' said Sharon. 'And why I eat so much. I keep thinking, if I keep *damaging* my heart, he's not going to want to hang on to it so much, is he? He's going to want to post it back, just to get rid of the thing. But I wanted you to know,' she said, and kissed him again, 'if you think I'm holding back. If you think I'm not putting myself into it completely. That's the reason why.'

And they had sex. He didn't especially feel she was holding back, but now she'd put the doubt in his head he couldn't not let it nag at him. And at the moment of climax, he thought, so that's adultery. That's it. I'm an adulterer.

'Ssh,' she said. 'What was that?'

He strained to hear. And yes, there it was again. A sort of scream, not too loud, but eerie, inhuman. And after that, an all too human one.

'Christ, what now?' muttered Sharon, and went to see. He followed her.

'What the fuck is *that*?' Denise from Marketing stood in the sitting room, pointing at his heart. It was shrieking in what could only be pain, high-pitched and plaintive. And it was glowing so brightly, with a fierce white light that lit the whole room – he saw moths dancing about in the spotlight beam. He had to get close, and shield his eyes, to take a closer look. The bone had spread again, and the remaining patches of pink were straining against it, bulging, livid.

'I don't need this,' said Denise from Marketing. 'I've got fucking work in the morning. I don't need to be woken up by someone's fucking heart.'

'Sorry, Denise,' said Sharon.

'Hello, Denise,' he said, and wished that he was wearing some clothes.

'I want you out of my flat,' said Denise from Marketing. 'Both of you,' she added, indicating the still wailing heart.

The rain hadn't yet eased off, but he didn't think Denise from Marketing would let him wait for a cab. As he walked the darkened streets, lit only by the heart's unearthly glow, its occasional cries sounded particularly loud, and passers-by would cross the road to avoid him. It was as he was getting into a taxi that his heart, which had behaved itself for ten minutes and done nothing more dramatic than hushed quivering, let out a shriek so agonised and despairing that the driver took off without him. He slipped off his coat, wrapped it round the tortured muscle – at first just to muffle the sound of its screams, but as he held it close to his chest, the chest from which it should never have been ripped, he believed it was more to give it as much warmth as he could. The heavens opened; his clothes stuck sodden to his skin. And all he'd say was 'ssh' and 'it's all right' and 'nearly there', and give little noises he hoped were comforting.

By the time he reached home, and opened out his bundle on to the kitchen table, the heart had almost completely ossified. There was one small streak of pink tissue, trying its utmost in spite of all to do its job and pump blood and oxygen around his body. 'It's all right,' he said softly, 'you don't have to try so hard. It's all right, I'll stay with you, I'm jolly well staying with you.' Within an hour it was dead.

'I'm sorry,' he said, and meant it. 'I'm sorry,' although he really couldn't see what else he could have done. 'Sorry,' but it hadn't been his bloody responsibility, had it? He left it, no longer gleaming, just a bony off-white, even the moths weren't interested any more. He'd decide what to do with it in the morning. He slept particularly well that night.

The next day at work a nervous Sharon approached his cubicle.

'I'm sorry about what happened,' she said. 'But I want you to know I really like you, and I'd love to try again...'

'I think,' he said, coolly, looking up from his work for the first time, 'I can do a bit better, don't you?'

And so he could. He soon realised that the worst a woman could do was to say no – and it's true that some *did* say no, but a lot didn't, and the fewer said no the more said yes. He didn't give a toss if they were married; if they broke their husbands' hearts, that was their lookout. He lost a bit of weight. He got himself a little stud earring – and, truth be told, it did make him look a bit stupid, but not *very* stupid, and, more importantly, not stupid *enough.* 'We shouldn't go back to mine,' said Denise from Marketing. 'Why?' he smirked, and so they did, and as they were humping away he liked to imagine the crying he heard in the room next door was something to do with him.

Three months later his wife came back. She was waiting for him on the doorstep when he got in from work.

'You could have phoned,' he said.

'You told me I could come around whenever I liked.'

'Not bloody likely. Anyone could be here.' He opened the door. 'You can come in for a bit.'

'Good news,' she said. 'My pangs have stopped.'

'Great news,' he said, and lit a cigarette. 'What's that got to do with me?'

'I made a terrible mistake,' she said. 'Or maybe it wasn't a mistake. Maybe I *had* to go away for a while. Just to realise that I love you, that I only love you. Maybe I had to put myself through that, put us both through that, just so I'd know for sure. Do you think?'

He just stared and smoked.

'All right,' she said. 'I admit, I did find someone else. He didn't treat me right. I tried to give him my heart, but it wouldn't do anything, wouldn't beat for him at all, it just lay there like a dead weight. And he said it smelt funny.' She fetched it from her bag, held it out for him to take.

'It does smell funny,' he said.

'I know.'

She continued to hold it out. He continued not to take it. At last she put it down on the table, between them, as a compromise.

'I've nowhere to go,' she said.

'There's the spare room. You can have it for one night. Just one night.'

She nodded. Waited for him to say something else. When he didn't, she nodded once more, then went upstairs.

He opened a bottle of wine. After he'd finished his second glass, he supposed he ought to see how she was getting on. Whether she wanted some dinner, he suddenly thought, maybe she was hungry. And he was surprised to feel some concern, where had that come from?

He went into the spare room. She'd been through the cupboards, there was debris all over the bed. From an empty shoebox she'd found his heart. She was holding it in one palm – he'd forgotten how, in death, it had grown so small and wizened.

'Put that back,' he said. 'That isn't yours any more.'

'Look,' she said softly. 'Look.' And she began to stroke it. She blew on it gently.

'It's not yours,' he said, uselessly.

And as he watched, the rock cracked. Pink tissue broke through the stone and bone. 'Look,' she said again. It was struggling, and then it managed a beat, and once it had managed one, it seemed all too happy to beat again. 'Look,' she said, and kissed it. The last of the rock crumbled away at her touch. 'I love you,' she said. 'Look. I love you. Look how much.' And she offered his heart out to him, as good as new.

Dazedly he reached for it. She smiled, nodded. He took hold of it. Looked at it, as it swelled with new life. And then he dug his fingernails in, dug them in deep, dug till it bled. 'No,' she said. And he began squeezing hard, so that one of the ventricles bulged then burst. 'No, stop!' And ripped it apart, tearing at it, pulling off gobbets of it, showering them on to the spare room carpet.

'I told you,' he said. 'It isn't yours. You gave it back.'

And his wife began to cry. He looked away in disgust.

'One night only,' he said, 'and then you find somewhere else to stay.' He wiped his hands on his shirt, then left, closing the door behind him.

'I'll get you back,' she said softly. 'It'll take time, but I'll get you.' And she looked down at the bloody chunks strewn all over the floor. And saw that, in spite of all the damage that he'd inflicted on it – all the damage they'd both done – the shattered heart still, stubbornly, beat.

This Creeping Thing

For Susan, love was just something which crept up on her. There was no such thing as falling in love, falling simply wasn't part of the process; the most Susan could manage would be an odd stumble every now and then. With Andrew there was no specific moment, nothing he did or didn't do, which convinced her he was the right one. But one night she was watching TV with him on the sofa, and it wasn't that they were cuddled up, it wasn't even as if they were watching anything romantic, it was probably one of those cop shows he enjoyed and she tolerated – but she looked across to him at one point, and realised there was a warmth inside her when she did so, something greater than affection. She was in love with him, she suddenly knew it, and she must have been for some time. She wondered how long, it might have been *ages*. It was funny, too, because she knew he loved *her*, and she'd been dreading that he might propose, she wouldn't have known what to say – she hadn't wanted to ruin what they already had, because even if what she felt for him wasn't love it was still very nice: they shared the same bed and the same utility bills, it was all working so well. But now she knew it *was* love, she decided there was no point in waiting any longer, she told him they'd best get married, right there and then in the commercial break. The love – it had just crept up on her. And a year and a bit later, when she was in hospital, and the nurse with the beatific smile was telling her to push and to breathe and all manner of things she couldn't have stopped even if she'd wanted to, and out came her baby son – and everyone congratulated her and the same nurse put the baby into her arms and said, 'Don't you just love him, don't you just love him'... and all she could think was, you think love is a choice, it's something you can *decide.* Obviously I'd love my son if I could, that would undoubtedly be the best thing all round, but it's not looking very likely, is it – this ugly red mass of gunk and tears, he's not exactly a heartbreaker. And just for a moment she felt a flash of hatred for Andrew, surrounding her like all the others, with happy tears streaming down his face, he'd been the one who had talked her into this, she'd managed to love *him*, didn't he realise that was hard enough? She hated him even as she loved him, even as he loved their son, even as she didn't. They called the boy Michael. And even Michael, Susan thought, maybe I'll love him in time. It'll just creep up on me. That's what love is, it's a creeping thing.

And it had been the same with Tom, the first time she'd laid eyes on him she hadn't wanted Tom at all. Not that he was called Tom back then. The naming of him was clearly her responsibility; that night at dinner, her parents still preening themselves with the thought of the lovely gift they'd bought for their daughter, her father said, 'Have you any idea what you're going to call him?' And she'd shrugged, and said, 'Tom.' Just like in the cartoons, it was the first thing she thought of. Her daddy looked a little disappointed that the new member of the household had a name that was so common, but he smiled, and said it was a good name, nice and solid, you knew where you were with a Tom. And her mummy just cooed and said, wasn't Tom just beautiful, she loved him already, didn't Susan just love him?

When Susan first opened the cat box and looked at the little ball of black fluff, it mewed up at her. It wasn't a very forceful mew, more of a high-pitched squeak. She could see it was very pretty, and it wasn't that she had anything *against* the thing, but it didn't seem much to do with her. 'We got you a kitten,' said her daddy, obviously. 'After the way you took care of that hamster, we thought you deserved a proper pet.' Even at eight years old, Susan couldn't see the logic in that. The hamster had died, hadn't it? Her success rate with animals was far from encouraging. She hadn't actually killed it, not as such – she'd fed it, she'd changed the water in its bottle, cleared out any pellets of crap from the cage – but these were all chores she'd fit in before she went to school and after she did her homework. Susan wasn't sophisticated enough to put her thoughts into any order, but deep down she supposed that if a creature could be killed by starving it of love, then she'd murdered Hammie the Hamster good and proper. And now she was going to be let loose on something even more demanding. She couldn't help but feel a bit irritated at the prospect.

And Tom did nothing to endear himself. He'd be waiting for her when she got home from school – and all day long at weekends! – mewing at her, following her about, this little bag of need and piss. It took him a good couple of months before he'd worked out the function of the litter tray, and even after he had (with Susan forced to clean up all the damp patches on the carpet, and take Tom and hold his face into the litter), it took even longer for him to perfect his aim. He was hungry, always hungry. 'Tom's old enough to be let out into the garden now,' her mummy said one day. 'He'll be scared, take him in your arms, walk around the lawn with him.' And so she did, reluctantly, holding Tom firm, his eyes wide, his head twitching back and forth as it took in this new world of clouds and birds and insects and rusting toys.

And he'd get lonely. 'When you're not here,' said Mummy, 'he spends the day searching the house for you. I try to play with him, but he's not interested. He knows whose cat he is, all right.' 'Look at the way he watches you,' said Daddy, 'that cat just adores you.' Susan thought it was creepy. She didn't like the way Tom had taken to sitting outside her bedroom of a night, crying to be let in. 'Go away,' she'd call out to him. If she opened the door to tell him off, he'd chirrup up at her and start to purr, and make a beeline for the bed. 'You've got a basket,' she'd say, 'it's in the kitchen, next to the litter tray.' And she'd pick him up and take him downstairs and drop him there, hard, and push on his back until he slumped over. 'Now go to sleep.' But he never stayed there, he sometimes made it back to Susan's bedroom before she did. 'He's getting a bit noisy,' said Daddy one morning at breakfast. 'Hard to sleep through all that wailing.' And for a second Susan thought that maybe he'd suggest giving Tom away, or at least chaining it down, putting some restraints on it, something. But instead her parents suggested that maybe she should just let Tom sleep in her room once in a while. Mummy knew she'd said she didn't want an animal on the bed, but he was ever so clean, he was always washing himself, and how could you resist a little love like that, didn't you just love him? And Daddy just said he'd like a decent night's rest. And Susan didn't like the idea at all, but she was only eight, and what her parents said was law. So the next night she left her door ajar. In strolled Tom, so arrogant, as if he'd always had visitation rights, and he jumped up on to the foot of her bed, curled up, and didn't stir again until morning. Susan thought Tom would disturb her, but he didn't make a sound, and he occupied such a little surface area on the duvet, really, she hardly knew he was there. And so from that point on this was where Tom slept every night, and it was funny how he did it – he was nowhere to be seen when Susan went to brush her teeth, but by the time she'd swilled the water and spat out the paste he'd materialised, already asleep on the bed, as if the sound of the tap and the scrubbing had summoned him.

And it was in such a manner, eleven years later, that Susan lost her virginity. She was studying physics at the University of Kent, in the final term of her fresher year. She'd resisted the attentions of boys very well so far, they didn't impress her much – so now they could go on student demonstrations and grow moustaches and smoke without their parents finding out, but they were just the same boys they'd always been, most of them popped home every other weekend so their mums could do their washing. She lived on the third floor at the halls of residence, towards the end of a long corridor of grey breezeblock and greyer carpet. One night David Parsons began to knock at her door. 'Please, Susie, can we just talk? All I want to do is talk.' Susan didn't like being called Susie, but David Parsons hadn't the wit to realise that. He lived further down the corridor, they used the same student kitchen and she'd even once given him some of her microwaved vegetarian lasagne, but she'd hardly have considered him a friend. Earlier that day he'd made a clumsy pass at her as she was doing the washing up. Not many students bothered with the washing up, and there was a lot of it to get through, so she had to stand there with her hands in soap suds for quite some time whilst he made his feelings plain. 'Go away, David,' Susan said now, 'I'm trying to sleep.' 'Okay,' said David. 'I'm sorry.' But the next night he was out there again, knocking at the door gently and getting her name wrong. 'It's gone midnight,' said Susan, 'and I've got a lecture in the morning about inertia. What do you want?' 'I know I could be so good with you,' said David. 'I'm sorry, I can't help it, I just want to show you how good.' 'Well, you can't,' said Susan. 'Can I just stay outside your room for a while?' asked David, and Susan said he could do whatever he liked, he could knock himself out. 'Thank you,' sighed David, 'I'll be very quiet.' And he was *quite* quiet, but he would occasionally tell her he'd fallen in love with her, and read her John Donne. He was an English lit student, she knew, he'd obviously just reached the Metaphysicals.The next morning the atmosphere in the kitchen was a bit tense. 'I couldn't sleep last night,' said Chloe Klass. 'Couldn't you just let him in, what's such a big deal?' Chloe was American and blonde and smoked roll-ups, she let every man into her room. So the next night when David came knocking, Susan opened the door. 'Oh,' he said, obviously surprised. He'd brought a whole hardback anthology with him.

Susan made them both a cup of tea. He hadn't much to say. 'I'm going to sleep now,' she told him eventually. 'Bye.' 'Can't I just stay?' he said. 'I'll just lie down beside you. I won't disturb you.' 'I suppose so,' said Susan, and she brushed her teeth, and got into her nightie, and to do that she had to take off her clothes, but she did it with her back to him, so it was all right. David got down to his underpants, got into bed. She lay there with her back to him, and he cuddled against her. And then she felt a little knocking, something hard and insistent just at the base of her spine, knock-knocking away. 'Are you going to do that all night?' she asked him, not angrily, merely curious. 'I could get some condoms,' he said, 'I've got some in my room.' 'Fine,' she said, 'if you want,' and he bounded up from bed so eagerly she thought he'd had an electric shock, he so rushed into his trousers he nearly fell over. He was back in a couple of minutes, a whole pack of condoms in his hand, and smelling all over of Old Spice aftershave. 'Here I am,' he said a little playfully. And they had sex, and it was all right, actually, it wasn't the best Susan would ever have, but it was far from being the worst. And afterwards David Parsons went back to his room, and he didn't bother her much after that, so that was all to the good too. 'Well,' said Susan to Tom, 'so much for that,' and Tom, who'd moved from the end of the bed when the jolting of David's body had got needlessly frenetic, and was now curled up on Susan's writing desk, gave a little yawn and stretched in indifference.

Susan was fourteen years old when Tom died. Her mum was waiting for her in the kitchen when she came home from school. Her face was ashen. 'There's been a car accident,' she said. And she explained how Tom had made it out into the front garden, he'd tried to cross the road, he hadn't made it. It was nobody's fault. 'Where is he?' Susan asked immediately, because she loved Tom now, she'd freely admit that. Sharing a bed could do that sometimes, it had just crept up on her. 'He's at the vet's,' said her mum. 'His legs are broken.' Susan demanded to know who had let Tom out the front door, she only ever let him out at the back, there was no road out back, and her mum said no-one had let Tom out, he'd squeezed out of the window all by himself, it was nobody's fault. What about the driver, asked Susan, the one who ran him over, the bloody bastard who ran him over, and her mum ignored the fact that Susan was swearing, she was clearly upset. There was nothing he could do, said her mother, Tom just came out of nowhere, indeed the driver had stopped the car and picked Tom up, he'd been knocking at everyone's front doors trying to find out who the cat belonged to, Tom would have died right there in the road if it hadn't been for him. It was nobody's fault. And then Mum put her arms around Susan, and Susan didn't want that at all. And Mum said she was going to have to be very brave, but Tom wasn't going to be able to walk again, and he was in a lot of pain. The vet was going to put Tom to sleep. Put him out of his misery. 'No,' said Susan. But it was the only thing to do, Susan had to be a grown-up, and her mum had only waited this long because she thought Susan might want to say goodbye, did she want to be there at the end? To see Tom one last time, and tell him she loved him, it was the humane thing, and it was nobody's fault. It was nobody's fault. 'No,' said Susan. And she went to her room. Her mother eventually knocked on her door. 'I'm going to the vet's now, Susan,' she said. 'Are you sure you won't come? It's up to you. But I don't want you regretting... I don't want you looking back and... It's up to you.' And at last her mum shut up, and Susan heard the front door close, and the sound of gravel as the car drove away.

Dinner that evening was a sombre affair. 'Well, well,' said Dad, 'life must go on!', and then he stopped talking, appalled at how callous he sounded. 'It was all very easy,' Mum said gently. 'Tom didn't suffer at all. Just a little injection in the paw, there was nothing to it, it was very quick. He was even purring. Do you know that, he was even purring.' 'What happens to the body?' asked Susan bluntly. Her potato held no thrill for her, she poked at it with her fork. 'Oh, darling, you don't want his body,' said Mum. 'That's not Tom, it's just a shell.' 'It'll be at the crematorium, I'd have thought,' said Dad kindly. Susan asked, 'Do you think he missed me? At the very end? Do you think he wondered why I wasn't there?' And Mum tried to work out which answer would be the most reassuring. 'I know he understood,' she said carefully.

And during dessert the tears started. They didn't come easily, but Susan could feel the need for them, all that water welling up in her head, she had to let it out somehow. She could only cry if she forced it out, if she thought about Tom very hard, and scrunched up her face – and keeping that position hurt, it actually hurt, and there were so *many* tears inside her, she'd no idea. 'That's the idea,' said Dad, but he looked a bit embarrassed. Her parents told her she'd feel better after a good night's sleep. She went up to the bathroom, she brushed her teeth. And she looked hard at her face in the mirror, that angry face, red now and blotchy. And she made a vow. She bunched up her hands into tight fists, glared at herself, furious that she was so unhappy. I'm not going to love again, she said. What's the point? What good does it do? I'm not letting anything in ever again. And that made her cry once more, and she got even angrier, she tried to drown away the tears with tap water, she got into bed and tried to sleep.

She knew she should have felt some surprise to hear the mewing outside her door. She opened it. 'Hello,' she whispered. Tom ambled in, at no more of a rush now he was dead, jumped up on the bed, and lay down. Part of her thought she must be dreaming, that's what her brain was telling her, but she wasn't, of course she wasn't. And she knew she mustn't think about it all too directly, because although this was real, Tom was definitely *there*, purring away at her, this was fragile, she mustn't ruin it, she mustn't chase the little miracle away. Tom tucked his head under his paws. The legs that should have been shattered stretched out as he yawned. 'You've had a long day, haven't you,' Susan said, and stroked his tail – and Tom looked up as if to say, thank you for all the affection, it's nice to see you too, but daytime is over, going to sleep now, night night. Susan sat up beside his sleeping body, stroking it ever so gently so she wouldn't disturb him. And she understood with a little start that this was because of her love, her love had been so strong that it had brought Tom back, that it wouldn't let him go. She'd never much *wanted* to love, it just crept up on her, but my God, she was *good* at it, look at what her love could do! It was a powerful force, this creeping thing. At some point she must have fallen asleep as well, her tears had exhausted her, and she'd have assumed she'd have simply slumped by her cat's side. But she woke to the sound of a knock at the door, and the lights were off, and she was under the covers, her head on a pillow. 'Susan?' called her mum gently. 'Can I come in?' Susan sat up fast, looked desperately for Tom – and she couldn't see him, he wasn't there, he'd just vanished in the night, or maybe he hadn't *ever* been there, she knew she hadn't dreamed it but maybe she had, and her heart quickened in panic. And then she made out the mound of little black fur, still fast asleep, obscured by a hillock of duvet.

Her mother came in. 'I just wanted to see how you were,' she said softly. And maybe it was because of the power she'd felt last night, but in a flash Susan could see how much her mother loved her, and how much that love was hurting, because her mum would have given anything to have made her daughter feel better but didn't know what to say or do. She was *aching* with love for Susan, but her love was useless, it couldn't bring back the dead, it couldn't do anything, and she looked so very awkward standing there in the doorway, so polite, as if talking to a stranger – 'Would you like any breakfast?' she asked. And Susan looked down at Tom, who stirred, blinked at Susan's mother without interest. She couldn't see him, so he didn't care. Susan felt a rush of pity for her mum. 'I'm fine,' she said. 'What you said. Better for a good night's sleep. I'll be down to breakfast in a sec.' Her mother nodded bravely. 'It's all right, Mum,' said Susan. 'Really. Come here.' And she got to her feet, and she opened her arms for a hug. Her mother looked surprised. But she came forward anyway, and Susan held her tight, 'It's all right,' she said again, 'it's all going to be fine.' And Susan didn't know it then, but in that moment the balance of her love had shifted, she'd never quite feel for her mother in the same way again; from now on Susan would be the adult, she'd take care of her mother, not the other way round, the love would be more open and more expressive but somehow patronising too. It'd be the same love she'd show her all those years later, after her mum had had her stroke, and was no longer aware she was even in a hospital, wasn't always sure of her own name, only knew that this confident woman standing by her bedside was her grown-up daughter who promised to protect her. 'It's all right,' she'd say to her mother, 'it's all going to be fine,' before turning to the nearest nurse and asking, 'So, how's my mother feeling today?'

Susan thought that Tom would be waiting for her when she got home from school, but he wasn't. But that was okay, she believed he'd be waiting for her when it was time for bed. Still not a sign, but she wasn't worried, she absolutely *knew* he'd be waiting for her once she'd washed. Even so, she took extra long brushing her teeth, just to give him more time to materialise. 'Hello, Tom,' she said as nonchalantly as she could stepping back into her room, she knew the magic wouldn't work if she gave it too much attention, she didn't even look to see if he were there before she greeted him. Tom stretched lazily out on the bed, chirruped a hello back. And she kissed him on the head and went to sleep. She was happy. Happier now than she had been when Tom was alive: he was all hers now, and only she could see him, and he was *proof* of her love, he wouldn't exist without it, it was good sometimes to have evidence that what you felt was real. 'I love you,' she'd say to him each and every night, 'I love you so much,' and these were things she'd never have said to him when he'd been alive. And Tom would flip over and show her his belly, as if to say, I love you too, Mummy, and quite right too, now give me a rub. 'We've been thinking,' said her dad a few weeks later. 'We could get you another cat.' 'I don't need another cat,' said Susan, quite truthfully. 'Not right now,' agreed Dad, 'it's a bit too soon.' 'I'll never need another cat,' said Susan, 'I'm fine, I'm happy.' One night she overheard her parents talking about her. Her mother used the word 'counselling'. 'What's to worry about?' replied her dad. 'She's not crying any more. Frankly, I *prefer* her like this.' And her mother spoke softly, as if she were just a bit scared. 'I just think she's a heartless little bitch.'

Susan didn't want to go away on holiday that summer. 'Let's stay at home,' she said. Her father took her to one side. 'You're growing up very fast,' he told her. 'There won't be many more family holidays. Indulge your mother, all right?' Susan kissed Tom. 'I'll only be gone ten nights,' she said. 'I'll be back home before you know it.' Tom looked supremely unconcerned, and Susan cried in spite of herself. The family flew to Spain, stayed in a hotel barely ten minutes' drive from the sea. Susan at last had a room of her own; even the year before, on that abortive trip to the Cotswolds, she'd had to share with her parents. 'You'd best not drink the tap water,' said Dad. 'It's coming out brown.' And he gave her some bottled water, and as she brushed her teeth that night at the bedroom sink it fizzed inside her mouth. When she lowered her head to spit out the paste Tom wasn't on the bed, and when she raised it again he was. He preened himself as if acknowledging the round of applause earned by a spectacularly good trick. It began raining the next day, and Susan's mother got food poisoning from something fish-like in a nearby tapas bar, and through the thin walls of the hotel Susan and Tom could hear her throwing up for days. 'Thanks, Mum, thanks, Dad,' said Susan on the flight home, 'I know that wasn't what you were hoping for, but it was the best holiday ever.' And Dad was clearly touched, and said what a lovely young woman she was turning out to be, and even Mum looked pleased.

* * *

From that point on, no matter which bed she slept in, Tom was always at the foot of it. He was there when she revised in bed for her GCSE exams, he was there for her A-levels. He was there at that New Year's Eve party when she was sixteen, and she fell asleep drunk on a pile of coats and teenagers in Jimmy Hall's spare room, and woke up to find Jimmy's twelve-year-old brother's tongue down her throat. He was there when she lost her virginity to David Parsons. ('I could get some condoms,' David had said, 'I've got some in my room,' and Tom coughed up a furball in disgust. 'I know, I know,' she told Tom, whilst David was off fetching contraceptives and masking body odour, 'but I've got to do it some time, let's just get it over with.') He was there when she first made love to Andrew, four years later, after he'd chatted her up in a nightclub. She didn't normally go to nightclubs, and she didn't normally respond to chat-ups either, but he had been ever so sweet and earnest, she thought it'd be rude to say no. They went back to Andrew's house, and she noted with satisfaction that at least the bed was made and clean. He kissed her on the mouth. 'Not just yet,' she said. 'I need to wash first. Can I borrow a toothbrush?' He looked surprised, but he found her one anyway. 'All right now?' he asked amiably, as she came out of the bathroom, and she looked down at the end of his bed, and smiled. 'I am now,' she said. And they had sex, and it wasn't love, but it was at least loving. And although Andrew obviously couldn't see Tom it was as if he could still sense something – whatever techniques he practised on Susan's body, he always took care not to disturb the invisible cat nestling by his feet. Susan was really rather impressed. After Andrew had fallen asleep, she looked down at Tom, and gave him the thumbs up. This one was a keeper. Susan moved in with Andrew two weeks later.

And years later, in the hospital, Tom was even there too, and Susan had to laugh out loud at the sight of him, in spite of the ordeal she was going through, with all these nurses busying around her in their starchy white pinnies, they'd *freak* if they'd known something as unhygienic as a cat was on the bed. Tom was there as her waters broke and her uterus contracted and God only knows what else, she hadn't read the book Andrew had bought about the subject, 'Don't you think, darling,' he'd asked gently, 'you might want to do a little research about your pregnancy, wouldn't that be useful?' And she'd thought, no, frankly, if this is the sort of thing my body's going to go through I'd rather not have to *study* it as well, it all sounds very unpleasant, tell you what, Andrew, it's not your uterine walls that are going to be bulging, why don't *you* do the homework for me? Everyone in the ward was being so frenetic, so constantly reassuring. 'Push, that's good pushing,' said the nurse with the beatific smile – to be honest, everyone was trying so hard to make her calm she'd have been quite panicked, if it hadn't been for Tom, supremely indifferent to the whole childbirth process, blinking bemusedly at all the strangers making such a fuss, she'd look at Tom and then she'd relax. 'Is there anything I can get you?' asked the nurse with the beatific smile, just before all that pushing started. 'Yes,' said Susan, 'I want to brush my teeth.' And the nurse had laughed, and said she wouldn't need clean teeth for what she was about to go through, and Susan had had to insist, 'Get me a bloody toothbrush, I want my teeth brushed *now*.' 'I'm here for you, darling,' said Andrew above her, and that was nice of him, he could hover over her in his smock if he wanted, but it was better that Tom was there, really. 'You're doing really well,' said the nurse, and Susan felt smug, she *hadn't* needed to study Andrew's books at all, she was a natural. 'Don't forget to breathe, those are good breaths,' the nurse went on through that beatific smile. And then there was pain, and Susan wondered how on earth she'd got into all this. It had been Andrew, asking her all the time for a baby, 'But don't you think we'd be a good mummy and daddy?' he'd asked. On and on he'd prodded, knocking at her door, knocking away, and Susan knew she always gave in if people knocked at the door for long enough. 'Okay,' she'd said, 'we can have a child, but it's *your* responsibility.' And he'd laughed, he'd thought she was joking, but she bloody well hadn't been. And now everyone was congratulating her, sorry, she'd zoned out there, the baby must have been born when she wasn't looking, how funny, she'd missed the whole thing. Beatific Smile was offering the baby to her, and she didn't want to hold it, but her arms were rising automatically, she took it. 'Don't you just love him, don't you just love him,' and all Susan could think was that she preferred her dead cat. And Tom was curious at last, he crept up the length of her body, and after what it had just been through Susan supposed that would have been quite painful, it helped that Tom had the light tread of a ghost. He stuck his face out at the baby, sniffed. And then something very odd happened. The baby stopped crying. It turned around, looking directly towards the invisible cat. It stared at Tom. It could see him. And Susan looked on in wonder, her new son could *see* her cat, it was a miracle, and she thought it would be all right. This baby was *part* of her, she could love this little miracle that had spilled from her stomach after all. And the baby extended one finger, slowly, thoughtfully. Then poked Tom in the eye with it.

'What shall we name him?' asked Andrew. He'd been asking the same question for months, and she'd always waved it aside, but now the baby was alive and real, it took on a new pertinence. 'I don't know,' said Susan. 'Why do I always have to be the one who names things? You decide.' So Andrew decided to call him Thomas, after his father. 'Not that,' said Susan. For the first few nights Andrew brought little Michael to sleep in their bedroom. Tom didn't like this at all. His fur stood on end, he hissed. And, with as much dignity as he could muster, he jumped down from the bed and walked out of the door. 'Tom!' called out Susan, to Andrew's surprise, but he wouldn't come back. By the end of that first week of motherhood Susan told Andrew she wanted her son in the spare room. 'I've been to Argos,' she said, 'I've picked up one of those baby monitors. Any problem, it'll beep at us or something.' That night she brushed her teeth so hard she thought she might make them bleed. Tom wouldn't settle at first, he lashed his tail and looked around warily. 'It's okay, the baby's not coming back,' she told him gently, and rubbed his belly just the way he liked it. Even so, it was the best part of a month before Tom regained his composure, and curled up by her feet in the way he did when he was relaxed.

If Michael had any further ability to see his mother's dead cat, he gave no sign of it. And by the time he was old enough for her to ask him outright, he'd found other distractions altogether – fizzy drinks and poseable toys and cartoon marathons on the Children's Channel. He wasn't a bad kid. Susan took care of him. She fed him and cleaned up his crap. And more besides, soon she was ironing his play trousers, rescuing Lego bricks from under the sofa, she was teaching him the alphabet, A for Apple, B for Bear, C for Cat. 'You spoil him,' she said to Andrew. 'Only because you don't spoil him enough.' They'd take him to visit his grandparents every other weekend. His nanna and granddad just loved little Mikey, 'Well, well, aren't you getting to be a big boy!' Susan's dad would say, and

Michael would chortle, because he knew he wasn't big at all, not yet, and Granddad would let him ride on his back as if he were an animal. One day Susan tried to speak to her mother privately, in the kitchen, whilst her father was pretending to be a giraffe. 'When you had me,' asked Susan, 'did you ever worry that you didn't love me enough?' 'No,' said her mother. Susan went on, 'How can you make yourself love someone? When it's what you really, *really* want to do, but you're not sure you've got it in you?' And her mother said nothing, just stared at her, then did the washing up.

'I've got something important to tell you,' Andrew said one day after he got home from work. He led her into their bedroom, and closed the door. He explained that he'd met this woman in Customer Services, and that they'd got talking, and one thing had led to another, and that he'd kissed her. He'd thought it was just a one-off, but they'd been at it again; there was a park near his office, they went there in the lunch break, they'd sit on a bench, they'd chat, eat their sandwiches, then snog. 'Are you in love with her?' asked Susan. No, Andrew said, and he'd never kiss her again, not ever, it was all over, he'd tell her the next day. It wasn't an affair, only kissing, he was sorry, he was sorry. 'I don't see why you're telling me,' said Susan. 'If it's all over.' And Andrew said he had to, this was important, wasn't it? 'Do you think I'd tell you,' asked Susan, 'if I were out snogging people, or having affairs? I think I'd give you that little respect, I'd keep it to myself.' Andrew asked if she ever had had an affair, and she said that chance would be a fine thing, when would she find the *time*, she had his son to bring up and feed and tidy after, look at her, in her baggy T-shirt, no make-up, who'd have her? Who'd have her? Andrew once more said he was sorry, but he felt something was very wrong between them. They'd fallen in love with each other so quickly, hadn't they, they'd both been besotted with each other at first. But now things were different. He wasn't even sure he liked her any more. And he was so scared of losing her. He was so scared he didn't have a wife any longer. He burst into tears, he actually cried, and Susan knew she should feel pity or something, but all she could dredge up was contempt. Even then she knew if she just put her arms around him and assured him it was all right, everything would work out. But she just couldn't. She told him she wanted to sleep on her own that night. He meekly retired to the sofa in the living room. She scrubbed hard at her face, washed all over, she felt dirty.

Tom waited for her on the bed. 'No, Tom, I don't want you tonight,' she said. 'Shoo!' And he wouldn't move, so she kicked at him – she didn't make contact, but he jumped off the bed all the same. She lay there in the dark. Soon enough she felt Tom work his way on to the pillow beside her. 'Not tonight, Tom,' she said again. But Tom ignored her, he put his paws around her, he held her, he snuggled into her back. He was five foot tall, maybe, shorter than Susan, her legs stretched out further than his, he was furry against her skin, but it wasn't too warm, and his tail wrapped around her and kept her safe. And Tom didn't knock away at the base of her spine, he didn't want anything from her, as they spooned he fell fast asleep, and then she was fast asleep too. In the morning she had breakfast with Andrew, and neither of them mentioned what had happened, but she gave him a forgiving smile, and the smile she got back was full of relief and gratitude.

When Michael was six Andrew suggested he be given a pet. 'He's a bit young, isn't he?' said Susan. At that age she hadn't even murdered her first hamster. But Michael wanted to skip hamsters altogether, he knew what he wanted, he wanted a cat. One Saturday they went down to the RSPCA. 'Now, all these cats need good homes,' Andrew told his son, 'because they're not wanted.' 'Why aren't they wanted, Daddy?' asked Michael, and Andrew didn't know. As Susan filed past the line of cages, all the cats pressed against the glass, crying for attention, crying to be loved. 'I'll wait in the car,' said Susan. 'You should stay, don't you want to meet the next member of our family?' 'I'll wait in the car,' Susan said. Less than half an hour later Andrew and Michael joined her, Michael carrying a cardboard box, all smiles. The cat he'd chosen to love was a young tabby, not as pretty as Tom had been. 'What are you going to name her?' Andrew asked, and Michael looked into the box he was cradling on his lap, studied the cat inside solemnly, and said, at last, 'Bubble.' 'That's a good name, isn't it?' said Andrew. Susan agreed it was very nice. Andrew bought Bubble a scratching post, a couple of furry mice with bells on, a basket to sleep in, and a dinner mat with the words 'A Very Fine Cat Eats Here' printed on it. 'For heaven's sake,' said Susan, trying to laugh, 'it's only a cat.' 'No,' said Michael. 'It's *my* cat.'

Michael set down Bubble in the centre of the sitting room carpet. 'Go on,' Michael encouraged her, 'explore!' But Bubble just boggled at the enormity of her new home. 'She'll adjust soon enough,' laughed Andrew. But Bubble didn't. She would hardly touch her food, even when Michael helped, tried to feed her with a spoon like the books suggested. Bubble hid under the beds, she hid under the chest of drawers, fur on edge, eyes wide in fear – and wherever she hid, she pissed. And she howled in the night so piteously, and it made Michael cry. 'What's wrong with her, Dad?' he'd sob. Andrew called the vet, and was told that some cats just weren't suitable for a young family, had the boy been pulling its tail, even in fun? Some cats just needed to be rehoused. And Michael wailed, saying that he loved Bubble, he couldn't live without her. And he was sure Bubble would love him too, she'd get used to him in time and love him right back. Susan tried to reassure Michael, but she knew love just didn't work that way. She knew that Tom was only protecting his territory. She'd never seen Tom outside a bedroom since he'd died, but now he paraded around the house like a general, always looking for the intruder. He'd spit in Bubble's face, he'd swipe at her with his claws out. And whenever Bubble was chased away, Tom would look back at Susan, and purr, and ask to be congratulated.

There was a card pinned to the noticeboard in Sainsbury's. Susan found herself reading it as the cashier scanned and bagged her shopping. It struck her as odd, but it wasn't until she was home and had put away all the fizzy drinks and the cat food that she gave it serious consideration. And then she got back into her car and drove all the way back to the supermarket. At first she thought the card had been removed – maybe it had never been there in the first place? – but it had only been obscured by an offer for a second-hand tumble-dryer. 'Pet Exorcist,' it read, and gave a phone number. Susan copied it down. She went home and made herself a cup of tea. 'Well,' she said out loud, 'there's no harm in just checking.' She called the number, and there wasn't even a personalised answering message, which wasn't very encouraging. I can stop this, she thought, I don't have to speak after the tone – but then did. 'I wonder if you can help me out,' she said politely. 'Could you call me back?' And then hung up, thought for a bit, dialled again. 'Hello, it's me. Actually, when you *do* call me back, could you use my mobile rather than my landline? I'd rather keep this private.'

* * *

An appointment was set for Thursday morning. On the telephone the man sounded reassuringly old, but when she answered the door to him she realised he must still be in his twenties. 'Oh,' she said. He was dressed smart casual, and carried a briefcase. His smile was polite and professional. 'Please,' she said, 'come in.'

'May I just wash my hands before we start?' he asked. And she directed him to the toilet. 'Would you like a cup of tea?' she asked, and he shook his head no, and said it'd be better for all concerned if they didn't prolong the moment. He knew this must be very hard for her, it always was. Then he closed the toilet door, and she heard the tap running, and she supposed he must have peed as well because there was a flush. He stepped out, smiled kindly at her, and said that they should get to it.

'Can I ask,' he said, 'is he a sick cat?'

'No,' said Susan. 'No, he's fine.'

'I see,' he said. 'That's a shame. It's always hard to euthanase a healthy pet.'

'It's not that I want to,' said Susan. 'But I can't cope any more.'

'I'm not judging you.'

'It was okay when I was fourteen,' she went on. 'Having my little ghost cat. But now I'm thirty-three. And there's a time I just have to grow up. Don't you think? I have other responsibilities. Don't I?'

'Really,' he said. 'I'm not judging you. Where is he?'

She showed him into the bedroom. 'He's not here yet,' she said. 'But he comes when I brush my teeth.' The man nodded. Susan hesitated. 'Shall I go and brush my...?' 'If you wouldn't mind.'

When she came back, Tom was on the bed, and the young man was opening up his case. 'Will it take long?' Susan asked. 'It's just that my son gets home from school at four.'

'It's all very quick,' he assured her. 'And all very painless.'

She looked at the needle he was holding. 'What's that for?'

'We'll just give him a little injection,' he said. 'An overdose of tranquiliser, that's all. And he'll just slip away. It'll be fine.'

'Oh,' she said. 'I wasn't expecting... It's just that when you said "exorcism", I thought you meant... You know.'

He just stared at her. 'How else do you think I can put a cat to sleep?' he asked her. And she didn't know. 'Do I have to watch?' she asked in a small voice. She was afraid she was already crying.

'It usually helps the animal to feel they're in the arms of someone they love and trust,' said the man gently. 'And it's usually good for the owner too. It's important that you were able to say goodbye.'

'Yes,' she whispered.

'Besides which,' he admitted, 'he's invisible to me. So I'll need you to show me where he is.'

She picked Tom up, held him close. 'I'm sorry, I'm sorry,' she said. She wanted to tell him she loved him, but it was hard to do with a stranger there. 'Now, Susan, I'm going to need your help,' the exorcist said softly. 'We need to find a vein in Tom's leg. That'll be the kindest place to give him the injection. So you're going to have to raise a vein for me, between your thumbs, that's it. So I can get the needle in as accurately as possible.' She didn't watch, but she felt him slide the syringe in close by her skin. She focused on Tom, stroking his head, making soothing noises, even though she was sobbing now, who could be soothed by sobbing? Tom began to purr. Then he gave a deep sigh, and put his head back, looking for all the world as if he were luxuriating in a drug fix. His eyes were wide open, and looked suddenly so very solid somehow. And Susan could tell him she loved him now after all, but there was no point, because he had gone. 'I'm sorry,' she told him anyway, and kissed the top of his head, and her tears streamed down on to the dead invisible fur. 'He wouldn't have suffered,' said the young man. 'And, right at the end, he had you there to love.'

She paid him and he left.

She sat down in the sitting room to cry, but the crying was over. Bubble mewed at her for food. 'Not now,' she said, and threw a cushion at her. She went back to see Tom, give him one final kiss. Then she went out to the garden shed, fetched a spade. She didn't think she need dig very deep, Tom was such a little cat after all, but it felt good to be hacking away at the lawn, she was out there digging for over an hour, she raised blisters on her hands. When she was satisfied with the grave, and when one of the blisters had popped open and she really couldn't dig through the pain, she went back to the bedroom to get Tom's body. It was no longer there. Or rather, she couldn't see it any more. She hesitated. And then she stooped by the bed, judging the place that she had left her cat, and scooped up a mound of thin air into her arms. She didn't think she could feel any weight in them, but she pretended, she liked to pretend. And gently, ever so gently, she went outside, and laid down her imaginary burden in the hole, and covered it with earth.

Susan mourned for weeks. If any of her family noticed, they didn't comment. Maybe they were afraid to.

And Bubble grew in confidence. She began climbing up the curtains. She killed her first baby bird, left its body in the kitchen. She ate a lot, and got bulky, undeniably bulky. Bubble would cry each night outside Michael's door. 'Please, Mum, can she sleep with me?' 'No,' said Susan. Bubble didn't care too much about the litter tray, and one day she pissed on the floor. 'For God's sake,' said Susan. 'Michael, your cat's made a mess again. Come and clear it up.' 'I'm watching television,' called back Michael. 'Now,' insisted Susan. 'It'll be over soon,' shouted Michael, 'I'll do it then.' She stormed into the sitting room, stood between her eight-year-old son and the cartoons he was enjoying. He glared at her. 'For God's sake, Mum, it's only piss,' said Michael. 'If it means that much to you, you clear it up.' 'You're a spoilt little shit,' Susan told him, and hit him hard across the face. The force of it knocked him off the sofa. Michael looked up at her, frightened, and too shocked to cry.

And, all of a sudden, love wasn't a creeping thing, it came at her in a rush. She looked down at her son, cowering on the floor, and was overwhelmed by it. 'Oh, Mikey,' she said, 'I'm sorry, I'm sorry,' and she offered him her arms. And he could have resisted, and if he had he'd have broken her heart, but he didn't. 'Mummy, I'm sorry,' he said as she hugged him, and she had to remember what he was sorry for, it was only piss, wasn't it, just piss? 'I love you, Mikey,' she said, and she kissed him fiercely on the side of his head. 'I love you, and don't you ever believe otherwise.' 'I know you do, Mummy.' 'And I'll never hurt you again. And I'll never let anyone or anything hurt you again. Do you hear me? Not ever.' That's the real power of love, not to bring back the dead, but to allow us to believe our lies so completely. That night Susan sat with Andrew on the sofa, and they watched a cop show. And in the commercial break she turned to him and said with a smile, 'What do you think Mikey would prefer, a brother or a sister?' Andrew's mouth fell open. She laughed at the sight of it, and then he laughed too. He was so excited by the idea that he abandoned the cop show altogether, they went upstairs and made love.

But in all the years ahead, she couldn't love Bubble. She tried, and she failed. There's only so much love a woman can feel.

Early one evening the phone rang. 'We're sorry,' said a nurse, 'there's been a car accident.' Susan tried to get answers, but there was too much to take in. 'I'll be over straight away,' she said. But she'd only just put Jennifer to bed – and she'd loved Jennifer at a rush too, from the moment she was born she knew that love wouldn't stop, and it never ever did. Susan didn't know the neighbours well, but they'd always been polite, and when Susan explained the situation as best as she understood it they agreed to look after the toddler for a few hours. When she got to the reception she said 'I'm here!' as if everyone at the hospital had been on tenterhooks waiting for her, and she had to give her name and wait for a doctor to come. 'There was a head-on collision,' he said, a doctor that looked professional but was too young, why were they all too young these days? Both her husband and her son were in a critical condition. Andrew had a lung punctured and a machine was helping him breathe, and Susan zoned out a bit after 'punctured', why choose a word that made her wince so? Michael had hit his head, there was possible brain damage. The bottom line was that both of them could pull through. Or either. Or neither. The doctor was sorry he couldn't be more helpful. He told her this must be very hard for her, it always was, and he didn't mind when she swore, he could see she was upset. They were in surgery now, but if she waited by her phone, they'd inform her the moment there was any news. So she drove back home again, her mobile phone on the seat, and she kept on taking one hand off the steering wheel to check the display, make sure she hadn't missed a call. She only stopped when she realised it was dangerous, that road accidents weren't just something which happened to other people.

She left Jenny at the neighbours' house. She had no words for explanations right now. She sat on the edge of her bed. She held a phone in each hand, the mobile in one, the landline in the other. She felt sick. She put the phones down, went into the bathroom, instinctively closed the door behind her. She threw up. She tried to take away the taste of the sick by brushing her teeth, but as she did so she felt a rise of vomit again, she leaned across to the toilet bowl and threw up bile and toothpaste. She brushed her teeth again. The taste didn't go away.

And as she brushed, she had a thought. She stopped dead.

How great was her love? If Andrew died, if Michael died – and she felt sick again, even putting that into her head so bluntly, but she persevered – if her family died, was her love strong enough to bring them back? Was her husband dying now, were the doctors switching off his respirator, would he vanish from the hospital and reappear here? And her son. Would his ghost be as she knew him, or would it have brain damage? Could she love him if he were a ghost without a brain?

She realised she'd left the telephones on the bed. She wanted to go and fetch them. Maybe the hospital had been ringing, even as she'd been sick. She put her hand on the doorknob. And then took it off again. What if her husband and son were out there already? What if they were waiting for her? What if her love was that powerful?

And then another thought struck her.

What if it wasn't?

What if she couldn't love enough? What if she couldn't bring them back, because she'd never loved them at all, not really, she'd just fooled herself all this time? It had all been just a lie, what she'd said, what she'd felt, everything? The only thing she'd ever given her heart to, it wasn't the man she'd shared the years with, it wasn't her own child, it was just a cat, nothing but a cat? And she'd open the door, and there'd be no-one sitting on the bed, and there never would be?

For the life of her she couldn't work out which was worse.

In the bedroom, the telephone began to ring.

14.2

Brenda said she loved me completely, but she didn't. Oh, she looked convincing enough, with her smiles and her blushes and the way she sometimes cast down her eyes shyly before speaking, and then might look straight at me and hold my gaze like glue. But it wasn't complete, it was only fourteen per cent proof. 'Oh,' she said, when we got the results back from the doctor, 'I am surprised,' and he smiled, and said it was really nothing to be concerned about. Fourteen per cent was a very good score; we had to remember the heart and the brain were very busy organs, they had a lot of other things to love, like food and sleep and pumping blood and stuff. 'Still, fourteen per cent,' she said. 'It doesn't sound very much.' And it didn't. He handed her the printout, and she looked it over, and then handed it to me, and I looked it over; fourteen point two is what it read, which doesn't sound quite so bad, but still I thought it was a long way off actually sounding *good.* Brenda sighed. 'I wish there was some way we could measure the amount of love in a man, it doesn't seem right the tests only work on women.' And the doctor agreed, a little stiffly, said that science was a funny thing, and showed us both to the door.

On the way home in the car Brenda began to cry, and I pulled us over so I could concentrate on being nice and understanding. She said she was so so sorry, and I told her it was all right, she could hardly help how little she loved me, fourteen per cent would have to do. 'Fourteen point two,' she said, and I said, all right, point two if she wanted to quibble. 'I'd do anything to improve on that fourteen point two,' she said, and so I got out the printout and we had a good long look at it. I suggested that maybe if she tried hard to love other things a little less then there'd be more room in her affections for me. Eight point nine on her brother, that was wasted love to start with, he was a dickhead. And she resolved to give it a go, and so as we drove on I listed the faults and inadequacies of all her family members to help her. She cried again, 'You're so good to me, I love you so so much,' and I smiled kindly, but thought, well, obviously not – and wondered whether by being quite so nice and understanding I had yet managed to give my percentage a significant boost.

That Sunday, as usual, we went to my parents for a roast dinner. Brenda loved these visits, I know; she'd pore over bridal magazines with my mother, picking out dresses and table decorations, and my mother would coo and say that she couldn't wait for Brenda to be properly part of the family, to be the daughter she'd always wanted, she loved her very much, she loved her easily as much as she loved me, her own flesh and blood. She offered Brenda seconds of dessert, and I gave Brenda a look, and shook my head, and she put her bowl back down on the placemat. Mum looked put out. 'You don't need to lose weight, does she, Arthur?' and my dad grunted, and Brenda explained that the diet wasn't to reduce her waistline so much as her passion for food. And quite right too, eating accounted for a whopping twenty-three point six of her love capacity, and I was damned if I was going to be usurped by my mother's apple crumble. I'd put her straight on to the diet myself, and enrolled her at the local gym, even found her a personal trainer. After we'd cleared away our plates, and Mum and Brenda had got out the latest issue of *Weddings Weekly*, Dad asked if I fancied a beer with him in the garden. Just the two of us – which surprised me, because the first thing Dad would normally do after Sunday lunch was retreat to the television and I wouldn't hear a word out of him for another week. We sat on the patio, and opened a couple of cans; it was spotting with rain, but we sat out there anyway. 'What percentage did Brenda get, son?' he asked, and I told him, and he grunted. He asked if I was worried to be marrying at only fourteen point two per cent, and I said I was a bit. 'Never told anyone this before,' he said, 'we lied to your grandparents. But for me your mother only scored a nine point eight.' I told him I found this reassuring; after all, they'd both done okay. 'Oh God, don't you believe it,' he said. 'Oh God, it's been miserable. She's never loved me enough, I should never have gone through with it. And the worst thing is, even that wore off. That's what love does. It wears off. She went and had a kid, and of course, she had to love *him*, didn't she? She had to use up some of her love on him. And guess whose love that came from, you guessed it, from muggins here.' He glowered at the garden for a while. I told him that we'd be okay, Brenda and I didn't want to have children. 'No children,' he said wistfully, 'just imagine.' And he opened a second can. I left him to it. When I went back inside, Brenda and Mum were having a girly chat and giggling about Brenda's personal trainer. They changed the subject when I came in. 'Dad's still in the garden if you want him,' I told Mum, and Mum shrugged.

Brenda certainly put in the hours at the gym. An unforeseen consequence of this was that she lost a lot of weight. Indeed, she dropped two entire dress sizes, and we kept having to order fresh wedding dresses, it all got very expensive. But there was a luckier consequence too. Brenda's mother died. Inspired by her daughter's efforts, and thinking that she'd too try to look good for the wedding day, she threw herself rather wholeheartedly into her own fitness regime. The heart attack she suffered on the exercise bike was so powerful that it took the very strongest of the personal trainers to prise her dead fingers off the handlebars. I was, quite naturally, elated. I couldn't expect that all the love Brenda had felt for her mother automatically devolved on me (twelve point four!), but I was surely in for a sizeable chunk. And I'd heard that sometimes recent widowers, stricken with grief, followed their partners shortly afterwards – I asked Brenda if she thought there was any chance her dad (ten point nine) would die soon too, and she said she didn't know, and I asked if she could ask him, and she always said it wasn't the right moment. But her dad's stubborn hold on her affections notwithstanding, I decided that it was high time we measured her love for me once more. I booked an appointment for her with the doctor. 'Do we really have to go through all that again?' Brenda asked, and I said, well, that's what all this has been about, hasn't it? I was dying to find out the results, she must have been too, surely!

I waved at her through the glass windows of her cubicle but she was too busy to wave back; they were strapping her down every which way, and they were injecting her arms and legs with some blue dye so that all the love would show up on the X-ray, and they were giving her something hard to bite down on for when the first lasers hit. I put on my protective goggles – some of the bright lights could be a bit hard on the eyes – and then the doctors lasered her naked body up and down, from top to toe, making sure that every little speck of love would be properly analysed and accounted for, none of it could escape. And it's funny – as I watched her face spasm, I realised that I loved that face no matter what. I could live with fourteen point two, if it were *her* fourteen point two, if that were the love she felt for me I should take it and be proud of it, my darling, my brave little Brenda. I told her that afterwards. I told her, sitting in reception, once we'd got the results. 'I love you whatever,' I said. 'I love you completely. And I don't care that my love outweighs yours, it's enough love for both of us to live on.' And Brenda smiled, and said, 'You're very sweet.' And she got to her feet, and said, 'I'll never forget you.' And as she walked away, as she walked out of my life, I believed that was true, and that that three point three per cent of her heart would somehow always be mine.

I saw her one more time. It was a few months later. My cousin Tim was getting married to a girl who clearly adored him – she loved him at twenty-four point six, they kept bragging about it in the wedding speeches. I was surprised to see that Brenda was there, and then I realised that my mum must have invited her; they'd stayed close, my mum loved Brenda, she said, she loved her like a daughter. I must say Brenda looked fabulous. She was there with her boyfriend, all six foot four of him, I'd guess, all strapping muscle and lean flesh. I avoided her most of the day, but later in the evening, after a glass of wine or three, I plucked up the courage to say hello. She seemed pleased to see me, as if she hadn't spotted me hours before in the church and looked away. 'You've met Anton,' she said, 'haven't you?', and I said I didn't think so, and she said, 'My fitness trainer, you bought me sessions with him – mind you, he doesn't charge any more!' And she laughed, and I laughed, and Anton laughed, and his skin was so tight I was surprised it didn't split with the movement. 'Get me a refill, would you, babe,' she said, and Anton took her glass and made for the bar. Brenda and I made small talk for a minute or two, and then I came right out with it, I said, 'And how much of your love do you give Anton?' She looked genuinely surprised, then laughed. 'Oh God,' she said. 'It's negligible. What, nought point two, nought point three.' And he was back, passing her her wine. 'But I tell you,' she said, winking at me, 'the lust levels are off the scale.' And with his hand now free he was at her arse, he was squeezing it, pulling at it. Yearning. 'Yes, all right,' she told him, 'I'm gagging for it too,' and with a smile to me that said, what's-a-girl-gonna-do? she let him take her somewhere more private.

Your Long, Loving Arms

In the end, it was the afternoons that were killing him. The evenings were fine. The evenings he could cope with. He wasn't working in the evenings, it was true, but that was okay, lots of people didn't work in the evenings. He'd play with Ben a bit, like a normal dad, might read him a bedtime story if Ben fancied it. Like a normal dad, and in a normal family too, he'd cuddle up with Cheryl on the sofa and they'd watch a spot of telly, and at last Cheryl would say that she'd best get to bed, she had to be up early in the morning. And he'd go with her, though he didn't have to be up early, not any more. And mornings were okay. He could ignore the mornings. At quarter past seven the alarm would wake them both, and Cheryl would kiss him on the head, and tell him she loved him, and get up to rouse Ben for school. At first he'd get up when she did, but she said there was no need, Steve, she'd say, why not lie in? Steve, you may as well lie in. And so he'd lie in, and shortly after eight he'd hear Cheryl and Ben leave the house and close the front door behind them. For the first few weeks he'd doze until nine-ish, then nine-thirty. Recently though he'd crossed the line; as he lay buried in the darkness he'd tell himself that so long as he was up by noon it'd be all right, that'd still mean he wasn't sleeping the entire morning. He wouldn't need to feel guilty, he'd still be normal. But now he was finding he wasn't opening the curtains till as late as twelve-fifteen, even twelve-twenty once. And as he'd blink out into the sunlight, he'd see that the world outside hadn't ended, the world had continued without him, and he was now firmly stuck in the afternoon, and it weighed down his very soul.

Yeah, in the end, it was the afternoons that did for him. That and the conversation he'd had after dinner one evening. Steve had asked Ben what he'd been up to at school that day, and he enjoyed doing that, Ben was always full of stories of new games he'd learned and new friends he'd made. But Ben just looked at him curiously and said, 'What did *you* do today, Daddy?' And he didn't have to justify himself to Ben, and Ben didn't even *want* to be justified to, he didn't really care, an hour before bed on the Xbox his grandparents had bought him would keep him happy. But Cheryl had just said, 'Yes, Ben, ask your daddy what he's been up to today.' And there was nothing accusing in it, it was as calm as you like, he couldn't even see Cheryl's face, her back was turned as she did the washing up. Steve hadn't answered, and there was an awkward silence – well, awkward to Steve, Ben didn't seem bothered, and Cheryl, Cheryl was still giving fierce attention to the dinner plates. Then Cheryl said something else, it didn't matter what, and it was just as neutral, and the subject was changed. They didn't mention it again; he didn't apologise for being out of work, and she didn't apologise for making him feel bad about it; they cuddled on the sofa, watched TV, then went to bed when Cheryl said it was time.

That weekend he went for a drink with Ray. Ray had been laid off the same time he was. He hadn't seen Ray for a while; at first they'd meet for a pint every few days, and they both took some comfort from that, in shared anecdotes and shared recriminations. But that was back when his unemployment had seemed like a temporary inconvenience, when deep down Steve believed the management would phone him up one day to say sorry and offer him his job back. 'Why not give Ray a call, see if he's up for the pub?' Cheryl would say sometimes, and she'd take a tenner from her purse and hold it out for him. And he knew it was his money too, really, some of that was his dole, but it felt like pocket money. Besides, he found Ray hard to face these days. He feared Ray was coping better with his redundancy than he was. But that weekend Cheryl had pressed him, maybe she felt bad about the dinner incident, 'go on,' she said, 'have a treat,' and waved the tenner in front of him. So he phoned Ray. Ray got in the first round, and he told Ray what he'd been planning. 'You must be joking,' said Ray. 'We're skilled labourers. We're engineers. You wouldn't catch me working in a fucking *garden*.' And Steve didn't dare tell Ray that garden shifts came later if you were lucky, they started you off in public parks and forests. During the second pint, Ray said, 'What you're forgetting is. That it's not our fault we were let go. It's not our fault.' During the third pint, Ray asked how much the Tree Scheme would bring in, and then said, 'Christ, we'll get more than that staying on the dole.' And Steve said that it wasn't about the money, it wasn't about fault, it was the afternoons, the afternoons were just getting longer, didn't Ray find the afternoons were getting longer and longer and there was no end to them? And Ray finished his pint, and said he'd go along to the training with him. You know, just to see what it was like.

Training lasted a day. 'Surprised you need a day,' said Ray. 'After all, all we do is just stand about, isn't it?' No-one wanted to sit in the first few rows of the seminar room, but the place was soon packed, and the latecomers had no choice. Free refreshments were available at the back, and dutifully Steve took his plastic cup of orange squash like all the others. At last a man in a suit stood up in front of them all. 'A lot of you here today,' he said. 'But not many of you will make the grade. You probably think there's nothing to this job. Some of you will think you're too good for it. But there's more to the tree than you think. Regulating the carbon dioxide intake, drawing nutrients from the soil with its roots. The tree is a very complex animal.' Steve spoke up and said surely it was a plant, not an animal, and Ray sniggered at this, and there was a tittering around the room, but Steve hadn't meant it as a heckle, not really. The man up front pursed his lips. 'Yeah, there's always some clever bugger who thinks he knows it all.'

Then the man turned on his overhead projector, and outlined on a whiteboard the differences between some of the major trees, those which were fruit-bearing, those which were not. He produced graphs of climate change, how an average tree might be affected by differences in rainfall. Then he said he was proud to introduce someone who'd been working as a tree nigh on fifty years, and a grizzled gentleman got up and tried to explain some of the practicalities of the job. He told stories that weren't very interesting and gave tips that were rather confusing, all with a grimness of tone that suggested he was imparting dark secrets of nuclear science. He stressed again that the tree was a complex animal. Then it was lunch: more orange squash, and some cheese sandwiches. 'Now it's time to get some experience in the field,' said the man, 'as it were,' and they all filed out of the seminar room, down the stairs, and into the private gardens of the company offices. 'We're going to start you off on sycamores. Sycamores are easy. Any fool can do a sycamore.' So everyone gave their best stab at a sycamore, and the man walked through the little forest that had sprung up, appraising their efforts. 'Good, good, keep steady, good, a little too feral, good.' Once in a while he'd take out a stick of white chalk and mark their sides with a little cross. Steve tried so very hard to be a tree; when the man looked him up and down it seemed to take forever, but Steve thought of Cheryl, and of Ben, and he didn't waver, he stayed rooted to the spot. Then, at last, 'Good,' came the grunt, and Steve was marked with a cross. 'We have your details,' the man announced to them all at the end of the day. 'If we want you, we'll be in touch.' And then Steve went home.

And for once Cheryl was waiting for *him* when he got home from work. She threw her arms around him, 'I'm so proud of you,' she said, and kissed him on the lips, 'I love you.' She'd made him his favourite meal, a treat for her working man. Even Ben was excited, and he raced around the house, shouting 'Daddy Daddy Daddy!' And although Steve was tired, he really had to laugh at the little feller, 'Daddy Daddy!' He half hoped that Ben would ask him over dinner what he'd done that day, but really was relieved he didn't, because he didn't know how to explain that he'd been a big hunk of wood. So they ate their spag bol to Ben's chatter, and Steve and Cheryl hardly said a word, but once in a while Cheryl would prod Steve with her foot under the table and give him a private smile. And for dessert they had ice cream, everyone's favourite. After Ben went to bed, they cuddled on the sofa as always, but they didn't give the telly much attention. Steve tried to explain that it had only been a training day, that there was no guarantee that there'd be a job at the end of it, and Cheryl said, 'I know you did your best. It'll all work out. I *believe* in you,' and they made love right there and then, and they hadn't done that for ages. It suddenly didn't matter to Steve whether he heard back from the Tree Scheme at all.

But he did. The very next morning he was woken by a phone call. He answered it blearily. 'Did I get you up?' said the man on the end sternly, and Steve checked the time, and saw that it was nearly half past ten, and assured the man he'd been out of bed for hours. 'I'm glad to hear it,' said the man. 'Now, listen. I want to offer you a job.' Steve thanked him. 'Don't thank me. This is a probationary period, all right? To see whether you have the right aptitude. So the pay will reflect that, you'll be on the probationary pay, all right?' Steve said it was all right, and thanked him again. 'Don't thank me.' Steve wasn't sure whether he should phone Ray, if Ray hadn't heard anything he didn't want to crow, but it was okay, Ray phoned him. 'You get the job too? Probationary pay. I nearly told them I had a bloody degree, I nearly told them to stuff it.' That evening he was nervous, and Cheryl told him that was to be expected. 'Tomorrow's a big day for you,' she said. 'For all of us.' She told him to take a bath, and he did, though logically he knew cleanliness really wasn't what the job was about. And at quarter past four the next morning he woke to the alarm, he was the one who kissed Cheryl and told her he loved her, he was the one who let her sleep in whilst he got ready for work.

Everyone had been told to meet outside the office at half past five sharp. Ray was there too, so were a few others Steve remembered from the training day. They too looked anxious, and were trying to hide it by horsing about and being noisy. 'That's it,' said their supervisor, 'get rid of all your energy now, whilst you still have the chance.' Then he bundled them all into the back of a van, and drove them to Clapham Common. 'When you've got more experience, you can choose where you want to stand,' the supervisor told them, 'but for now, leave that up to me.' He planted Steve far away from Ray, and away from the lad he'd said hello to in the van, and for a while Steve felt a bit lonely, and then reasoned there wouldn't be much chatting anyway. There were two breaks scheduled during the day; as his first, Steve picked the eleven o'clock slot, and Ray did too. As the trees gathered around, forming an impromptu copse, stretching their limbs and smoking their fags, Ray said, 'Christ, this job's boring, isn't it?'

And it was boring, of course it was. But Steve soon realised that being bored wasn't so bad. On that first day the sky was overcast, and so the common didn't get many visitors, but perhaps that was just as well. It meant that Steve could concentrate on not wobbling. Not wobbling, he quickly discovered, was the key. Once he had the not wobbling sorted, he'd have the job down pat. And he learned that the odd wobble was fine, so long as you didn't fight it – lean into the breeze, and you could turn it into a *sway*. The second day the sun came out, and with it the lunchtime workers, with their thermos flasks and their sandwiches. One of them sheltered in Steve's shade, and Steve expected he'd be jealous of him, this man in a suit, having a proper job, doing something respectable. But he wasn't. He actually wasn't: he peered down at the man's face, and saw it creased with stress; he was just trying to grab a quick bite in peace, but his mobile phone kept on ringing, it rang no less than three times, and each time the man would put his sandwich down and take the call, and each time Steve heard him pleading to someone on the other end, yes, the contract would be ready by Tuesday, yes, the contract would be ready by the end of the day, please bear with him, please bear with him, please. And Steve felt sorry for the man, he wanted to protect him, and to shield him as best he could with his branches. It was funny – after an hour or so you didn't feel the stiffness in your arms. First they numbed, then felt like something detached from the body altogether. And when the breeze fluttered his leaves, Steve thrilled to it – the wind just teasing them, they didn't seem so much blown about as stroked. He'd zone out, and sometimes he'd think of the common, and how many different shades of green there were, no patch of grass the same. And sometimes he'd think of his family. That if he was moved off probationary pay that maybe they could have another baby, he knew Cheryl would like that, and Ben deserved a little playmate, someone he could look after. Maybe Cheryl and he could even get married at last. And sometimes he'd think nothing at all.

By the end of the second week Ray had had enough. 'To hell with this!' he shouted, and Steve was sure the whole common must have heard him. 'I'm out of here!' The supervisor told Ray that was fine with him, he was no use anyway, he didn't have the aptitude, he just didn't have the aptitude. But for now he'd have to finish the shift, if he wanted any pay at all he'd bloody well get back to work. 'Christ,' said Ray, but did as he was told, dragging all his roots behind him and back into position. On the way back in the van Ray wouldn't shut up about it all. 'You're being exploited,' he told the other trees. 'This is the worst job in the world. I'd rather work for McDonald's.' The other trees looked uncomfortable and didn't say much. 'You don't have to rush off, do you, Steve, you've time for a pint?' But Steve told Ray that he'd best get back home, his family were waiting. Some other time maybe. 'Yeah,' said Ray, 'maybe,' and he went. Steve felt rather relieved that Ray wouldn't be on the common with him any more. He liked Ray and all, but he let the side down. He was a troublemaker.

That evening Steve told Cheryl what Ray had said. Cheryl was quiet for a while, and then asked, a little uncomfortably, whether maybe Ray was right. 'You gave the job a go,' she said. 'Darling, there's no need to stick it out if you don't want to.' And Steve assured her he was fine. He liked the job. He did, really! Couldn't Cheryl see that? Isn't that what he'd been telling Cheryl every night as they cuddled? 'Well, yes,' said Cheryl. 'But I'd always thought you were just putting a brave face on it. It all sounds horrendous.' No, no, Steve said. He was really getting to grips with it.

'Oh,' said Cheryl.

And besides, Ray had been exaggerating. It wasn't all just hard graft, there were lighter moments too, lots of them. For example, there was that time with the two teenagers. They sat under Steve's branches, and they told each other that they loved each other, and they snogged. And both the declarations of love and the snogs that punctuated them were so forceful that Steve suspected this was the first time for them both; they were so so young, they'd not used the 'love' word before. Steve rather liked them. They were sweet. 'I love you,' said the boy, 'and I'm going to prove it.' And he got out a Swiss Army knife from his jacket, pulled out the blade, and Steve was alarmed, thought the boy was going to do something terrible to himself, or to her: he wondered whether he should break character and call for help, but that was strictly forbidden. But it was all right, the boy just wanted to carve their initials into the bark, and Steve felt relieved – right up to the point that he remembered the bark was *him*. 'What happened to you?' said Cheryl that night, and he told her the whole story, and they had a good laugh about it. 'And what's that around the initials, is that supposed to be a heart?' Steve supposed that it was. Cheryl said, 'Oh dear!' and laughed again, and wondered whether it could all be removed by laser surgery. And Steve pointed out that it wasn't a tattoo, that wasn't the way it worked. 'Oh dear!' laughed Cheryl. And then, 'But what a romantic gesture.' And Steve hit upon an idea, and he told Cheryl that she should carve their names into his bark. 'No,' said Cheryl. 'Do you really think I should? Won't it hurt?' Steve said it wouldn't much, and she said he was being brave, and he said he wasn't really, and she said, no, she liked it when he was brave. 'Okay,' said Cheryl, and grinned, and looked so excited, and went to fetch a knife. 'Whereabouts should I do it?' And Steve told her that she should carve her heart higher than the teenagers' heart, this was *proper* love they felt, not some school crush. Their heart should take precedence. 'Here goes,' she said, and began to chip out a heart: high up like he'd said, just below his throat. Cut deep, Steve said, unless she wanted the bark to grow over. So she cut deep. And she cut an arrow through the centre of the heart, and then carved their names either side. Their full names, not just their initials, if it was worth doing it was worth doing properly, and Steve was secretly relieved his name only had five letters. Then she laughed at her handiwork, and Steve couldn't see properly, so had to go and take a look for himself in the mirror, and he laughed too, and said she'd done a great job. And then they kissed. And then Cheryl cleaned the knife of the sap and the little smear of blood.

Pretty soon Steve stopped taking his scheduled breaks at eleven o'clock. He preferred to work through, he didn't want to break his rhythm. For a while he was still obliged to take the one at half past four, because by then he'd be bursting for a pee – but he then learned that with just a little concentration he could convert all his waste matter into chlorophyll and pump it out into his foliage. It wasn't necessarily textbook stuff, but hey, it worked. In the van to and from work he didn't talk much to the other trees, and they didn't talk much to him; he couldn't tell whether they were just wanting to maintain their focus as he was, or just didn't like him. And he honestly didn't care either way. One day the supervisor came to Steve and told him that he'd noticed his common or garden sycamore was now showing signs of becoming a *variegated* sycamore; Steve wasn't sure whether this was a good thing or not, but the supervisor said that the extra effort was appreciated, and gave him a friendly slap on his trunk. And only a few days after that, the supervisor asked Steve if he could have a private word with him away from all the other trees. He asked Steve if he fancied being an oak. 'One of the oaks in St James's Park has gone sick. Don't know what, some sort of fungus, doesn't matter. Would you be my new oak?' Steve was surprised and flattered and just a bit scared; he wasn't sure he had what it took, I mean, to be an oak was every sycamore's dream. 'You've got what it takes,' said the supervisor. 'I don't want you, you know, to get above yourself. But I'll tell you, you're the most promising oak I've seen in years.'

After his shift Steve went home and told his family the news. Ben didn't say much, he never said much any more. 'Will there be any extra money?' asked Cheryl. Steve said he didn't know. He'd only be a probationary oak, after all, they couldn't expect much. But that was hardly the point. He'd be in St James's Park! That was just an acorn's throw from Buckingham Palace itself, some days the Queen would look out of her window, and guess what she'd be looking at, Ben? She'd be looking at his daddy! What did Ben think of that? Ben very politely asked if he could be excused from the dinner table, he had homework to do. Steve expressed surprise that Ben was doing homework – he was too young, surely? Cheryl said, 'He's been doing homework for weeks now. I don't think you remember. I don't think you listen.' She washed up in silence for a while. And then Steve told her that he was even being allowed to choose which oak he wanted to be, there were so many different types of oak, you know.

They trusted him with that decision, all by himself. He thought he might go for a sessile oak, partly because he admired the way that its acorns weren't carried on stalks but directly on the outer twigs, and partly because he just liked the name. Cheryl coolly said that it sounded like he'd already reached his decision, and Steve said, no, no, he'd welcome her input, she'd every right to help choose what sort of oak tree her husband was going to be. She banged the plates down in the sink and left the kitchen.

The other oaks were set in their ways and standoffish. Sod them, Steve thought, and put his efforts into being the best sessile oak he could. He liked the park, he sheltered a better quality of picnicker there. He loved all the tourists, and all their different accents, and that they were always so excited by everything, and took photos all the time, and he liked to imagine they'd flown all around the world from their own countries just to visit him, they were there to see him. He knew it wasn't true, not necessarily, but it sent a warmth of pride from the tips of his upper branches right down to the furthest ends of his roots. And in the evenings at home he'd study, he'd pore over gardening books and encyclopaedias and the latest academic dissertations about oak care theory. Just so he could be expert. Daddy was doing his homework whilst Ben was doing his! – and he'd tell Ben that, and he thought Ben found that amusing, he couldn't quite be sure. He'd explain to Ben why the oak was the best tree in the world. There was a reason it had been adopted as a national emblem in England and France and Germany and the USA and Poland and Latvia and Estonia. And he'd tell Cheryl that after that time of unemployment all he'd wanted was to be a normal man again. But he now believed he was actually *good* at this, special, she was living with a man that was special. He loved his afternoons now, they were long and rich and full of sunshine and birdsong... 'Don't you care,' asked Cheryl, 'that your own son is scared of you? He's *scared* of you. Doesn't that bother you at all?' That pulled Steve up short. He'd never hurt Ben, he never would, he loved Ben, this was all for Ben, for them both, he loved them both. 'He doesn't know what you are any more. He thinks you're a monster.' With all his talk of trees, that's all Steve would talk about any more, just bloody trees – and Steve didn't raise his voice, he pointed out to Cheryl as gently as he could that he *was* a bloody tree, what did she bloody expect? 'We came to see you this afternoon,' said Cheryl. 'Ben wanted to see where his daddy worked. We came to see you in the park.' Silence. 'You didn't even know he was there.'

She told Steve she didn't love him any more. She'd tried, but she'd given up trying, she had to give up now. She was so sorry. And she gave him a sudden hug, and held on to him fiercely, buried her head against his hard mottled chest, and began to cry. Steve looked down at her, and thought she looked so small, and she couldn't reach her arms round him of course, it was almost funny – she was so small he could barely feel her. 'I don't want to lose you,' she said. She kept on saying that, over and over again. They went to bed, and she sobbed, facing away from him. And he wanted to comfort her, to protect her, but he didn't know how. He reached out for her, he brushed her skin, and he wasn't sure she'd want that, he thought she might tell him to stop, but she didn't tell him to stop, and she didn't stop sobbing either. And he held her in his arms, his long strong arms, and she accepted them gratefully. That's how she fell asleep at last, gripping on to him, her fingernails cutting thin little slits into his bark. When the alarm woke them the next morning she smiled at him, and kissed him, and for a moment Steve thought everything might be all right. And she asked him to move out.

Sometimes in the park a family would approach him, and the father would say, 'Do you want to play in the tree?', and the little boy would say, 'Yes! Yes!', and the mother would smile nervously and say, 'Now, be careful,' and the father would lift the boy into Steve's branches, and the boy would squeal with joy, and Steve would hold him tightly in those branches to keep him safe, and he'd think, Ben, he'd think, it should be Ben I'm holding, I should be holding my own son. And then the thought would be lost upon the breeze.

He tried phoning Ray once. Ray wasn't in. He didn't try again.

One day he was alarmed to find a ridge running across his midriff, over where the navel used to be, right around his body and back again. He was quite certain there'd been no trace of it the day before. He hadn't felt anything even approaching alarm for quite a while now, and wasn't quite sure what to do with it. So at the end of the shift he told his supervisor. 'Oh, that's a ring!' said the supervisor. 'All trees get those. That means you've been doing this job a whole year. Congratulations!' Steve thanked him. 'Don't thank me. A whole year, hey, that must mean you've got a holiday due. Have you taken a holiday yet? You're owed a holiday.' Steve informed the supervisor that he hadn't taken a holiday. 'Well, you must then. No arguments!' Steve asked him what sort of holiday he ought to take. 'God, I don't know, I'm not a travel agent,' said the supervisor. 'Somewhere sunny. I don't know. With a beach.' So Steve dutifully went to the travel agent's, and an excitable young assistant there told him that yes, there were *lots* of sunny holidays she could recommend, and *plenty* of them came with beaches. And she booked him one right there and then to prove it. 'Just the single passenger, is it, sir?' she asked.

The aeroplane was full of noisy families. Steve usually liked noisy families, but now he wasn't there to shade them they made him feel awkward and somehow sad. Once he'd cleared immigration a shuttle coach took him and the noisy families to a noisy hotel. 'I hope you like your room, sir,' said the bellboy, and Steve said that he did, even though the bed was too soft and too too small, and whenever he turned on the TV something Spanish came out. He sat on the bed to have a think, but no thoughts came to mind. So he got changed into his T-shirt, his shorts, and his sandals, he put on sunglasses and sun lotion. In the mirror he looked at the heart that Cheryl had carved into his skin, and on a whim he covered it up. Then he went for a walk on the sand. He left strange footprints behind him.

He'd walked for a couple of hours, maybe three. The sun was beginning to set. He stopped at last, and stared out to sea for a good few minutes, unmoving, unthinking. Then he turned to the nearest palm tree he could see, and told her that he admired her fronds.

The palm tree didn't reply.

Steve didn't do a lot of talking any more, so he wasn't sure he'd got it right. Maybe he just thought he'd spoken. Maybe the words hadn't actually come out. He found that happened sometimes. So he told the palm tree again that he admired her fronds.

'I heard you the first time,' said the palm tree. 'We're not supposed to fraternise.' Steve apologised. And then said that he didn't know whether she'd be interested, but maybe Steve could buy her a drink? He was staying at a hotel. Somewhere, back there, he didn't know where exactly, but they served drinks, he was sure of it. Maybe he could buy her one.

The palm tree didn't say anything, and for a moment Steve thought he'd have to come right out and say all that again, and that would be such an effort. But he was just summoning up the breath to do so anyway, when the palm said, 'Are you married?'

Steve had to think about this for a while.

'Yes,' he said, at last.

The palm tree seemed to shrug. 'All right, señor. One drink. Just the one. At your hotel.' Steve thanked her. 'Don't thank me,' she said. 'But only after my shift, okay? I've got to finish my shift first.'

'I can wait,' said Steve. And he sat down beneath her shade, rested his head against her bark, and closed his eyes. And let the crash of the waves against the shore lull him to sleep.

At the Crease

A lot of this story is about my father, and I suppose I want to apologise to him for that. But I can't help it, it's all true, or at least, I've always remembered it this way, and the entire relationship with him has been based on it, so, really, if that isn't truth, what is? Everyone who knows my father will know how much cricket means to him. Each year he'd cheer up at the start of a new season, then sour once more when it was over. It was always on the television, on the radio as he drove me to school, there'd be copies of Wisden spilling over the shelves in the spare room. He'd watch it, he'd read it, he'd *study* it, and he'd once in a while even play it, for a local team that got together now and then, but he didn't enjoy that so much, he said they didn't take it seriously. He loved cricket, no question. But there was a time when he loved me too.

He was there when I was born. And, so the story goes, once the doctors had done all their business, he'd picked me up in his arms and looked at me carefully. Didn't kiss me, no, nothing like that, didn't even hug me, just gave me an inspection. And he announced to the entire medical staff there assembled that one day I was going to play cricket for England. Now, of course, this is not a story my father ever told me. Had the prophecy come true I'm sure there'd have been no stopping him, but I clearly didn't play for England – just look at me – so he might have looked a fool. Mum told me the story, but despite that I trust it anyway. Yes, she was prone to exaggeration, bless her, and yes, by the end, she didn't seem to have much idea what was going on in that nursing home of hers. But however often she told me the story of my birth, the details never changed. The pride on my father's face, the absolute *certainty* in his voice. I was to be a cricketer. There could be no alternative.

And for the next few years he put his plan into operation. The boy would need to be taught, and taught in the best conditions possible, no matter how long that would take. My father counted out twenty-two yards in the back garden, and called it a cricket pitch. Then he attacked it. First he destroyed all the flower beds that were in the way. Then he rolled the ground as flat as he could, trying to iron out each and every bump, he'd lay spirit levels across the grass, peer at them, and tut. Then the grass wasn't good enough, he dug it all up, planted new grass, in a reddish soil that looked to me as if my father was going out to that garden and *bleeding* on it – and Mum told me this was nearly true, she'd see the blisters on his hands as he worked those extra hours each day transforming a nondescript lawn in Surrey into something that could rival Lord's. And these may be my earliest memories, my father outside panting his breath out on that garden, he *belonged* outside somehow, it always seemed somewhat odd to see him indoors. He'd set out nets to ward off the birds that came to feast on the new seed, and I remember over dinner how he'd keep peering out of the window, then run outside if even the smallest sparrow got too close. One evening, I could have been no more than three, I looked from my bedroom and saw him spread-eagled on that pitch of his, trimming it with a pair of scissors.

And my mother had her part to play. She worked on the cricketer, taught him how to walk and talk, to read, to go to the toilet all by himself. And when my father saw I'd accomplished these skills to a level of reasonable proficiency, he decided it was time that the really important lessons could begin. 'I've got a surprise for you!' he told me one day, and he ruffled my hair a bit, the way he did when I was good. He gave me a bat, all of my own, he said, well done! And I don't suppose it was really full size, but it seemed enormous, almost as big as me, and I had to grab it with both hands straining just to lift it off the ground. It's not a toy, he told me sternly, it was an *instrument*, and if I couldn't handle it properly he'd take it away, and I begged him not to. I didn't really want the bat all that much, it didn't seem much like a present at all, but it was *mine.* He took me to the garden, let me stand on the grass I'd always been told to avoid on pain of death. He lunged a few balls at me, and I swung at them every which way, but never managed to hit them. So he taught me how to hold the bat, to aim my left foot where I thought the ball was going to bounce. And I hit one, I think it was an accident, and though the impact hurt my hand my father seemed so delighted I couldn't help being delighted too and quite forgot to cry. 'That's it, that's the idea!' he said. 'You're going to be world class, you'll see!' 'I'm going to be world class,' I told Mum that night when she tucked me in, and she smiled at me, but didn't say much.

And so passed my first cricket season. All day on weekends, and every evening when my father came home from work, racing to beat the traffic. In he'd come, where's my leg-spin bowler? he'd call, where's my little England captain? And he'd be angry if I wasn't already wearing my whites, I'd be wasting good sunlight. He taught me how to bowl, to wrap my fingers around the seam, never to *throw* the ball, but to let it loose at the right moment, my arms soon perfecting that strange windmill motion that looked so balletic on the TV. He taught me how to catch, that I had to cushion the ball with soft hands. 'Otherwise it'll hurt,' he said, 'like this,' and he threw the ball straight at me, and he was right, it was very painful. 'Try to think yourself at one with the ball,' he'd say sometimes, at others 'try to think yourself at one with the bat,' and I'd nod – I soon realised it was simpler to pretend I could think such things, I'd put on a frown and look serious. But it worked. Somehow it worked. And I'd get that hair ruffle, not every day, but now and again, I learned how to protect the wicket, I could bowl sideways-on, and once in a while I'd even enjoy it.

One day, quite unexpectedly, summer ended. I was wearing my whites when my father came home, and he said we couldn't play in this weather, we'd ruin the pitch, and he didn't talk to me again until March. He went back to the grass with his pegs and his seed and his scissors. I told Mum I missed Daddy, and she said she knew I did. I started school, I learned maths and spelling and how to play games that weren't like cricket at all, I hadn't realised there were such things. I even made some friends, I went to their houses after school, one of them had a swing in his garden! And then one day my father smiled over dinner, said that he was pretty sure it was nearly time, maybe even this weekend, he'd checked the weather. And that was it, Saturday morning it was out with the stumps and on with the pads, and I was trying to remember all that bowling and batting stuff, and there wasn't time for swings any more.

It'd be unfair to say that was my whole childhood, making friends in the rainy months, then losing them when the sun came out. But there's some truth to it; I wasn't unpopular, just vaguely anonymous. The one chance I had to shine was in the cricket team – because all that practice had paid off, by twelve I was really a decent batsman and a talented bowler. I even played once; I even won. My father came to watch. Sat there on the boundary, frowning. On the way home he told me he'd spoken to the sports teacher, asked him his methods, and judged him as an amateur. 'You deserve better,' he said. So that was that. My greatness was not to be tainted by the bungling of others.

* * *

I told my mother I'd had enough of cricket one day after school. Hadn't planned a rebellion, it just started. She didn't have much to say, carried on with the cooking, and told me to do my homework. But that night over dinner she suggested to my father that all this cricket business had gone far enough. My father, for all his faults, was not a man who lost his temper; if I fumbled a catch, he let me know I was pathetic without even raising his voice. But this was different. He asked me to leave the room, and then rounded on my mother so loudly I could hear it all the way upstairs. 'Do you want him to be a nothing?' he yelled. 'Do you know what that feels like?' And then I heard crying, and I thought it was my mother, but it may very well have been my father. Actually, do you know, I think it was.

I'd like to pretend this triggered the revolution – but it happened weeks, maybe even months later. I was batting, and putting in no effort. My father would bowl, and I'd barely move my bat. 'Come on!' he said. 'This is no way for an England captain to behave!' And he bowled again, and this time I deliberately blocked it with my arm, I let it hit me, I let it sting. The pain was what I wanted. 'Don't you ever hurt me again!' I shouted, and I advanced on him, waving my bat. He didn't back away, he knew I wouldn't strike him. And then, and I don't know why, 'And don't you ever hurt *her* either!' And that was it, he visibly flinched, and I realised I'd gone too far, and I had no idea whether he'd ever touched my mother, but for a moment I had the thrill that he might have. He stared at me, I stared at him. I lowered the bat. It was over. He walked away without a word. The next day he took the stumps and the bails, he took the bats, and he binned the lot. Within weeks the pitch had its first weeds, by winter it had all but disappeared.

To say that my father and I never talked again would be nonsense, but we never talked about cricket again, and maybe that's the same thing. When I was fourteen I started smoking and at seventeen had an ear pierced. But he didn't seem to notice; whatever game I was offering him, he didn't want to play. So I gave up the cigs, let the hole grow over, it didn't matter. I thought my mother would be pleased I'd broken free, but all she said to me was that I could have held out a little longer. I told her I'd been holding out my whole bloody life, and she just smiled sadly. When I was eighteen I passed my exams and went to university, and left home for good. A week later she sent me a letter saying her duties were now over, and she was divorcing my father. And I understood what she'd meant. She never married again, said she'd done all that. And then she fell ill, and then she lost her marbles, and then she died. And it was at her funeral that I saw my father again.

He was looking good, actually. Not as old as I'd have expected. We talked, rather shyly, but it was all right, we exchanged addresses. That was months ago, and I haven't written, and nor has he, but he might, I keep thinking he might. It's nearly Christmas, he might. And I think. I used to laugh at him for what he said when I was born, but at least he was there. I wasn't at the birth of my son, and a few months later Linda had taken him away, she didn't hold on like Mum did, she didn't want to play my games either. Last I heard they were in the States, someone else will be teaching my son stuff, and it won't be cricket, they don't do cricket over there. And I could have taught him cricket. I could have taught him *something*, maybe. To bowl. I was good at that. I was good at bowling, I think.

I've no idea if my father still likes cricket. When we talked at Mum's funeral, somehow it never came up. But I'm sending him this Wisden for Christmas. And writing inside it.

A lot of this story is about you, I'll say. And I suppose I want to apologise to you for that. But I can't help it, it's all true. Or, at least, I've always remembered it this way.

Luxembourg

It's not that they thought it wasn't worth reporting, it was just a matter of deciding where to schedule it. It wasn't a human interest story, after all, and it wasn't an issue of national concern, how could this possibly affect the average British voter? And global importance, well, no, clearly not. It was something quirky, something a little whimsical, a story that would amuse rather than educate, distract rather than inform. And that's why the disappearance of Luxembourg didn't headline the news, but was announced instead somewhere just between the sports round-up and the weather.

It wasn't even as if anyone could ascertain for how long it had been missing. It's not like Luxembourg was a country people were in the habit of looking at. A housewife in Belgium said that on Wednesday she'd thought to pop across the border, go to this grocery store she knew, the milk was always cheaper there. When she found out there was no longer a Luxembourg to pop across to, nothing but water stretching off as far as the eye could see, she'd turned right round and bought her goods from the supermarket in Antwerp. She said it was a bit of a schlep to get there, and she might end up paying a bit more, but at least they were *reliable.* And no, she hadn't bothered to report the missing nation for a couple of days. When asked why, she said she was always mislaying things, there was no point in making a fuss, they usually showed up again sooner or later.

Juliet had never been to Luxembourg. Colin had. Sometimes she'd ask him what it was like there. 'Oh, you know,' he'd say vaguely, and shrug. And she'd smile, and nod, and change the subject, but she didn't know, that was the whole point, why else would she be asking? Sometimes he'd be a bit more forthcoming. 'It's got nice architecture,' he'd say. 'Yeah, some of the architecture is quite nice. Quite European.' Juliet didn't know Europe very well. She'd been on a day trip to Dieppe when she'd been at school, and there'd been that summer holiday near that beach in Tenerife. Both times it had rained. She'd asked whether one day she might go to Luxembourg with him. She still had her passport, look. And showed him the photo of her inside, with that bemused expression on her face as the flash caught her by surprise. And he'd laughed, and said, no-one *chooses* to go to Luxembourg. He'd find them somewhere better than

Luxembourg, just wait and see! Maybe on their anniversary. But the anniversaries had come, and then gone, several of them now, and that photo of her in the passport was looking terribly young now, she wasn't sure the customs people would let her through.

When Juliet saw the news story, she felt the urge to call out for Colin, she thought he'd find it interesting. But then she remembered. He was on one of those business trips of his, in Luxembourg, he did a lot of business in Luxembourg these days. Even at that very moment she thought he'd be enjoying himself, sampling the drizzly weather and the architecture. She settled down to watch the whole programme, stupidly she half-wondered whether Colin would get a mention. But they didn't talk about Luxembourg for long, soon it was time for *EastEnders*. So she watched *EastEnders* instead. She supposed there was nothing to worry about. She supposed if there was something she ought to be doing, someone would soon tell her to do it.

The next morning Juliet got up early, watched the news before going to work. She was a bit sleepy, so may not have been concentrating hard enough, but she was pretty sure Luxembourg wasn't mentioned at all. She asked the other girls at the supermarket about it, but none of them knew what she was talking about. Mrs Wilson, who was deputy manager, but also did turns on the patisserie counter, so wasn't as big a deal as she thought she was, said she'd heard *something* about a country disappearing, but was certain it was Liechtenstein. And that gave Juliet some hope, she didn't think even Colin had visited Liechtenstein, she might still have a husband after all – but that night she watched the evening news, and there was an item about it, just a very short item, and it *had* been Luxembourg all the time. 'Country still missing,' said the report. 'Experts baffled.' They had a financial boffin in, to work out how much the nation's absence would affect share prices and the FTSE – and he concluded it wouldn't make the slightest difference. And there was an editorial about it in *The Sun*, in an article entitled 'Luxem-gone!', neither the title nor the contents of which made any sense whatsoever.

All that could be said with any certainty was that a nation of some half a million souls had been yanked out of existence. Fifty miles long by thirty-five miles wide, it was as if one of the jagged jigsaw pieces that had made up Europe had simply been taken from the puzzle by its cosmic player. Not that many alluded to this being the handiwork of God – it was all very well some tub-thumpers claiming it was divine retribution for the evils that Luxembourg had stood for, but since no-one could work out what Luxembourg's stance had been on *anything*, it wasn't very convincing. A few theories did the rounds. Some said it was because of continental drift. It was unusual, admittedly, for a landlocked country to be drifting, but just because it had never happened before didn't mean it hadn't happened now. Others blamed it on global warming. They suggested that perhaps Luxembourg had been using a higher than average number of aerosol deodorants or CFC-bearing fridges per capita, and if someone could only conduct a few surveys on the ecological habits of Luxembourg's populace, they could prove it. It was hardly their fault, they said a trifle defensively, if there was no Luxembourg populace left to survey.

But the sad truth is that there weren't *that* many theories, because there wasn't that much interest. It had only been Luxembourg, after all. For a few days the nations of the world waited to see if anyone else would vanish – and when no-one did, they heaved a sigh of relief. And, it must be said, looked at their neighbours sideways on, and felt a twinge of disappointment too.

The only remaining flicker of interest was not in Luxembourg itself, but what had been created in its absence. Small as a country it may have been, but the gaping puddle it left behind was considered to be rather on the large side. France called it 'La Manchette'. Belgium called it 'La Mer Belgique'. The Germans went one better, gave it the name 'Fehlenderangrenzenderlandsee' – if anyone referred to it as something else, they put their fingers in their collective ears and pretended not to understand. There were quite heated discussions between the three countries, and even hints that all or any of them might be prepared to go to war to claim this fresh territory. And then the USA stepped in, and said they were all being very silly – if they were going to behave like children, none of them could have it, so there. So it was named Lake Stars-and-Stripes. Everyone seemed satisfied with that. And with this last matter solved, Luxembourg dropped off the world's radar again, and every nation on the planet could get back to what it had been doing in the first place.

Juliet didn't find that so easy. Colin may have been away on his business trips rather a lot, but her life still had revolved around him

– if not his direct presence, then at least anticipation of his weekend returns. The weekend had always been about Colin, he ran through it like lettering through a stick of rock. On Saturday they would go out and do the shopping, and that night they'd curl up on the sofa and watch a DVD. If the movie wasn't too long, or if Colin wasn't interested in the special features, afterwards they might make love. That first Saturday she'd still half expected him to turn up; the night before she had, as always, vacuumed the house from top to bottom. Not that he ever commented, but she knew he'd notice if she didn't bother, she wanted the house to be just perfect for the time he was there. She adapted quite well, considering – she just pretended it was a Thursday instead, a Thursday without work, a long Thursday evening maybe, and carried on as normal, she was quite used to being on her own. But come the second weekend she found it all quite frustrating. She didn't know how much food she should buy on the shopping run, and the DVD wasn't nearly so much fun without Colin talking through the whole thing – she looked at the house, all newly cleaned, and wondered why she'd bothered. She began to fixate on his absence. It became a solid thing, somehow, she didn't know that absence could take up space, but it did – Colin wasn't there when she got up in the morning, Colin wasn't there when she went to bed, and he insisted on not being there at any time intervening – in a strange way, his very absence filled the house more completely than his presence ever had. She supposed she mentioned Luxembourg quite a lot at work, rather too much even. Mrs Wilson took her to one side and told her to stop going on about it, she was boring everyone to bloody death, and since Mrs Wilson was speaking to her at that moment in her capacity as deputy manager, Juliet supposed she'd have to listen. And that seemed fair enough, she was beginning to bore herself too. And on the third Saturday in a row, as she lay there in bed, on her own, indisputably on her own, and there was no love-making to be had, not even a sniff of it, Juliet told herself it was high time she did something about it all. She supposed there must be many people out there who'd lost family when Luxembourg vanished – but since the overwhelming majority of them had been in Luxembourg too, there was no-one she could compare notes with. She decided that Colin was dead. Once she put it like that, without fanfare, without qualification, everything seemed so much simpler. And seeing that he was dead, she decided too that she really ought to be grieving, that's what was called for at times like these. She stood in the bathroom, looked at herself in the mirror, practised expressions of sorrow and loss. It was hard work. In truth, she *did* feel sad, but, thinking about it, she felt sad pretty much most of the time, she wasn't sure Colin's death had very much to do with it. She had hoped that being sad already would be a help, that it wouldn't take much of a leap to get from her normal state of faded ennui into an appropriate display of grief. But just when she thought she'd got a handle on that grief, that it was finally taking shape, she'd lose her concentration and slip back into her usual sadness again. And wonder afterwards whether she'd been kidding herself, what she'd begun to feel wasn't anything even like grief, not even in the same ballpark, it was just hunger or tiredness or boredom. Juliet had no experience of mourning, didn't know what it was she was reaching for. She'd never lost anyone; her siblings, her aunts and uncles, they were all still about, all still kicking. Her parents had stayed stubbornly alive – they were getting on a bit, and Juliet couldn't see what they actually *did* with all that life, but they were there anyway, if not exactly energetic, still nowhere yet near death's door. She'd have to try to mourn a bit harder, really put her back into it, she stared at herself in that mirror of hers, she practically *gurned* with the effort. She tried to visualise Colin as a corpse. But it was no good, he always just looked asleep, it made her drowsy just to think of him, it made her want to get into bed beside him and cuddle. And if she tried to imagine him with his eyes open, the facial contortions she put him through to make him look sufficiently deceased just gave her the giggles.

Colin's family felt sorry for Juliet, of course. They'd never much liked her, this shy girl that Colin had married so suddenly, pretty but not quite pretty enough, always hanging in the background at social occasions, never speaking unless she was spoken to and not speaking anything of interest even then, always too eager to pass the phone straight to Colin without saying more than the quickest of hellos. But they didn't dislike her either; there was nothing to dislike. They could quite appreciate the awkwardness that Colin's disappearance must be putting her through, and even if their sympathies had not yet been conveyed via greeting card or phone call – they wouldn't want to interfere – they were genuine enough. But when she invited them to Colin's funeral, they were somewhat irked. 'He's not been in Luxembourg a month!' his mother told her.

'Some people go on *holiday* longer than that!' She went on to tell her, in no uncertain terms, that there was no body, so he couldn't legally be pronounced dead, and even if there *were* a body, it would barely have cooled yet, what was her bloody rush? And Juliet told her quietly that she needed to move on. It was time. She had to move on. And although Colin's mother might have thought that Juliet was a brazen slut, that she obviously had some new man already lined up to take Colin's place, that she'd probably *wanted* Colin dead, yes, actually *wanted* it, so she could cop off with the nearest feller, that really wasn't it at all. Juliet just didn't feel she could accept Colin had left her until there was something official to tell her so. She asked the vicar if there could be a service at the church – no, there was no body, not yet, but she thought Colin'd have preferred cremation if that was any use – and was told that, sorry as he was for her loss, it wasn't quite a loss big enough for him to help her with. So the funeral became a wake, held at her house that Sunday, and all Colin's family and friends could come and pay their respects if they wanted to. Not many did. She'd been out on the shopping run the day before, had massively overcompensated on the sausage rolls and the scotch eggs, she'd be picking her way through them for months.

As she was washing up in the kitchen, Dave came in and asked if he could help. Dave said that she was the widow, she shouldn't be doing all the work. And Juliet said he could do the drying if he liked, there was a towel hanging by the saucepans. Juliet liked the sound of 'widow', it gave her a buzz, and all day long she'd been waiting to feel something. Dave was three years younger than Colin, and would look a bit like him too, if only his hair were greyer and he were a bit fatter and he wore glasses. He'd come up from Leatherhead with his wife Sheila and their four-year-old son Tim, who'd been running around the house all afternoon pretending to be a dinosaur and who was clearly not making any better a stab at this grieving thing than Juliet was.

'Do you miss your brother?' she asked Dave, as she handed him a cake knife.

'Oh yes,' he said. 'Well, sort of. I mean, I only see him at Christmas.' He dried a couple of cups, and some saucers, and a fork. 'I'll probably miss him at Christmas,' he said.

They carried on washing up for a while. And then something got very confused, because he was supposed to be drying, but now his hands were in the sink as well, he was washing away at the cutlery with the spare sponge. It wasn't the largest of sinks, so their hands kept on bumping into each other.

'Do you miss him?' asked Dave.

'Oh yes,' said Juliet.

'Do you miss kissing him?' asked Dave.

Juliet thought about this. 'I suppose I do,' she said. 'Yes.'

'I miss kisses too.'

Juliet said, 'But Sheila hasn't been in Luxembourg,' and Dave said, 'I know.' And then his face was all over hers, cheek and neck, and finally he found his way to her lips, and she thought, oh yes, I was right, I *had* been missing this. They dripped soap suds on to the floor. He pulled away. 'Sorry,' he said. 'Sorry. I've wanted to do that for such a long time. Forgive me. I shan't do it again.' And he left the kitchen.

That night he phoned her. 'Oh, hello,' she said. 'Did you make it home okay?'

'I've got to see you again,' he whispered at her. 'I'm sorry, I'm sorry.' She supposed that would be all right. He said he'd make it over to her on Saturday, he'd find a reason to be out for the day, just leave it with him. And even though it was now arranged, and this was only Sunday night, he managed to find a reason to call her every night that week to confirm all was still well.

She broke her shopping habit, went out on Friday evening. The supermarket wasn't as crowded, she wondered why she'd never done it on Fridays before. And she made Dave a nice lunch for when he arrived. He didn't want her potato salad, though. The first thing he did was to wrap her in his arms and kiss her all over, even before he'd taken his shoes off, even before his coat. Realistically Juliet had known they probably wouldn't draw the line at kissing, and there might be a bit of sex involved. She just wasn't prepared for how much. 'Oh God, I've missed this!' he shouted out, somewhere during the fifth bout. And Juliet said she'd missed it too, and she meant it, but she thought to herself she hadn't missed it quite enough to *shout* about. Dave looked just like Colin, but they felt so very different; Juliet had imagined that in the dark she could have pretended they were one and the same, fair exchange, no robbery – but his hands were all over her, she wasn't sure where he'd want to touch next, and it wasn't in the dark, was it, even with the curtains drawn the sunlight was streaming in, she could see *everything*. And that was a bit disconcerting at first, and not necessarily all that pleasant, but it lent a definite thrill to the proceedings. Around half past five he said he'd have to head home now, it was a long drive ahead, and Saturday traffic was probably rubbish. And she surprised herself by actually minding. 'Don't go,' she said, 'not just yet,' and, uselessly, 'I've got potato salad in the kitchen.' 'Can we do this again?' he asked her. 'We've got to do this again.' 'Oh yes,' she said. 'I bloody love you,' he said, and kissed her, and drove away, and although she decided it'd be better to ignore that last bit, it replayed in her head a lot over the following week.

The next Saturday she didn't bother with the potato salad. She'd had a good think about what she should be feeling during the sex, about how much pleasure there ought to be – and she was able to get that right, she was very proud of herself, she'd caught the expression exactly. And then it occurred to her – my God! – she really *was* enjoying it, without consciously having to try. That made her panic a bit, she was lying there next to Dave when she realised that Colin was fading away, he'd been there in her head but now he was disappearing, how could he just disappear like that? This was grief, she thought, finally it was here, and she wasn't sure when she cried out whether it was out of the relief or the sudden loss knotted in her stomach. And Dave hadn't known why she'd cried out either, but he held her tight, he held her until she felt better and he told her that he loved her. He was using the 'love' word quite a lot. She told him once in a while not to be silly, and he said it wasn't silly, the last thing in the world it was was silly, it was *love*, didn't she deserve to be loved? And she asked him if he didn't love Sheila. It wasn't meant to be accusatory, but he went very quiet. He told her he had loved Sheila, of course he had, but that love had just gone. He didn't know where. It didn't make sense. How could something as important as love just fade away, what could it be worth if it could vanish so easily and without cause? So Juliet said that maybe he'd feel the same about her one day, and he denied that, he said this was a different kind of love, this one was solid. They had sex again after that. And then he got a bit tired, and asked whether she had anything to eat. He was bloody starving! And she wished she'd made the potato salad after all.

* * *

'I've told Sheila all about us,' he said one Saturday. 'We're getting a divorce.' Juliet wasn't entirely sure that she wanted him leaving his wife for her sake – she'd only just got used to the idea of feeling grief and feeling pleasure without now having to feel guilt as well. Dave assured her it was all right. Sheila was pretty angry, and his mother was absolutely furious, for some reason, Juliet might want to avoid answering the phone for a bit. But this was good, they'd no longer be living a lie, and better still, he could now spend all weekend with her. Friday evening to Sunday! He'd stay all week, of course, but his office was in Leatherhead, he could drop his marriage but not his job, that'd be silly. And it worked fine for a while. He wouldn't want sex the minute he got through the front door any longer, there was no need, they had all the time in the world now. He'd help her with the shopping on Saturdays, in the evening they might watch a movie. Then they'd make love, and it was fairly good, but Juliet couldn't help but notice it was getting that bit more perfunctory, the hands weren't quite so keen to explore, they stayed pretty much north of the equator. Colin hadn't been a passionate man, but he'd had his moments, it had taken two years of marriage before the sex had got stale. With Dave it had taken a little under three months.

Juliet supposed it was her fault, she must just suck the spirit out of people. And she didn't *want* Dave to be like Colin, she didn't want to think of Colin at all. But it was like prodding a sore tooth, she couldn't help it, and Dave was so like his brother it'd only take the right set of nudges from her and he'd become Colin entirely. She nagged him and watched for grey hairs, she put extra mayonnaise in his potato salad to fatten him up. And already as she lay beside him in bed, as they shopped, watched DVDs, she thought, he may not be Colin quite yet, but look! Colin Mark II can be seen peeping through. 'I love you,' he'd tell her, so bloody often, and she'd believe him, but she'd choose half the time not to hear. 'Let's have a baby,' he said to her, 'a baby of our very own.' 'But you've got Tim,' she said. 'Fuck Tim,' he said. 'I want a son with you.' And he worked hard at that, Colin had never wanted a child, that made Dave different, didn't it? Didn't it? After they'd put the work in, he'd fall asleep and she'd lie in his arms. How long would he stay with her? How long could he love her? She'd started dreaming of turning on the news one weekday morning, and finding that Leatherhead was in the headlines, that Leatherhead had vanished from the face of the earth.

And that's what she wanted, too; she wanted Leatherhead to fade away, and take Dave with it, just so she'd know, just so she'd finally *know* it was over and done with. She was practising already in front of the bathroom mirror, she was practising her grief, this time she knew just how she was going to do all those reactions. And although he hadn't vanished yet, he hadn't done a Luxembourg on her, as she cuddled next to his sleeping body she began to mourn. 'I love you,' she said. 'Oh God, I love you.' And she began to cry. This is grief, she thought, I'm getting *so* good at this! It hurt so much. If only he'd disappear.

But Leatherhead didn't disappear. And Luxembourg came back.

Mrs Wilson said she'd seen something on the news about it last night, hadn't Juliet heard? She was surprised, she'd always thought Juliet considered herself quite the Luxembourg expert. Juliet didn't believe her, but one of the girls at the checkout confirmed it. Juliet asked if she could take her lunch break early, just go and check, and Mrs Wilson said she didn't think anyone could be seen to be taking lunch at half past ten, it'd set an unfortunate precedent. And Juliet thought, sod it, and it made her feel good to think that, and she went out to her car anyway, without permission, and drove home. She turned on her mobile, and Dave was there, he'd left four messages, 'Phone me,' he said, and, 'We have to talk.' So she called him from the car. 'You've heard the news?' he said. 'I'm coming over. I've left the office, I'm coming over right now. We need to talk about this.'

Luxembourg had been misplaced in the middle of the Pacific Ocean. Juliet hadn't known much about the Pacific Ocean, but she now found out it was *vast*; you could drop a country in it easily, no sweat, say, twice the size of Luxembourg, and never expect to find it. The people of Luxembourg hadn't even noticed they'd been transplanted for a day or so; they were a bit puzzled by the warmer weather, but they weren't going to complain. And then it dawned on them they were aboard an enormous raft, a thousand square miles floating untethered out of the reach of civilisation. They peered over the edge. They found out that as wide as this raft was, it wasn't very thick – it was just a sliver of a nation, really, no more than three feet deep. And so the authorities had set up a rota, and the population had taken it in turns to lean over the side, and paddle their way to the nearest country. They had thousands of miles to cross, but they really put their backs into it, it had taken them a little less than a year before they were close enough to Samoa to get a mobile phone signal and call for help.

And the best news was, as far as anyone could determine, pretty much everyone in Luxembourg had survived the incident. There'd been a few deaths, of course – old age, illness, suicide – but it looked as if they were the sort who'd have died anyway, all the dead looked fairly old or sick or fundamentally depressed. And there'd been some instances of cannibalism, where some of the populace had panicked and thought they might be about to starve: but these cases were few and far between, and no-one had been quite sure why they'd resorted to such desperate means in the first place. After all, the cattle and the vegetation had been unaffected by the vanishing act, and besides, all the grocery stores had stayed open and kept normal hours.

So there was no reason to believe that Colin wasn't alive, and well, and would soon be coming home. 'How do you feel about this?' asked Dave. He was sitting with her in the kitchen, looking very stern. And she didn't know how she felt, actually, did she need to *know* just yet, why did there always have to be a reaction to everything? She said she was excited. 'No, how do you feel about us? What's going to happen to us?' And she hadn't even *started* to consider that. 'Do you care at all?' he asked. And he said that he loved her, that he'd told her many times, but she'd never been straight with him, she'd never given him that love back. And she wanted to say that of course she loved him, she let him share her bed and her potato salad, what was love if not that? And she *did* tell him she loved him, she did it at least once a day, she counted; she just made sure he wasn't there at the time, or made sure he wasn't conscious, or made sure he was just out of earshot – and even now she didn't say this to him, it didn't seem fair to offer up love when she'd never been sure she was free. And he called her a bitch, said that he'd ruined his life for her, abandoned his wife, his kid, it was all her fault. It wasn't her fault, she began to say, it was *Luxembourg*, Luxembourg had done this to them, it disappeared for no reason, now it had popped back, how could a small European country be her responsibility? But he was having none of it. He left the house, if she wanted Colin rather than him that was up to her. He'd see whether Sheila would take him back, maybe if he said sorry, if he apologised for the rest of his bloody life.

And, as it turned out, Sheila *did* take him back, but only under very stringent conditions. Apologising for the rest of his life was just the start of it.

Metal hoops were hammered into the ground, studding the whole coastline. Ropes were threaded through. And, on a count of three, a whole flotilla of helicopters winched Luxembourg into the air, flew over to Europe, and lowered the errant country back into position. It wasn't a perfect fit, it was hard to get it into the hole exactly. Some of the extremities had to be chopped off, they lost the whole of Schengen and all the bits of Hinkel that were worth a damn. But they did the best they could, they stamped and kicked the towns that were bulging out into place, and Luxembourg was once more part of Europe. Only three feet thick, it bobbed on the water, and everyone was warned not to walk too heavily in case they made it spring a leak.

And Colin came home. 'Hello,' he said to Juliet. 'Hello,' she said back. And neither were sure what to do, they both felt a bit shy. She had wondered whether seeing him on the doorstep once more would fill her with a romantic passion, that they'd sweep each other up in their arms, and never stop kissing again, never stop making love. It wasn't quite like that, but it was affectionate, they gave each other a hug. 'Would you like some lunch?' she said, and he said he would. She asked him what the ordeal in Luxembourg had been like. 'Oh, you know,' he replied, and shrugged. He noticed she was pregnant. That's right, she said. He said he didn't blame her, she'd have thought he was dead, he'd have slept around a lot had she been the one who'd disappeared. 'What was he like?' he asked. 'Was he better than me?' 'Oh,' she said, 'you know.' He nodded, ate his potato salad, said he'd never ask her again. To his credit he never did. She just hoped that the baby growing inside her looked nothing like her husband; it'd be hard to explain. But a few months later out it came, and it didn't, it looked like every other baby, a bald bad-tempered old man.

For a while the marriage improved. They had conversations when they did the shopping, he picked movies to watch on DVD she might actually like. And the lovemaking was never exciting, not exactly, but it wasn't a ritual any more, it felt at least like making love. 'I didn't know what I was missing,' he said. 'I've been such an idiot.' And yes, in time, it all sank back into routine again, but they'd shown each other it didn't always *have* to be like that, they could make it all work so easily if they could just get round to bothering, and maybe that was enough. And Colin was an excellent father, he knew just what to do; Juliet rather envied him that, it took her a lot of thought to decide how a mother should behave. 'We're happy,' he said one night to her, quite unexpectedly. 'We're actually happy, aren't we?' And she agreed. They were.

One day, about twenty years later, he told her he had cancer. It was eating away at him, it had been for ages apparently. The doctor had told him that morning, that's why he had to speak to her like this, that's why he had to sound so serious, oh God, don't be upset, oh God. Because it wasn't too late, the doctor had promised him, there were treatments, they mustn't give up hope. But the doctor was wrong, it was much too late. And all the treatments in the world could do nothing more useful than make Colin's death terribly, terribly slow. Juliet was always there for him. She drove him to the hospital. She fed him soup, even when he wasn't hungry, she told him he had to keep his strength up. And she mopped it when he threw it all up, she never commented, never made him feel bad. As she watched, he got older and weaker, his hair whitened then went altogether, his paunch disappeared into thin air. And she wished he'd vanish with the paunch. She wished she could wake up one morning and know he'd just evaporated whilst she'd slept, so painless, so simple. She now knew how to react, she could do the grieving thing now, she'd been right, it *was* easier when there was a body. And this time everyone came to the funeral, all the family were there to see him off. Not Dave, of course. Dave had died from a stroke two years previously. Juliet hadn't mourned; she'd decided then and there to save it all up for Colin.

A few weeks before he died, Colin told her he had something to confess. He didn't want to hurt her, but this was something he had to do. She waited patiently as he tried to find the words. 'I was never in Luxembourg,' he said.

She asked him what he meant.

'I was having an affair,' he told her. And he explained how he'd lied the whole time, invented business trips just to get away from her. He'd seen this woman on and off for years, he wouldn't say her name, it didn't matter any more – and Juliet agreed, it didn't. When Luxembourg had vanished it had seemed like a godsend. One little item buried late in the morning news, and his life had changed in a trice, he was free, and there'd be no need for a divorce, no need to make Juliet feel bad, because it had never been her fault, it had been him, all him. A break, clean and simple. He'd moved in with his lover. They had barely lasted a month. Some relationships are better at arm's length, he said, sometimes the reality of living together just gets in the way. He knew he couldn't go back to Juliet. How could he explain where he'd been? And then one day Luxembourg had returned. It had given him a second chance. He began to cry.

'It's okay,' she said. 'It doesn't matter now.'

And she could barely make out his voice through the tears. 'That's not it,' he said. 'I miss her. I'm sorry. I miss her. I'm sorry. I'm sorry.' And she held him in her arms, and she kissed him. And she cried too, because she knew what he meant, it was wrong, but sometimes she felt exactly the same thing.

One day she decided to take a holiday. Her husband was dead, her son was at college. What was to stop her? She renewed her passport, had a new photo taken for it. The old one looked so young now, so gauche; the picture that looked out now at the customs officials was confident, and hard, and expressive, that was a face that had *felt* things.

There wasn't much tourist interest in Luxembourg. Even after twenty years of good behaviour, it still had its reputation. And people said they felt seasick there, especially near the edge – you could see the whole country rise and fall on the water. Juliet liked Luxembourg. She liked the architecture. She knew it wasn't the *real* architecture, of course; the surface of Luxembourg was so thin all the heavy buildings had been torn down and replaced with balsa wood replicas. But that was okay, Juliet knew that Luxembourg had to have changed, that there'd have to be a Luxembourg Mark II. She was wise enough to know that's what happened to things which come back, things you'd thought had been lost forever.

She bought herself a caffè latte, and sat beneath the light flatboard spires of Luxembourg's very own Notre Dame Cathedral – not as grand looking as the one in Paris, but perfectly okay as far as cathedrals went, perfectly acceptable, they'd done a good job. She wondered whether she was tempting fate by coming here.

She wondered if it would all disappear, and take her with it, and this time there'd be no going back, no reprieve discovery in the Pacific, no last minute returns, they'd all vanish forever and never be heard of again. Well, she thought to herself, we'll see. And she decided that if she vanished, she'd just accept it. And if she didn't, she'd go home, and get on with the rest of her life. Either way, she wouldn't complain. She'd give herself, and Luxembourg, and their twin destinies, until she reached the end of her coffee. She sipped at it, without rush, and admired the architecture, and smiled, and enjoyed the day.

Sharp

The most interesting thing about my wife was the way she died. Don't get me wrong, she wasn't a *boring* woman, not as such, you could pass the time of day with her perfectly innocuously. But she wasn't a wit, she wasn't a wag. She didn't have much conversation, and the opinions she had she'd stolen either from me or from afternoon television. When we went to parties she'd be introduced as Pete's wife, you know Pete, they'd say, he works in computing. That's how she was defined. That's how she liked it. Since her death, if I go to parties – and believe me, I get invited to a lot – it's all changed. This is Janet's husband, they'll say, and point at me, and I'm supposed to smile and take it. This is Janet's husband, you know Janet, she's the one who got her head chopped off by revolutionary guerrillas in Africa.

I find it all rather irritating. Janet didn't deserve to die like that. Janet didn't deserve to die, alone, friendless, amongst strangers, part of someone else's war, her neck cut clean through with a machete. If you're going to die, then your death should at least reflect the way you lived your life. Janet ought to have had a heart attack straining for the television remote, or, at a pinch, been electrocuted by a power surge whilst flicking channels. I don't think the way she went was fair. To me, principally. And, come to think of it, it wasn't fair to Janet either.

I first heard about it on the news. Janet had been the only English passenger on the tour bus, that's why the press made such a big deal about it. Had there been even one other British national on board she'd probably have got less attention, but, just my luck, she was travelling with a bunch of Germans. Shortly after the news broke, journalists came to the house to interview me. My mum gave me a call, 'I've seen you on the telly!' she said. Over the next few days the facts came out. The bus had been stopped by a group of rebel soldiers, fighting for some sort of independence or another. They'd killed the driver, then taken all the tourists off the coach, one by one, and killed them too. 'I hope it was quick for her,' said my father-in-law at the wake. 'I know it sounds awful, but I hope she was first. I wouldn't want her to have had to watch all that.' I agreed for form's sake, but I thought it was unlikely. Janet had always been such a patient woman, she was never the sort to jump queues, that was one of her finest qualities. I imagined her sitting there on the bus, uncomplaining, waiting her turn. That's how I like to think of her, one of the reasons I loved her. 'I bet it *was* quick,' I lied, and my father-in-law nodded. He looked ever so smart in his best suit, partly because they were laying his daughter to rest, partly because there were journalists there who wanted to interview him too.

'But what was she doing in Africa in the first place?' When I get invited to these parties, the women buzz around me like moths to a flame. They ask me all about Janet, what was it like to be married to a celebrity? I do my best not to disappoint. And, usually, there'll be one woman who buzzes that bit harder than the rest of them, fanning the competition away, she'll be the one who'll ask the obvious question. 'What was she doing in Africa, and why weren't you with her?' And sometimes I'll make up a story, and sometimes, if I've drunk enough, I'll tell her the truth. How one evening I'd come home from a hard day's computing. Janet was excited, her eyes shining, her bags packed. 'I'm going away for a while,' she said. 'I need to find myself.' I asked her what she was talking about. 'I've wasted my life,' she told me. 'I've done nothing. I am nothing. It's time that changed.' I wondered where she'd got this idea from, and I checked the *Radio Times*, and sure enough, that afternoon there'd been a programme about female empowerment. I told her that it was ironic she was the one breaking away, because I was the interesting one. 'Don't you think it's ironic?' I said. I asked her if I could at least drive her to the airport, and she told me not to worry, she'd phoned for a taxi. Then she left.

And sometimes, if I've told her the truth, and sometimes even if I haven't, the woman at the party will take me back to hers. And there we'll have sex, because I'm quite the catch, I'm a celebrity, I've appeared on all the major channels, I was even on a chat show discussing the intricacies of African politics. Afterwards she'll fall asleep, but I never do, all that talk about Janet gives me insomnia. I'll get up, I'll pace a bit. And think how we never know what the best time of our life will be. I thought it might have been when I fell in love with Janet, or that day she accepted my proposal, or our wedding. But Janet peaked right at the end, it was perfect, she always had her proudest achievement ahead of her. And I hope I haven't peaked yet. Please God I haven't peaked. The woman from the party might stir, 'What's wrong, Phil, come back to bed.' It's not Phil, I tell her, it's Pete. 'Whatever. Come back to bed.' And I do.

Be of Good Cheer

I'm afraid you're not going to like Gillian very much. But I don't want you to get the wrong impression. There were good days, many good days, when we were able to find some sort of equilibrium. She'd sit across from me at breakfast, and she'd smile, very cautiously, and she'd say, 'You know, I think today is going to be a good day.' And then the smile would get a bit broader, now that she'd committed to the idea there was no going back, and she'd relax, and I'd relax. And although neither of us would get carried away, we couldn't afford to get too complacent – they were precarious things, those good days – from that moment on, by and large, everything would be just fine. By and large. There were plenty of good days, that's what I'm saying, that's what I want you to remember. I couldn't have managed otherwise.

I find myself forgetting the real Gillian. Looking back at our time together, I too can fall into the trap and see her as a selfish bitch. And of course she was selfish, how could she not be? But when you were actually with her, and you looked into her eyes, those beautiful eyes of hers, so deep you thought you were going to drown, she'd seem to be saying, I'm sorry, I'm sorry, I know what I'm putting you through, please forgive me – and you did, that was the thing, she'd lower her head bashfully even as she said the most hurtful things, and you'd want to say no, please, raise your head again, let me look in those eyes, do what you want to me but let me drown in those eyes once more. She was a monster, yes, but she was *trapped* inside the monster, begging me to find a way to set her free. Help me, she'd say, as she'd insult me once more, please help, as she drew tears and blood.

And it wasn't as if she hadn't given me fair warning. Even on that first date, sharing a chicken pasanda at the local tandoori on Kensington High Street. 'I've something I have to tell you,' she said, and she did that lowering of the eyes thing. 'I have a condition.'

'What sort of condition?' And she told me. I didn't take it very seriously at first.

She explained it was why she could only be a temp. 'I can't stay in any job too long. I can't let anyone get too comfortable around me.' We'd met over the photocopier; I'd been wanting an excuse to speak to her for days. When I tried to correct a jam, she slammed my hand in the paper feed. She was so elated that she accepted my invitation for an Indian there and then. 'I'll have to move on soon, I think,' she said, absently tearing her peshwari naan into threads. 'People are already beginning to accept me, remember my name. Pretty soon they'll be asking what I watched on telly last night, and where I get my hair done, and then you're on the slippery slope to friendship. I can't allow that.'

'But you seem fine to me,' I said. 'I mean, I'm happy, aren't I?'

'You're not happy,' she told me.

'Yes, I am.'

'No-one's that happy on a first date. Too much pressure, too awkward. That's why first dates are safe.' She smiled at me. 'You don't really like me,' she said, 'and I don't make you feel good about yourself. I couldn't be with you now if I did. It wouldn't be fair.'

We ate our curry in silence for a bit. I felt irritated. She, on the other hand, positively seemed to bloom. And then, suddenly, I saw her wince sharply.

'Are you all right?' I asked.

She nodded, waved my concern away, took a sip of lager. Then winced again, and this time she couldn't help letting out a gasp of pain.

'Is there anything I can do?'

'I thought we'd be safe here, this restaurant is so very dingy. No-one could be very happy here.' I blushed, I'd chosen it because I thought it was rather nice. 'But there's a couple come in, can you see them?' I looked, and at the far side of the restaurant a man and woman, chatting away, were taking seats. A waiter was asking them if they wanted anything to drink. 'Oh God,' she said. 'They're going to be here for ages. I think we'll just have to go.'

'I'll deal with it,' I said, and got up. She looked at me in surprise. I must admit, I was pretty surprised as well. I'm not a confrontational man, nor, it must be said, a very spontaneous one. So I had no idea what to say, or whether I'd have the guts to say it once I'd thought of it. The couple were kneading each other's hands, eyes not for the menu, only for themselves. It took them a moment to realise I was standing over them. The man looked at me, and blinked. 'Can I help you?'

'You seem happy,' was the best I could come out with.

They smiled, exchanged glances. 'Yes,' he said. 'Yes,' she said, 'it's my birthday.' 'It's her birthday,' he said. 'Oh. Well done.' And then, a moment of inspiration, 'how old?' 'Bit of a milestone,' she said. 'A milestone,' he agreed, 'forty.' 'Forty!' she laughed, 'dear God, forty!' And he laughed too, clasped her hand again.

'You don't look it,' I said. 'I'd have thought you were pushing fifty.' The man looked up in surprise, his jaw literally dropped. Birthday girl looked as if she'd been slapped. 'Really,' I went on, babbling now, 'you're really very very ugly. Both of you, in fact,' I added, but sensing instinctively the best place to attack, and pointing at the woman, whose eyes were now brimming with tears, 'but, you know, especially you.'

I half expected him to thump me. I wouldn't have blamed him, he'd only have been protecting his girlfriend. Just as I'd been protecting mine. And that thought gave me a sudden thrill, *Gillian's your girlfriend*, and it made me stand my ground. But he didn't thump me. He just sagged into his chair. The woman looked at him in horror, and then realised he wasn't going to defend her, perhaps because she wasn't worth defending, perhaps because he agreed with my assessment of her looks. And I felt a bit like a lemon just standing there, so I sort of nodded, muttered a 'sorry' (which could have ruined everything, but didn't appear to make much difference), and walked back to my table. I stole a look back; they were no longer holding hands.

'You made them very unhappy,' Gillian said.

'Yes,' I said. 'I feel awful.'

'I know,' she said. 'And that's the icing on the cake.' She lent forward, gave me a little kiss on the cheek. 'Come on,' she whispered. 'Let's get out of here.'

Her condition didn't have a name. She told me that doctors hadn't given it one; in fact, most of them refused to acknowledge the condition even existed. 'They just tell me I'm faking it,' she said. I could see she wasn't faking it, the way that her body would suddenly seize, her muscles contorted, her hands rigid like claws. And me standing there, watching her in the throes of agony, useless, unable to do anything to help. The first thing she'd feel would be an itching, only mild to begin with, and soon after she'd break out into hives. 'Look at the hive marks,' she said, 'look, there on my arms,' and they didn't look all that dramatic really, but I'd look closely, and yes, I suppose there were little bumps and spots. 'I mustn't scratch them,' she went on, 'that just makes it worse, but I *have* to scratch them, it's impossible, I just *have* to.' And after the itching and the scratching, the pain. I asked her where the pain came from, but she just told me it was everywhere, that everywhere hurt, it was all burning – and it was true, as I watched those attacks of hers, they never seemed to start from a consistent place. What a cruel allergy to have. If you reacted badly to pollen, or to cat fur, you just did your best to avoid flowers and cats. But when the thing which triggers so much anguish is as nebulous as other people's happiness, when the least show of pleasure from the remotest stranger can set you off – it was unspeakably unfair on her. That first night Gillian took me back to her flat. She stripped off, and I admired her naked body – it was without blemish, you certainly couldn't tell it harboured such a debilitating illness. And I kissed it all over. She didn't kiss me back, she said she was frightened I might hurt her if I enjoyed myself. In fact, that first night I didn't get to take my clothes off at all. And we made love, or as best as my trousers would allow, on the most uncomfortable sofa she had. It had a loose spring, it kept on boring into my back, whichever direction I turned to try to get new purchase on Gillian's body, there it'd be, boring away for all it was worth. Next morning I looked like a pincushion.

And that's how I began to go out with Gillian. Because she was an invalid she took up a lot of my time, and friends complained that I was ignoring them. We're really *happy* you've found someone, they'd say, we'd really *enjoy* meeting her – and, of course, that was the problem. But I didn't need them. I had Gillian. To celebrate this decision, I bought her a bouquet of dead flowers and chocolates well past their sell-by date. She looked bemused when I gave them to her, and I explained. She burst out laughing, 'You silly,' she said, '*I* don't have to be unhappy!' And she gave me a kiss. 'Only you, darling. Only you.'

'I'm a cripple,' she'd tell me. 'Don't say that,' I'd reply. 'Why not, it's what I am. I'll be a cripple till the day I die, and if you don't like it, you can piss off like all the others.' On good days, when she was feeling a bit brave, she'd put on a little lipstick – just enough, she'd say, so she wouldn't stand out, she was terrified of people's attention, she just wanted to vanish into the background – and she'd maybe walk to the shops. On bad days, anything could set her off. She could detect happiness through walls, from a car driving past the house, from a child playing on the pavement. And she'd double over in pain, gasp for breath, and then would start the tears. I wanted to care for her, I *enjoyed* caring for her. One night in front of the television she snapped, 'What are you so happy about?' And I hadn't known I was, but I supposed it was because I *loved* her, I realised I loved her, she was mine and no-one else's, and I just couldn't take my eyes off her. 'Well, stop looking at me, it hurts, stop fucking looking at me.' She stopped temping, better that I support her with my earnings, better that she didn't risk an attack outside. And I'd work extra hours, and come home late, exhausted, flop down on the sofa. And she'd look up from the telly, see me in my misery, and say, 'That's it, darling, that's the idea.' And I'd feel my heart lift again, and I had to force it down just in case it upset her.

However much I'd try to protect her, though, it wasn't always enough. Some nights I'd come home, and she'd be furious. 'Where have you been? I've been stuck in this bloody house all day, I'm bored to death.' And I'd explain, of course, I was trying to make sure she'd never have to go out and get hurt, she didn't want to get hurt, did she? And she'd say, 'I'd rather be hurt than put up with this.' It was hard to know where to take her. We went back to the dingy Indian restaurant, and we found a dingy Greek, and a dingy Moroccan too. I'd feel so nervous throughout the whole thing, just in case someone enjoyed their starter or their couscous. I'd take her to the cinema, making sure that the film was suitably depressing first. But it wasn't enough to see films about depressing subjects, about heroin addicts or holocaust victims. Good films, no matter how dour, were still curiously uplifting, sent a ripple of unity around the audience that quite made Gillian gnash her teeth in distress. So we had to go and see *bad* films about depressing subjects, where the heroin addicts were badly acted, the holocaust victims badly lit. Only then, as we watched on the big screen suffering on a cheap budget, could Gillian sit bathed in some beatific peace. Looking across at her over my stale popcorn, seeing her smile lit by the flickers of cut-price gas chambers, it almost made Auschwitz seem worthwhile.

Sex, of course, was the hardest thing of all. She'd lie next to me in the dark, stiff, cold. And if I'd reach out to stroke her, even the slightest touch, she'd growl, or say no, or do nothing at all, stay as stiff and cold as before, and that somehow would be the cruellest thing. This could go on for weeks, months; and just as I was sure

I'd never have sex again, as my senses dulled and I began drifting off to sleep, there she was, suddenly, she'd climb on top, pinion my arms down hard, and straddle me. Sometimes the operation was all but over by the time I'd woken up and realised what was going on. And I'd try so hard to avoid climax, to prevent that moment of joy bursting out and ruining everything. As she pummelled me with her hips I'd imagine my mother, and then that wasn't enough, and I'd have to imagine my mother being dead, all sorts of deaths, cancer, tumours, run over by a bus. And even that wore thin after a while, and I began to associate my mother's demise with being shagged in the dark, the very thought of her blood flowing would give me a hard-on. If, in spite of my best endeavours, Gillian felt I was getting happy, she'd whisper in my ear as she pumped away, 'Your cock is tiny, it's like being fucked by a gerbil,' but she said it so softly, that even though the words hurt they didn't leave a mark. In the same way that when the insults couldn't throw me off my stride, and she had to resort to her fists, her little hands raining down on me from every direction, she never made a bruise. She took great care that way.

With all these little complications in place, I was shocked when she called me at work one day to tell me she was pregnant. 'How do you feel about that?' I asked, and she said, 'I don't know, how do *you* feel about that?' So I told her that a baby was out of the question. It was hard enough to control the happiness of other adults around her, how could she manage with a baby? Sure, a baby might be miserable a lot of the time, it'd scream in hunger, or in fear, or because it was teething. But what if it suddenly came out with a laugh, babies could do that sometimes, who could know what stuff they were laughing at? Better to abort it now, I said. Better to rip it out of your belly right this second, before it grows up and hurts you. And she thought about this for a moment, and then said, 'You know what would make me happy? Really happy? A family. A real family.' And she told me that we must get married, it wouldn't be right for the child to be born a bastard. So I went out and bought her a ring and came home early and proposed. She made me get down on one knee to do it, 'Do it properly,' she said, 'on one knee', and afterwards she pushed me over and said she'd think about it. My mother wasn't very happy when I phoned her with the news. 'What do you see in that dreadful bitch?' My parents didn't like Gillian very much. Of course, that suited Gillian perfectly;

whenever she was feeling bad, she'd give them a call. She wouldn't say anything, just breathe at them, and listen to the rage and despair on the other end, it almost seemed to *nourish* her. 'We won't come!' said my mother. 'If you go ahead with this, we won't be there!' 'Fine, I don't want you to be there.' 'And you tell her to stop phoning us, all hours of the night, we know it's her, she does it again we're going straight to the police!' I hung up on her. Gillian was standing by, smiling sadly at me. 'Don't worry, darling,' she said, '*we're* your family now.' And she patted her stomach. There wasn't a bump there yet, it was still too early, but I knew what she meant. We were married three weeks later; we were lucky, it was raining.

And from then on it was all about the baby. The bigger she got, the more exhausted Gillian became: she barely had the energy to raise a hand against me. Whenever I got one of those niggling waves of contentment, she'd just lie there on the sofa, and look imploringly up at me, as if in the hope I could save her the effort and batter myself. And the kicks in her belly took it out of her too. 'Are they happy kicks or sad kicks?' I asked. 'Well,' she'd shrug, 'I'm not coming out in hives, so I'm guessing whatever's inside is pretty pissed off.' When the nine months were up, and the baby was done, we dutifully went off to the hospital to get it. Out came this girl, screaming for all it was worth. I pointed out that it didn't seem very happy, and the nurse told me I'd have to expect that, I had to remember that this baby had been somewhere nice and warm and safe where nothing could hurt it, and now it was out in the big wide world; it'd learn to be happy in time. I said that if it tried anything like that I'd soon knock some sense into it. And the nurse looked so shocked, and Gillian held the baby tightly to her, and said, 'Don't you ever hurt my baby. I won't let you *ever* hurt my baby.' And I laughed and said I was joking, of course I was joking! And, do you know, I probably had been.

Neither Gillian nor I discussed it, but I knew we were both worried that the baby might inherit its mother's condition. But it seemed perfectly normal. It liked ice cream, it didn't like baths; it liked laughter, it didn't like the sound of its father being beaten up. Indeed, whenever Gillian felt the urge, she'd look at me, put her finger to her lips, usher me into the bedroom, and close the door. 'Try not to cry out,' she'd say, 'I don't want to upset her.' She'd punch me less and less often, anyway. She hardly had the time, not now she was bottle-feeding and nappy-changing and rattle-shaking and saying 'coochie coochie coo' every five minutes. 'She's perfect, isn't she?' she asked me one night in bed. 'She's perfect, and we made her, *we* made her all by ourselves. Thank you. Thank you. I love you so much.' And she cuddled up to me and kissed me and nibbled my ear, but the nibbling was wrong, she barely used her teeth at all. And I froze, and pretended I was asleep.

'There's a Disney film playing at the cinema,' she said one day. She was beaming with happiness, and seemed to be enjoying the soft paste of apple and parsnip as much as our daughter. 'Let's all go as a family!' I pointed out it was a *happy* film, we couldn't possibly go. And she beamed that bit more, and said it didn't matter so long as our little princess was happy – if she were happy, so was Gillian. So we all went, and during the bit where Baloo was singing of bare necessities whilst floating down a river on his back, the baby looked her mother right in the face and said, 'Mummy.' And Gillian began to cry. I thought it might be because of all the laughter – that Baloo was such a *happy* bear – but it wasn't that at all. 'I'll always love you, and you'll only have what's best for you,' she promised our daughter, right there and then. 'I'll always love you.'

I got up whilst Gillian was still asleep. Took the baby, caught the train to London. 'Look, London,' I said, 'we're going to have an adventure!' I bought myself a ticket for a cruise on the Thames – she got to go free, there are some advantages to being a baby. 'Look, Big Ben,' I said. 'Look, the Tower of London.' It was a cold weekday in spring, but the boat was still packed, God knows where they found all those tourists. 'Look, look at all that lovely water.' I held her up to the edge so she could see, and I could so easily have slipped. I was so miserable, but without her everything would be all right again. Okay, I'd still be miserable, but it'd be the right sort of miserable, it'd be a useful miserable, Gillian would have all the misery I could offer, she could suck it out and drink it in, as much as she liked. But I couldn't drown my daughter in the Thames. No more than I could drop her from the Whispering Gallery, or abandon her on the Northern Line. 'Where have you been?' asked Gillian. 'I've been frantic!' And I explained I'd taken my daughter out for an adventure. 'Isn't that nice of Daddy?' she cooed. I left the next day.

* * *

I thought my friends would be pleased, especially those who'd told me my relationship with Gillian was 'unhealthy'. 'You can't just walk out on a young child!' they said. 'Without even an explanation, even a goodbye!' So I moved away, found myself new friends. A new job. Even new girlfriends, once in a while, I even came close to liking one of them. But at the end of the day, no matter how much she sulked and stormed, it really wasn't the same thing. One Christmas, on a drunken impulse, I sent a card to my parents, telling them where I was. They didn't respond. But soon afterwards my sister phoned to tell me my mother had died. And there was a strange mix of emotions – grief, of course, and the sick knowledge I'd been estranged from someone who loved me and cared for me and for all that love didn't want to hurt me, and for no good reason I'd now never see her again. And also that my mother was dead, *really* dead – and as my sister described the illness to me, I pictured her in her final moments, and I couldn't help it, I couldn't stop thinking of those nights with Gillian, no matter how hard I fought it down there was an enormous erection growing in my trousers.

And one day, another phone call. 'It's Natalie,' said the girl on the end. It took me a good thirty seconds to realise Natalie was the name of my daughter.

She asked to meet me in a bar. I couldn't see how she'd be allowed in one. I didn't recognise her, of course. She had to identify me from an old photograph. 'You've aged,' she said. She was surprisingly tall, dyed red hair, four studs in each earlobe.

'What do you want to drink?' I asked.

'Rum and Coke.'

'How old are you?'

'Twelve. But I can get away with it.'

She probably could, too. But I ordered her a Coca Cola. She pulled a face. I began the speech I'd been rehearsing on the train down to London. 'It's perfectly natural that you'd want to find out who your father is,' I said.

'Come off it,' she said. 'I don't care about that.' She stared at me coldly, and I could see that her eyes were nothing like her mother's, just smudges of mascara. 'It's Mum. She still wants you.'

'Does she know you're here?' And she smirked, and I realised that of course Gillian did, she'd *sent* her. 'How did you find me?' That smirk again. 'Where is she?'

'Same place you left her.' Natalie didn't bother to finish her Coke.

Gillian had been expecting me. She looked nervous and thin. And the eyes, you could still drown in them probably, but you might need to be weighted down. 'Come in!' she said. 'Just give me five minutes, and then I'll be ready. We can go out for dinner.'

'We don't have to go anywhere,' I said. 'Not if it'll cause you any pain...'

'No, no. We'll go out. Five minutes.'

We went to a dingy Indian restaurant. I'd like to say, for symmetry's sake, it was the same one in which we'd shared our first date. But it wasn't. 'Will this do?' asked Gillian. 'Is this all right? I hope it's all right.'

'How are you feeling these days?' I asked her.

'Oh,' she said. 'Up and down. You know. I have a condition.'

Into the restaurant poured a party of businessmen. Laughing, already a bit drunk, their ties askew. I got up. 'I'll deal with this.'

She was obviously hurting. 'No, really,' she said. 'I can control it better these days.'

'No problem,' I said. And I went up to them. I didn't need to say anything. Years living with Gillian had taught me you didn't need to be obviously rude to spoil someone's evening. The right look of contempt and the job was done. That's how fragile happiness is, it doesn't take much to destroy it. And even after all this time without my wife, I still had the knack.

'Thank you,' she said. We ordered chicken pasandas. 'Did you ever love me?' she asked suddenly.

I was honestly taken aback. 'Of course I... In all those years. I never once laid a finger on *you*. I never once hurt *you*. Did I?' I'd raised my voice a bit, but not so much that anyone was going to interfere. The man on the table opposite me saw the nervous woman flinch, but decided to concentrate all his attention on his onion bhaji. 'What do you want, Gillian?' I asked.

'With Natalie... I thought everything was going to be all right. If she were happy, then *I* was happy, it was simple. And if she wasn't... then I'd *make* her happy. That was all there was to it. I loved her that much. I couldn't imagine loving someone so much they could actually *fix* me. Can you, could you imagine that?'

'No,' I said.

'But now... Well. You've seen her. Haven't you?' I said nothing. She looked exasperated. 'She's into boys. And parties. She wants a tattoo, for Christ's sake!' I still said nothing, took a mouthful of chicken. It wasn't very good. 'What makes her happy is no longer what makes me happy.'

'So, what do you expect me to do about it? Talk to her? Why should she listen to me?'

'We can make another one. I'm still young enough, just about. If we move fast.' Her hand reached for mine in excitement, and her eyes gleamed, and I could see a trace of the old beauty in there after all, hidden away, not quite dead yet. 'And I'll get it right this time. I'll love her and make her happy and she'll make me happy and I'll never feel this pain again...' And she winced. Someone, somewhere, was enjoying their chicken pasanda in spite of the chef's best efforts. 'It has to be you,' she said softly. 'Who else would put up with me?'

We went back to the house. The bedroom didn't look like it had ever been mine – she'd moved the furniture around, given the walls a lick of paint so many years ago the pink I'd never seen before was already fading. 'How did you want us to do this?' I asked. 'I don't want to hurt you.'

'No,' she said. 'Hurt me. I don't want you to hold back. Not any more. After all I've put you through, I want you to *enjoy* this. And maybe,' she said, 'we'll get a better child that way.'

So we had sex. She kept on telling me it was okay, I mustn't worry about her condition, I should do it harder, faster, do anything that would make me happy. But I was doing my best already. And then it was all over, and I rolled off.

'You held back,' she said. 'You didn't have to.'

'I didn't,' I replied. 'That was very nice. Thank you.'

'You held back. If you'd *enjoyed* it, I'd have felt it. I felt nothing. Not even an *ache*.'

'What can I say?' I put on my socks. 'Best I've ever had.'

And then she came at me. 'Bastard!' she cried. 'I wanted to make you happy! Why wouldn't you let me make you happy?' And her fists were all over me, every which way, not like it used to be, back in the day every single one of those punches would have hit home, not a single one wasted, I'd grown to admire it – but not now, they were all over the place, one of them even drew blood. No technique at all, the old Gillian would have been disgusted. And soon she wasn't hitting me any more, not really, there was the odd flail now and then but that hardly counted, she'd given herself up to tears, and she was in my arms, and for God's sake, I was comforting her, I was actually *comforting* her.

'It was wonderful,' I said. 'Ssh now. It was great.'

'Do you promise?' she sobbed. 'I made you happy?'

'Very happy.' And I carried her back to bed, and lay her down, and stroked her hair, and she fell asleep. And I wondered whether I'd still be there when she woke up.

Jolly Roger

'May I have your embarkation card, sir?' So Roger juggled all his papers to try to find it, his passport, his itinerary, the e-ticket his son had printed off the computer for him. 'No, sir, it's the pink one,' and her well-practised smile never even wobbled, and the woman at check-in gave Roger no reason to believe she was impatient with him.

The couple in front were already posing for the camera, arms around each other. The photographer told them to smile, 'You're on holiday now!', and they giggled, moved closer. Honeymooners, thought Roger vaguely, or no, not married, they're giggling a bit too much for that. He wondered if there was going to be a lot of giggling in the week ahead, supposed there was, and nearly turned around and walked away. But he didn't want to test the non-wobbling smile of the cruise line any further, and, besides, its owner was talking to him again. 'Just the one of you, sir?' she asked kindly. 'You don't have to have the photograph taken, not if you don't want. It's more for the couples, really.' And she looked so very sympathetic. He felt a flare of irritation, wanted to tell her he wasn't single, thank you very much, he was married – and then realised that he was nothing of the sort. There wasn't time to take her advice, the giggly couple had been dispensed with, and the photographer was waving him forward. He stuffed all his papers into his hand luggage for neatness's sake. 'Now smile!' commanded the man behind the camera, 'you're on holiday now!'

Roger's stateroom was on the Aloha deck. 'Aloha!' chirped the elevator voice cheerfully. He found his stateroom easily enough – every door had a name on it, ready and welcoming: his read, *Mr Roger Kennedy, Mrs Deborah Kennedy*. 'Stateroom' sounded more impressive than it actually was; it was clean and beige and rather smaller than his bedroom back at home. A television was mounted above a minibar, and on it an attractive American woman was talking through an ever-widening smile about the many shipboard activities Roger could enjoy; a desk was filled with leaflets detailing much the same thing. He supposed it might have looked a bit more plush had they reserved a cabin with a porthole, but it was there Roger had drawn the line.

'It costs nearly two hundred pounds more,' he had said. 'We're not paying two hundred pounds for a hole.'

Deborah had tried that usual trick of hers with the watery eyes. It usually worked, but not this time. Not to the tune of two hundred pounds. 'You promised me luxury,' she'd said. 'We'd be able to look at the sea.'

'We'll be *surrounded* by the sea,' Roger had then pointed out. 'Odds are we'll want somewhere we can get away from it.' He'd been wrong, he now realised. Without a view, the room was a claustrophobic cell. Deborah wouldn't have liked it. She'd have been silent now, surveying the room with displeasure, and starting to sulk, and he'd have felt guilty in spite of himself (after all, he'd still paid for the bloody holiday, hadn't he?).

And then he saw the rabbit. 'Aah, sweet,' she'd have said, and given that smile that made her look like the girl he'd fallen in love with, and less like the fortysomething with a weight problem. The rabbit might just, he supposed, have saved the day. It was sitting on top of the pillow. Of course, it wasn't a real rabbit. It had been made from a hand towel – body, tail stub, floppy ears, the whole works – and a couple of chocolates in silver foil were studded into the head to make eyes. Underneath the rabbit was a little card. 'JESUS WELCOMES YOU,' it said, and Roger wondered whether on cruises towel animals were the equivalent of a Gideons Bible, but then it went on, 'I am happy to be your steward and to make you comfortable. If you need anything, do not hesitate to call me on my pager,' and it gave a number. Roger plucked out one of the rabbit's eyes, and ate it. It was minty. Deborah, he knew, would have eaten both.

He unpacked his suitcase, put his shirts and trousers on hangers, stuffed underpants and socks into a drawer. He opened the safe, and into it went his passport, his wallet, his English and European currency, and Deborah.

There was a knock at the door. He opened it. A short man in a uniform beamed at him.

'Hello, sir!' he said. 'I am Jesus.'

'Hello, Jesus,' said Roger.

'I am your steward.'

'I saw your card.'

'Is good.'

'I saw your rabbit, too.'

'Yes, sir.'

Roger wanted to ask about the rabbit, but couldn't think of any question more burning than 'why?', and that seemed a little rude. Instead he just flapped his hand towards it. Both Jesus and Roger regarded it solemnly. It regarded them back with its one remaining eye. Jesus waited politely for Roger to say something else. When Roger didn't, he continued.

'I welcome you,' said Jesus, 'and wish you good holiday. I am happy to be steward and make you comfort. If you need anything, do not hesitate call pager. I'm from the Philippines,' he then added. He gestured a hand towards the bedside table, and Roger turned to see what he was wanting. There was the silver foil from the chocolate Roger had eaten, scrunched up. He passed it across, this little bit of rubbish he'd made, it disappeared into one of Jesus's pockets, and in a trice the room was as perfect as before Roger had arrived. Then Jesus turned to go.

'There is one thing,' said Roger. 'Can you work the safe? I thought there'd be a key, but it's all a little more electronic than I expected.'

'Is simple,' said Jesus. 'You type in secret code, so? And turn the knob.' Jesus watched approvingly as Roger did just that. 'Is good.'

'Good,' agreed Roger. 'And to open it again, I...?'

'Type in secret code, and turn the knob. Sir, the other way, sir.'

'Thank you. Do I give you a tip or...?'

'At the end of the cruise, sir. But if you have an express wish to...' Roger had just locked the safe again; now he unlocked it, gave Jesus a fifty pence piece, locked it a third time. 'Thank you. Is good,' and the coin vanished as swiftly as had the chocolate foil. And Jesus left.

At five o'clock the ship set sail from Southampton. Everyone was pressed against the railings, looking down at the sea and pointing at it as if they'd never seen water before. The waiters were offering cocktails of rum and fruit, and were all so enthusiastic about them that Roger thought it'd be churlish not to buy one. He sipped it through a straw as he stared out at the coast. On land crowds of people were waving; the passengers were waving back, and Roger waved too, putting on a smile and feeling like a fraud. And in spite of himself he couldn't help thinking of that movie in which the ship turned upside down and all the passengers drowned – what was its name? Deborah would have known.

The cruise had, of course, been Deborah's idea. 'Julie's just sailed around the Med,' she told him one day when he got home from work. 'She says it's *luxury*. That's what we should do. Sail around the Med a bit.'

'It's pretty expensive, isn't it?' he'd said, but he'd only had the energy for token resistance.

'Julie says not. Julie says it pays for itself, because all the food is free, and all the drink. Well, not the drink. And you get to go to all these lovely places, and there are swimming pools and televisions. I just think,' she'd said, and he knew she'd already checked the prices, 'I want to go on a cruise just *once* in my life.'

But she hadn't been that lucky. And there was so much to think of that Roger had entirely forgotten about the holiday until the funeral. There his son had been, in that suit which wasn't a proper suit, and after he'd made the right noises about the cremation and the canapés, he'd said, 'You still going on that cruise then, Dad?'

'What? No. No, I don't think so.'

'Oh, you should. I mean, it's all paid and everything.'

'Yes, you should,' cooed his son's latest girlfriend. 'That sounds so lovely, a cruise, that sounds so *romantic*.'

'It'll take your mind off Mum,' said his son. 'You know. You've been through a lot. Haven't you? God. We'd give our eye teeth for a cruise. God.'

'Why don't you go instead?' asked Roger.

'No, thanks.'

The next day Roger phoned up the cruise line. 'I'd like to cancel the booking,' he said. 'My wife's dead.'

'Did you take out insurance, sir?'

'I don't know. I expect so. Yes.'

The girl checked on a computer. 'I'm afraid you have no insurance, sir, and so we can't offer you a refund.'

'Oh.' And he was about to say the money didn't matter, he didn't care about the money, when all of a sudden he bloody well did. He bunched his free hand into a fist, began to pace angrily. 'Oh.'

'I'm sorry for your loss.'

He wrote an angry letter to the cruise company. In it he used the phrase 'cynical exploitation'. He rather enjoyed writing it – so much so, in fact, that he put it to one side and set to work on an even angrier second draft. It was fun to use words he knew he'd never even countenance in everyday life, and it became a little project for him to look forward to when he came home from work, a spot of dinner from the microwave, an hour or so on the complaint letter, then a little telly before bed. And he felt too that at last he was able to let something *loose.* His irritation at how banal the funeral had been, at how average the catering was. At the unfairness of having to put up with so much sympathy, and the way he wasn't allowed to mind, wasn't allowed to turn to all these well-wishers popping up all over the place and tell them to sod off, that he had to be *nice* to them and thank them, thanks, even though they were putting such stress on him, it was easy to show grief, you just had to look sad, but showing grateful grief was so much more of an effort. At how suddenly Deborah had died, a heart attack in Sainsbury's, one moment picking out clementines in the fruit and veg section, the next his wife on the floor, and the fruit bouncing about and rolling everywhere and getting underwheel of the trolleys, all the shock of it, but even worse, the *embarrassment.* By the fourth draft of his complaint letter he'd called the managing director 'a cunt' – called him it rather a lot, in fact, because he liked the way it looked on the page – and it didn't matter because he knew he wasn't going to send the letter, he was going on the cruise after all. He'd now found the perfect reason to do so.

The tour operators had sent him lots of bumph about his holiday, and one thing that he remembered was that for the evening dining formal dress was compulsory. Roger changed into his suit, put on a tie, cuff links. He hadn't worn the suit since the funeral and it felt odd to be giving it another airing so soon. His reservation was for the second sitting in the Riviera Room, on table 197, at the back, near the window. There was a five-course menu, most of it using the word 'terrine'. Table 197 seated eight people, he was the first to arrive. He chose the chair with the least advantageous view of the sea, since he wasn't planning on looking at it very much. His companions joined him in dribs and drabs – all in T-shirts and comfortable trousers. One man in a baseball cap told him that the formal dinner was tomorrow night, that Roger had misread the instructions.

'Not to worry,' said the baseball cap's wife, 'you'll just have to come in a T-shirt tomorrow whilst we're all dressed to the nines!' And they all laughed, not unkindly. They went round the table introducing themselves, and Roger promptly forgot their names. Three couples and one elderly lady on her own, probably in her early eighties. Two of the husbands discovered they supported the same football team, and became lifelong friends over the prawn cocktails. The wives talked about shoes. The elderly lady gamely tried to talk to Roger. 'Have you ever been on a cruise before?' she asked.

'No,' Roger replied. And then, because he felt he should, 'Have you?'

'Oh yes,' said the lady. But she was sitting two couples and four mushroom terrines away, and to have pursued the conversation further seemed more effort than it was worth. So she nodded at him instead, smiled, and turned her attention back to the wife extolling the virtues of her flip-flops.

That night he slept well. The gentle rock of the boat made him drowsy, and although he would stir at the sound of couples talking in the corridor outside his cabin, he always nodded off again soon afterwards.

There was another full day of sailing to be had before the ship reached its first port of call. A helpful newsletter had been popped under his door, presumably by Jesus, and it promised a 'Fun Day at Sea!' Inside it Roger read of an arts auction on deck nine that afternoon, of quoits and trivia quiz competitions, of the daily AA meeting in the Razzmatazz Club. He put on some cotton jeans and a short-sleeved shirt and took a morning walk on the lido deck. There was a chill in the air, but this hadn't deterred most of the passengers from taking up sun loungers, coating themselves with lotion, and lying around hoping to be basted. The swimming pool was full of children; the jacuzzi seemed to have a two tattoo minimum requirement; the all-day buffet bar was full of people queuing for cheeseburgers and rum babas; the gym was all but empty. A huge video screen on the main deck played videos of other cruise holidays passengers could book *right now* and at *special rates* down by the Purser's Office – all the people in the film were beaming and laughing, and all the people watching them on deck looked fraught or bored, as if waiting to be told their holiday had already started.

There was such a listlessness to it all that Roger felt he could have carried out his little ceremony right there and then and no-one would have noticed. But he felt self-conscious, this was a private thing of his own, he wanted neither witnesses nor as backdrop music a karaoke version of the Macarena. He went back to doze in his stateroom, but was woken by a knock on the door.

'I'm sorry, sorry,' grinned Jesus. 'I'll come back later.'

'That's all right,' said Roger.

'Are you not going to dinner, sir? The formal dinner. All very nice. Lots of pictures taken, lots of fun.'

'I'm not very hungry.'

'Are you enjoying your holiday, sir?' asked Jesus. 'You got the newsletter I left you? Lots of activities, lots of fun.'

'Oh yes,' said Roger. 'I am having fun.'

Jesus didn't look convinced. 'Don't you worry, sir. Jesus make sure you have fun. You leave to me.' And he closed the door.

Roger opened the safe, took out what he needed, and left the room. He tried to fit it in his jacket pocket, but it made such a peculiar bulge that he took it out again. It wasn't as if anybody would look at him anyway – a plain man in slacks carrying a small urn. The deck was dark and deserted; they'd been crowding round the sides the day before, but the passengers had already got bored with the fact they were ploughing through the sea at twenty knots, and were indoors trying to forget it with casinos and dancing and variety entertainment. There was no roll, no sensation of movement, and against the black horizon you couldn't tell the ship wasn't standing still. It was only when he peered over the edge of the rails, and looked straight down – far down, a good ten metres – and saw the water being churned around and sucked under and spat out, that he could appreciate how fast they were travelling.

'Do not throw any objects over the edge,' a sign said. 'We are committed to protecting the environment. Put rubbish in the litter bins provided.' And more. 'Do not throw your cigarette butts or ashes over the side, as wind could blow them on to a lower deck.' Roger had always treated authority with the greatest of respect. Deborah had not, and had made him anxious whenever she broke the speed limit, or joined the express checkout at the supermarket with more than five items in her trolley. It was in the spirit of Deborah, then, that he decided to flout regulations on her behalf. He stole a look up and down the deck, then took the lid off the urn, and climbed up on the first rung of the protective railing.

'Hello,' he heard. 'Roger? It is Roger, isn't it?'

And he climbed back down again. He didn't recognise the old woman at first. She was now dressed for the formal dinner. Her hair was up, and she wore a ball gown which sort of twinkled when it caught the light – Roger supposed it must have had little sequins on it or something. She was fully made up, too, and her mouth was now a gash of thin scarlet. She held a cigarette. 'You looked as if you were going to jump off,' she said, but amiably enough, without apparent alarm.

'What? Oh good God, no. No.'

'It's a long way down,' she said.

'It is,' he agreed.

She looked at him hard, and one eye squinted as if to avoid the sunlight. Since it was dark, he wasn't quite sure why she did that. 'Loneliness can be hell,' she said. 'Believe me. I know.'

'I'm sure,' he said. 'No, really, it's all right. I was just...' And he vaguely gestured with the urn.

She tapped her cigarette ash over the side. 'I don't really smoke,' she said. 'But, you know, it sort of suits the dress.' She tapped again. 'My husband smoked. He actually knew how to smoke. I just copied him when I had to.' It was true, she wasn't even smoking now, not really. Never inhaled, just tap-tapped away. 'What is it you do?'

He told her, and she didn't pretend to be impressed. He liked her for that. Caught in the moonlight, with only the flash of the deck seven disco behind her, she didn't look nearly so old. 'What do you do?' he asked.

'I go on cruises,' she smiled. And she did that squint again. 'Do you mind me asking how old you are?'

'Forty-three,' said Roger.

'That's awfully young,' she said. 'Was it recent?' And she didn't wait for a reply. 'So young, I'm so sorry. And there's been no-one since, has there, of course not.' She reached out for the urn, nothing forced, nothing demanding, just a little gesture really. And he didn't know why, but he gave it to her. She weighed it in her hand, smiled just a little, then gave it back. It didn't feel quite so important to Roger somehow, seemed lighter in his hands.

They both stood at the railing for a while, watched the night sky and the sea, tracing where one ended and the other began. Not looking at each other, but not uncomfortably, she tapping ash, he clutching his. He felt her hand reach for his hand, and took it, but still didn't look at her, knew that looking would be wrong, would break something. 'It can be hell,' she said at last, and only then did he feel he could face her, and there she was, all scarlet gash and twinkling gown, and he thought her eyes were twinkling too. Tears, maybe? Or something else? She held his gaze for a long time. 'What's your cabin?'

'Um. A636.'

'Yours is closer.' She threw away her cigarette without even a final puff.

'I don't think you're supposed to do that,' he said.

She shrugged.

They didn't say a word in the lift. 'Aloha!' chirped the elevator at last. Roger ushered her into his room, and carefully shut the door behind them. There was a 'Do not disturb' sign, but he thought hanging it might look a little crass. He put the urn down on the desk. 'It's not a big room,' he said. 'Is yours a big room?'

'Mine's got a porthole,' she said.

'That's nice.' He looked around the cabin, as if this were all as new to him as it was to her. 'Would you like a drink?' he asked.

'Do you have one?'

He opened the minibar. 'No,' he said.

She kissed him on the mouth. That little thin gash of red against his lips, and her tongue poking its way past them. Just as Roger thought he might begin to enjoy it, she stopped. 'Thank you,' he said, and then he thought, I'm going to make love to a total stranger, not making love, it won't be love at all. And he was about to clear all the leaflets off the bed, all the details about the cruise excursions, all the discount vouchers for the jewellery shop. But she didn't seem to want a bed. Without a word she got on to her knees, and pulled at his trousers.

'Oh,' he said, and his hand moved to help her. A little impatiently she brushed it aside, this was clearly something she wanted to do herself. And she had his flies down, and then his pants, and it was only as she took his penis in her hand it occurred to him what long nails she had, more like talons really, varnished as scarlet as her lipstick (probably the same brand). Ever so sharp, one false move and she could slice his penis open, like a sausage, and all the sausage meat would spill out – he really must take care, he decided, not to make any false moves. And then, to his alarm, that's exactly what the penis did, it woke up with a lurch, it stiffened and stood to attention so suddenly and Roger felt an absurd urge to tell it to watch out, be careful of those red razors, you could cut yourself! But she was careful, she plucked it gently as if picking out a piece of fruit, and popped it into her mouth.

My God, thought Roger. Deborah hadn't ever liked that sort of thing. They'd had sex, of course, lots of times, and she'd even kissed him down as far as his navel, but she'd never ventured any further south. 'You don't mind, do you, darling?' she'd asked early on. 'But the thought of it, it makes me want to throw up.' His nameless new friend had no such qualms, she was smacking her lips all round it, and he really felt he ought to do something to help, he looked down at her grey hair bobbing away on the end of his dick as if it had just *grown* this elderly woman somehow. He wanted to give something back, even just a show of affection. He ran his hand over her hair, and he saw it wasn't so much grey as silver-streaked, and it felt starchy to the touch. It felt a bit awkward doing that, and since the mouth and tongue were still so busy licking and sucking and nibbling, the rest of the head barely seemed to register that it was being patted like a cocker spaniel. He wasn't sure what to do with the hand now, though, so he gripped the edge of the desk, and his fingers brushed the urn. He didn't want to think of the urn. Or what was inside it. Or *who* was inside it. He closed his eyes and tried to concentrate on the matter in hand, he thought the best way he could help the old woman now was to come as quickly as possible, he imagined she'd be down there till she suffocated otherwise, slobbering away until her breath gave out, and then there'd be two dead ladies to deal with, that didn't sit well with him at *all*. So he put all his effort into getting excited, he really tried. *The Poseidon Adventure*, he thought, that's what the film was called.

Eventually, of course, she had to give up. As she pulled away, he pretended he'd reached orgasm. 'Mmm,' he said, 'thank you.' His penis splashed wet but flaccid at his thigh, the erection hadn't lasted long. 'Thank you,' he said again, and gently helped her to her feet. 'That was really nice.'

'Are you sure?' she asked.

'Oh yes.' And he smiled at her. The scarlet lipstick hadn't even smudged for all that effort. He did hope she wouldn't want to be kissed on the mouth now, considering where it had been. But she didn't appear to, and accepted the little peck on the forehead as if expecting him to aim nowhere more tender.

'Well now,' he said. 'Well. What can I do for you? I mean, I could do the same in return. If you like.'

'Can I have some toothpaste?' she asked. He tried to work out exactly what she wanted him to do to her with it, and then realised. 'Of course,' he said, she nodded, and went into the bathroom. She left the door open, and he saw her squeeze some paste on to her finger and use it as a brush. He blushed, and looked away. For some reason this seemed something too intimate, he was embarrassed. But turning around, he found himself looking at the urn, and that was pretty embarrassing too; he could at least lock that away in the safe, and so took the opportunity to do so.

She stepped back into the bedroom, smiled him a minty smile. 'That's better,' she said.

'I'd still like to give you something,' he said.

'You have.' And she kissed him on the cheek, like an aunt, just a little peck – and her mouth was so small it was hard to believe it could have opened so wide. She walked to the door. 'Late-night bingo in the Pirate Lounge,' she explained, and left him.

The first port of call was Vigo. Roger had never heard of Vigo before, but didn't hold that against it – after all, there were lots of places he hadn't heard of, it didn't mean they were rubbish. However, Vigo *was* rubbish. He watched it from the coach, as a tour guide told them of its history: 'Our principal export is granite,' she said. 'We are very proud of our granite. Out of the window you will see houses, made from Vigo granite.' The way she pronounced 'granite' made it seem rich and exotic, and you could almost believe it was, until you looked at the houses in question. In his lap Roger held a Spanish phrasebook, which he wouldn't need, and the urn, which he wouldn't need either. He had wondered whether Vigo might be a good resting place for Deborah, but really, she deserved rather better.

At one rest stop the tour coach parked by three enormous anchors mounted on a plinth. Roger supposed they must have some historical significance, but the guide was only interested in pointing out where the nearest toilets were. Deborah would have known, she'd have studied all the travel books before they'd set out, she'd have told him – and for a moment he felt a yearning for her so strong that it almost left him winded. And he knew, with some guilt, that he wouldn't have much *wanted* her to explain the history of the anchors, or of Vigo, or of Spain in general, that he'd probably have snapped at her, and she'd have sulked – but at least it would have been some human contact. And then they'd have got back on the coach, and Deborah would have perked up at some new sight she could talk about – a lump of granite, maybe – and all would have been well. He looked around him. Some of his fellow passengers were taking photographs of the anchors; others, photos of the toilets. He'd rather hoped that his new friend might be here, but there were many tour coaches, she must have caught another.

As the rest stop drew to a close, and Roger took his seat once more, he saw another tour coach pull up. Another guide opened the doors, another set of passengers got off – and there she was amongst them all. He got to his feet, squeezed his way to the exit past those still getting on. 'We're ready to leave, sir,' said the guide. But there was no greater urgency in her voice than when she'd been discussing the mercantile strength of Spain, so he ignored her.

He hurried up to the old woman. Although she didn't look *old* as such, that wasn't fair. She looked *mature*, that was it. Her face was rather elegantly framed by a wide sun hat. 'Hello!' he said.

'Oh,' she said. 'Hello.'

'How are you?' he asked stupidly. 'How was the bingo?' he asked, even more stupidly. The coach honked its horn. 'I like your hat.'

'Thanks,' she said.

The coach honked again. Everyone onboard was glaring at him, and one couple were taking a photograph. 'I think,' she said, 'they want you to go.'

'I could go on your coach,' he said.

'It's full.'

'You can come on mine.'

'But I've only just got here,' she pointed out. 'I haven't seen the sights.'

'There aren't any sights,' he promised. 'Unless you like anchors. Do you like anchors?'

She frowned, did that squint again, sizing him up. He waited. 'Well,' she said, 'I'm sorry, but I *do* like anchors, yes.'

One final blast on the horn, very long and very angry. He smiled, and said casually, 'Enjoy them then! And see you at dinner!' And he got back on to the coach, pretending that all the tutting was nothing to do with him. He looked for her out of the window, and he thought she was looking for him too, it was hard to tell under the hat. He gave her a wave that was a little too cheery. Nothing for a few seconds, then she gave a wave back, of sorts, and turned her attention to the splendour of Vigo.

And she didn't come to dinner. He'd arrived early, bagged the seat next to him. He'd dressed up, too, put on his suit once more. 'You've got it wrong again, this is casual night,' Mrs Flip-Flops told him. Roger didn't even stay as long as the entrée, told the table he needed the toilet, and left. No-one seemed to notice. Maybe she was eating elsewhere. He went to the Steakhouse Bonanza on deck five, the twenty-four-hour buffet on the sun deck, even the Burger 'n' BBQ bar up near the pool (although he'd already decided that burgers would not be to her taste). Nothing. So much food on the boat, there seemed no end to it, enough to feed a small nation, all being pumped out to keep a bunch of fat holidaymakers all the fatter – so much food, and she wasn't eating any of it. He went back to his cabin.

'Bloody hell,' he said.

There were towels everywhere; it was a menagerie in towel form. Roger's eyes were drawn at first to the monkey suspended from the light fitting by one of the hangers from his wardrobe; the puff of the air conditioner made it rotate a little. But then, peering behind the primate, he saw that the dressing table boasted another rabbit and – what was it? a hedgehog? or, perhaps, an armadillo? On his pillow there were a couple of white mice, on the sheets a duck and the flat triangle of a manta ray. But the biggest animal of all was the elephant. It was too big for the bed, and sat in the centre of the carpet. A couple of beach towels had gone into the main body; hand towels made its ears, a flannel its little tail, and, best of all, the rug that had covered the toilet had been taken, rolled up tightly, and inserted into the head to form an exaggerated parody of a trunk. It was the pièce de résistance of all towel animals, it was a work of loving genius. Roger boggled at it, wondered how it could even stand up. He peeked under its massive bulk, timidly, not wanting to topple the structure over.

And then he picked up the phone, and called Jesus's pager. He sat on the bed and waited for him. Chocolate eyes from all the creatures bore into him, unflinching, cold. It was a good ten minutes before the steward arrived.

'You like?' he said, with a big smile. 'You have fun?'

Roger had had time to work out three very distinct ways to explain to Jesus how he felt. He forgot them all at once. 'You're sick,' he said. 'Sick.'

Jesus's smile faltered. Then he beamed anew, as if he'd misunderstood.

'What is this?' said Roger, and reached for the elephant and pulled out its innards. 'What is this?'

'Is pot.'

'No. Is not pot. Is my *wife.* You sick... It's my bloody *wife.*'

Jesus looked at the urn, around which he had built his towel construct, frowned. 'No,' he said. 'Is pot.'

'Shit,' said Roger. 'You fuck.' And he got up from the bed swiftly. He wasn't going to punch Jesus, he was sure of that, but Jesus backed away in alarm, got his head caught in the monkey. 'What did you do, open my *safe*? Yes, you saw the combination, didn't you, thought you'd have a little game with my wife. What the hell is wrong with you?'

'The pot was on the table,' said Jesus.

'No, I put it in the safe.'

'It was on,' said Jesus, with a new coldness, 'the table. I wanted you to have fun. Okay? I wanted to make you happy. And you come at me with your shit fuck. Well, you're the shit fuck, I spent long time making those animals, I spent *twenty minutes*, because you're so miserable, you never smile. The people on this ship, every week they come, they pig themselves on food, they laze in the sun, they *lazy.* But they *smile,* and Jesus, he smiles back, puts on the accent a bit, makes the English not so good, hey? But I speak English fine, and you're the shitfuck, you Mr Shitfuck. That your wife?' And he pointed at the urn. Roger nodded dumbly. 'She lucky woman. She die to get away from you, hey? Maybe she kill herself? Shitfuck.' And Roger at last *tried* to hit him, but really, it was so feeble, and Jesus sidestepped it easily. And with a gentleness that was so much more insulting than a punch would have been, he pushed Roger back on to his bed. Roger sat there, stared up at the little Filipino steward, who even now hadn't once raised his voice, and who even at this late stage somehow contrived to flash him a grin. 'I only wanted,' he said, 'to make you happy.' And then he went.

And for the first time since Deborah's death, Roger cried. The tears just flowed out without any effort, he almost felt detached from the whole process; he just sat there and felt the water stream hot down his cheeks, and waited for it to stop. He reached for the nearest towel – which happened to be the duck – and wiped his face with it. Then he ate the chocolate eyes from the duck, and then, for good measure, those from the manta ray as well.

Because, in a way, he supposed Jesus was right. Maybe Deborah had just been eating to kill herself. Or, if not exactly to die, at least to make herself happy, to give herself the little joy which he so plainly couldn't. If she hadn't keeled over in the supermarket she'd have keeled over somewhere else eventually. Perhaps she'd have made it on to the cruise, and she'd have had the formal dinner, and then gone to the steakhouse, and then on to the buffet and the Burger 'n' BBQ; she'd have keeled over on the Mediterranean instead. 'Come on,' he said to the urn, and he got up, 'let's get this over with.'

This time he didn't care if he was seen. Shit the regulations and fuck them. He walked straight up to the railings, took the lid from the urn, and without further ceremony, tipped it over the side. Nothing came out. Roger hesitated. Dazedly, he looked inside to see if the ashes somehow had clogged together, or had got stuck, or needed to be prised out with his fingers.

The woman at the purser's desk was called Kylie, so he assumed she was Australian, but when she spoke it was with the same flat lack of interest as the Vigo tour guide. Maybe she *was* the Vigo tour guide, he couldn't remember. 'How can I help you?' she asked.

'I want to report a theft,' said Roger.

'Yes, sir?'

'It was Jesus. He got into my safe. This urn used to be full, almost to the brim, my wife was a big woman. Now look at it.'

The purser asked, 'Was there anything else missing from your safe? Your wallet? Any valuables?'

'No.'

'Just the urn.'

'Not the urn, obviously. I still have the urn. I'm holding it, look.'

The purser took it, looked it over, gave it a sniff. 'And this urn contained a powder of some kind?'

'A powder? No. Well, yes, if by powder you mean...'

'Because it's left quite a sweet smell. You will know, I hope, that transporting certain powders is an offence. Failure to declare it at customs...'

'It wasn't that sort of powder. It was my wife.'

'Your wife was in the urn?'

'That's right.'

'You brought your wife onboard.'

'Yes.'

'And does she have a passport?'

Roger stared at her. 'No. No, look. She's dead. Isn't she? I mean, obviously.'

The purser didn't even flinch from his stare. 'Either you transported her onboard as a passenger, in which case she needs a passport. Or as a powder, in which case, failure to declare it at customs is an offence, and may even be seen to contravene the Misuse of Drugs Act.' Roger didn't know what to say. 'I would hope, sir, that the contents of your urn *remain* missing. I think that would be the best thing for you, wouldn't it?' And she confiscated the urn, behind her desk. 'Now, was there anything else?'

Roger said feebly, 'He also called me a shitfuck.'

'What was that, sir?'

'Jesus. Called me a shitfuck.'

'Well, sir,' said the purser. 'Maybe that's because you *are* a shitfuck.'

Roger opened his mouth to say something, then closed it again.

'Yes,' said the purser, as if giving the matter some consideration. 'Yes, I think that you're a shitfuck. We've had complaints about you, sir. Harassment. A certain Irene Knowles says you've been stalking her.'

Roger was about to tell her he didn't know an Irene Knowles, but then, 'Is she an elderly woman? Sort of grey hair with silver bits in?'

'I am not at liberty to describe passengers' hair.'

'That's her, isn't it? No, look, you've got it all wrong. She was the one who approached *me.* Came to my cabin last night, most surprising, and then she...'

'... and then she what, *sir*?'

But Roger couldn't say, because he could hardly believe it himself.

'Mrs Knowles is a regular passenger, sir. We're all very fond of her. I think you'd better keep away from her from now on, don't you? I think you'd better keep your nose out of trouble. Smuggling illegal substances, slandering your steward, and sexually intimidating the elderly. This is a pleasure cruise, sir, we just want to make you happy. But there are limits. Do you understand?'

'I suppose so.'

'Do you understand?'

'Yes.'

'Goodnight, then, sir.'

He went back to his cabin, picked his way through the debris of gutted animals, and lay on the bed. With his remote control he turned on the TV. The American woman with the wide smile was still enthusing about the shipboard activities, and he watched her, wondering where she got so much energy. The programme was on a half-hour loop, and some time during his second viewing Roger began to see something more mocking in her smile, it wasn't a smile so much as a sneer, and there was an anger behind her eyes, they were blazing with *something*, and whatever she might claim it wasn't an appreciation of the ship's beauty salon. And second time round, too, the passengers in shot looked so much *older*, the kids playing in the pool weren't kids at all but people steeped in a second childhood from which they would never escape.

And at some point he must have fallen asleep, though he certainly didn't remember turning off the television or the lights. And he dreamed of Deborah, she was alive, and she was on the cruise with him. 'Thank you for bringing me here, you've made me so happy,' and she *was* happy, by God, was she happy!, 'this is *luxury*, darling,' as she waddled her way around the deck. At least he assumed it was Deborah, but she was so fat, her face had got so wide and chubby its features were all flattened into nothingness, but she was doing that thing with her watery eyes when she wanted her own way, so it *had* to be her. And the purser was taking him aside in complaint, 'Sir, your wife has eaten all the food on the ship, there is no food *left*, you've got to stop her, shitfuck.' And Deborah was starting on the passengers now, biting into them, then wolfing them down, and sure, she couldn't move very fast to catch them with her great bulk, but they were so *old*, and there weren't many places they could run, the uncaring Mediterranean Sea all around them. 'Darling, I'm hungry,' she said, and reached out for Roger, and he knew he'd give in to whatever she asked, because he *always* gave in, didn't he, and he only wanted to make her happy, that was all he had ever wanted, he just hadn't known how, it was so easy at the beginning but then she'd had the kids and then she'd had the depression and then she'd swelled up like a balloon. 'I'm hungry,' she said, and she touched his cheek, and it wasn't even flesh, her hands were coarse like towels...

He forced himself awake. But the towels were still there, lapping at his face. Holding back a scream he wriggled free, scrabbled for the bedside lamp. In a moment the room was flooded with light. And then he really did scream.

There was a man hanging from the ceiling right above his bed. Not a real man, of course, but something almost as grotesque – a series of large beach towels knotted together to make up the torso, and the legs dangling from it. It had been one of those legs that had been brushing against Roger's face. And the whole thing was suspended from a noose, made from nothing more remarkable than a twisted flannel – but it had to be more than that, surely, how could it have taken the weight? A hole had been pinched in the head to form a mouth, opened in an expression of comical surprise, as if the towel man really hadn't *expected* to spend his cruise holiday hanging in a cabin after all, he'd as soon as play the bingo instead, what a turn-up for the books! But those inevitable chocolate eyes of silver wrapping gave the face a colder, dead expression.

Even in his terror, Roger couldn't help but admire the *detail* in Jesus's work. It made the animals of his past exhibitions look like the juvenilia of a dilettante. The body must have taken hours to construct and hang. And that's when the impossibility of it all struck Roger; Jesus must have been in his room all the time he was asleep, and standing on his bed right over him. Roger prodded the bed – it was a firm mattress, but not *that* firm, and the room was rocking gently on the waves. There was no way that Jesus could have been here for that long, balanced over him so precariously, and carried out such delicate work, without waking him up. And yet there it was, Jesus's masterpiece, twisting to the roll of the sea. I can come and get you any time, that's what the hanged man was saying. I can come and get you and you'll never even *know*.

And suddenly the noose broke. The towels fell on him in a heap, and Roger gibbered with fear, pushed them off, ran to the cabin door and the safety of the corridor outside. He got his breath back in a series of shuddering gasps. He saw that the name on his door had been obliterated, crossed through so many times and so ferociously that he could no longer make out any letters at all.

Up the corridor Roger could see the names on all the other doors had been left respectfully intact, and that each one represented a person safely asleep in their beds having a lovely holiday. He read a few of them. And without making any real decision about it, began looking for the name Irene Knowles.

It was a large ship, comprising over a thousand staterooms. He had no real sense of the passing of time, but when he finally found Irene Knowles's cabin, on Dolphin Deck, it was four in the morning Southampton time, five in the morning Vigo time, and God only knew what time where the ship was now headed.

Roger hesitated. Then knocked. There was a good minute's wait, and he thought there wouldn't be an answer. But he didn't move away, he had nowhere to go, after all. And eventually the door opened.

The old woman looked at him. Except she wasn't that old, she wasn't even what you'd call mature, she looked rested and calm and secure. She was in a nightie, and he only now thought to check what *he* was wearing. To his surprise he was still dressed in his suit, he hadn't changed since dinner, but it was now all rumpled from where he had slept in it, the jacket creased, the tie askew.

'I got all dressed up for you,' he said uselessly.

She asked him what he wanted, and he didn't know how he was going to answer. And then he replied anyway, 'I want my wife. I want my wife back.'

She thought about this for a moment, then gave a curt nod. 'Give me a moment,' she said, and closed the door. He supposed she was putting on some clothes, but when she opened up a couple of minutes later she was still in her nightie. It was Jesus who was now dressed. Jesus stepped out of the cabin, and Roger moved aside to make room for him; Jesus gave him a smile, Roger couldn't tell how mocking, and then disappeared down the corridor. 'You'd better come in then,' said Irene Knowles.

Her cabin was exactly the same as his, except hers had a porthole, and his a hanged man on the bed. 'Jesus finds me my widowers,' Irene said. 'How did you know?'

'I didn't,' admitted Roger. 'I still don't,' he added.

'Why do you want Deborah back?' Roger had been pretty sure he'd never told her his wife's name. 'Is it to say goodbye? It's a bit too late for that, isn't it?'

'No, I don't want to say goodbye.'

'Or because you love her? You're in love with a little pile of ash?'

'No, I don't love her,' and it was true. 'I haven't loved her for years,' and that was true too, but a bit of a shock for him, all the same.

'Then why do you want her?'

'I don't know,' said Roger. 'But I put up with her for over twenty years, so I think she's *mine*.'

Irene thought about this. 'I suppose that's fair,' she said. 'All right,' and she gave a sigh, 'all right,' and her hand went for his flies.

Roger began to tell her that he wasn't in the mood, but as she pulled his penis out from its little hiding place it made a liar of him and stiffened. 'Oh,' he said, and Irene gave a humourless smile. And then she swallowed it whole.

Once again he felt he really ought to do something to help. But her hair was no longer silver-grey, but a shiny gold blonde, and he wasn't sure how she'd feel about his getting his hands over it. His penis felt warm in her mouth, and then she *started* – and it was as if the warmth had been turned off. And her breath became cold, almost icy, and she wasn't sucking at him this time, she was blowing. His cock was still stiff in there, he could feel it, but he worried that this was because it was getting frosted. He wanted to tell her to stop, but he didn't dare – it wasn't a breath now, it was a wind, he looked down at Irene's face and her cheeks were all puffed out with the effort, her eyes were bulging too – and it was almost *funny*, it was the least erotic thing he had ever seen, this beautiful woman with her face all swelled up like a trombone player in mid-blast. But he was too scared to laugh, too scared that she'd blow harder, or that she'd stop blowing altogether before she was done, and that might even be worse. But just as he felt he couldn't stand any more, that he'd either cry out with the pain, or laugh at the very look of her, it was all over – and she pulled away.

She sat there on the floor, saying nothing.

'What now?' he asked.

'Give me a moment, can't you?' she snapped. She got up, went to her bathroom. 'Toothpaste,' she said, and she closed the door on him, he wasn't welcome to look this time, but, sure enough, he soon heard her brushing away for all she was worth.

When she came out, his penis was still erect. He couldn't believe how erect – it was embarrassing, to be honest. She sized it up, nodded. 'It's ready,' she said.

She knelt back down, took hold of it. And began to tap on it with her finger. Not too hard, but firm. Tap tap tap along the stem. She did this for about ten seconds, and just as Roger was about to ask what she was doing, she took hold of his hand. 'Cup it,' she said, 'no, under here,' and moved it into position under the tip. And that's when the ash began to spill out.

He was so surprised he almost dropped it. 'Careful,' she said. 'Do you want your wife or not?' And on she tapped, and out of the end of his penis poured a steady trickle of ash. Truth be told, it didn't feel like anything very much, he felt detached from the process. He just sat there and felt the ash stream hot into his palm, and waited for it to stop.

After a few minutes the cock at last began to droop. 'Just the dregs,' she said, holding it straight, and shaking it out. And she'd finished. She got to her feet and walked over to her dressing table. Reached inside her handbag for a cigarette, lit it.

Roger looked at the mountain of ash in his hands. 'I don't suppose you've got an urn, or some sort of container?' he asked. 'I sort of lost mine.'

She said nothing for a while, her back to him, hardly seemed even to notice he was there. When she turned around she seemed surprised he'd stayed. She frowned at him through the veil of smoke.

'There you are,' she said. 'Much good may it do you. Or me.' It may have been the light, but she looked very tired, and very frail. She didn't smoke the cigarette, just tapped at it, tap, tap, tap.

He made his way up to the top deck, dribbling ash all along the corridors. He kept his two fists tight, holding on to as much of Deborah as he could, but as he climbed the stairs and the ship lurched, he decided it'd be prudent to use the handrail and that one fistful would be enough. He sat on a lounger in the dark, staring out at the sea. He considered letting the remaining ash go over the side, but he looked down at the waves, and at the still beauty of the water, and then he thought of his wife – and he realised that the Mediterranean deserved better.

And so he just sat there, with Deborah, until dawn. And when the sun appeared so did the waiters, setting up the Burger 'n' BBQ, the ice cream sundae bar. The ship neared land. It reached a port. It docked. Roger didn't know where.

About an hour later an announcement was made that passengers were free to disembark, to explore the city with their tour guides. Roger queued up with the rest of them. He knew he was supposed to take his passport, but that was back in the cabin, and he knew he'd never be going there again. No-one asked for it anyway; in fact, no-one gave him a second glance.

The first thing he did was find himself a litter bin. It was marked with a language he didn't recognise. He opened his fist at last, emptied the ashes inside. There weren't many ashes left, to be honest. Then he went off to find a local.

'Excuse me,' he said. 'Where do all the people from the cruises go?'

The man stared at him, didn't understand.

'The tourists,' he said. 'Where?'

The man pointed.

'Thank you,' said Roger. And set off in the opposite direction. He wondered where he was, and how far he would get before he found out.

Crumble

At half past four in the morning she woke with a start beside her husband, and realised she'd fallen in love with him for the third time.

She hadn't noticed up until then that she'd ever fallen *out* of love with him particularly – but she must have done, obviously; just compare now with then, *this* was love, it made a mockery of the lukewarmth of before. She looked at him, his bulk caught by the little light coming through the curtains. He was sleeping on his side with his back to her. From this angle she couldn't make out the belly sprawled out the other side from it, but it wasn't that she was pretending it wasn't there, its absence or presence had nothing to do with this fresh rush of love; and, besides, she'd grown used to the belly, she'd watched it grow all these years, she'd been the one who'd cooked the food that had made it swell, you could almost say she was responsible, that she'd *nursed* it into shape, it didn't repel her, certainly had she first met him with a belly like that she'd have hardly spared him a second look, but not now, it was just part of him, it was just him. You get used to stuff. It was surprising what stuff you got used to. And stuff doesn't change.

Or so she'd thought. Or so she'd hoped. Lying there beside him, somewhat poleaxed by this strange new raw love she felt. And it wasn't lust either. She knew that she could tap him on his shoulder now, wake him up, tell him she wanted sex; he'd have been a little surprised, and bleary most likely, he'd probably yawn through the whole thing, but he wouldn't say no, he wouldn't ask why, they'd have sex right then and after he'd turn right back, swing the belly away, fall back asleep. She knew she could make the magic happen. But it wasn't sex she was after, and hadn't been for a while actually, and he hadn't seemed to mind, or hadn't commented on it at least, and with him that was the same thing, all his little complaints these days were in comment form.

She stared at him. She couldn't see the little brown spots on his back, that as time went on looked less like freckles and more like pockmarks. She couldn't see them, no, but she could picture them anyway, oh they were there all right. She wondered whether by staring at him for long enough there in the half dark, by painting all those little spots into place, she could shoo herself back out of love again. She concentrated. It didn't work. She sighed.

Where had it sprung from, this love that wasn't sex, that wasn't familiarity, wasn't putting-up-with-pockmarks, that instead made her guts feel like water, made this man seem at once like the most important thing in the world – no, more, the whole world itself, that from now on her every thought would be about him, that when she was with him that would *be* the world, and when she wasn't with him she would only think of returning to him, that was what it was all about?

She got up. She had to think about this.

He didn't stir. She took one look behind her to make sure of that, then turned away, made herself open the door, leave the room, shut the door behind her. She didn't want to start doing all that looking again, once she looked for long enough she might not want to leave, she wasn't going to go through all that again.

The first time she'd fallen in love with him she could barely remember. She supposed it must have happened, she got a marriage and a mortgage out of it. But she couldn't recall an actual *reason*, a moment when it hit her, *this is the one*, this will be the father of your child and the keeper of your cheque book. And she'd looked so young back in those days, of course, they still had the wedding photos on the wall in the spare room, just in case guests wanted to take a look – and she'd got her hair in something like a hive, what had she been thinking, and the face it framed was so naïve and vacant, peering out of the picture frame with such smugness, I'm a wife now, it said, I'm an adult – my God, what would a kid like that know of *love*? Maybe there wasn't a first time. Maybe it hadn't happened at all.

She did remember the second time she fell in love with her husband. But it was a love based on misunderstandings and half-truths. She didn't want to think about it. Let's not go there.

She'd now reached the kitchen. She didn't know why she was in the kitchen, she didn't want anything from the kitchen. She thought she might just leave the kitchen, then, go to some other room altogether, but then she decided that since she was already in the kitchen she should turn that to her advantage, see what the kitchen had to offer, make herself a cup of tea or something. But she didn't want tea, and even though she boiled the kettle, when she opened the fridge door to get out the milk she saw the bottle of wine beneath it and thought she'd rather have that instead.

She poured the first glass with a shaking hand. She hadn't noticed until then she'd been shaking. Maybe it was the shaking that had woken her up.

The second time she'd fallen in love with her husband he hadn't even been there. She'd taken a part-time job in the library, it was good to get out in the afternoons, and her daughter was now old enough to walk back from school by herself, and there she'd been, stacking shelves, and the love came on her all at once; she didn't know what had sparked it off, it wasn't as if she were even in the romance section. It winded her and she doubled over with the force of it and she began to cry. And everyone gathered around and asked her if she was sick, and she said she was, and it wasn't entirely a lie, because there was a taste in her mouth that made her nauseous. And they asked her what was wrong, and she said she didn't know, and that *was* a lie, because she definitely did – it was the full *clarity* of her love that was so overwhelming. She was told to go home, could she drive okay, she should drive home and put herself to bed. But she didn't want to go to bed; it was all she could do not to drive straight to her husband's office and tell him how much she loved him, and indeed she was nearly there when she got a better idea, she turned right round across the dual carriageway and headed home after all. When her daughter got in she found her mother preparing a candlelit dinner for two. She was surprised, but not as surprised as her mother, who had all but forgotten she even *had* a daughter; she told her to go to see her Auntie Jackie, she liked Auntie Jackie, didn't she, here's the bus fare, quick, off you go. When the husband came home from work he was tired and not really up to big shows of enthusiasm, but he did his level best. 'My God,' he said, looking at the serviettes, at the best china, at the steak, at his wife dressed in the little jewellery she owned, 'what's all this in aid of? And where's Sally?' And they sat down to eat, but she didn't feel much like eating, she just wanted to watch her husband eat, every forkful of meat put into his mouth. 'Is everything all right?' he asked her. Then Jackie phoned and asked what was going on, Sally had just turned up on the doorstep, 'Is everything all right?' And she asked whether Jackie would mind looking after Sally for a few days, actually no, she didn't know for how long, she didn't want her around for a while. And Jackie asked what was the matter, and she explained that she was in love, she was in love, she was blissfully head over heels in love – and Jackie sounded a little shocked, and said, 'Who with?' At which she'd taken offence. 'My husband, of course. My husband.'

And she wanted to kiss him, and yet she didn't want to kiss him, because she wanted it to be something elemental, when they kissed she wanted to feel she was drowning in him, and she knew somehow that when they actually got down to it, it'd be just – well, it'd be just *kissing*, wouldn't it – but she couldn't stop herself, she needed to try anyway, she was shaking as her head neared his, and her lips pouted and so did his, she thought partly in surprise, and then they met and oh God! it *was* elemental, she *was* drowning, who'd have thought it, it was perfect and she was in love, oh she was so in love. Then they had sex, and she knew intellectually he was giving the usual performance, she knew his technique so well, half a minute's suck at the breasts for foreplay, then on and in – but that didn't matter, now she loved him as she should and she thrilled to every touch. She stayed awake that night, watching him as he slept. The next morning she asked him to stay with her, and he looked confused, and said he had to go to work, what about work? She didn't go to the library that day, she drove instead to his office and sat in the car park looking up for his window, she didn't exactly know which window was his, but there were three likely candidates, and all day her eyes darted between them hoping to catch a glimpse. And every song on the radio was about them, every song was a love song, even the ones that weren't. And everything she did she imagined as an anecdote to share with him later, and she bought new candles for each romantic dinner she cooked, and Jackie kept calling and she eventually just had to tell her, 'I don't care about Sally, and I don't care about *you*, now go away.' And she'd cry a lot, and sometimes in the bathroom she'd dry heave, and sometimes stuff would come out.

'You need to see a doctor,' said her husband.

She asked him whether he loved her. She demanded to know.

'Yes,' he said uncomfortably. That's why she needed a doctor.

The doctor was very sympathetic. He asked her if she was depressed, and she thought it'd be simpler to say she was. He prescribed her some medicine for that. He asked her if she was in any pain, and she thought for a bit, and decided that she might be. So he gave her medicine for that too.

She took the medicine, and the crying stopped, and Sally came home, and she went back to the library. And she was still in love with her husband – desperately, desperately – but she was able to hide it from him, it was her secret. 'Are you okay?' he'd ask, and by that he'd mean, 'Are you normal?', and she'd say yes, and knew she was lying. But eventually it really wasn't lying, it was a sort of truth, and then it *was* the truth, and she didn't need the medicine any more. She loved her husband, of course she did, in her own way – but you couldn't expect it to be intense after so many years of marriage.

At half past five in the morning, he woke up and realised that his wife wasn't next to him. He reached out and touched the space in which she'd been sleeping. He didn't know why he did that.

He wondered where she was.

He wanted to tell her he loved her.

It was a new idea, that. He wasn't sure where it had come from, but he could see nothing wrong with it per se. He did say he loved her quite a lot, and she to him, every time he left for work, 'love you', 'love you too', every time they turned out the bedroom light, 'love you, good night'. And he didn't necessarily want to make this 'love you' any bigger than those, but it did feel more important, it was a real urge.

He supposed she must be in the toilet.

He missed her.

He considered getting up, going to find her. 'I love you,' he'd say. He wondered how she'd react. She might be pleased. She might be bashful. She might be pissed off, actually, even after thirty years of marriage the toilet door was still the one that was closed to him. 'I've a right to *some* privacy,' she'd say. He wasn't sure a declaration of love would cut much ice with her if she heard it squatting on the loo.

And it was so warm in the bed, it'd be a shame to spoil that.

He would stay awake. He'd lie on his back, he could never sleep on his back, he snored. Yes, he'd stay awake for her, and when she came back to bed he'd be waiting. He'd tell her he loved her. 'I love you,' he'd say. Most likely she'd say the same thing back. And then he could go back to sleep.

He missed her. He wanted to tell her he loved her.

He listened for a flush.

At half past six in the morning she finished the bottle of wine. She tipped it over, but no, nothing more to come out. She thought about opening a new one, but that seemed an awful lot of effort. And, anyway, she didn't like wine.

This was it, then, the difference between being in love and being in Love, and they were nothing alike, the first was safe and it was restrained and, no, it wouldn't inspire great poetry, and no, it didn't make her heart swell to burst, but it was *kind*, it had kindness to it, it was the love of ironing his underpants and of going to the supermarket a mile and a half away just to get him in his favourite brand of chips. And, yes, sometimes she wanted her heart to burst, sometimes it made her sad that she hadn't got that, that she wasn't excited to see him, wasn't excited by the *thought* of him, sometimes it made her sad that all she'd believed about love when she'd been a girl had got so watered down and routine, but it didn't make her *very* sad, not too sad, not really. And this other love, this new love, it'd take her life and throw it into turmoil; and she quite liked her life the way it was, she knew where everything was, she wasn't sure she could cope with the disruption. The very chaos of all those feelings she hadn't had for years itching away at her, it'd be such a mess.

She thought of him upstairs and her guts squeezed again, and her heart leapt, and she knew she'd fallen in love, and it made her so happy and it made her so frightened.

And yet, maybe. Maybe. Maybe this time it would work. There were just the two of them now. Nothing to get in the way. He was nearly retired, he only went into the office twice a week on a consultancy basis, she *could* keep him home with her this time; Sally had gone, moved out years ago, and even if she hadn't found love of her own, not really, she still had a child to show for her efforts; there was no job for her at the library any more, in fact there was no library, they'd closed it down and turned it into a chemist's. She could go and see her husband. She could go upstairs to their bed, shake him gently awake. Tell him what had happened. Tell him that her life had changed forever, the sheer weight of what had taken place; the love was back, could he take it, could he take what she was offering? She loved him. She loved him. And maybe he'd be pleased. Maybe. Maybe he could give that love back. Maybe. Maybe, even a bit. And she wasn't sure her heart could take it, all the flips and turns of it, all that would be squeezed out of it, all the extra beats it'd need to make – it'd kill her, this love, she knew it. If he accepted it, it'd finish her off. But what a way to go, was there a better way to go? What a romantic way to go.

She was so happy and so so frightened.

She rinsed out the empty wine bottle with tap water, and put it in the recycling bag. Then she went upstairs.

She supposed that would change too, that a woman who had given in to the throes of love wouldn't care much about the environment. She wondered if that would be the last bottle she'd bother to recycle.

She hesitated outside the bedroom door.

If he wakes, she said to herself, I'll tell him. I'll tell him I've fallen in love with him. And if he doesn't stir, if he doesn't even bother to stir, then I won't. I'll close that side of my life to him. Close it off to *me.* Forever. It's up to him. After all this, it's up to him.

She turned the knob on the bedroom door. She wouldn't cheat, either. She wouldn't make heavy footfalls, that'd be unfair. But nor would she enter the room on tiptoe. She'd just walk in, the way she had thousands of times before, and look at him, and find out what the rest of their lives would be.

And so she did.

Oh well, she thought. That's that then.

He had turned in his sleep, she saw, and was now on his back. She hadn't seen him sleep on his back very often. The belly pointed straight upwards, like a hillock. He was snoring.

She wasn't to be in love after all. But looking at him now, listening to him. That seemed the right thing.

She went to the bathroom, rummaged around the back of the cabinet until she found the pills. She'd never thrown them away. They were years past their expiry date, but she didn't suppose that mattered. She swallowed two doses, washed them down with tap water. The taste was bitter. Then she went back to bed at last, climbed in next to her husband, to the whole rumbling mass of him. And she lay there, waiting for the medicine to work, for her love to crumble.

George Clooney's Moustache

I tried writing this on toilet paper but it's hard writing on toilet paper because the paper's so thin it breaks. And you can put some sheets together to make it thicker but that's not much better and you have to write so slowly to keep it from breaking that by the time you reach the end of the sentence you forgot how it started and you forget what it was you wanted to say anyway, and anyway you get through a lot of paper like that. XXXXXXXX **He** caught me, I knew he would, he's smart like that, I was taking so long in the bathroom that he began to bang on the door asking if I was all right and I said I was all right, and I flushed, but he said if I didn't open the door he'd break it down and so I did. I should have flushed away my writing first while I was at it but I just didn't have time to think and he picked it up and he read it and I thought he'd get angry because a lot of it was about him, well all of it really. But XXXXXXXX **he** didn't say anything bad and he said if I wanted to write he'd get me some proper paper if it meant that much to me. And a pencil too, not a sharp one, he'd seen a film once about how a sharp pencil could be used as a weapon and stuck into someone's neck and that was funny because I think I've seen that film too but I couldn't remember what it was called, neither of us could, we laughed about that. And I told him I'd never do that to myself, I'm scared of blood, and he looked a bit shifty and said he'd been more worried I'd do it to him actually, and I hadn't even thought of that and said I wouldn't, we laughed about that. So XXXXXXXX **he** gave me this pad and this pencil. And told me I could copy out what I'd written on the toilet paper if I liked. But I didn't want to, he'd been so nice about the whole thing and what I'd said on the toilet paper wasn't very kind. I didn't want to write anything for a while, I didn't know what to say any more, and he'd ask me sometimes about it over dinner, have you started writing yet, but he said it nicely, it wasn't a nag and didn't come out sarky. And so eventually I thought I'd better write something after he'd gone to all that trouble, and so I did, and this is it.

Over breakfast he read what I wrote last night. He said it was very good, but that some of the grammar needed a little work, that it wasn't always easy to read, and I asked about my handwriting, and he said that was good, and about my spelling, and he said that was good too, it was just the grammar, I could do with a few more full stops. So I'm going to do that. When I remember. I'll try. He said he'd have to change just one thing, and he crossed out a few words with a pen, and handed it back. And he'd crossed out all the times I'd used his name, he'd put 'he' instead, he said that he should never have let me know his name in the first place, that was a mistake. So I could carry on writing, but no more names. And I said could I use another name instead, it'd get a bit much calling him 'he' all the time, and he said that was all right. And George told me that he was glad I enjoyed the pad and the pencil, that they'd been a present. And that I'd get more presents, so long as I behaved, so long as I did what I was told. I told George I would and he was so pleased. He asked what I was going to write next and I couldn't think what, and he said I should write about what I know. But I don't want to write about my life before, if you're reading this you probably know it already, it's probably not much different from yours. So I'm going to describe where I am. I don't like descriptive bits, I'd rather tell stories, but here goes. There are three rooms. (Actually there are more than three rooms, but I only get to go in three of them. There's the kitchen, but I'm not allowed in there because it's full of sharp things, George keeps it locked with the bolt he took from the bathroom. And there's the room which has the front door in it, I don't go there.) But there are my three. There's the sitting room which is where we eat our breakfast and our dinner and it's got a television in it and George watches the news a lot, and sometimes he watches other things too, sitcoms I think because I hear laughter and it isn't George's. Then there's the bathroom, but you know about that, it's only different now because he took the lock off. And then there's the bedroom which is where I am now, I spend most of my time here. George keeps it locked but he lets me out when I need to, when it's time for breakfast or dinner or when I need the bathroom. The walls are a bit old and have wallpaper on which is a bit old and when I get bored I can count the stripes but I don't need to be bored now because I have the pad and the pencil and I can use them instead. And that's enough for tonight and I'm going to sleep now, night night.

He asked me why I'd named him George. But he wasn't angry, he was smiling. Puzzled though. And I told him it was because he looked a bit like George Clooney. And he laughed and said he did not, and I said he did too, and I laughed as well. And actually I suppose he doesn't look much like George Clooney, not really, what I mean is that George Clooney has nice eyes and my George had nice eyes just like his, and you know how George Clooney has got a sort of square jaw, well my George has nothing like that but it's a nice jaw anyway. And the real George Clooney doesn't have a moustache the way my George Clooney does but still never mind. So if you're the police and you're out there looking for him then they're not that alike really, to be honest there's no point going after George Clooney. And George said that I was right, he did watch sitcoms, he couldn't only watch the news it'd do his head in. He was sorry if it disturbed me, he could turn the volume down if I liked, and I said that was okay, I liked to hear the laughter. And he said that if I was very good that could be another present, he'd let me watch a sitcom some time, not now but soon. I thanked him for that. And he said it was very odd there was nothing on the news yet, it'd been over a week now, you'd have thought there would be something. I said I didn't know, maybe they were keeping it a secret, and he said it just didn't make sense. Then he told me he'd wash up breakfast and he put me back in my room. And a bit later he came back and said why not, we'd watch a sitcom that night, he'd come and get me when one was on. I'd been very good and I deserved a present. (And I think he liked the fact I'd called him George.) And it's funny, I suppose I'm writing this for George now. I thought at first it was for Daddy, or Paul, or Jessie, although Jessie couldn't read it she's only two, but Paul could read it to her, he's a really good dad like that. But this is for George now, isn't it? Hello George. You really do look like George Clooney, I was being silly before, except for the moustache. And George came and got me and took me into the sitting room, he had the lights off and there was only the light from the TV screen, it was like going to the cinema! And I said that, do you remember, and you laughed, and we sat down on the couch and watched Friends. And it was an episode I'd seen before but that was okay, I pretended it was new and laughed anyway, I didn't want to hurt George's feelings. Although of course you've just read this, George, you know that now, sorry. Sorry. It was a great evening, a bit like a first date, and I hope we can do it again soon.

I'm in love with George Clooney! I am. I'm shaking as I write this, can you tell, I hope my handwriting isn't too wobbly, but I'm so relieved too. Just to let it out. I love you, George. Let me tell you why I love him. I love his body, no not like that. I love his eyes. I love his teeth. I love his neck. I love his nose. I love his face, it's a kind face, and I know George has had to do some bad things, I know that's why I'm here, but you can tell from his face he doesn't really want to, and there are some people out there who don't do bad things but their faces aren't kind and you can tell they'd like to do bad things but can't get round to it and I think that's worse somehow. It's a nice face and I love the way it smiles. I love his arms. I love his chest. I love his stomach. I love his hands. I love the way he's got bits of hair growing on his hands. I love his legs, I haven't seen much of his legs yet, but it's February and it's cold and I can't wait for August when it gets hot and he'll get into his shorts. I love his hair, I want to run my fingers through it, I bet it tastes like butterscotch. I don't just love his body. I love his voice. I love his smell, it's a nice smell, I can't work out what it is yet I'll come back. I love the way he cuts up all my food for me in the kitchen. I love the way when he locks me in my room he smiles first and says good night and then he turns the key quite slowly so that it feels like he doesn't want to say goodbye yet. I love the way last night we watched Friends again and it was a better episode this time, Chandler and Joey were funny and it didn't have the monkey in it. And George didn't laugh at it, and nor did I, we let the TV do the laughing work for us. And after Friends George turned over and we watched the weather and then a documentary about plastic surgery, I don't know how people can go through that. And there was a late film and George said did I feel like staying up for it? And I said yes because it was nice just sitting there with him and being close to him and smelling him and I bet his hair tastes like butterscotch. And during the film George leaned over and he kissed me and he said sorry sorry was he being too forward and I said no he wasn't and he gave me that smile I love and took my hand in his hand with all the hairs on it. And he took me to his bedroom. And I thought it'd be like mine with all the old stripy wallpaper but it wasn't, there were silks and rugs and mirrors on the ceiling and a big four-poster bed. And he put me on the bed and it was the softest bed I'd ever felt and the sheets were like velvet they were like butterscotch. And we made love right there and then he was gentle but not too gentle and he was rough but not too much, he was in me and through me and George was all around me and all about me and there was nothing but George. And then he kissed me on the lips gentle and rough and that was the nicest thing of all and told me I was the best he'd ever had and that was a nice thing to hear because he is George Clooney after all. And then he took me back to my bedroom and said goodnight and did that slow key thing and I wrote all this. I love you, George. I'd marry you if I weren't married already.

I remember what he smells like. It's sweat. But a nice sweat, I love it.

George is a bit cross with me and making me write this. He wants me to say that what I wrote last night wasn't true. Well, some of it's true, watching Friends was true and it didn't have the monkey in it is true and the plastic surgery documentary is true. But nothing about the sex. George wants me to point that out. He said he'd be in enough trouble as it is for what he'd done without lies, and I said the sex was very loving and he said he didn't think the police would see it that way. So sorry I made that part up. And he wants me to say I made up the bit about being in love with him too. So sorry I made that up. (But I didn't, it's true, I love George Clooney.) And he said what was this about August, it'd all be over long before then, it should be over by now, why wasn't there anything on the news about it? And that he thought I should take out my pencil and write a letter to Paul or to Daddy and say what George wanted. He'd written one but they'd just ignored it, from me they'd know it was real and he meant business. And I said no. He looked surprised. So was I. I couldn't imagine saying no to George Clooney. But this pad and this pencil are for writing to George, these are love letters to him only. I'm not going to write to my husband with them, that would be cheap and nasty. And George got cross again and said that if I didn't write the letter he'd punish me, I wouldn't be allowed to watch TV any more and I said good, that plastic surgery thing was horrible it had given me nightmares, doing things to their breasts and to their lips, I don't know how people can go through that. And he promised if I wrote the letter he'd buy me some butterscotch, he thought I might like that, and I said I'd write it if I got the butterscotch first and he thought about it and then said yes. So I'm locked in my room again and he's at the supermarket and I'm having a nice dessert tonight and I'm meant to be writing the letter now but I'm writing this instead and I'm telling you now I won't write the letter even so. I don't love Paul any more, I love George. When George took me I missed Paul at first, and Jessie, and Daddy, but if they wanted me they'd have come and got me by now, they wouldn't have let this happen. They don't deserve me the way George does. And I'll try and eat all the butterscotch before George reads this or he'll know I was breaking my promise and take the butterscotch away, sorry George sorry. But what we have, George, is good and pure, and I can't let you spoil that, George, I'm doing this for you, George, it's for you, George. When I think of what I wrote about you at first on that toilet paper it makes me ashamed. Hurtful things. I'll never do anything to hurt you again.

I've been a very naughty girl, and I'm sorry, properly sorry this time not like last time. And George was quite right to be angry and do what he did, and to be fair he only hit me the once and that was to get me to shut up. It's not entirely my fault, though, I'm not trying to get out of it, but I'd never have thought of the pencil if he hadn't put the idea in my head in the first place. But then George points out that I must have been writing with the side of the pencil, trying to sharpen it to a point, I must have been planning it quite on purpose, so I don't know what to think. After I stuck the pencil in his throat I didn't wait around, he was making a strange squealing noise I didn't like at all, and there was blood everywhere. Besides I was trying to escape. I rushed for the front door and I think that's where I made my big mistake, because it's in a room I hadn't seen before, I'd arrived with that blindfold on, and I wasted too much time looking around and taking it in. Then I remembered that George was behind me, I could hear the squealing getting closer, and I got the chain off the door and got to turn the key but didn't get to do the bolts before he reached me. And I suppose if I hadn't been distracted by that new wallpaper and stopped to count the stripes I might have got outside. As I say he only hit me the once and he didn't break the skin, and I think that was fair because I'd certainly broken his there was blood everywhere I don't like blood. And we didn't watch Friends for days, and he didn't let me have my pad and my pencil either, not for days. But the pencil hadn't been that sharp, I hadn't killed him or anything, and George is such a kind man he forgave me in the end. He gave me back my pad, as you can see, and he gave me back my pencil, but he makes sure that I only write when he's there to watch, but I like that better, it's nice to have his company. And we were watching the news tonight and something lovely happened, it said that Paul was dead. Paul was dead, and so was Jessie, and so was Daddy, and it was okay, it was all quite painless, they wouldn't have felt a thing. This meant I was a free woman I said, and George turned to me and smiled and said that was all he was waiting for, and he took out a ring. Diamonds I think yes, and he got on his knees and proposed and of course I said yes. We went to his room and made love again, and it was even better this time now we were engaged, it was official and everything. And I told him I was sorry I had tried to run away. And he said it was okay, and he kissed me, and told me that if I ever tried anything like that again with the pencil he'd be forced to kill me. And then he held me in his arms, all night long with his arms around me, never leaving me, except for the bit in the middle I got up to write this.

George has started smoking. He'd stopped years ago he said, but he's been feeling tense. He looks tense too. And at night I can hear him walking and making the floorboards creak, I don't think he's sleeping much. I wasn't sure at first how I felt about the smoking. Daddy used to smoke, but stopped when they made it bad for you, and Paul doesn't smoke, and Jessie doesn't smoke, and I don't think Paul and I would have let her anyway. But I don't know, I think I like it with George. It makes him look rugged. He's asking me why no-one's reported my disappearance, don't my family want me back? And I said that Paul probably knew I wasn't in love with him any more and was doing the decent thing. That didn't make him any less tense, not one bit. I asked him if I could cook dinner for him to help him unwind, and he looked at me a bit strangely then sort of shrugged and said why not. It was lovely to see the kitchen, all the saucepans and spoons and knives and sieves, all silver and gleaming, it quite took my breath away. He wouldn't let me do any of the sharp stuff, but it was nice us doing the meal together and I made him my speciality. We ate our beans and chips in the sitting room and I think George enjoyed it as much as I did. Afterwards he lit a cigarette and I asked if I could have one, a little shyly actually. And he said he'd nearly finished the packet he needed them, but he'd get some more tomorrow, a lot more, I could have one of those. And I told him they made him look rugged. And that I loved him so much, I loved his hands and his teeth and his neck, I loved his arms, all I didn't love was his moustache, George Clooney didn't have a moustache, the real George Clooney, it spoiled the effect, it spoiled everything. He didn't say anything for a while, just sat there and smoked. I asked him if he was all right. And he said he was just working out what to do now. What should he do now? And I told him not to worry, I'd take care of the washing-up for once. And I did.

I'm worried about George. He's behaving very oddly. He hardly said a word when he let me out for breakfast, and he didn't touch his Rice Krispies. He smoked the last of his cigarettes, then said he was going out to buy some more, and locked me in my room. When he let me out for lunch I told him he'd promised me I could have a cigarette today, and he didn't say anything for a while, then handed me the packet. He lit it for me. I'd never smoked before and it was pretty horrid but I worked out it wasn't quite so bad if you don't put it in your mouth. I asked him if I looked rugged and he said he didn't know, so I asked if he could take me to the bathroom so I could look in the mirror, and we went and looked and I don't think I looked especially rugged, not like George does. But then I'm not sure I want to look rugged, so long as one of us is rugged that's all right with me, I asked George if he could do the rugged stuff on his own and he said sure. I told him that when we had a baby we'd see how it went, if it were a Jessie we wouldn't let it smoke, but we would if it were a Jimmy, he could be rugged like his father, we'd start him young, we'd start him right away. I asked him when he thought we could get to work on that, the whole baby idea. He didn't say anything for a while again and then said he needed to go out. I asked him why and he said he needed some cigarettes. I pointed out he'd only just bought some and then asked if he was getting extra in for Jimmy and he said yes that was it. He took off in the car so quickly it didn't dawn on me for a while he'd forgotten to lock me in my room. That was very exciting. I could go to the bathroom when I liked, I could turn on the TV and watch whatever I wanted, there was nothing good on though. I even opened the door to his bedroom, I hadn't been inside and my heart was pounding, I was so excited, and it was everything I hoped it would be, it had the silks and the mirrors and the four-poster bed, I couldn't wait for George to come home with his cigarettes so we could start making babies there. And eventually it occurred to me I could open the front door if I wanted to, and that the bolts weren't drawn and the chain wasn't on, I could get outside if I wanted to. Get some fresh air maybe. But I didn't want to. Not really. It wouldn't smell of George out there. I wanted George. I want George. I hope he's back soon. He's been gone hours, I hope he hasn't got lost. If he's not home soon he'll miss Friends and his beans and chips are getting cold.

George woke me up with a shout. He didn't scream of course, George Clooney wouldn't scream, but it was a definite shout. I went to see if he was all right. He seemed very upset. He told me that he'd been in Belgium. I said that was nice, what had Belgium been like, and he said he didn't give a shit about Belgium, Belgium was just as far as his car had taken him before he needed to sleep for the night. It was impossible, how could he be back here? I said that maybe he'd only been pretending to be in Belgium, I did that sometimes, when I got bored I made up stories and sometimes they seemed almost real. Though, as far as I could recall, never stories about Belgium. And why was I still here, he asked, didn't I realise it was over, he'd set me free? And he shouted a bit. He went to the front door and opened it and told me that I could go, what was I waiting for? It was over. And I hadn't wanted to go outside yesterday when George was gone, I certainly didn't see the point now he was here. And I told him that wasn't how love worked, you couldn't just open someone's heart and close it again when you'd had enough, I would always be waiting for him, I was his life now, there was no escape. He told me to leave and I said I wouldn't. He called me a stupid bitch and I forgave him, I forgive you George I know you're very tense right now, but I'm not sure you should be encouraged, I may have to punish you for that. He went to the kitchen, came back with a knife, kept on jabbing at me with it. He said he didn't want to hurt me, he'd never wanted to hurt me, had he? He hadn't hurt me, not much? I agreed, and said that it was his very tenderness that had captured my love, his very distinctive rugged tenderness. I'll kill you, George said, I'll kill you if I have to, and I told him that Paul had killed me once, or maybe he'd just tried to kill me, it was so long ago this was before we had Jessie and became a proper family and Paul realised he loved me after all and George would feel the same when we had a proper family George just you wait and see, and then George killed me.

George Clooney screamed. I thought that was disappointing. I do hope he doesn't disappoint me again. I poured him his breakfast cereal but he wasn't hungry. He told me that this time he'd nearly made it to America, after he'd killed me he'd locked my body in the bedroom then gone straight to the airport then caught the next flight out, he'd only shut his eyes for a little nap and here he was again. He was very upset by this and I felt very sorry for him. He asked to be freed. Please let me go, he said. I'd let Paul go, hadn't I? But Paul was a special case, I said, how many times do you get gazumped in your affections by George Clooney? I couldn't just stop loving George, I told him, it wasn't like a tap, it was real this love it wouldn't be denied. But if he did everything I told him to, I'd do my very best, I promised, I'd harden my heart to him, I'd try to get bored of him and let my passion for him die. What did he have to do, he asked? Convince me that you love me, I said. That you live for me, that you live only for me, you won't try to run again, will you George, that isn't love, but I'll lock you in your room anyway from now on, I know how hard it can be sometimes to do the right thing and listen to what your heart wants. Love me blindly love me desperately love me entirely love me without end or hope of end. And maybe I'll get bored of your love, what's more boring than that? And finish your breakfast. I'd made him his breakfast, the least he could do was to finish it. He ate his Krispies, and then I poured him a second bowl, and then a third, and then more, I could have made him eat those Krispies all day but then I got bored, you see George, I can get bored, there's hope for you yet. Then I kissed him, hard on the lips. I told him he was allowed to respond. I loved him, I said. I loved his hands and I loved his eyes and I loved his teeth but the only thing I didn't love was his moustache. In fact I disliked it. In fact I hated it. In fact the very sight of it made me want to hurt him. George Clooney didn't have a moustache, my George would be better off without one, my George would be safer. And he said he'd shave it off right away, and I said no, I couldn't trust him with sharp objects, not any more. I'd have to shave it off for him. I fetched a knife from the kitchen. He asked for shaving cream and I said there was no need for that and he began to cry and I told him that he had to keep still he mustn't flinch, if he kept still and didn't flinch I wouldn't cut him, but he was crying so much he flinched so I did cut him, I took off his upper lip. I don't like blood, I'm scared of blood, but sacrifices have to be made. He looked a bit funny now without a lip but at least he's also without a moustache, it's not such a bad trade-off. And now I told him I wanted us to make love, I wanted to have butterscotch love. I wanted him inside me, not one scrap of him could get away, and to make the point I took the gobbet of flesh that had been his lip and popped it in my mouth and swallowed it down. And he threw up, and I'm sure I don't know why, I was the one who had eaten the disgusting thing. We had sex, and it wasn't as good as I remembered it, and I made allowances I knew he was scared and confused, and bleeding quite badly actually – but it was all right, I closed my eyes and I pictured the four-poster bed and the mirrors and even a fountain, why not, a little fountain in the corner, and I smelled him and he smelled of sweat but it was nice, it was a good sweat really, I love it.

I'm not convinced yet but he's at least trying hard. The effort he puts in is quite touching. I cut up his food for him and he always looks so grateful and says please and thank you, and I keep his hands tied for the meal so I have to feed him every single mouthful and he always remembers what I told him and to smile after each bite. If I'm stricter with him than he was, it's just because I love him more than he did me, I see that now, but he'll learn, there's so much time to learn. Sometimes I'll let him out of his room when Friends is on, though he hasn't actually watched one yet, I keep the blindfold on, he doesn't mind, he's lucky, the best bit is hearing the audience laugh and wondering why. And I light him cigarettes and let him puff away, he looks rugged like that, and I don't let him hold the cigarette because it might burn him, and I suppose that having it fed to him like a baby cuts down a little on the ruggedness but I can pretend I'm good at pretending I'm so good at it. Sometimes I get him to smoke a whole pack in one go to see if he'll be sick, and sometimes he is. And at other times we'll make love. And when he's not busy with the eating and the smoking and the sex he's got a job to keep him occupied. He sits in his bedroom and writes me letters. Just to let me know what he feels for me, to show me I'm his one and only. This is his latest:

and they're getting better, I don't accept them unless they're neat and tidy. I haven't given him a pad yet, and I'm not sure I ever will. Writing on toilet paper is slow work, but it makes you really think about what you want to say. And you have to be careful, because toilet paper breaks so very easily.

Love in a Time of Sharing

Mary didn't want to open envelopes that weren't addressed to her. It seemed rude, and intrusive, and besides that it was none of her business, she had enough to do as it was without poking her nose into other people's affairs. But still the postman kept bringing them. Each morning her heart would sink as she heard them plop through the letterbox and on to the front door mat.

Every few days she'd call Simon about the problem. 'Mum,' he'd say, ever so patiently, 'just open them. It's all right. Most of them will be rubbish in any case. And anything you don't understand, just put it to one side, and I'll look through them when I come over at the weekend.' He always came over on Sunday afternoons, though he didn't always stay for long. 'Mum, you haven't even *looked* at these,' he'd say. Of course she hadn't; each day she'd scoop them up and put them in a drawer in the kitchen so she wouldn't have to look at them, isn't that what he had told her to do? 'You do know Dad wouldn't mind you opening them,' Simon said. 'There's nothing he'd get in the post he'd want hidden from you, is there?' But Mary explained it wasn't what Patrick wanted, it was what *she* wanted, and she knew it was silly, but she just didn't want to open envelopes that weren't addressed to her. Sorry. Had he time for a cup of tea and a biscuit? Oh. Well, give her love to Catherine and little Rachel, maybe next time he could bring them too!

But one morning something different came. She was just about to put it in the drawer when that very insistent difference caught her attention. 'Patrick and Mary Johnsen', it said. Yes, the name had been misspelt but the letter was clearly intended for her, or, at least, *half* intended for her. Mary stood with the envelope in her hand a full minute, not knowing what to do. She wished it had simply been addressed to Patrick, by now it'd have been shut away and she wouldn't have to think about it. But that was her name, and she knew her duty. She slit it open with a knife.

'Congratulations!' said the letter, in big bold red writing. Mary blinked. She was well used to commiserations, but recently congratulations hadn't been so forthcoming. 'You may already be the lucky winner of £50,000 in cash, or a holiday for two, or dominion over life and death, or a digital camcorder! If you can reveal three anchors on the scratch card enclosed,' – Mary checked, there was indeed a scratch card – 'then one of these star prizes* is guaranteed! And reply within 48 hours, and you'll also receive this fabulous gold-plated fountain pen, absolutely free!'

Mary phoned Simon right away. 'Mum, I'm in a meeting,' he said. 'Are you all right?' Mary told him that she may already have won £50,000 in cash, or a holiday for two, or dominion over life and death, or a digital camcorder. She heard Simon sigh patiently. 'Mum, they always tell you you've won a holiday for two, or dominion over life and death, it's what they always say. It's rubbish.' Mary went on to explain that all she needed to do was reveal three anchors. 'Just chuck it in the bin, Mum. Okay? Listen, I'm in a meeting. I've got to go.'

'All right, Simon,' said Mary. She always did what Simon advised, and to be fair to her, she fully expected she *would* chuck the letter in the bin. But before she did so, she decided she was gasping for a cup of tea. And then that nothing would complement the tea better than one of those digestive biscuits she kept in for Simon's Sunday visits. And by the time she'd finished her tea and finished her biscuit, she thought she might as well look at the scratch card more closely. She could always chuck it in the bin afterwards.

'It's simple,' said the card. 'With a coin just scratch off three squares. If you get an X, then bad luck! You won't have won a star prize*, but remember, if you reply within 48 hours you can still receive a gold-plated fountain pen absolutely free! If you reveal three anchors, you will have won one of our star prizes* – £50,000 in cash! A holiday for two! Dominion over life and death! Or a digital camcorder! Now, get scratching, and get winning!' Mary opened her purse, wondered what coin would be best for the job. She had one of those two-pound coins, and a few coppers. She selected a two pence piece, she didn't want to seem ostentatious.

'Mum, I'm still in a meeting,' said Simon. 'Of course you got three anchors. Everyone gets three anchors, everyone's a winner. That's the point. Because you then have to call a premium rate number to get your prize, £1.50 a minute or something, and they'll keep you on the phone for ages. It's a waste of money. It's a scam. It's a con. Chuck it in the bin, Mum, like I said. Now I've got to go, no, the meeting isn't over yet.' Simon always sounded so patient, he was a good lad, Patrick had been so proud of him, well, they both had been, hadn't they? And Mary did indeed take the scratch card, and the letter, and the envelope they had come in, and binned the lot.

But that evening she was watching *Coronation Street*, and she thought, well – it might be a waste of money, but it is *my* money. She'd saved enough buying the supermarket's own rather than the brands she preferred, even though Simon urged her to buy what she liked. 'You've plenty of money, Mum,' he'd say, 'you've nothing to worry about. If you want PG Tips, get PG Tips.' And Mary knew suddenly that this *was* something she wanted, she'd call that phone number anyway, she'd get the letter out of the bin and find out what her star prize could be. She found it, smoothed it straight, decided she'd call first thing that next morning. That would be exciting. She was excited already. She wasn't sure she'd sleep that night. And then, reading the letter again, she discovered that the number was a twenty-four-hour hotline, she could call them *now* if she wanted. That took her so by surprise she made herself a cup of tea. And her heart was fluttering as she picked up the phone and dialled.

'Welcome to the Prize-winners' Hotline!' said a man chirpily, and Mary began to speak, and when he carried on talking right over her she realised it was a recorded message. She was always doing that, Patrick used to laugh and said she'd been caught out by the robots again – and then she'd laugh right back, and point out he'd been caught out just as often as she had! 'Listen for the claim code on your scratch card,' the man told her, 'to find out what star prize you've won. Then stay on the line to leave your contact details. And best of luck!' She waited for sixteen minutes, while in the sitting room *Coronation Street* turned into *The Bill*. She hadn't won £50,000 in cash. She hadn't won a digital camcorder. She had won dominion over life and death. 'Leave your name and your partner's name after the beep,' the man advised her. 'And thank you for calling the Prize-winners' Hotline!' Mary explained that she was Mary *Johnson*, and spelt it because they'd got it wrong last time, and that her husband was Patrick Johnson, and she gave them her address and said she was in every day so they could send the prize whenever they wanted, and if she was out doing the shopping which she had to nip out for every now and then she wouldn't be long but if they couldn't stop then Mrs Singh next door would look after the prize for her until she got back. And she thanked them for their generosity, it was so very kind of them, and then the phone beeped at her again, and she hung up.

* * *

Mary didn't know what shape her prize would be, but she thought it'd be nice and discreet: she decided on it arriving in a small cardboard box, something that would sit snugly on her palm. She waited for the postman each morning, but all he brought were ever more envelopes that weren't addressed to her. One day she got up early, sat by the front door, ready to open it when he arrived. 'Hello!' she said. He stepped back off the porch, startled. 'You don't have a parcel for me, do you?' asked Mary. 'I'm expecting a parcel. It'll be a small cardboard box, I expect, probably this big.' And the postman said he hadn't got a small cardboard box for her today, but he'd be sure to keep his eye out for it. She thanked him, tried to hide her disappointment, and closed the door.

It didn't come in a parcel at all. She nearly missed the letter addressed to her, she was ignoring the envelopes altogether, stuffing them into the kitchen drawer without a second look. 'Oh, my goodness!' she said, as she saw the words 'Mary and Patrick Johnsen' – she noted with some pride that her name was first now, even if they had still spelt the surname wrong. Inside there wasn't dominion over life and death – but the next best thing, it told her where she could pick it up. Mary and Patrick Johnsen were formally invited to a prize-giving presentation at a hotel the other side of London, at eleven o'clock in the morning the following Friday; the presentation was to last no more than two hours, and refreshment would be provided. Mary didn't know what to do. She hadn't been into the city for years, not on her own, she wasn't quite sure she could remember how to do it. Her first instinct was to call Simon, but then she'd have to admit she hadn't chucked the letter into the bin as he'd told her, and he'd been so good to her these last few months, she didn't want to seem ungrateful. At last she put this new letter into *another* drawer in the kitchen, one where Simon wouldn't think to look that Sunday, and gave the matter some thought.

Mrs Singh didn't know London very well either, she said it was so expensive out there. But Mr Singh read the letter, and gravely studied his *A to Z*, and told Mary that getting to the hotel was easy, there was nothing to it. She could do the whole journey in three buses, look. On the Thursday afternoon Mary wasn't all that certain she was even going, but by the evening she'd got out her best clothes and hung them up on the wardrobe door. She got up first thing next morning, put on her hat; she hadn't worn the hat since the funeral, but this was a special occasion. On each of the three buses she rode on the upper deck and looked out at the city. It felt almost like a holiday. She hadn't been on holiday in quite a while. She didn't see any famous landmarks, but it was fascinating nonetheless. Once a year, on their anniversary, Patrick had taken Mary into London for a special meal at a nice restaurant. As the years went by, the restaurant he chose had been closer and closer to home, this last time it had only been a few minutes' walk from the house, but Patrick and Mary still thrilled to the expedition regardless. There Mary would have the fish and Patrick would have the steak, and they always laughed about the steak, there'd been some joke about it, though for the life of her Mary couldn't now remember what.

'Is this the place?' Mary asked a smiling woman outside the hotel. 'I've come to collect my prize.' 'Yes, this is the place! Come in, come in!' Inside they were all smiling too, young men in suits and gelled-back hair. 'Take a seat at a table,' said one of them, 'the presentation will begin shortly.' 'And then I get my prize?' asked Mary. 'After the presentation, the prizes, yes,' said the man, and Mary was reassured. There were tea and biscuits to be had, but Mary had already had tea that morning before she set off, she didn't want to be greedy. All the other prize-winners were in couples or in families, Mary seemed to be the only one on her own, and she felt a little stab of loneliness, Patrick would have *loved* this. A man with a smarter suit and a wider smile than anyone else rose and stood in front of them all. 'Welcome, welcome!' he all but chuckled, 'we're going to have a great time today, ladies and gentlemen. And we've got some great opportunities for you, that I know you're just going to love. But to kick it off we have a short film that will explain everything. Lights, please, Jerry. Yes, now.'

'Everyone likes holidays,' said the woman on the screen, and she spent the next half an hour expounding on the subject. Then the lights came back on, and one of the smiling young men in suits sat down at Mary's table. 'Hello,' he said. 'I'm Jeff. You must be Mary.'

'I am Mary,' Mary confirmed.

'And I'm going to be your personal representative this afternoon.'

He opened his briefcase, and produced a whole stack of papers and brochures and forms and leaflets.

'Really?' said Mary. 'I'm sure there's no need for that. I'm only here for my prize. Aren't there people you'd rather spend time with?'

Jeff's smile got even wider. 'No, Mary, we like to take extra special care of our prize-winners. And where's Patrick? Couldn't he join us today?'

'I'm afraid not,' said Mary.

'Oh dear.'

'I'm sorry.'

'That's all right.'

'He's dead.'

'Oh,' said Jeff. 'I see.' For a moment he looked quite upset, and Mary thought how sweet that was of him. A lot of people had looked upset like that since Patrick had passed away, but they had at least *met* him. Jeff began to put all the papers and brochures and forms and leaflets back into his case. 'I'm afraid this opportunity is for married couples only. We did say that on the forms. In the small print. Look.' And he took one of the leaflets back out from the briefcase, looked it over, and then jabbed at it with his finger. Mary squinted at it dutifully. 'If your circumstances have changed, you really ought to have let us know.'

'I read everything I could,' said Mary. 'There was an awful lot to get through, and my eyesight isn't what it was. And it was such *very* small print, I thought it probably wasn't important.'

'No, no, Mary, it was very important. Oh dear.'

'Oh dear,' agreed Mary. 'I have *been* married, though. For over forty years. I was quite good at it. Looking around the room, I'm quite sure I've at least as much experience as everyone else. Even if they've been able to keep their husbands alive.'

'It's not that,' said Jeff. 'The opportunity does require a modicum of financial commitment. Something which might be more suitable for a couple.'

'Oh, I've got money,' said Mary. 'Lots and lots of it. To tell you the truth,' she dropped her voice, a little shyly, 'I've rather too much. I don't know what to do with it all! I've offered to give some to Simon, that's my son, but he says, you hang on to it, Mum, you might need it for a rainy day. Patrick always made sure I was well provided for. He said that if there was one thing he could be certain of, this was when he was dying, and he wasn't a religious man, he said he didn't know whether there'd be anywhere for him to go on the other side, but if he could be sure of one thing after death it was that I wouldn't go hungry.'

'I see,' said Jeff at last. 'Well, look. It's very unorthodox. But let me just go and check with my supervisor. I shan't be a moment.'

'All right,' said Mary. Jeff smiled at her, and she smiled back warmly. She watched him as he went to the back of the room and spoke earnestly to a man in a suit. She saw him point at her every now and then, and on the third time she waved at him. He came back to join her.

'Good news,' he said. 'We'll be able to offer you our opportunity after all.'

'That is good news, isn't it?'

'We can get right down to it now. That's great.' He got all the papers out of his briefcase once more. 'And, obviously, we're sorry for your loss.'

'It's funny,' said Mary. 'But sometimes it does feel like a loss! That I've just got careless and mislaid him somewhere. I'll wake up some mornings and he won't be in the bed next to me, and I'll wonder where he's gone, I'll wonder if I put him down somewhere silly like I do with my handbag or the front door keys. And then I remember, of course, he's dead, and sometimes I'll be relieved, he's dead and I haven't just dropped him in the supermarket, it isn't my fault. And sometimes I'll cry. One or the other. There are good days and bad days. I was told that'd be the way.'

'Sure,' said Jeff. 'Now, you've seen the presentation video. Did you understand it?'

'Oh yes,' said Mary. 'Everyone likes holidays. It all seemed very straightforward.'

'That's good, Mary, that's great. And do you have any questions about anything you saw?'

'I do have one,' said Mary.

'That's what I'm here for.'

'The woman who did the presenting. I know I've seen her somewhere. I've been racking my brains but I can't place her. Do you know?'

'I think,' said Jeff, 'she used to be in *Coronation Street*.'

'Oh yes, that's it,' said Mary, and smiled. 'She was lovely in that. That explains it, she had her hair done differently.'

'So,' said Jeff. 'Everyone likes holidays. And if you could pick a holiday, Mary. Somewhere you'd like to go. Where would it be?'

'Oh,' said Mary. 'I don't know.'

'Don't hold back,' smiled Jeff. 'Anywhere in the world. What would be your ideal holiday destination?'

'You sound a bit like Patrick,' laughed Mary. 'Every year he'd say this to me, shall we go on holiday in August, Mare? Get away for a few days? Best to book it now. Where would you like to go? And I'd laugh and say, Patrick Johnson, you know I can never choose. I've enough to worry about just deciding what to cook for your dinner! And besides, I know that look in your eyes, I know you've already got somewhere in mind! And he did, you know, his eyes, they'd be *shining*. Oh, we went all over, we went everywhere.'

'Well,' said Jeff. 'Where was your favourite?'

'They all blur into one, really. There was a place we went to, it had lots of cathedrals. That was nice, where would that have been? Or maybe it just had the one cathedral, but it was very big. That was nice. Do you know where that is?'

'Not offhand,' said Jeff.

'Patrick wasn't a religious man, but he liked a good cathedral. That's sturdy, he'd say, you can tell they really put their backs into building that. He liked to work hard himself, you see, so always appreciated it in others. And then another year there was a beach. Patrick said they're all baking in the sun, these people, they must know something we don't, let's give it a try! But he didn't take to that at all, dozing there on his deckchair, he said he felt basted like a chicken. We went for a meal on the seafront, and he had a steak, and I asked him how it was, and he said it wasn't as well done as he was. Oh, we laughed a lot at that. Whenever we had steak, from that time on, we'd laugh. We used to laugh so much.'

'How about,' said Jeff, producing a brochure, 'we take Majorca.'

'I'm not sure they have cathedrals in Majorca.'

'No, I know. Just as an example.'

'Oh, I see. All right.'

'Do you like the sound of Majorca?'

'Oh yes,' Mary said. 'But they all sound nice, don't they? Every single place in the brochures, they all sound lovely. I mean, it makes you wonder. Maybe everywhere *is* lovely. Maybe if we just stopped, and looked around, and kept our minds open a bit, we wouldn't need to have holidays at all. What do you think?'

Jeff looked about. The presentation hall didn't look lovely. His colleagues were all standing over their customers, bulldozing them into sales. Some had already got a signature on the dotted line, Jeff could recognise the difference between the practised smile and the grin of triumph and lucrative commission. 'Do you want a cup of tea?' he said. 'I think it's time for a tea break.'

'That'd be very nice,' said Mary.

'I might even rustle up a biscuit.'

They drank the tea, and munched on their biscuits. 'Don't worry,' said Mary. 'You're doing a very good job.'

'Do you think so?' asked Jeff doubtfully.

'Oh yes,' said Mary. 'I'm really enjoying myself.'

'So,' said Jeff, sliding away their cups and sliding the shiny brochure back into position, 'Majorca. Let's take a look at our Majorcan apartments.' He showed Mary page after page of bedrooms and bathrooms and TV lounges. Mary said they looked very nice. 'They *are* very nice,' said Jeff, and laughed. 'This is a lot nicer than where I live! In fact, quite a lot of our customers say it's nicer than where *they* live as well!'

Mary looked at the pictures carefully. 'It's probably nicer than where I live too.'

'Well, there you go. And this summer you could be *there*, Mary!'

'Oh no,' said Mary. 'I'd rather be in my own house. It's where all my stuff is.'

'But this could *be* your house,' Jeff explained. 'As well. That's the point, don't you see? For one week a year, this luxury flat in sun-drenched Majorca can be yours and no-one else's.'

'It has a balcony,' observed Mary.

'It does have a balcony. Do you like balconies?'

'I do like balconies,' said Mary.

'Well,' said Jeff, seizing upon this, 'the apartment's balcony is one of its prime features.'

'We had a balcony on one of our holidays,' said Mary. 'I can't remember which. I can't remember whether we saw cathedrals or beaches when we stood on it. It was very nice, though. We'd stand out there every night as the sun set, and if it was a little chilly, we'd hug. It was nice when it was chilly. When we got home, Patrick told me he'd build me a balcony of my very own.'

'I thought he might have,' said Jeff.

'It was meant to be a surprise birthday present,' said Mary. 'Which was a bit silly, because it was outside the bedroom window, it could hardly be kept a secret. Patrick had to apply for planning permission. It was only a little balcony, but you see, the council are very strict. He got some advice from a builder, he did it all by himself, said it wouldn't be a proper gift to me otherwise. And that may have been the problem, because when the council came they said it was structurally unsound. And Patrick and I had been out there four weeks already, staring out at the sunset, hugging against the chill, not that there's much of a sunset in Finchley, it had felt perfectly safe to me. But we weren't allowed on it again. Patrick wouldn't have let me out. He said, Mare, I'm not having you risk your neck for a sunset. I keep plants on it now. And I can water them fine, if I stretch out with the long watering can.'

'Right,' said Jeff. 'That's a shame.' And he fell silent for a few seconds. Tried again. 'But I'm quite sure their balconies are safe. You could enjoy many a sunset there.'

'It's very nice,' agreed Mary.

'It's a big apartment,' said Jeff. 'You mentioned Simon, he's your son? Does he have a family?'

'Oh yes,' said Mary. 'Catherine, his wife, she's a sweetheart. And they've a little girl, Rachel.'

'Well, what could be more perfect? A family holiday in one of these apartments is absolutely ideal. All staying with Granny. What do you think?'

'I think Simon has enough of me as it is,' said Mary gently. 'Oh, I know he loves me. He tells me to ring whenever I want something, bless him, and I do ring rather a lot, and he's always so patient. I can hear it in his voice, that patience, it's something he just slips into whenever we talk these days. And I'd ring less, I don't want to disturb him, he's got a family of his own now, he doesn't want his mum there every other minute, and I don't want to hear that patience because it makes me cry. All that patience, he doesn't mean to, but he makes me cry. But I ring anyway. I don't know why. I keep ringing. I think,' she said with a smile, 'they'd probably rather holiday on their own.'

'Well, maybe,' said Jeff, 'they could go without you. Because that's the joy of timeshare. They make perfect gifts. I bet Simon likes holidays, doesn't he?'

'He does like holidays.'

'And little Rachel, I bet she just *loves* holidays, am I right?'

'Everyone likes holidays,' agreed Mary. 'That's what Vera Duckworth said.'

'Just think,' said Jeff, 'you could ring Simon this evening. And he'd come to the phone, as you say, sounding all patient. Just imagine how his voice would change if he was told his wonderful mum had bought him a luxury flat in Majorca! His darling, generous mum, he'd never just sound *patient* again, would he? He'd sound grateful. Every time you'd ring, he'd sound so grateful. "Thanks, Mum," he'd say, "I love you."' Jeff's eyes were shining. He was moved.

'It'd be quite a surprise,' said Mary.

'It would, wouldn't it? It really would.'

'What do I have to do?'

'We don't ask you to pay all now,' said Jeff. 'That's the beauty of it. We want this to be easy and convenient for you. This is a holiday, holidays should be *fun*!' And he got out some forms. 'And the most fun way is to do it in monthly instalments, Direct Debit, at a very competitive rate.'

Mary looked at the papers. 'I'd usually get Simon to look these over first,' she said. 'But then it wouldn't be a surprise, would it?'

'No, it wouldn't,' agreed Jeff. 'Quite right. You have me there.' He watched as Mary signed her name.

'And it'll be nice,' said Mary, 'to think of Simon on holiday. Once he was born, of course, it was all about Simon. Patrick would say to me, where shall we go on holiday this year, and we'd laugh. Because it wasn't for *us* any more, Patrick wanted to show Simon the world. Let's open his eyes up to it all, Mare, he said to me, let's show him all the cathedrals and beaches we can. And Simon was such a good traveller, even as a baby, all the other kids would be screaming on the plane, and I never got used to it myself, I felt like screaming myself sometimes! But not him, he'd be staring out of the window the whole flight, he was so fascinated by it all.'

'And you put your card number here,' said Jeff.

'And then, on one holiday, I don't remember where, as I say, they blur into one. But it was somewhere foreign, I know that, because we couldn't speak the language, and Patrick had left the phrase book back in the hotel by mistake, we didn't know the word for "police". We lost Simon. One moment he was holding Patrick's hand, the next he was gone. We'd lost him, like a bunch of keys or a handbag. And Patrick called his name, Simon, Simey, where are you? All around the cathedral, or the beach, wherever it was, and people told us to shush, so it was probably a cathedral. And he said to me, oh, Mare, what if we've lost him for good? And I told him not to say that, don't ever say that, but he began to cry. Right in the middle of all these foreigners and tourists and stained glass windows, and this was a man who *never* cried, he was so solid, you see, he was sturdy like a cathedral.'

'What happened?' asked Jeff.

'Oh,' said Mary, and smiled. 'Simon turned up eventually. I don't think he was gone more than half an hour. It was all right. Don't look so worried!' she said, and took Jeff's hand. 'Bless you, it was all right in the end!'

'Yes,' said Jeff.

'"But what if I'd lost him, Mare?" That's what he kept saying to me. And that next year, a holiday was never mentioned. Spring into summer, not a word. So one day I went out to the travel agent. I'd never booked a holiday before, it was all a bit of a mystery. And I came home, and I said, right then, Patrick Johnson, three tickets to Majorca, we leave next Friday. And he got angry, and I said, darling, you darling man, we can't hold on to his hand forever. We're proud of him, of course we are, all parents are proud of their kids. But he's got to grow up. Just so one day when I speak to him on the phone he'll sound patient at me.' She was quiet for a while. Then said, 'I didn't make a good choice. Majorca was terrible. It was cold, and it rained all week.'

'Oh,' said Jeff. 'Maybe I should find you an apartment somewhere else.'

'Not to worry. I won't be going, shall I? It's for Simon.'

'I don't think,' said Jeff slowly, 'my parents are especially proud of me.' Mary blinked at him in surprise. 'Sorry. Forget that.'

'I'm sure they are,' said Mary. 'I'm sure they're very proud. Dressed as smart as that. I'd be proud of you. I am proud. And I don't even know you!'

Jeff smiled, and it was a real smile, a sad smile. 'I don't think they are. Not in a job like this.'

'But you're very good at your job,' said Mary. 'It's worked on me, hasn't it?'

'Yes,' said Jeff quietly.

'And it's funny, that. Because everyone likes holidays, I know. Everyone likes them. But some years back, after Simon had grown up, and he'd seen everything we could show him. And Patrick said to me, do you know what, Mare? Let's not go on holiday this year. All these beaches and bastings, we've done it all, and the only thing I want now is you. It's you. Let's never go on holiday again. Let's just shut the doors tight, pretend we're away, it'll be just the two of us. And I don't want to make you blush,' Mary added, 'but then we went upstairs, and we made love. And the final signature here, is that right?' Jeff nodded, and she scribbled down her name one last time. 'And sometimes now I wake up in bed, and wonder where he is, and whether I've lost him.'

Jeff took hold of the forms and tore them up.

'Oh,' said Mary. 'Are you all right, dear?'

The man with the smarter suit and the wider smile came over. 'What's going on?' he said.

'Mrs Johnson doesn't like holidays,' said Jeff.

'Of course she does. Everyone likes holidays.'

'I quite like holidays,' said Mary.

'No,' said Jeff. 'You don't. You really don't.' He looked away from her, up to his boss standing over him. 'She really doesn't. Please.'

The man in the smarter suit frowned. He didn't speak for a while. 'Okay,' he said at last. 'Okay. Then Mrs Johnson should go home. Mrs Johnson should leave and not waste our time any longer.'

'She really should go home,' said Jeff.

'I just said she should go home, Jeff. I just said that, didn't I?'

'What about my prize?' said Mary.

The man in the suit looked at her. 'What?'

'My prize. I came to collect my prize.'

'You get your prize,' said the suit, 'when you buy one of our apartments. It says so in the small print. You should have read the small print.'

'Oh, come on,' said Jeff. 'Give her her prize.'

'She should have read the small print.'

'For Christ's sake,' said Jeff. 'We're drowning in the stuff back there. Give her a bloody prize. For Christ's sake.'

'Fine,' said the man. 'Fine. She can have a prize. She can have a prize, then she can go home. What do you want? There's a fountain pen, or there's a disposable camera. Up to you.'

'I want dominion over life and death,' said Mary. 'It says I won dominion over life and death.' And she held out her paperwork, all the letters she'd kept safe in that special drawer in the kitchen, she even held out the scratch card she'd used. The man dumbly took them from her, looked them over, then tutted with annoyance he'd even stopped to give them a glance.

'If we had dominion over life and death,' he said, 'do you think we'd be needing to flog shitty timeshares?' He reached into his briefcase. 'Pen, or camera. Your choice.'

'Go for the pen,' said Jeff. 'The camera's rubbish.'

The man held them out. The gold plating of the pen was already rubbing off. 'I'll go with the camera,' said Mary, pointing instead at the box, the cardboard box she'd been imagining, the small cardboard box she'd been expecting in the post.

'Enjoy,' said the man. He gave her the box. 'Jeff. You come with me.' He glowered, and Jeff nodded, and both turned and walked away from her, and were soon lost within the crowd of suits.

The meeting hadn't taken two hours as promised. By the time she was on her second bus home it was nearly dark. And Mary held on to the little box tightly all the way. She didn't open it. She didn't want to open it. She knew that if she opened it she'd only find a camera inside. And what did she need a camera for? What would she want to photograph now?

She opened her front door, pushed against a pile of envelopes. She'd left that morning before the postman had arrived. She sighed, stooped to pick them up, to shut them away in the drawer.

'Don't worry,' said Patrick. 'I take care of all that, don't I?' And she looked up and saw him there. And she knew it wasn't her Patrick, not exactly. It was the Patrick of her stories. She could see the difference in his smile. This was a Patrick who had made a joke about getting sunburned, who hadn't moaned all week. This was a Patrick who had actually finished building the balcony, not given up halfway through. This was a father who had been able to cry amongst all those foreigners, without shame or embarrassment, when he thought he'd lost his child.

She wanted to fly into his arms right then and hug him. But she knew she'd have plenty of time for that now.

'Hello, Mare,' he said. 'Kettle's on. I'll make you a nice cup of tea.'

Not About Love

Of course, in principle, I'm revolted by the whole thing. It's this idea of turning everything into a competition. We're taking artists and reducing them to the level of contestants on a game show. All these prizes and award ceremonies, does everyone really need to be liked so badly? What's the big deal about being *liked*? The great writers I've admired over the years, they didn't need to be popular. Do you think Proust would have accepted an award? Do you think Dostoyevsky? I mean, okay, I'm not comparing myself to Proust, not exactly, I know I'm not in the same ballpark, but, you know, I'm trying, isn't the trying the point? How can I ever write something of the majesty of *À la Recherche du Temps Perdu* if I'm forever looking over my shoulder, wondering if it's going to appeal to the judges, whether it will win me prize money and a glass paperweight? I like to think, I don't know, if Proust *had* been nominated for an award, if *his* publisher had phoned him up, and said, 'Great news, Marcel, you're up for Best French Novelist Writing in a Memoir Form,' he'd have baulked at the very suggestion. 'My art is my art,' he might have said. 'It's not there to be categorised, to be *nominated*, to be held up in comparison to other artists and judged against them. It is what it is, take it or leave it. *C'est ça*. Now sod off.'

That said, I must admit, I had no such qualms accepting my nomination, and told my publisher so. 'I should hope you've no bloody qualms,' he said, 'the favours I had to pull in just to get you on the shortlist.' The ceremony was to take place in two weeks' time, in an arts centre in Liverpool, and an invitation was already in the post; dress should be formal, but not too formal, I wouldn't need to rent a tux or anything. 'This'll be good for sales, won't it?' I said, and my publisher agreed it couldn't hurt, with any luck I might be on royalties soon. This was my second collection of short stories, and attention in the press had been perfunctory at best. My debut had had a few decent crits, but this follow-up was seen as a typical sophomore effort, trying too hard to impress. Indeed, the words 'sophomore' and 'effort' had featured, either linked or apart, in every major review we'd received. I hoped that the nomination would prove the critics wrong, that they'd read of the shortlist in their newspapers over breakfast and choke on their Weetabix. I confess I was excited. I couldn't keep still all afternoon, kept googling my name on the internet, opened a celebratory can of beer. I've always prided myself upon a certain literary dignity, and I'm ashamed to confess it, it took three hours and two cans of Stella for me to recover the appropriate authorial mien.

I took my book from the shelf. I hadn't given it a good look in days. Called *Love Songs for the Shy and Cynical*, it was a collection of meditations on love, upon the fragility of it, its cruelty, its shifting definition in today's junk culture, etc. You know the sort of thing. It had quite a long title, and my publishers warned me that that wasn't commercial – go with Adjective Noun, they said, or, if you really want to raise their eyebrows, Noun Exclamation Mark. But I'd been adamant. I smiled at the cover, fingered the lettering, then flicked through. All these words I'd written about love. Each and every one copyrighted to me.

The short story is the perfect medium in which to write about love. What is love, anyway, if not a series of short stories? It's such a fleeting thing, the passion of it here today and gone tomorrow. I'm not talking about the *trappings* of love, they hang around your neck forever like a dull weight – children, marriage, mortgage, fitted bedrooms with double beds. That isn't love, just unfortunate by-products of it. They're the things that take up all our time and demand all our attention, but that's no more experiencing love than a visit to the travel agents to buy your medical insurance is experiencing a holiday. When we reflect upon the great loves of our lives, really, it's just anecdotes we mean. Snatches of happiness, glimpses of something overwhelming we can't grasp, short stories. When I look back at the time with my wife, I think I could sum up love, the time I really felt love, in no more than three or four anecdotes. I bet that's about the norm. Three or four, I bet that's pretty good, actually.

You might think that a bit cynical. But consider the popularity of the love song. Love summed up in four minutes, just four minutes' worth of words, and most of those words repeated in the chorus, and most of *those* drowned out by drum beats. Now that's cynical. But we listen to them anyway, they're all that plays on the radio, every song a love song – we *want* our love to be handed to us in bite-sized chunks between the news and the traffic reports. Personally, I find that a bit cheap. Personally, I don't think you can squeeze the whole meaning of love into such a tiny space. Short stories are best. You can give love just that little bit of attention it deserves, the whole experience. Three thousand words should do it, four thousand if you're being a bit flowery.

I tried to explain something of this to my mother when I phoned to tell her about my nomination. She gently reminded me that she'd read my book, my singular views on love were very clear. She congratulated me and asked if I thought I was going to win. 'Oh, I wouldn't have thought so,' I laughed. 'I'm not quite enough part of the *establishment*.' And anyway, as I pointed out, I didn't actually want to win, winning awards damaged your artistic credibility, no good writer has ever won awards, did Proust? She asked if there was any prize money, and I said it was a thousand pounds, and she said that was nice, I could go on a nice holiday with that. She asked if I'd phoned my father to give him the news. I hadn't. 'Oh, you must,' she said, 'he'll be so thrilled.' I said I was surprised the two of them were talking, and she got a little irritable, and said they'd been talking quite happily for nearly a year, she'd told me that, they'd put all that behind them now and were friends. 'Give him a call,' she said. 'Really. It'll mean the world to him.'

So I did. I hadn't spoken to him in a few weeks, he was about due. He took a little while to answer, he was somewhere in his seventies and not as fast on his feet as he should have been; normally I'd have hung up and tried my luck later, but I was very patient, this time I waited. 'Hello, son,' he wheezed at me.

We exchanged pleasantries for a bit. I asked him how he was and he said he was fine, and he asked me how I was, and I said fine. 'Fine is good,' said Dad. Then I told him about the award nomination for my book.

'Which book is this?' asked Dad.

'You remember the book. I gave it to you for Christmas.'

'Oh yes,' said Dad. 'But that was ages ago. I thought you might have written another one since.'

'No,' I said.

I told him all about it, the going to Liverpool, the prize money, the not having to rent a tux. 'That's nice,' he said. I told him it wasn't nice. It was a big award, this, actually, something of an achievement even to get this far. It was an honour, this could change my career, could change my life.

'That's great,' said Dad. Not, as I pointed out, that I actually wanted to win, artistic credibility and all that. 'No,' said Dad, 'I can see that.' We talked about other things for a while, and I was about to hang up, when Dad said, 'This award ceremony of yours. Will you be going with Janie?'

'I hadn't thought,' I said. 'I wouldn't imagine so. No. No, I won't be.'

'Can I come?'

I was genuinely astonished. 'Why?' I said, at last.

'It's a big deal, isn't it? I'd like to be there for you. I'd like to support you.'

'I'm not going to win.'

'No, I know that.'

He'd put me in a very difficult position. How could I say no? 'No, Dad,' I said. 'They're only going to give me the one hotel room, I expect. You won't want to share a room, will you?'

'Oh, I can live with that,' he chuckled. 'Why not? You are my son, after all. It'll be an adventure!' And somehow, by the time I'd put the receiver down, I was bringing a guest with me to Liverpool.

The next morning I called my publisher and told him I wanted to discuss accommodation. He said that wasn't his job, and if sorting out a hotel meant so much to me, here was the number of the award admin faculty. So I called them, and told them I wanted two rooms rather than just one. The woman at the other end had initially been very chirpy with congratulations, but she could tell I was talking business; she said she could have a word with the finance department to see whether they had the budget to afford a hotel room for me, but she was quite sure it wouldn't stretch to two. So I asked her to give me the number for the hotel, and I called them directly, and found out how much a second room for my father would cost. Then I called back the admin faculty and said I'd be happy with just the one room after all, but that it'd need two beds. I didn't recognise the woman at first, her voice had hardened somewhat. All in all, it was a busy day.

I waited out the next two weeks. I tried to work, but it was hard to write anything fresh with the weight of my old stories on my shoulders. So I went out to the bookshop to check out my fellow nominees. There were five of us in total; one of the books was still in hardback, but I could pick up all the others cheaply enough. I was delighted to discover that one of the books was definitely worse than mine, it was a dreadful collection of lumpen prose and shallow stories, and I hadn't enjoyed a read so much in ages. I could spot the winner, though, straight away. The author was from Scotland, which was still going through a phase of fashionable earthiness; I'd been raised in Surrey, which hadn't been artistically credible since the eighteenth century. Her stories were lyrical and spare and issue-based and just a little boring. The third story in had a woman confronting over breakfast porridge the father who'd serially abused her as a child. It had award stamped all over the bloody thing.

At last the big day arrived. I met my father on the concourse at Euston station. I hadn't seen him since Christmas, and he'd lost weight, and his skin was baggy and yellow. He was in an old suit that was too big for him. 'You're not going to wear that tonight, are you?' I greeted him. He chuckled, and said this was his good luck jacket, he always wore it to award ceremonies. I laughed politely. 'No, but seriously, you're not going to wear that.'

We found two seats together on the train. I got out a newspaper, he got out a pristine copy of *Love Songs for the Shy and Cynical.* 'You're only getting around to reading it *now*?' I asked him. 'No, no,' he assured me. 'Just refreshing my memory.' He put on his reading glasses. It was hard to concentrate on my sudoku when I knew he was next to me, frowning at my words, licking his finger before he turned over each new page.

Eventually he put the book down. 'I don't get it,' he said. 'I'm sorry,' he added, and I could see that he was. 'I thought you said they were love stories.'

'They are *about* love,' I said.

'So all this stuff about Luxembourg disappearing...'

'It's a metaphor,' I said. 'Obviously.'

'Oh.' He looked at the book unhappily. He seemed uncertain whether to pursue this any further. If this had been one of our phone calls we'd both have found a reason to hang up by now – but here we were, side by side, sharing the same arm-rest, and we hadn't even reached Watford yet. 'And all the people who read this... You think they're going to get that?'

'Yes.'

'All those judges?'

'Well. I'm nominated, aren't I?'

'Right,' he said. 'I don't know. I mean, I know I'm not an expert like you. But it just seems a bit of a cheat. I mean, if your book says it's going to be love stories. I mean, you've been in love. Haven't you, with Janie, and I was, with your mother, still am. Of course I still am. Maybe you could have written about that.' I looked at him. 'Sorry,' he said. 'I'm not an expert. Are they all... all your stories, are they like that?'

'Yes,' I said.

'Right,' he said.

He wanted to stretch his legs, so I let him out. He brought me back an egg sandwich from the buffet. 'I couldn't remember if you'd turned vegetarian or not.'

I thanked him, ate the sandwich. And then I closed my eyes and pretended to sleep. I was trying to think of a really good acceptance speech; I hadn't prepared one, I felt that if I had it would have jinxed the whole thing, but that said, I didn't want to get up on to that podium with nothing to say looking like a prawn. Not that I thought I was going to win. Not even for a second, I knew I wouldn't. And didn't want to anyway. Next to me I heard my father fall asleep for real, I could hear the snoring. After that I was able to think about an acceptance speech with my eyes open. I came up with something which postulated on the value of the short story's craft, and traced its historical development from Guy de Maupassant through Anton Chekhov and Raymond Carver to me.

The hotel was only two minutes' walk from the station. The receptionist gave us a pair of electronic keys, and directed us to the fifth floor. 'I think he thought we were gay,' chuckled Dad in the lift. 'Do you think that?' The room was clean and anonymous. It had coffee-making facilities, a TV, a bathroom, and a large double bed.

'I asked for a twin,' I said.

'Oh, it doesn't matter,' said my Dad, already trying the mattress out for comfort. 'It's nice and soft. Which side do you want? We'll be all right. They've got free biscuits, look!' He grinned at me from ear to ear, and took the wrapping off a custard cream. 'This is like a holiday,' he said. 'It's nice to spend time with you. I haven't shared a bed with anyone since your mother left. Have you shared a bed since Janie?'

'No,' I said.

'She tell you we're talking again? Your mother and I. I know she's not coming back to me now, I accept that. But at least we can still be friends. I think that's better somehow, maybe, I think. Maybe that's what it's all about.' He turned on the television. The default screen welcomed me by name, as nominee of the Verity Lonsdale awards. 'My God,' said Dad, impressed. 'This really *is* a big deal, isn't it?'

I changed into my suit, and talked my father out of his. 'The jacket makes you look like a tramp. We can get away with the shirt and tie.' And then we walked to the arts centre. 'Hello,' I said to a smart young woman at the entrance, 'I'm here for the Verity Lonsdale.'

'He's up for a prize,' said Dad, and beamed. 'He wrote the one about love.'

'Oh yes,' she said. 'I *did* enjoy that. And such a clever theme, love's a universal, isn't it, we can all relate to that. Do please help yourselves to drinks. They're still preparing the auditorium.'

There was even champagne. I took a glass for me and a glass for Dad. Suddenly I was being hugged, and I pulled back, and realised that it was my publisher. He was wearing a better suit than I was. 'Hey, hey!' he said. 'Here he is!' He'd never hugged me before, he'd probably been drinking for some time. 'Are you excited? Think you're going to win?'

'I don't really want to win,' I said.

'Yeah,' he said. 'And who's this?'

'I'm his dad,' said Dad.

'Yeah? Great! Well, you must be very proud of him.'

'I am proud of him,' agreed Dad.

'Yeah, he's good, isn't he? So, read his stories, then? Got a favourite?'

'I like the one about Luxembourg,' said Dad.

There was an announcement that the auditorium had now opened, could we all make our way there with our drinks. There was a queue for the lift. 'You go on ahead,' said my publisher. 'I'll get another round in first.'

I realised who I was standing behind. 'Oh, hello!' I said. The woman looked around. 'I recognise you from your photograph.'

'I recognise you from yours too,' she said, in a light Scottish accent.

'Yes.' On the website her photo was in black and white, and she was unsmiling, and looked as austere and forbidding as an empress. She looked much the same now, even seeming faintly monochrome with her pale skin and her black dress. I shook her hand. It was cold.

'I read your book,' I said. 'Loved it.'

'Thank you.'

'So. Best of luck for tonight. Bet you win!'

She nodded. Then turned around again.

'Are you nervous?' I asked. She sighed, turned back to me.

'What's there to be nervous about? It's already been decided, hasn't it? We can't do anything to affect the outcome now.'

'I know,' I said. 'But we might have to give a speech if we win.'

She shrugged. Another set of people got into the lift. We all shuffled forward. The next would be ours. 'Did I say I read your book?' I asked.

'I haven't read yours.'

'Oh.'

'That's the problem with these award ceremonies. You meet all these other writers, and how awful if you've read their books, and hated them, and have to make small talk, and pretend that they're any good. So I don't bother any more.'

'Oh,' I said. 'Perhaps you'll read it afterwards.'

'No,' she said. 'I *hate* being told what to read. Lists of books, all up for prizes, I'll choose my own books, thank you. I'm not going to buy what a bunch of judges tell me to. And I don't think your book sounds very appealing.'

'It's about love, though,' I said. 'That's a universal.' The lift doors opened. She got in. I hung back, thought I'd wait for the next one.

'Good luck,' said Dad. And then, cheerfully, as the doors closed, 'I'm his dad!'

In the auditorium the people in suits and dresses were still milling about, but now in ever tighter circles, anticipating the evening's climax. At the far end of the room a single microphone stood on a table. Next to it was a glass sculpture I could only assume was the award. And on a large screen, playing in rotation, were the faces and biographies of all the nominees. I could see at that size how my left eye was smaller than the right. I idly wondered whether that would affect my chances of victory.

A man I'd never met before approached me. 'There's someone very important who wants to meet you,' he said, and stood back to reveal an old lady, standing at probably no more than five foot tall, eighty years if she was a day. Her hair had blonde highlights, her mouth was a smear of pink. 'This,' he said, 'is Verity Lonsdale.'

'Hello,' I said, raising my voice a little in case she was deaf. She offered me her hand; I took it as if she were the Queen. I felt an urge to curtsey.

'Thank you so much for writing your book,' she told me. Her voice was younger than her face. 'And for attending our celebration of the short story and what it can achieve.'

'Oh, no problem. And, of course, thank you for having me.'

'It's a good book, isn't it?' said my dad.

Ms Lonsdale frowned, and half her wrinkles smoothed out. 'Well,' she said. 'I think it's a *curious* book, certainly. Yes. It made me very curious.'

'Thank you,' I said. 'I do my best to be curious.'

'I have to ask,' she said. 'What an *intriguing* idea, a book of short stories about love. Why ever did you do it?'

'I think that the short story is the perfect medium in which to write about love,' I told her. 'I mean, what's love, really, but a series of short stories?'

'Yes, yes,' she said, and waved her hand a little so I'd stop. 'Yes, I read your back cover blurb. But it's bollocks, that, isn't it?' And she smiled charmingly through the pink. 'Love isn't a short story at all. It's an epic poem by Dante. It's the complete works of Shakespeare. It's a writer's entire oeuvre; look at Stendhal, Flaubert, Lawrence even, it's vast and it bursts out of whatever tries to contain it. Short stories, I thought, when I got your book, this I *have* to see. How daring, how cheeky, how *arrogant*. I read your book with *huge* interest.'

'Thank you,' I said again.

'But it's not about love at all. Not at all. Your stories, they *hide* from love. All the silly jokes you play, all your little bits of absurdism, the heart in the Tupperware box, the rabbit with wings – it's all amusing for a while, yes, but I kept on saying, when's he actually going to *engage* with the subject? When's he going to drop the gimmick, and make me *feel* something?'

'It couldn't be that bad a book,' I said. 'It got nominated, didn't it?'

'Oh, I don't select the books, I get cleverer people than me to do that. I just put up the money. But it made me wonder. And forgive me for asking. Throughout the whole clever, oh yes, clever, but passionless read. Have you even ever *been* in love?'

'Of course I have.'

'Of course. Forgive me. I just never recognised the love you describe. I've been in love so many times. Had love affairs, some brief, some lifelong. But none of them have been shy or cynical. And none of them, I can assure you, have been short stories.' She darted a glance to the man who'd introduced us, and he moved in to flank her. 'But don't get me wrong. It's a *fine* book. With many fine things in it. The very best of luck.'

'I think the book's great,' said Dad.

'Well, that's good,' said Verity Lonsdale.

'I found it all about love. It made me feel something.'

'I'm glad to hear it,' said Verity Lonsdale.

'I'm his dad. I'm very proud of him.'

Verity Lonsdale gave my dad a sweet smile all of his very own.

'Don't listen to him,' I said. 'He's not even read it.'

Verity Lonsdale was shepherded away to meet fresher meat. 'I'm assuming,' said Dad, as I took another glass of champagne from a tray, 'that she's someone important?'

'Yes,' I said. 'I think so,' I added. 'To be honest, I first heard of her two weeks ago.'

The lights dimmed a little. Conversation hushed. I looked around for my publisher, but he'd joined another group altogether. All I had was my dad. 'Are you nervous?' he said.

'It's already been decided, hasn't it? Can't do anything to affect the outcome.'

'I'm nervous,' said Dad. 'I wish I had my jacket.'

'What on earth for?'

'It's my lucky jacket. I always wore it to award ceremonies. You remember, I used to get a lot of nominations? Back in the seventies, when I was in advertising?'

'No.'

'You do,' he said. 'I even won a few times. Those chunks of glass in the sitting room, remember? On the window sill?' But I didn't. 'All I'm saying, son, as someone who's been to a ton of these things. It's just a circus. A bit of a laugh, nothing to take too seriously. If you lose, it doesn't matter a fart, does it?'

'Shut up,' I said. 'You're making it sound as if I'm *going* to lose.'

I did. One of the judges took the microphone, welcomed us all to the prestigious Verity Lonsdale Awards, and in one moment I was a nominee, and the next I was a loser. The Scottish woman won. She made a speech about the short story, and traced its history from Katherine Mansfield through Flannery O'Connor and Angela Carter to herself. And she praised all the other nominees, and said that it was an honour to be in the same room with us, so many writers she'd so long admired.

The champagne tasted a bit acrid. I saw the winner surrounded by well-wishers, people shaking her hand, all waving fresh copies of her book they'd just bought at the display. She was trying to talk and autograph at the same time, and seemed to be doing a marginally better job at the latter. My publisher came to find me. 'Hey, bad luck, matey,' he said, 'but we gave it a shot, didn't we?' 'I didn't want to...' 'Yeah,' he said, and then went off to get a copy of the winning book signed by the author.

'Here,' said Dad. And from his bag he took out a copy of *Love Songs for the Shy and Cynical.*

'What's that for?'

'I'd like you to autograph it, please,' he said. 'For your dad.'

'Don't be ridiculous,' I said.

Scottish Woman was still signing away. I drained my champagne. 'Excuse me,' I said, 'barging through! Excuse me, so sorry, I'm not being rude, I'm a fellow writer.' I reached her, offered my hand. 'You won,' as she took it, 'told you!'

'Yes,' she said, in that soft voice of hers.

'Many congratulations.'

'Thank you.' Someone was taking a photograph of us. I let go of her hand.

'I must just say,' I said, 'embarrassing confession here. But I've always been a big fan of your work. I've read everything you've done.'

'Really?' she said.

'Oh yes.' I tried to recall the titles I'd seen displayed in her biography. 'That first book of yours, *Imagining Others*, was good. In fact, I loved it. In fact, reading it, it's what made me want to be a writer. I wouldn't be here today if it weren't for you. In a very real sense, my own book is your book as well.'

'God,' she said, and looked impressed.

'In fact,' I said, ploughing on, 'when my publishers told me who the other nominees were, I wanted *you* to win. In fact, I was more excited about the prospect of being in the same room with you now than the prospect of winning a literary award of my own. Isn't that something?'

'It certainly is something,' she said. She still looked surprised, but not necessarily pleased. 'That means a lot to me, but...'

'You'll have to read my book now,' I joked, 'and see what monster you've created!'

'But,' she continued, hard, 'I really must get back to my autographs.'

'That story you wrote,' I said, 'about the child abuse. Worth the cover price alone. It was exquisitely written. I knew, when I read that, that you'd win. You can't go wrong with a bit of child abuse, the judges love that. I don't mean that they love child abuse, ha! I'm sure they're against it in real life, ha!'

'No, I understand what you're saying.'

'But I have to wonder. I don't know. If it might have been more of a surprise had it *not* been about child abuse. Something of a twist, right at the end. I'm not saying we should all be Roald Dahl, I know short stories can't all be Tales of the Bloody Unexpected. But, out of curiosity, did you ever think of putting in a twist?'

'No.'

'I don't know,' I said. 'Maybe as a child you *were* abused. Maybe it was important for you to write that, therapeutic, whatever. I wasn't abused, you see. I had a loving family when I grew up. In Surrey. I was never denied love. It was never withheld from me. The way it is in *your* story, the word was never redefined as something violent or obscene. My parents gave me nothing to write about, they didn't even split up till I was in my thirties, that's how fucking considerate they were. I just think it puts you at a rather unfair advantage, awards-wise, that's all I'm saying.'

'Please,' she said. 'Please leave me alone.'

'That's enough,' said Dad.

I turned around. I hadn't seen my father angry in years. The pudding of a man, I didn't think he was capable of it. My mum had confided to me, during the divorce, that had he even once raised his voice, even showed the least passion that his marriage was collapsing about him, she'd probably have called the whole thing off and stayed.

'I'm sorry,' Dad said to Scottish Woman. 'He's drunk, and tired, and disappointed. Congratulations on winning. I haven't read your book, but I'll be sure to look out for a copy.' And then he pulled me away.

By the time we'd reached the corner of the room I could see the anger had dissipated, the pudding was already back in charge. 'Oh dear,' he said, as if that were reproof enough, and smiled weakly. 'Look, there's a posh meal after this. But I don't think we'd better go. I think we're a bit tired, aren't we? I'll make our excuses, and we can go back to the hotel.'

'Sure,' I said.

'We can have fun without them, can't we? Just you and your old dad.'

'Sure,' I said. 'Bring it on.'

A flare of irritation over his face. 'I thought it'd be good to spend some time with you,' he said. 'I know that after your mum left me, we lost touch. Probably my fault as much as yours. But I had hoped, I don't know, that now you and Janie have split up...'

'Wait a moment.'

'That in some ways we had something more in common. That we could be friends maybe.'

'Just wait,' I said. 'For a start, Mum left *you*. And I left Janie. I'm not the loser. Completely different. And we haven't split up. It's only temporary, I expect. I might go back to Janie soon. I just couldn't live with her whilst I was writing. I found I can't be artistic in a domestic environment.'

Dad said nothing for a while. Then, softly, 'You're an idiot.' And he gave me his bag.

'What's this for?'

'Take it back to the hotel.'

'Why? Where are you going?'

'Me?' he said. 'I'm going out to enjoy a posh meal.' And he walked away.

At the hotel I looked at the in-room dining options. There was a burger I rather liked the sound of. I phoned down to order it. It cost fifteen pounds! That was outrageous. The receptionist told me that it would be half that price if I could only make my way down to the restaurant. But I never wanted to leave my bedroom, never again. So I paid the excess. It took nearly an hour to arrive. It was good.

I tried the television, but there was nothing on. So I took from my father's bag his copy of *Love Songs.* I hadn't actually read it since I'd checked the galley proofs nearly a year ago, and then I'd been looking for typos, I wasn't trying to enjoy the stories. I was surprised I'd forgotten the details of what happened in them. I lay on the bed and read my book. Some of it was as Verity Lonsdale had said. I wanted to cross out entire passages with a pen. But other bits made me smile. Other bits made me proud.

I autographed the book for my father. 'Dear Dad, Best wishes.' Then signed my name. I felt foolish doing that, as if that was something he needed reminding of! And then I read another story. And then I thought for a while. And I wrote him a PS. The PS took three sides of my small handwriting. Then I dozed for a while.

Eventually my dad came back. He looked apologetic. 'I'm not stopping,' he said. 'If that's okay. Verity has... well, she's asked me back to hers. I think she's taken rather a shine to me.'

'Verity Lonsdale?' I said. 'Really?'

'I came back for this,' he said. He picked up his lucky jacket. 'I really haven't shared a bed since your mother left, you see.'

I nodded.

'I'll stay if you want, though. If you feel I'm running out on you.'

'No, Dad,' I said. 'That's fine. Go and give her one from me.' That sounded a bit odd, but I didn't pursue the idea, and nor did he, and he grinned, and I grinned back. 'I signed your book,' I added.

And even though downstairs there was passion waiting from a woman whose love affairs had never been short stories, he read my PS. A short story about love of his very own, for him, and for no-one else. He finished it, nodded, smiled. And took it with him.

And I phoned Janie. 'I'm sorry to call so late,' I said. 'I'm sorry.'

'No,' she said, 'I was waiting up. I was hoping you'd call. How did you get on?'

'I didn't win. And I really really wanted to.'

'I liked your book,' she said. 'That's the main thing.'

'That's the only thing,' I said. And I told her that all the love stories in the book, however shy, however cynical, however clumsily and imperfectly expressed – they'd all been for her and all been about her.

'Are you coming home now?' she asked.

I thought. 'Soon,' I said. 'Soon. There's just one more story I have to write.'

Listen:

One Last Love Song

Listen.

There was once a little boy who was in love with love. It was the first thing he thought of when he woke in the morning. It was what he hoped to dream of when he went to sleep at night. At school he'd think of love during his lessons, geography, physics, gym. He didn't see the point of geography or physics, he didn't see the point of gym; love was so much more important, surely, and so much more interesting, he didn't see why they couldn't just study that. His grades weren't very good.

Of course, the little boy had no first hand experience of love. He was, after all, a little boy. But on his eighth birthday his parents had bought him a radio, all of his very own. He kept it in his bedroom. And after he'd done his homework, and he'd done his chores, it was to the bedroom he'd go. He'd lie on the bed, turn on the radio, and listen to the love songs that came out. And there were so many! He listened to the ones that were sheer celebrations of love, telling the world how great love made them feel, and how unashamed they were of that, they were in love and that was all there was too it – there'd be drums, probably, and loud guitars, and the songs would be fast, and it would sound as if the singers were almost laughing over the words. These songs made the boy happy. And, when he was a little older, he listened to the other love songs. The songs that were about *wanting* love, crying out for love, wondering where love had gone – or, even more despairing, about being in love that wasn't love after all, or *was* love but the wrong kind of love. These songs were much more confusing. They made the boy sad. And, in a funny way, they made him happy too, even happier somehow than the happy songs had.

He learned what love was. A matter of getting the right notes in the right order. And hoping that the right words didn't get in the way of those notes and spoil everything.

By the time he was twelve, after countless evenings of diligent study, the boy had heard every single love song in the world. And he liked them all. He had his favourites, of course he had. He had two hundred and eighty-nine favourites. But there wasn't one love song he didn't respect, and which hadn't taught him something.

He never intended to compose a song of his own. But one night, as he dreamed about love, a tune began to play in his head. He'd absorbed so many songs, they were as much a part of his life as breathing or eating. And somehow the best bits of the best of them had got mixed up in his head, and produced something new. He woke up with a start. He didn't know how to write music. He didn't know how to record his voice. So he made himself stay up all night, walking around the house, singing the new song under his breath over and over again so he wouldn't forget it. When his parents got up at dawn they were shocked to see their little boy shivering with exhaustion, the catchiest of melodies on his lips. They listened to the song. The boy couldn't really sing very well. And he had to explain where the drums and guitars came in. But the parents exchanged glances in awe. 'That,' said his daddy gravely, 'is a love song, all right.'

Daddy didn't go to work that day. He phoned a friend, who knew someone who knew someone who might be able to help. Daddy took his little boy to see this man, and for a fee the stranger wrote down the song with staves and treble clefs. 'Is that it?' said Daddy. 'That's his song?'

'That's his song,' said the man, pocketing the money, 'and we never met, right?' And the little boy took the paper on which his song was now inscribed, and he didn't recognise it like that, but it still gave him a thrill of pride to see it. And then he just keeled over, fast asleep, right there and then. He really was very tired.

Daddy went to the post office for the right forms, and filled them in. And the next day, as instructed, he took the little boy into the city to get his love song registered. Mummy made them sandwiches for the trip. The government buildings were stone and grey. There was nobody on reception; a notice at the front told prospective songsmiths to take a ticket and wait until their number was called. It also said that there must be no smoking and no littering and, in particular, the humming of unregistered music was expressly forbidden. Daddy and the little boy took seats. A number was called, and a man at the far side of the room got up, stretched, and shuffled through swing doors down a corridor. The little boy calculated that there were one hundred and twenty-eight people in the queue ahead of them.

There were no other children in the waiting room. Mostly men with beards and raincoats, each holding in their hands a post office form and sheets of music paper. 'Is everyone here to get their song registered?' asked the boy.

'I think they must be.'

'Why do we need to get songs registered?'

'Well,' said Daddy, and handed him a sandwich. 'Otherwise, it'd be chaos, wouldn't it? Look around.' The little boy did. 'Without registration, there'd be another one hundred and twenty-eight songs in the world for us to listen to.'

'That doesn't sound so bad.'

'One hundred and twenty-eight doesn't sound bad,' agreed Daddy. 'But that's just today! There'll be another one hundred and twenty-eight tomorrow. Maybe more! You'd end up with a world that has so many love songs in it, we'd be swamped in them. We wouldn't know what to listen to. We might miss out on the one thousand good love songs we'd enjoy because we couldn't find them amidst all the bad ones we wouldn't.'

The boy liked his sandwich. It was tuna. It was the seventeenth best sandwich filling in the world. Across the aisle an unkempt man with grey hair glared at him. The boy didn't know why. The boy was glad when, a few hours later, the man's number was called. He didn't see him again.

At last it was the boy's turn. His daddy nudged him from his drowse. 'Come on,' said Daddy, and offered him his hand. The boy was really too old now to need his hand held, but he took it gratefully. They walked through the swing doors, and down a long corridor. They only stopped when they found a cubicle that had a door open. 'Come in,' said the clerk inside the cubicle. And then, on seeing the boy, 'Composers only. That's protocol. You'll have to leave your little boy outside.' 'I'm not the composer,' said Daddy. 'My little boy is.' The clerk blinked in surprise, just the once, then regained his composure. 'Very well,' he said, and ushered them in, and in spite of protocol, he didn't ask Daddy to leave. The clerk held out his hand for the form. Daddy gave it to him, and the clerk read it briefly. Then the clerk held out his hand for the song. And, taking it, fed it into the computer on his desk.

'Aren't you going to read it?' said Daddy.

'No need. The computer is wholly impartial, it's not affected by quirks of personal taste. It measures the song on timbre, metre, rhythm, and cultural importance.' The computer whirred as it made its assessment, and the clerk smiled thinly at the little boy. 'Shan't be long now.' And then the computer made a happy little ping. This time the clerk didn't bother to hide his surprise, and blinked repetitively.

'Does that mean,' asked the boy, 'that my song is one of the top thousand in the world?'

'Yes,' said the clerk. 'Yes. It would appear so. Yes. If I... just check my... yes.' He tapped away at his keyboard. 'It's nine hundred and fourteenth,' he said. 'Well done.'

With a new respect, the clerk went on to explain to the little boy that the Government would now be purchasing his song and all future rights appertaining. The boy would receive a handsome stipend once a month, index-linked to adjust for inflation. That he should start listening to the radio, because he'd be hearing his own song playing there soon! 'But what happens,' asked the boy, 'to the song that's nine hundred and fourteenth already?' 'Well,' said the clerk, 'that'll become nine hundred and fifteenth. It'll shuffle down the rankings. They'll all shuffle down, until they reach one thousand.' 'And what happens,' said the boy, 'to number one thousand?' 'Quite right,' said the clerk approvingly, although the boy couldn't see why, he'd only asked him a simple question, 'I'll deal with that right now.' And he turned to his computer, tapped on his keyboard for the shortest few seconds, and erased Elvis Presley's *Blue Suede Shoes* forever.

On the bus ride home Daddy realised that they could now have afforded a taxi. Taxis were the fourteenth best transportation in the world, whereas buses were only at three hundred and forty-seven. 'Never mind,' he laughed. 'Taxis only from this point on! I'm proud of you, son. Not a bad day's work, eh?' And the little boy agreed. 'I'm going to write some more songs now,' he said, 'I'm already getting ideas!'

But he didn't have time for writing for a while. The boy was famous. Truth to tell, the press wouldn't usually have taken much interest in the story. Every few months someone or other was breaking a song into the bottom hundreds of the canon, shoving aside others which had only just been put in. And it may have been the nine hundred and fourteenth best song in the world, but it was also the eighty-seventh worst, which didn't sound half so impressive. But the boy *was* twelve years old. That was something which caught the listeners' imagination, and his song was rerecorded in many different styles to sate the interest, reggae, rap, a cappella. The boy was referred to as a genius in the making, a wunderkind, a veritable Mozart. Mozart was a famous composer. He'd managed to get no fewer than fourteen songs into the top thousand, he was really very good indeed.

At school he'd been so dreamy he'd barely made an impression. But now he was the epitome of romance. He won the hearts of all the girls, and quite a few of the teachers as well, one or two quite got into trouble over him. He barely noticed, he looked on in some bemusement as his classmates wept for his love, as his form mistress was disciplined by a tribunal and put on probation. And he didn't stay at the school for long; he had no need for geography or physics or gym any more, and the boy could now afford a special education in which he could focus upon his gifts. He learned how to write in musical notation, he learned to pick apart the songs he'd once enjoyed so uncritically. He wrote a few songs, and of course everyone in academe buzzed with expectation, what fresh classics might he be concocting under their very noses? But they were to be disappointed; the boy always destroyed these efforts, saying that they weren't good enough, he wasn't yet ready to give a second masterpiece to the world. By the time he graduated his original song had slipped down the rankings, and was now nine hundred and thirty-third. One of his fellow students at last managed to catch his attention, and then to catch his heart. She was the envy of all her friends, and received a couple of death threats from the most jealous. As they walked down the aisle, with his mummy and daddy looking so proud, and the boy no longer quite a boy, no longer quite a wunderkind, the song that was played was his own. The bride had chosen it especially. She said it was that song that had made her fall in love with him. Of course it had been. At this point it was the nine hundred and forty-seventh best love song in the world.

The fact was, the boy didn't like the song very much. No matter how much it was digitally remastered, or reremastered, he heard it for what it was. A melange of other people's songs that had just got lucky. There was love in it, and it was *his* love, but it wasn't the love it pretended to be – a love for the love that others feel is still a borrowed love, it's hardly love at all. The boy knew he had to find within his heart some passion that was sincere. He dedicated himself to his wife. He knew that she loved him, and that ought to make him love her – but was it really a love strong enough to produce a good tune? He worked on it. He studied her from every angle. He'd adore the nape of her neck, he'd delight in the kink of her nose. He taught himself to feel ecstasies over the little jokes she made he knew really weren't that funny at all. And at last he thought the preparation was over. He wrote a new song. He read it back critically. He prised it apart, put it back together, tweaked the chorus, softened the guitars a bit. He thought about destroying it. He was all set to tear it up. And then he realised how much it would hurt him, to lose even one note of it. It was finished, his second attempt at love. His previous effort was now ranked at nine hundred and seventy-four.

As a composer in the top thousand, he could bypass the usual registration process. He didn't have to queue. He could come to the city with his post office form and his sheet music, and no matter how busy the office, the doors of the cubicles would be flung open wide for him. 'Hello, sir!' said the clerk, 'and welcome!' The clerk fed the new song into the computer. The computer whirred, but it didn't ping, it grunted. 'Oh!' said the clerk, checking his readout, much surprised. 'Better luck next time.' And took the song from the feeder tray, and shredded it before the young composer's eyes.

Maybe his love had been too clean, he hadn't fought hard enough for it. He began to have affairs. Nothing major at first, just the odd grope with likely-looking women in the back of pubs; he was no longer hailed as a genius, but telling a pretty girl he'd written the nine hundred and eighty-second greatest love song was always an ice-breaker notwithstanding. Seeking further inspiration, he moved on to afternoon trysts, and then evening trysts, and then weekend trysts. A five-day fling with identical blonde twins provoked him to compose a full seven-and-a-half-minute ballad. The computer rejected it, as it did all his other songs. The doors of the registration office were still flung open wide to him, but with markedly less enthusiasm. His wife left him. She said that she no longer knew him. She said that maybe she never had. He wrote a song about how that made him feel. The computer didn't care. His daddy died. Quite unexpectedly of a heart attack, there was no warning. His mummy, who had never raised her voice to him, who had bought him a radio and made him tuna sandwiches, told him that his father had been so appalled by the way he'd treated his wife that the shame had killed him. The composer cried for days. He wept it all out into a new song. The computer barely gave it a blip, let alone the much-sought ping. The clerk studied the readout and said, yes, the computer could see that the composer in question was upset, and it offered him its condolences. But that didn't mean he'd written a good song.

One day a bar pianist in Portugal hit the news. Afonso Guttierez had been playing his own songs to customers as they ate their tapas, and had been persuaded by concerned friends to take a selection of his work for registration; it would only have taken one disgruntled diner unhappy with the calamari to shop him. He offered fourteen songs. Eight were rejected, but that still left an unprecedented *six* that were accepted automatically by the Lisbon computer. The pianist was thirty-four years old, but in spite of that still hailed as a new wunderkind, a new Mozart. All six of the songs ranked higher than our composer's effort, which now came to rest at a precarious nine hundred and ninety-seven. The composer decided that he needed to get a song accepted into the canon immediately before he lost his placing altogether, and for the next few nights worked hard on his latest masterpiece – he pushed and prodded at all of his feelings, dredging his heart for something that might sound beautiful. But it was too late. By the time he took his new work into the city everything had changed. Fired up by his success, Guttierez had returned to his bar, and written up for submission a further fifty-eight of the songs he'd squirreled away over the years. All fifty-eight were accepted. When our composer reached the office, he found he now had to queue like everybody else. He had to take a ticket and wait his turn. And when he at last reached a cubicle, tired and angry, it was only to find that his childhood success had been erased, deleted from the computer, wiped from the world's iPods. The clerk apologised. He fed the new song into the computer. It was rejected.

'What if I wrote a song that wasn't about love at all?'

The clerk said, very slowly, 'I don't think that's possible.'

'It has to be possible.'

'Every song expresses love for *something*,' said the clerk. 'A few hundred years ago, love of God was all the rage. Now it's all about love of sex. Give it another hundred, it'll be love of silicon chips, who knows? But in any good song, there's always a love you can't get around. And that's love for the music itself. That'll always be there. You can't beat it.'

'A man can try,' said the man who had once been a composer.

For two long months the man worked hard. Fortified by broccoli and lukewarm beer, he cut out anything from his diet which might excite his taste buds, anything which might get translated accidentally as passion in melodic form. The stipend had been withdrawn, so he was obliged to go out to work during the day, concentrating on his music only once his shifts were over. He wasn't trained for anything, so took on a series of menial temp jobs, stacking shelves, stuffing envelopes. But even that helped, he was able to channel the numbness of the day into the numbness of his music. He composed through the night, every night, his desk turned so he was facing a blank wall, and every time he came up with a note that even reached for emotion he'd quash it. The music wasn't bad; he couldn't simply afford to be bad, anyone could write *bad* music. It took a very certain sort of genius to write something instead that was so good and so fully formed, and yet stillborn.

He went to register his song. He took the day off work. They'd just have to find someone else to hold a placard advertising golf sales. He took his ticket. He waited. There was a little boy across the aisle sitting with his father, no doubt thinking this whole process of assessment and rejection was some fun day out. He glared at him and made him cry. He went to the toilet. His face looked haggard with lack of sleep, his hair had greyed.

The song was fed into the computer. It whirred for a bit, and then whirred some more. The screen froze. The clerk had to get out the manual, turn the computer off and then back on again. 'Well,' he said, at last, 'it's not a love song. We don't know what it is, but it's not a love song. And so it's outside our jurisdiction. It doesn't need to be destroyed.' He took the sheet music from the feeder, and instead of shredding it, handed it back to the composer.

'You'll buy it?' said the composer.

'God, no.'

On his way home, for want of something to do, the composer read over his song. He didn't finish. He left it on the bus behind him.

He vowed he'd never write music again. He needed a career, something permanent, something he could commit to. He applied for a job at the local McDonald's; McDonald's was a fast food chain specialising in burgers, and the six hundred and sixth best in the world. He was much older than any of his fellow workers, they all thought that was impressive. And he worked hard there, he began the week as a mere team member but by Thursday he was team leader, he had five gold stars on his name badge and he was on a roll. His managers were in awe, they'd never seen anyone scale the ladder of the convenience food industry so quickly, he was astonishing, a wunderkind. He loved his job. He flipped the burgers and wiped the tables and gave service with a smile, this was something he was good at. The restaurant played an endless stream of muzak, simplified versions of the love songs he'd once admired and competed with. And sometimes they played Guttierez.

One day the televisions all reported breaking news. The world had a new best love song. Nothing composed in the last fifty years had even made it near the top ten, there was something so established about those classics that was just hard to beat. But the latest from Afonso Guttierez had taken the number one spot, knocking down into second place some ditty by Verdi. Always one to shy away from publicity, Guttierez had only reluctantly agreed to a TV interview, in which he mumbled in broken English that he was pleased people a-liked his song. People more than liked it; it was adored. Everyone played it for their loved ones, and although doing that was immediately a cliché, it somehow wasn't, because the song seemed to speak personally to whoever heard it, it was universal but was also specifically about *them.* The former child prodigy, former composer, gave the song a listen. He didn't much care for it.

He couldn't have explained why he caught that flight to Lisbon. Why from there he took a seven hour coach trip into the Portuguese hinterland. He didn't know what he was going to do when he found Guttierez. Only that by now Guttierez had three hundred and four songs in the top thousand, and, if that wasn't bad enough, the other composers of the world had cottoned on, they were writing their songs in the *style* of Guttierez; they weren't quite as good as Guttierez, of course, but they were perfectly suited for adaptation as background music, for elevators, for supermarkets – there was suddenly a strange sticky homogeneity to the music of the world, and there was a new name already coined for it, it was used freely and without shame by all the critics and all the disc jockeys, and that name was Guttierezesque. He'd been working so hard at his Big Macs to make a bit of money. Now he'd blown all his savings. Some of it had gone on the fare to Lisbon, the rest had gone on the gun.

* * *

They said that the genius of Guttierez was that he didn't appear to compose his songs at all, he'd just play at the piano and somehow they'd pour out. It was why he was so extraordinarily prolific. He said he needed the audience, that before his success he'd tinkered away before customers in a bar, and that he couldn't change the way he worked now. That was why, shy as he was, he still performed. He'd sold up the small bar, of course, and now owned a large restaurant. The food was only adequate, and was served on paper plates and with plastic cutlery to minimise the clatter of knife and fork. But no-one came to Restaurante Guttierez to eat.

The maître d' asked if he had a reservation.

'No, I'm sorry. Can you squeeze me in?'

'I'm sorry senhor, tonight we're fully booked.'

'I see. Can I reserve a table for tomorrow?'

'Senhor, we are fully booked for the next five months. Senhor Guttierez, he is very popular.'

'Please. I need to see him. I've flown all the way from England.'

'We have many visitors from England, senhor. From Japan, from Australia, from the Americas, from all over the world.'

'I'm begging you. I'm a composer too. I compose love songs. I used to compose love songs. We're the same, him and I. We're the same. Please. Please.' The maître d' let him in.

He was given a little table at the back, with two chairs. He looked at the menu. The wine cost a fortune. He couldn't afford it. He ordered a carafe.

At last the lights dimmed, and Guttierez appeared. He shuffled towards the piano. He was just a little man, a little man. He was wearing shirt and tails, like a concert pianist, but they didn't really fit him, he looked scruffy. He darted a glance at the audience, but didn't look at them directly, didn't want them there. There was a smattering of applause, but Guttierez ignored it. He sat down at the piano.

The team manager from McDonald's carefully took the gun from his coat pocket.

Guttierez frowned at the piano. As if it were something he was trying to remember, trying to place. He raised a finger. He hesitated. He dropped it on to a key. Plonk. It was a C. He thought about this, then raised the finger once more, thought a bit further, then dropped it on to the F. Then back on to the C. Then back on to the F. He gave this some consideration. He took his hand away from the piano altogether, stared at it once more. Then raised his hand, raised his finger. Held it in the air – then let it fall, at last. Back on to the C. Then faster, another C, another F, another C. Then the single finger exploring further, excited, picking out other notes, at random, a mess.

Our hero wanted to laugh. Guttierez wasn't worth killing. He wasn't worth the price of a wine carafe. He got up to leave.

'No,' said the woman beside him.

He hadn't realised there *was* a woman beside him. That someone had taken that second chair. He couldn't make her out in the dim light. She said something to him in a whisper.

'What?'

'*Escute*. Listen.'

So he listened. And there wasn't much to be impressed by. Not for a while. But then Guttierez visibly relaxed. The notes began to smooth. They still seemed random, at least at first – not so discordant now, even pleasing to the ear, nothing special of course, nothing of any worth – but then that was all stripped away, it was as if it had been a game all along, those notes weren't random, they'd been building up to something, building up a rhythm, you could hear those simple Cs, those Fs, every now and again being picked out, as if winking at an audience who had taken them so much for granted before, we're building up to something, they said, we're building up to... and here on the top of them there was...

He gasped. And was flooded by the music.

Guttierez opened his mouth. For a while nothing came out. The fingers continued to dance upon the piano, the music hadn't reached his head yet, the mouth hung open, waiting for it to do so. And then words tumbled out. Guttierez was not a great singer. He didn't have to be.

He didn't know what Guttierez was singing about. He didn't have to.

He didn't have to know anything.

He wasn't a composer any more, or a man who had once been a composer and had given up, or a man who had once been a composer and who could never give up, not really, no matter how much he failed. He was a little boy. He was a little boy who listened to love songs. He was a little boy in love with love.

He turned to the woman, and he could barely see her. It dawned on him that this was because he was crying.

She put what she was holding on to the table, and with her hand now freed, reached for his. He looked at her closely. And he knew that he loved her. It wasn't that she was beautiful, it wasn't that. But she was there. She was there, amongst the music.

'Listen,' she mouthed, and he nodded happily. She held his hand tightly. It was smaller than his, but strong, stronger. He saw that she was crying too. He saw what she'd put upon the table. He saw that she too had come with a gun.

He didn't know what he could ever say to her, whether he could ever find the right words. But for that moment he was in love, and it was the fullest and richest love he'd ever felt. He gazed at her, and she gazed at him, and they listened. They listened. And hoped that the love song would never end.

Acknowledgments

Writing this book has been made a hell of a lot easier thanks to the support and enthusiasm of a huge number of friends. They've urged me on, told me they were impatient for the next story, and in a few cases, have taken rather too much delight in pointing out factual or grammatical errors. Apologies for anyone I've left out!

Justin Ackroyd, Guy Adams, Jon & Carolyn Arnold, Lois Ava-Matthew, Rosalind Ayres, Elizabeth Baines, Christie Baugher, Mel Beattie, Lindsey Bender, Deb Biancotti, Lyn Boundy, Erykah Brackenbury, Nicholas Briggs, Debbie Challis, Xanna Eve Chown, Paul Cornell, Frank Cottrell Boyce, Sue Cowley, Ailsa Cox, Karen Davison, Sue Everett, Nev Fountain, Mark Gatiss, Vikki Godwin, Laura Goodin, Kate Gowers, Matthew Griffiths, Simon Guerrier, Toby Hadoke, Jason Haigh-Ellery, Steven Hall, Lisa L Hannett, Robert Hoge, Fiona James, Martin Jarvis, Stephen Jones, Alisa Krasnostein, Tanya Lemke, Alison Macleod, Adam Marek, Kirstyn McDermott, Dan McGrath, Suzanne Milligan, Steven Moffat, Ian Mond, Mark Morris, Simon Murgatroyd, Andy Murray, Heather Murray, Liz Myles, Tara O'Shea, Sarah Pinborough, Wena Poon, Charles Prepolec, Jody Richardson, Rebecca Riley, Kim Rose, Rhonda Scarborough, Will Shindler, Mandy Slater, Angela Slatter, Cat Sparks, Gill Spaul, Katharine Straker, Daren Thomas, Lee Thompson, Lucy Toman, Trudi Topham, Gabrielle Trio, Simon Kurt Unsworth, Beryl Vertue, Sue Vertue, Stephen Volk, Peter & Jo Ware, Dave Whittam, Clare Wigfall, Fiona Williams, Sean Williams, Vanessa Williams, Philip Wolff.

Particular thanks to Ra Page at Comma Press, who got this whole short story thing going in the first place. I've never had so much fun writing in my life, and that's down to your original commission. I'll always be grateful.

To my family, Mum (Joyce), Dad (Dennis), and Still-Just-a-Kid Sister (Vicky).

But especially to my wife, Jane Goddard, who's heard every single one of my love songs – and forgives me when I'm out of tune.

For further information on Rob and his work, check out www.robertshearman.net